W9-CFB-628

GRAND CENTRAL
PUBLISHING

LARGE
PRINT

ALSO BY LEILA MEACHAM

HISTORICAL FICTION

Roses

Tumbleweeds

Somerset

Titans

ROMANCE

Ryan's Hand

Crowning Design

Aly's House

Dragonfly

A NOVEL

LEILA MEACHAM

LARGE PRINT

Grand Central Publishing
Hachette Book Group
1290 Avenue of the Americas, New York, NY 10104
grandcentralpublishing.com
twitter.com/grandcentralpub

First Edition: July 2019

Grand Central Publishing is a division of Hachette Book Group, Inc. The Grand Central Publishing name and logo is a trademark of Hachette Book Group, Inc.

Print book interior design by Thomas Louie.

Library of Congress Cataloging-in-Publication Data

Names: Meacham, Leila, 1938- author.
Title: Dragonfly : a novel / Leila Meacham.
Description: First Edition. | New York : Grand Central Publishing, 2019.
Identifiers: LCCN 2019001971| ISBN 9781538732229 (hardcover) | ISBN 9781549121838 (audio download) | ISBN 9781549150098 (audio book) | ISBN 9781538732212 (ebook)
Subjects: | GSAFD: War stories.
Classification: LCC PS3563.E163 D73 2019 | DDC 813/.54--dc23
LC record available at https://lccn.loc.gov/2019001971

ISBNs: 978-1-5387-3222-9 (hardcover), 978-1-5387-3398-1 (large print), 978-1-5387-3221-2 (ebook)

Printed in the United States of America

LSC-C

10 9 8 7 6 5 4 3 2 1

In dedication to Ann Ferguson Zeigler,
again.

The sun on the hill forgot to die, and the lilies revived, and the dragonfly came back to dream on the river.

(Welsh inscription)

THE CAST OF CHARACTERS

THE AMERICANS

(Bucky) Samuel Barton, civil engineer
OSS code name: Lodestar
Working name: Stephane Beaulieu
Bridgette Loring, fashion designer
OSS code name: Labrador
Working name: Bernadette Dufor
(Chris) Christoph Brandt, track-and-field coach
OSS code name: Lapwing
Working name: Claus Bauer
Brad Hudson, fly-fisherman
OSS code name: Limpet
Working name: Barnard Wagner
Victoria Grayson, fencer of foil

OSS code name: Liverwort
Working name: Veronique Colbert
Alistair Renault, OSS case officer, chief of station for French Affairs, aka the man in brown

THE GERMANS

Major General Konrad March: head of the Abwehr, the German intelligence agency in Paris
Wilhelm March, the general's son
Sergeant Hans Falk, the general's aide-de-camp
SS Colonel Derrick Albrecht, chief of the counterintelligence division of the security service of the Reichsführer (SD)
Sergeant Karl Brunner, the colonel's aide-de-camp

THE FRENCH

Beaumont Fournier, author
Nicholas Cravois, the Black Ghost
Madame Jeanne Boucher, owner of the Paris fashion house La Maison de Boucher

Claude Allard, riverboat captain and owner of a fishing tour company in Paris
Jules Garnier, director of personnel at the Sorbonne
Madame Gabrielle Dupree, proprietress of a boardinghouse and landlady to Bucky
Madame Adeline Gastain, neighbor to Major General Konrad March
Maurice Corbett, chief of detectives, French National Police
Sister Mary Frances, mother superior of the Convent of the Sisters of Charity
Jacques Vogel, director of the L'Ecole d'Escrime Français
Henri Burrell, Alistair's man in Paris

EXPLANATIONS OF GERMAN MILITARY ORGANIZATIONS

Wehrmacht: the German Army
Abwehr: the German intelligence agency, a branch of the German Army
Schutzstaffel: SS

Waffen SS: the military arm of the SS
Allegemeine SS: the administrative arm of the SS
Sicherheitsdienst: the security service of the Reichsführer, operating under the Allegemeine

CHAPTER ONE

SEPTEMBER 1962

Cambridge, Maryland

The man in brown snapped shut the book he'd been reading and looked up with a stare of disbelief. There was no doubt about it, absolutely none. The five-member team the author described in this obscure little book about clandestine operations in German-occupied France during WWII was the same group he'd sent into Paris in the fall of 1942. Four had made it home, one barely, the last left behind dead, buried in an unmarked grave on French soil. Or so they'd all believed...

Alistair Renault sat very still. Eerily coincidental that he should have read that chapter in *The Greatest Ruses of World War II* today, almost twenty years after he'd watched the most amazing team of covert operatives he'd ever trained take off in the predawn darkness from England into enemy territory. In three weeks the team was to have met in Paris for a twenty-year reunion. The date, long canceled, had been suggested, insisted upon, by the team's missing member. Alistair wondered if September 23, 1962, was as stuck in the others' minds as it was in his.

He turned to the author page to read again, but with more interest, the credentials of John Peterson that qualified him to write *The Greatest Ruses of World War II*, a subject on which few had greater knowledge and none more experience than the man in brown. Mr. Peterson's sparse qualifications, the lack of footnotes and a bibliography, and the so-so writing, plus its publication by a little-known university press in 1956, would not have enticed a serious reader of WWII literature to give his war chronicles a try, but the title of the book, set on a low shelf in the local library, had caught Alistair's eye. All through his reading, he had wondered about the validity of the man's research. The acknowledgments page made no mention of persons from whom John Peterson had received assistance or the sources he had consulted. For all the reader knew, the author could have made up the dramatic content and labeled it nonfiction. Alistair did not recognize the names in the book's cast of characters, but he knew that the chapter detailing the clandestine activities of a five-agent team code-named Dragonfly that had operated in Paris during the city's darkest years was factual—at least up until the claim in the shocking climax. He should know: He was the man who'd run the operation. Whether the ruse the author had described at the chapter's conclusion was bogus, he didn't know. He suspected it was, against a flickering hope that it wasn't. He intended to find out.

John Peterson, bald, bespectacled, lackluster, appeared from his photo to have been in his late forties in 1956. He'd be pushing seventy today and, if still living, was probably retired. Madison, New Jersey, was a little over a four-hour drive away. Before requesting John Peterson's telephone number in New Jersey, of which there must be a slew, he'd try Madison High School, where Peterson had been an American history teacher. Perhaps a talkative school clerk would give him all the information required for Alistair to locate him in Madison, and he would take a little motor trip to the Rose City to introduce himself to John Peterson.

He was indeed fortunate to be referred to a loquacious clerk who had handled student registration for the school since its founding in 1920. "Forty-two years I've been here," she said proudly, and to Alistair's questions replied, "Oh, Mr. Peterson's been gone from Madison for a long time. He and his wife divorced...No, I don't know where he relocated or even if he continued teaching. My guess is that he took off to travel around Europe. He was a big one for Europe."

"Europe..." Alistair mused. "Any special country?"

"He liked France."

Would she know if Mr. Peterson was still alive? Alistair asked.

"We haven't heard of his death, and I believe we would have," the registrar said.

What about his ex-wife? Maybe he could locate Mr. Peterson through her?

A snort. "That hussy disappeared with her paramour right after she took Mr. Peterson for everything he had, poor man."

Alistair thanked her, hung up, and then asked the long distance operator for the number of the book's publisher in Trenton, New Jersey. No such listing was available. The publishing house had probably gone defunct years ago. Alistair was not disheartened, for he was still in touch with an organization that could locate the most elusive persons of interest. He'd place a call to a buddy at the CIA with whom he'd served in the OSS, the Office of Strategic Services, and put him on to John Peterson's tracks.

Meanwhile, he'd telephone the surviving members of Dragonfly to ask them to find and read the last chapter of *The Greatest Ruses of World War II*.

Surprisingly, he found them all at their places of work on this late Friday afternoon. They were still young and active at forty-two and, though scattered all over the country, had remained in his life and one another's since their first reunion in New York City on the twenty-third of September in 1945, forever bound by ties that transcended blood, lifelong friendships, and career attachments. Initially, it had been their doing, the remaining in touch, unusual in a business where war-weary operatives were only too glad to shake themselves free of their case officers as soon as their missions were over. At first he had resisted continuing the association—the idea of it was so foreign to him—but the team had held fast, and after a while he had responded with pleasure to their phone calls, visits, and invitations to weddings, christenings, holidays, and milestone celebrations. The four who had returned, along with their spouses and children, had become the closest to family he'd ever had.

He telephoned Labrador first. He had never stopped thinking of the members of Dragonfly by their OSS field names, just as they had never dropped his military rank when addressing him. It was always *Major*, never Alistair.

Labrador met his summary of the last chapter of John Peterson's book with a shocked silence that lasted a long five seconds. Alistair waited as his listener gnawed at the possibility that there might be a grain of truth to the author's preposterous claim, but then protested, "I don't believe it. The others all say they watched the execution from their cell windows. Peterson just made up that cock-and-bull ending to fit his 'ruse' scheme."

"I'm inclined to think the same," Alistair said, "but I want you kids to read it for yourselves and get back to me with your analysis. Meanwhile, I am going to try to track down John Peterson."

"If he's not living, we'll never know."

"There are ways to find out. I'll begin working on it."

"Good grief, Major, what if...his conclusion is correct?"

"Then we'll go from there and follow the path to wherever it leads." (No one said *Good grief* anymore, a throwback to the '40s, Alistair thought, amused.) "The book is out of print, I'd think. If you and the others can't locate a copy, I'll xerox the chapter and mail it to you."

The others received Alistair's news with the same degree of shocked silence, for the last chapter of *The Greatest Ruses of World War II* maintained that the missing member of Dragonfly had survived the firing squad that three of the group had witnessed. The execution had been carefully planned to fool the Nazi SS. Comments ranged from an explosive "Nonsense!" to expletives prompted by rage at the cruelty of the author's claim. None of the team members had ever discussed their exploits with anyone nor had they been approached for an interview by a man named John Peterson.

After the last call, Alistair pushed back from the telephone. What if the chapter's conclusion was correct? What if the missing member of Dragonfly was alive and well and living in Europe as the chapter claimed? The execution had occurred on June 11, 1944. It had been eighteen years since three members of the team had witnessed the brutal death of one they had loved and still mourned. What if Dragonfly was not missing one of its wings after all?

There might be one quick and easy way to find out.

The man in brown drew open a desk drawer and pulled from it a thick set of files, each labeled with the names of the candidates who eventually became Dragonfly. He'd absconded with the files after President Harry Truman terminated the OSS in October 1945, putting him out of the job he was born to do until the CIA had snapped him up. If he had left them, the dossiers would only have gathered dust in locked-away, classified government files, their names and missions forever forgotten along with those of other courageous men and women who had risked their lives for their country. In the back of his mind, Alistair had a notion that someday he might write his own book, telling of the bravery and selflessness of five young people who had volunteered for infiltration into the city of light gone dark.

Unable to find a current phone listing for the missing dragonfly's parents, Alistair then dialed the private number of his friend at the Central Intelligence Agency in Langley, Virginia, and after speaking with him, took the weighty collection of files to his easy chair, attempting to ignore a pack of Lucky Strikes in the drawer of his armchair table. But the urge to smoke overpowered his doctor's warning that his lungs were a puff away from emphysema. This situation called for a nicotine fix. He settled the bundle on the table, lit up, took off his shoes, placed his socked feet on the chair's ottoman, and reached for the first file.

Along with his other epithets, Alistair had been

known as "the ferret" when it came to searching out information on a subject. Flipping through the candidates' intimate details and mental and physical qualifications, he mused on how these collections showed the kids' mettle even then. Prodded by John Peterson's specious, poorly written version of Dragonfly's years in Paris, Alistair thought that he just might decide to write that book after all, tell the derring-do tales of five young Americans code-named Labrador, Liverwort, Lodestar, Limpet, and Lapwing. He would begin in May 1942.

THE RECRUITS

CHAPTER TWO

MAY 1942

Washington, D.C.

The members of the choir of Saint Luke's Episcopal Church on Fifteenth Street in Washington, D.C., referred to him as "the man in brown." Even after two years of singing with them the Sundays he was in town, few knew his full name of Alistair Renault, and no member could claim to know him at all. Dressed in his drab brown attire, he appeared on Wednesday evenings for choir rehearsal just as the body of thirty gathered in the church chancel and did not linger for coffee and cookies and fellowship afterward. The choir director considered Alistair's the most magnificent singing voice ever to come under his baton and would have appointed Alistair lead tenor if only he could have relied upon him to be present every Sunday, but he understood that the man had a government position of a hush-hush nature that precluded his regular attendance.

On this particular day, this same man of mystery slid a sheet of paper listing names, addresses, and personal details of each across a large mahogany desk. The recipient was Colonel William J. Donovan, known as Wild Bill Donovan to friends and foes. The desk belonged to the director of the Office of Strategic Services, better known as the OSS, the country's first national spy agency, whose conception had been discussed in the White House in 1940. The office had become official the following year, before Japan's surprise attack on Pearl Harbor in December 1941 and Germany's subsequent declaration of war against the United States. The paralyzing global uncertainties of that spring had confirmed America's need for a centralized intelligence system set up to collect and analyze timely and accurate information as a means to plan military strategy against the enemy should the U.S. be drawn into a worldwide conflict. This aim was to be achieved primarily by the insertion of agents trained for covert operations into hostile territory. President Franklin D. Roosevelt signed it into existence by executive order and chose as its head Wild Bill Donovan, the most decorated officer of World War I, in civilian life a prominent

Wall Street lawyer before being recalled to active military duty in 1942 with the rank of colonel.

The organization had since grown to become a full-fledged agency and had moved from its crowded temporary quarters to a more spacious home atop historical Navy Hill in northwest Washington. Colonel Bill Donovan now directed his bustling and burgeoning outfit from a high-ceilinged corner office on the first floor of an establishment that, because of its secrecy, had come to be nicknamed "the Kremlin." His deputy and second-in-command waited for his boss's reaction to the list while he enjoyed the cool mid-May breeze flowing through the tall, open window with its bird's-eye view of the Potomac River.

"I see you've circled five names," Donovan said to the man in brown. "Why these five?"

"Brad Hudson and Christoph Brandt speak fluent German with an understanding of French learned in high school. If they come onboard, they'll be given a refresher course. Samuel Barton speaks French like a native with a college minor in German. Bridgette Loring is fluent in French and German, as is Victoria Grayson. Besides their understanding of the languages, their personal skills and fields of study make them the most qualified for the assignments I have in mind. Also, none is married." Alistair's level gaze conveyed what did not need to be stated between the two men: *They were therefore dispensable.* "Only one comes with serious family responsibilities—Brad Hudson, so he may not be a player," he continued. "Samuel Barton, the graduating civil engineer, actually sent in a request for an application form, and I've an appointment to meet with him in Oklahoma City, his hometown, on Monday. Victoria Grayson of Williamsburg, Virginia, you know about. She's the fencer of foil who came to my attention in 1940."

"Ah, yes, of the Virginia Graysons. Family's richer than God," Donovan said. "Let's hope she goes for it."

"Our Paris asset is in place and expecting her."

Bill Donovan laid down the list and eyed his deputy appreciatively. "It was a stroke of genius how you got these names, my friend."

Alistair accepted the compliment with a slight nod. His boss's trust was what he liked most about working for Wild Bill Donovan. He allowed Alistair to do his job without requiring him to trot every idea or plan by him for interminable study or—God save them!—from the quagmire of a committee. Investigation and recruitment of a special few for certain missions was the purview of the man in brown. Early last year he had hit upon the idea of contacting college professors of particular disciplines to obtain the names of students fluent in German and French the agency could approach "to serve in a special capacity for the security of the United States." The letter, written on OSS stationery, asked for any known details of their personal lives. These were listed by category: family, friends, interests, hobbies, social affiliations, religious preference, proclivities, temperament, political views, and the like. The psychology of the letterhead of a highly secret government agency had worked, and he'd heard from an amazing number of professors from whose replies he had compiled the list in his boss's hands.

Wild Bill said, "Tell me about these boys and girls. Where are they now? I mean, where are they in life?"

Alistair warmed to the subject. "All of them were born in 1920 and have turned twenty-two or will shortly. By all accounts, Samuel Barton, nicknamed Bucky, is eligible for the draft, but his name has not yet been drawn. Bridgette Loring is graduating Stephens College with a degree in fashion design and illustration. Apparently, she's the next Coco Chanel and has been offered a job with the J. L. Hudson Company in Detroit, but she is holding out for a designer's position in a house of high fashion."

"The fashion district in Paris should be a tasty inducement," Wild Bill commented.

"Victoria Grayson and Christoph Brandt have graduated and are employed, Victoria as a French translator for G. P. Putnam's Sons in New York, and Christoph as a high school teacher and track-and-field coach in Austin, Texas. He goes by Chris and resents the use of his German given name."

"A good sign," the colonel said, "but why hasn't Brandt volunteered? He's been out of school two years."

"He failed his physical. He was born absent a thumb. He tried to argue his way in, but the medics wouldn't have it. According to his professor friend, who volunteered all the information you're reading there, Christoph did everything he could to show the docs his missing thumb wasn't a handicap, but they didn't buy it. He's quite an athlete."

The colonel grunted and consulted the list again. "And Brad Hudson?"

"Brad Hudson is the only non–college graduate. He lives in Meeker, Colorado, and works for a lumber company. He's the one deferred from the draft because of family obligations. His father died in a lumberyard accident, and his mother and sister and the two kids they've taken in off the street, a brother and sister, now depend on him for putting food on the table."

The piercing blue eyes of Wild Bill Donovan rested upon him. "What's he doing on the list?"

"He's fluent in German."

"So?"

"He's also a very proficient fly-fisherman."

"And how does that help us?"

"So is Major General Konrad March."

Wild Bill Donovan rolled his chair back from his desk and settled deeper into its worn leather with a pensive steepling of his fingers over his lips. "I see. What makes you think you can entice Brad away from his family?"

"I don't. Fact is, I doubt it, but he's worth checking out. He has all the qualifications essential for the job—the only candidate I've uncovered so far. I have some days coming, so I thought I might pop down to Colorado and get in a little fly-fishing when the rainbows start running."

Colonel Donovan nodded his assent. "How about the others? How amenable do you think they will be?"

"I don't know, Bill. It depends on the degree to which they hate the Nazis. Bridgette Loring's grandmother was tortured and her grandfather murdered by the Germans in the last war. The sister of Brad Hudson's mother married a rabbi, and they were caught up in one of Hitler's first pogroms to rid Germany of Jews. Victoria Grayson's grandparents live in London, and her brother and fiancé are flying Spitfires for the RAF in the American Eagle Squadron. Samuel Barton's mother has close affiliations to antifascist groups in Paris."

"What about Christoph Brandt's allegiance? I see here his parents are the descendants of the founders of their German community in Texas. New Braunfels, is it?"

"Can't answer your question until I interview him, but from his professor's comments, the kid chafes at being associated with his heritage, especially now."

"What about romantic entanglements? These kids are of the age to be involved with somebody, and from their physical descriptions they are all extraordinarily attractive. Won't that be a detriment?"

Alistair shook his head. "For the assignments I have in mind for them, their looks will be an asset. As for romantic attachments that have occurred since I compiled my reports on them, again I won't know until I interview them."

"So what's the next step?"

"The three that I won't be contacting personally

will be receiving letters that will include a telephone number to call. If they respond, I'll have their calls flagged to be put through to me immediately."

"And if you don't hear?"

"Then I'll pay them a visit if the budget allows it."

"It allows it. When will these letters go out?"

"Tonight." From a folder marked TOP SECRET the man in brown removed three letters slipped under the flaps of their addressed envelopes and placed them before the OSS chief. "All I need is your signature to make the invitations official."

Wild Bill Donovan barely glanced at the first letter before affixing his signature to the rest of the lot. "I hope to God that I'm not signing their death warrants," he murmured.

CHAPTER THREE

BUCKY / LODESTAR

Norman, Oklahoma

Make a wish, Sam!" Penny Parker, Samuel Barton's girlfriend, giggled into his ear.

"But don't tell us what it is, Bucky," his college roommate admonished, "or it won't come true."

Bucky leaned toward a chocolate cake ablaze with twenty-two candles. He imagined that everyone at the long restaurant table believed they could guess his wish, but they'd be wrong. They were all as well lit as his birthday cake but for his mother, who sat sober and unsmiling across from him. He felt her tension and could easily read her wish, her prayer, for him in her eyes: *Please God. Let my son survive the war.* The same wish for themselves sobered the faces of his University of Oklahoma fraternity brothers. Of the four, two were already in military uniform, their draft numbers called before they could complete their diplomas, and were home on brief leaves before their deployment overseas.

They had cause to be worried. The war was going badly for American forces and their allies in both the European and Pacific Theaters. Europe lay under the Third Reich's domination after an almost unbroken chain of battlefield successes, and now the German Army was effectively advancing into Russia. In southeast Asia, U.S. forces had surrendered at Bataan and Corregidor, and the Imperial Japanese Army had occupied most of the islands in the South Pacific. His other Phi Delta Theta buddies would be joining up to serve their country immediately after graduation in a few weeks. Only Bucky remained uncommitted, a situation everybody expected to change with the next drawing of the military draft numbers, but Bucky had other plans.

The honoree puckered his lips and drew in a full lung of air to annihilate the candles with one blow. All twenty-two flickered out. "Atta boy, Bucky," his father said across the table, joining in the guests' riotous applause. So far, his pudgy face, flushed from food and drink and high spirits, had managed to deflect the concerns on his wife's.

One of his fraternity brothers sang out, "Tell us how you got the name *Bucky*, Sam!"

"Yes, son," urged his father, eyes alight with devilish amusement. "Tell your friends how you happen to be called Bucky."

Bucky, who preferred to be called Sam since leaving high school, batted away the request with his hand and with forced good humor called down to his friend who'd made it, "Another time, jerk face, when you're sober enough to remember."

"*I'll* tell 'em!" Horace Barton boomed out. "Nothing to be ashamed of." He turned expansively to the group, ignoring the warning Monique pressed on his arm and Bucky's embarrassed look. "When my son was born, he was very sickly. Colicky. Cried all the time. Threw up a lot. Couldn't keep food down. That went on for a while until I told him, 'Buck up, boy! Buck up!' That was before he could talk. When he finally did, he'd heard 'Buck up!' so often that when he was asked his name, he'd say 'Bucky'! And that's how he got the handle he goes by." Horace beamed his pride around the table for his hand in making his son the man he was today.

"Did," Bucky corrected his father. "I go by Sam now, Dad."

"Because he's no longer that sickly kid, I can assure you," Penny purred knowingly and snuggled closer, warming his ear with her breath.

Bucky subtly wiggled his shoulders as a hint to Penny to undrape herself from his arm. It was warm in the private room of the restaurant, and her perfume and the waft of the blown-out candles were stifling. He was mad at her anyway for smuggling in a case of champagne and beer and bribing the waitress to keep quiet about it. Oklahoma was a dry state with strict laws against the sale and imbibing of alcohol in public. He felt suffocated from the heavy food and beer in his belly, the cigarette smoke, and the revelry that had begun to have a desperate edge to it, as if his friends' loud jests and tipsy laughter could drown out the voices of gloom and uncertainty hanging over their futures. Tomorrow when their heads cleared, the voices would resound louder than ever. He supposed it would be impolite to have the waitress box the cake to take home, but he didn't think he could endure the long ritual of having it cut and served and eaten at the tail end of his party. He'd had enough of his birthday celebration. He wanted to get his mother out of here. He wanted to go home.

This birthday bash had been his father's idea and thrown at his insistence. "It'll do your mother good to get her mind off her worry over you and the war news in France. Besides, this is the last one you'll have before you're drafted, and you know that I like to show off what I can do for my family," he'd argued. But Bucky suspected a big part of his father's reason for the party was his own fear that this birthday might be his son's last.

The girlfriend of one of his fraternity brothers leaned forward and slurred, "So, Bucky, wha... branch of the service are you...gonna sign up for if your draft number isn't called this next go-round?"

At a signal from his mother, the waitress approached the table and, in chagrin, Bucky watched her whisk away the cake to be taken to the kitchen and sliced. They wouldn't be skipping dessert after all, and he wouldn't be able to escape the question he'd known was bound to pop up.

"I won't be sure until I finish investigating my options," he replied. "I want to sign up with whatever organization will let me put my engineering degree to good use."

"Oh, I see," she said, but, clearly, irritatingly, she did not. Ever since the war began, his friends, classmates, parents, and his father's close business associates had noticed that the usually decisive Bucky seemed mysteriously disinclined to discuss his military service "options" after graduation, which made them wonder if he was holding out for a noncombatant but essential government job stateside. Was Sam Barton, model of young manhood, pride of his parents, star athlete, class leader, school hero, taking the safe and cowardly way out?

The girl flopped a hand carelessly. "Oh, well, who can blame you if you want to play it safe? Those Nazis are horrible people, and the Japanese are worse. The atrocities they're committing make your blood curdle."

Penny shot her a scathing look. "Good God, Babs! What gave you the idea that Sam wants to play it safe? He wants to use his professional skills in the most effective way for the war effort. And I doubt you can *see* anything given the amount you've had to drink."

Penny's reprimand signaled the end of the fun. The cake was served in near silence and hardly touched during strained conversation. Penny refused a serving, saying, "I'm watching my figure so Sam will." After the first round of coffee, everyone folded their napkins and pushed back from their plates. It was Saturday evening, and most had to be in their rooms on the university campus by twelve. Bucky would be driving his parents home to Oklahoma City and staying for the rest of the weekend. Anticipating that his father would drink more than usual at the party, Bucky had insisted on being the one to drive their car, but he really wanted an excuse to keep an appointment at seven on Monday morning. He had arranged to meet a man at a coffee shop before catching the bus back to Norman for his midmorning finals.

Behind the wheel of his parents' Cadillac, Bucky noticed that his father's expansive mood, encouraged by the beer, had vanished. Horace Barton had purchased the car in anticipation of the nation going to war. Automobile manufacturers would be converting their plants to military production of arms, munitions, trucks, tanks, and planes, he predicted, "and the home front will not see another new civilian car roll off assembly lines until the end of the war, whenever the hell that will be."

His assessment had been right and in line with most of his astute commercial and business decisions, as evidenced by the success of his trucking company and its notable survival of the Depression. That he adored Monique Barton, Bucky had no doubt. After almost twenty-three years of marriage, the feeling his rough, bombastic father had for his lovely, refined French mother still bordered on adulation. "Imagine the luck of an old high school dropout country boy like me winning the hand of a beautiful, educated woman like your mom," he'd say to Bucky. "Never let me hear you say a cross word to her, son, you hear me? The belt if you do."

"Yessir," Bucky would dutifully reply, as if he could ever disrespect his mother, but he had learned that Horace Barton's idea of parenting was to instruct by empty threat, for Horace Barton would never lay a hand on his son, even if Bucky had been the sort of child to test his concept of good conduct. His father loved him without bounds. Of that, Bucky had no doubt, either, and he was happy to make him proud.

Looking into his rearview mirror, he saw his father glance worriedly at his mother and reach for her hand. She had not spoken the whole drive, and the car vibrated with her deep silence. "It will be okay, sweetheart," Horace said soothingly. "Your sister in Paris will be fine. The Germans treat the upper-class French with respect, and *should* Bucky decide to join the Army Corps of Engineers, it doesn't send its bridge builders into combat. If Bucky is sent overseas, chances are he will be given an assignment far behind hostile lines, ready to step up to do his stuff when the path is clear." Horace reached forward and popped his son on the shoulder. "Right, son?"

"If you say so, Dad," Bucky said. From his mother's

expression, his father's assurances had the effect of a sprinkler bottle used to put out a house fire, and she turned her head to stare out the window. Bucky added no words to comfort her. They would have been meaningless and untrue, as were his father's, for in the First World War, Horace Barton had seen firsthand what the Germans could do to the French population. Also, Bucky would not be volunteering for the Army Corps of Engineers, as his father assumed. The unit he planned to join would not assign him to build bridges but to destroy them from deep within enemy territory.

But all that would remain a secret until he discussed the details with the man at Kelly's Coffee Shop on Monday. It wasn't only patriotism that had urged him into the meeting with the man from the Office of Strategic Services, but an even deeper secret that Horace Barton could not know—could *never* know. At fourteen, Bucky had overheard a private conversation of his mother's and learned that the man in the back seat of the Cadillac was not his father. His real father lived in Paris, a high-ranking officer in the French military whom his mother still loved.

CHAPTER FOUR

The truth had come to light in the winter of 1934. Bucky's mother and her sister, Aunt Claire, visiting from France, had thought they were alone in the house. It was four o'clock in the afternoon. His father was at his business, and Bucky was supposed to be at piano practice four blocks away, but his teacher's husband had met him at the door to say that she was ill and there would be no lesson that day. Bucky considered spending the unexpected gift of freedom at Rob Hamilton's house, but it had seemed somehow wrong not to be where he was supposed to be, so he'd gone home consoled by the thought that there would be enough time to have a cup of hot cocoa and a cookie without spoiling his dinner. He let himself into the house through the back kitchen door, feeling again the kick of loss at the absence of his black

Labrador retriever. He'd thought many times afterward that if Pepper had not died earlier that month, he would never have discovered his mother's secret. Pepper would have alerted her to his presence.

He did not call out that he was home. His early arrival would have startled and alarmed his mother before he had a chance to explain. She was jumpy when it came to him, he supposed because he was her only child. Voices were coming from the living room—his mother's and Aunt Claire's. He set his book satchel in the kitchen chair he occupied each evening to do his homework, hung up his jacket and cap on a peg in the mud room, and started down the hall toward the sound of the voices. His mother and aunt were speaking French in what sounded like a serious, high-strung conversation, and Bucky would have to decide whether he'd disturb them to ask for cocoa. Just before arriving at the living room door, he heard his aunt say, "Does Horace know the boy isn't his?"

"*No!*" his mother cried. "And he never will. Oh, my God, how can it be that Nicholas is still alive? They told me he was killed in an ambush in October of 1919!"

"The French occupation of the Rhineland was a confusing time. Chaos everywhere," Aunt Claire said. "Remember it took days to quell the German resurgence. The Belgians, not the French, were in charge of identifying and listing the names of the dead on the casualty lists."

"So the Belgians mistook another French body of the same rank that looked enough like Nicholas Cravois and pronounced him dead, when all along he was lying in a ditch by the side of the road. Oh, God, Claire..." Monique Barton's voice trailed off in a stifled cry, and, frozen where he stood, Bucky heard the wood floor creak and pictured his mother walking in circles about the room clutching her throat as she always did when agitated.

"You are not to blame yourself, Monique. By the time Nicholas had regained consciousness and got in touch with his family, you'd learned you were pregnant with Samuel and had married Horace. What else were you to do, *ma chérie*? You thought Nicholas was dead."

The creaking of the floor stopped. Bucky imagined his mother whirling to his aunt. "But why didn't he get in touch with me, for God's sake?" she said.

There was silence, and then his aunt answered gently, "Really, Monique, why would he? It was too late."

"Does he know he has a son?"

"He knows *you* have a son. He does not know the boy is his."

"*Mon Dieu*, Claire, why did you tell me this now? Why didn't you allow me to remain ignorant?"

"Because Nicholas is now an influential general in the French Army, slated to become one of the youngest marshals in French history and well known for his antifascist views. His outspokenness against that little mustached worm, Adolf Hitler, makes news. His name may well be mentioned in the American newspapers, and I didn't want you to learn of his survival that way. Has Horace ever suspected..."

"No, never." More silence, then: "How...does he look? Nicholas?"

A pause. "Handsome, strong, commanding. I see much of him in Samuel, especially his eyes."

Bucky backed away, returned to the kitchen, collected his satchel, cap, and coat, and pedaled against the icy wind as fast as he could to Rob Hamilton's house, his second home. There, alarmed at Bucky's pale face and strange look, Mrs. Hamilton made cocoa for her son and his best friend, served piping hot. At dinner that night, Bucky took only a few bites of coq au vin and pushed his peas and carrots around on his plate. His parents did not ask him about his piano lesson and seemed not to notice that he kept his eyes on his food. His mother and aunt were full of bright, nervous chatter, the kind adults engaged in to cover awkward situations.

His aunt left for Paris the following morning and that afternoon after school, Bucky biked to the county library and asked the kindly librarian to help him locate information on the French occupation of the Rhineland in 1919. Also, he wanted to know what *antifascism* meant and what a marshal of France was. His questions had to do with World War I, the librarian said, leading him to shelves full of books on the subject since so many in the county had served in that global conflict. Was he researching for a history report? she asked.

"You could call it that," Bucky said.

They found a book about the swift and brutal French suppression of German resistance in the Rhineland, which had originally been a German territory. The librarian, whose husband had been killed on the Maginot Line, read over his shoulder. "Served the Jerries right!" she declared.

That evening Bucky leaned in close to the bathroom mirror to study his eyes, a source of embarrassment when he was younger. They were thickly lashed—"girl's eyes," they were teasingly called in elementary school. Now the girls thought them sexy. They were hazel with flecks of blue and green that alternated in dominance depending on the color of his shirt. He wondered about the man from whom he'd inherited them. At fourteen, Bucky had already decided that, though Horace Barton was a good dad and he wouldn't have traded him for anyone else's in the world, he did not want to be like him. He loved him dearly and respected him, but he did not admire him. But Bucky thought he might wish to emulate the "strong, commanding" man who lived across the ocean and was opposed to dictators and fascism, the man who as a marshal of France wore seven stars on his shoulders and carried a blue baton...the man his mother saw when she looked into her son's eyes.

Behind the wheel of the Cadillac, Bucky touched the breast pocket of his sport coat in which he had tucked the letter from the man at the Office of Strategic Services. He might need it as a form of identification when he met him at Kelly's Coffee Shop Monday morning.

CHAPTER FIVE

BRIDGETTE / LABRADOR

Stephens College, Missouri

Bridgette Loring stepped back to appraise her creation, displayed on the wire dress frame formed to match the measurements of her best friend and college roommate, Gladys Bradbury. "That gown is utterly breathtaking," her friend said beside her. "God, I hope I don't ruin it for you, Bridge."

"The judges will be looking at the dress, not you," Bridgette said, "so relax and enjoy the stroll down the runway."

"I'm afraid I'll lose my balance when the cameras pop," Gladys said. "What if they blind me, and I fall?"

Bridgette turned away with a flash of annoyance at this latest "what-if" on her friend's roll of problems that could derail her entry from winning a highly competitive spot on Edith Head's list of the five

"Most Beautiful Designs." The celebrated costume designer for Paramount Pictures was the main judge of the evening wear in tomorrow's annual May fashion exhibition at Stephens College to showcase the talents of its seniors graduating with degrees in fashion design and illustration. Each student was required to exhibit a garment of their own creation in the runway event billed as a style show, but it was really a competition to catch the attention of talent scouts from some of the most prestigious clothes manufacturers in the industry.

However, at this year's May event, the prime catwalk audience seats reserved for these fashion reconnoiters would be mostly empty. Bridgette had learned that few rooms had been booked for the judges at the Pennant Hotel, where they usually stayed. War rationing had hit the fashion industry especially hard as people were urged to "make do and mend" so that fabric manufacturers could focus on war-related textiles. The government needed wool for uniforms and silk for parachutes, maps, and bags for gunpowder. The military draft had drained factories of their workers, and transportation of goods had been hampered owing to the rationing of fuel and rubber tires. The contestants' hopes for an internship centered mainly on Edith Head, but all understood she might have come merely to judge the style show as a favor to her longtime friend, the dean of the college's School of Fashion Design.

Bridgette knew differently. The dean had confided to Bridgette that she had invited Edith Head to judge the style show primarily to see Bridgette's work. "She won't know what gown is yours," the dean had told her. "That would be unfair to the other girls. That's why I haven't sent Edith your portfolio. Your entry will be your only chance to get your foot in the door with her. If she likes what she sees, then I will show her your drawings. Needless to say, this conversation remains between us."

When Bridgette had tried to thank her, the dean had said, "I'm not doing this for you, Bridgette, but for the school. If Edith Head takes you on, you can understand the benefit of the publicity to Stephens."

Bridgette hoped she wouldn't regret her decision to ask Gladys to model her creation in lieu of its designer. Most of the entries would be worn by the same students who had conceived and seen their garments through to construction, but Bridgette hadn't the height to do justice to her slinky evening gown nor the heart to give the honor of modeling it to another girl. But Gladys as usual was afraid of failure, and while Bridgette's creation would have to speak for itself, the model had a lot to do with showing it to its best advantage.

"Okay, so tell me, and don't avoid the subject this time," Gladys said accusingly. "If you make Edith Head's list, and she asks you to come work for her, will you be going to California?"

Bridgette concentrated on testing the drape of the skirt, unnecessary since her sharp eye, merciless as a stiletto, told her no final stitch or adjustment was required. The toga-inspired, floor-length sheath in shimmering scarlet jersey with its inlay of rhinestones on its single shoulder was ready to go, but she could not meet the disappointment bound to flare on her best friend's face when she heard her answer.

"Yes, I will, Gladys. I've given the J. L. Hudson offer a lot of thought and decided that I'm not going to accept it. I'm not keen on moving to Detroit for a marketing career with a retail store chain. I'm a women's clothes designer, not a fashion marketer and manager. Short of going to Paris as an apprentice in one of the big couture houses—which is now out of the question with the German occupation on—can you think of a more exciting place to intern than in Paramount's costume division under Edith Head? Of course I'll take the position if it's offered.

Imagine creating clothes for Bette Davis and Olivia de Havilland! Besides, I want to get my grandmother out of the Michigan winters."

"California is a long way from home, Bridge, and a move might not be good for her. You know she's not well."

"All the more reason to move her to a warmer climate. The change will be the best medicine for her. She's taken the news from France terribly hard. I have to go, Gladys. You have to understand that."

Bridgette's voice softened as she turned to look at her friend, crestfallen at the thought of their inevitable separation. Hardly a day had passed since the first day in kindergarten that she and Gladys Bradbury had not been together. They were as close as sisters. Even when the Bradbury family went on vacation, Gladys wrote to Bridgette every day, and sometimes her father would allow her to make a long-distance telephone call just to hear Bridgette's voice. Her friend had been thrilled when Bridgette was offered a position with Hudson in Detroit. Gladys had accepted a job as an elementary school teacher in one of the suburbs of the city, and her middle brother, Mike, who'd always had more than a brotherly interest in Bridgette, was an architect in a firm that catered exclusively to the wealthy Grosse

Pointe area. For years, Gladys had dreamed of Bridgette becoming her sister-in-law, but now it was not going to happen.

Bridgette put a consoling hand on her roommate's shoulder. "We always knew we'd go our separate ways once we graduated from college, but that doesn't mean we can't visit each other. That's what planes are for."

Gladys flexed her shoulder irritably. "Oh, you'll forget about me once you're among all those rich and famous movie stars, hobnobbing with the likes of Ginger Rogers and Fred Astaire."

"I doubt very seriously I'll be keeping that kind of company. I'll be like a little mole slaving in the back room and never see the stars I'm sewing for. But that's just my dream talking, and we're getting way ahead of ourselves. For all we know, Edith Head may be here only to judge the show and not to scout for interns, and I may not get an invitation even if she is offering. I'll have plenty of competition."

"Oh, if she's offering, you'll get it. You and Miss Head both speak French."

That was true. Bridgette had researched Edith Head and learned that the famous designer had begun her working life as a French teacher in Hollywood, but Bridgette hoped to be offered an internship based on more than the language they shared. Feeling another jab of irritation with Gladys, she said, "Let's go get some lunch," and took a final look at her creation before drawing a protective muslin sack over the form, one of many such shrouded dress stands about the room. Beneath their protective hoods were the formal evening entries of the other competitors. They looked like ranks of headless ghosts, each standing apart from the others, silent, wary, and threatening. Bridgette was the last exhibitor to check her design, and they were alone in the room but for the student assistant who would sit guard until two o'clock, when the door would be locked until it was time for the staff and student designers to prepare for the style show that Saturday evening.

"All set?" the assistant asked as Bridgette and Gladys gathered their purses to leave.

"All set," Bridgette said. "We're going to the dining hall."

The assistant snapped her book shut. "Great. You girls are the last, so I'll lock up the shop and go get some lunch myself after I drop off the room keys in the chairman's door box."

"We'll wait for you if you care to join us," Gladys said, the invitation surprising Bridgette. Whenever possible, she liked to keep Bridgette to herself.

On the way across the parklike campus, crowded today with groups of family members and friends arrived for graduation week and commencement on Sunday, Bridgette looked around at her alma mater. She would be forever grateful for the all-inclusive scholarship that had made it possible to pursue her dream of a degree in fashion illustration and design, but she wondered if she would ever return to Stephens. She'd always concentrated on the here and now with an eye to the future. She had made friends at Stephens, but she expected time to break those college ties as roads led on to other roads, new places, new faces. She was one to be grateful for the memories of the old but was eager for opportunities to make new ones. Gladys, on the other hand, never missed a school reunion. She clung to every person, place, and thing that had ever been a part of her life, possibly because they represented safety and security and familiarity and spared her the risks of the unknown. Bridgette realized, sadly, that perhaps her childhood friend was right to wonder if they'd remain as close as they were.

Gladys asked as if she'd read her thoughts, "We'll always be best friends, right, Bridge?"

A trace of irritation with her friend still lingered. "If time and distance allow it," she said.

A disappointed silence fell between them. "Well, let's just make sure they do," Gladys said after a while.

Bridgette thought about her friend's remark as they walked along among the ancient oak trees and academic edifices. Detroit was four hours from Traverse City, a long way from home to Gladys. When Bridgette was younger, she had envied her best friend's large and loving and wealthy family. She'd wondered what it would be like to be doted upon and indulged, denied nothing, petted and protected as the youngest, but as Bridgette had matured, she'd felt herself lucky to have been brought up by a thrifty grandmother who did not believe in coddling. "Too much kneading the dough ruins the bread, and too much sugar spoils the yeast," her grandmother always said. Bridgette came to realize that her tougher childhood had promoted in her ambition, initiative, and confidence. Those particular attributes were lacking in Gladys because her privileged birth had not required them. If her friend ever decided to try her wings, her family would swoop in to catch her before she fell. Bridgette planned to spread her wings and fly, but far from Detroit and Traverse City, Michigan, and she would not fall.

CHAPTER SIX

In the dining hall, the three girls joined a table of others who, like Bridgette, had no family coming for commencement. Gladys's parents and five older brothers, along with their own families, would be arriving late that afternoon to witness her graduate from college. Gladys had her own car on campus, and Bridgette would ride back to Michigan with her on Sunday after the Baccalaureate ceremony, her little two-seater adding to the convoy of Bradbury vehicles. Seeing the throngs of visitors about campus on their walk to the dining hall, Gladys had said, "Oh, I do wish your grandmother had been well enough to come, Bridge."

Sincere as it was, Bridgette saw through her friend's expression of concern. To boost her argument for Bridgette remaining in Michigan, Gladys would drive home the point of her grandmother's ill health at every opportunity. "Well, you know Angelique Duvalier," Bridgette said. "Her pride would never allow her to accept transportation and accommodations that she couldn't pay for, but it was good of your folks to offer. She and I will celebrate my graduation and my birthday when I get home."

At the table were several rivals of Bridgette's in the dress competition, and an undercurrent of tension prevailed despite the girls' cordial relationships. Privately, everyone agreed that Bridgette's design would top the list of Most Beautiful Designs and win the coveted invitation to fly out to Edith Head's studio in California for a chat. This consensus was in contrast to earlier reservations about her choice of style, color, and fabric. The selections were considered unpatriotic. Experts had long agreed that during wartime, fashion elements should be restrained, refined, and unadorned, but Bridgette's view differed. Color and luxury of fabric and embellishments were a great foil against the ugliness of war, she maintained. The instructor had shaken her head at her most gifted student's obstinacy, but it was Bridgette's decision, and she had given her the go-ahead to make the biggest mistake of her four-year tenure at Stephens College.

Now it appeared that Bridgette's elegant, unabashedly glamorous scarlet jersey creation might win the day against the gowns of the other girls who had heeded the established mantra. Bridgette had experienced many competitions—debate, chess, sports—and had learned never to anticipate victory before it happened. Something could always come along to gum up the works, and sneaking a taste of dessert before it was served robbed it of its full flavor later, as her grandmother would caution. So today she concentrated on another "last" of her college experiences. Never again would she eat the dining hall's tasteless rice pudding.

Talk centered on the speculated arrival of Edith Head and how long she would stay. Bridgette noticed that Gladys, usually the more talkative of the pair, had sunk into a strange, reflective mood, made more puzzling by her sudden move to get up from the table.

"Where are you going?" Bridgette asked.

"To the Pennant to see that all is in order with my family's rooms. I'll see you later."

Bridgette stared after her, surprised that she had not been asked to go along. Her roommate hardly went anywhere without her, and now that Bridgette's packing was done, she would have enjoyed getting off campus as a break from all the family activity that made her wish that her grandmother had come.

After lunch, Bridgette decided to make a last pass by the campus post office. After today, the combinations to the seniors' mailboxes would be changed, and they'd no longer have access to them. Unexpectedly, she'd received two letters, an official-looking one with a return address in Washington, D.C., and, equally surprising, one from Steve Hammett, a classmate and her tormentor from junior high school, the guy responsible for her hated nickname, Slugger. She opened Steve's first.

Dear Bridgette,

I'm just writing to say good-bye as I've recently joined the army and will be going to Fort Sill, Oklahoma, for training. I've been assigned to the 45th Infantry Division. I hope you don't mind, but I got your address from your grandmother. I just wanted to say, in case I never have a chance to express myself in person because of the war and all that I'm sorry if I caused you any distress in school. I only wanted you to know how much I admired you for being so gutsy, you being so small and cute and nobody expecting such gumption from a girl like you. I understand you're graduating from college with high honors like you did from high school. May I say I'm not surprised. I cut your picture out of our yearbook to take with me overseas because that's where we're eventually going. I wanted it to remind me of what we're fighting the Nazis for. Take care of yourself, Slugger, and maybe give me a thought now and then—a kind one, I hope.

Yours sincerely,
Steve Hammett

Bridgette's eyes stung when she'd finished reading. She could now look back on Steve Hammett's pestering of her in junior high school with more understanding. He had meant her no disrespect and had shown his admiration for her in the only way he knew, having been brought up motherless by a drunkard father. Steve had been considered the bad boy of Traverse City's junior high school. Tall and brawny and darkly handsome in an oily, cheap, Hollywood way, he had all the girls mad for him except Bridgette. He sat behind her in ninth grade English class, and she'd finally had enough the day he traced the faintly visible lace pattern of her slip through the back of her white silk blouse with the eraser tip of his pencil. She'd whirled around and given him a tongue lashing, and he never bothered her after that. But all through high school until the day they graduated, she'd had the sense that he had his eye on her. She wondered now if he'd been watching out for her, making sure she stayed safe. Bridgette wished him well in the army, a life that might suit him to a tee—if he lived. Gladys would be as surprised and moved as she when she showed her the letter. Imagine Steve Hammett carrying her yearbook picture in his wallet! Bridgette hoped it would bring him luck.

The second envelope contained a greeting from the director of the Office of Strategic Services, cosigned by his deputy. Bridgette had never heard of the government organization. The letter's content was surprisingly personal, containing intimate details of her short history, including her coming graduation from Stephens College. The correspondent wrote of his knowledge of her grandmother's torture and her grandfather's murder in Germany during World War I, and concluded by asking if she would be willing to meet with him to discuss how she might "do her part to rid France of the Third Reich's evil domination." A telephone number was listed below the sender's name.

Bridgette folded the letter and reinserted it into its envelope, slightly disconcerted that a Washington agency had somehow sniffed her out as having cause to fight the despicable Nazis, but her degree was in fashion design and illustration. What contributions could she make to assist France? She might be tempted to reply if she didn't feel in her bones that tomorrow she would be offered an invitation to interview with Edith Head. Besides, she must take care of her grandmother. After her first thought to toss the letter into a campus waste can, Bridgette reconsidered its private nature and slipped it into her purse with Steve's.

Back at her dorm in Columbia Hall, she was given a note from Gladys saying that her family had arrived at the hotel; she would spend the night with them and meet Bridgette for breakfast the following morning. Bridgette felt a smart of disappointment. There had been many times during the past four years when she would have welcomed a break from Gladys's constant presence, but tonight she was feeling at sixes and sevens and could have used her chatty company and the pleasure of being with her boisterous family. Bridgette thought it odd that Gladys, excessively solicitous about her, had left her on her own tonight of all nights, when the dorm was practically deserted and the dining hall closed. Students had been given a sack lunch for their supper.

She shook her head at her mood. Since when had she depended on Gladys Bradbury to fill her time? And she had no right to presume that she'd be included in tonight's private family gathering when the Bradburys had been kind enough to invite her to join them for the celebratory dinner tomorrow evening. By then, the style show would be over, and she might well be dining in the restaurant of the Pennant Hotel with the dean and Edith Head herself.

Rather than sit alone in her room, she went downstairs to the reception room with a book to read and pen and paper to write a reply to Private Steve Hammett. The return address listed his home in Traverse City, and Bridgette hoped his drunkard father would forward it to his military unit.

Time passed quickly after all. Students and parents passed through the reception room and stopped to chat, and the desk crew invited her to eat her sack lunch with them in the anteroom behind the reception counter. By nine o'clock she was bored with her book and tired of her chair and decided to walk across campus to mail Steve's letter. A breeze had risen, fanning her face and discouraging the mosquitoes, and she found herself enjoying the walk before she returned to Columbia Hall to bathe in the floor bathroom she'd have all to herself tonight.

Bridgette had just left the campus post office when she glanced toward Walter Hall and saw a light briefly flare in the first-floor window of the fashion design department. She stared, thinking she may have imagined the flash, but there it appeared again, the brief beam of a flashlight. It had come from the room holding the exhibits. Startled, alarmed, curious, Bridgette ran toward the entrance of the building and let herself into the front door of Walter Hall quietly, her heart knocking. Someone unauthorized was in the exhibit room; otherwise, why not turn on the lights?

Without thinking beyond the numbing fear that the exhibits were in danger, Bridgette marched to the closed door of the design room and flung it open. She flipped on the blinding overhead fluorescents, and her mouth fell open. The dress stands stood denuded of their muslin shrouds and beautiful gowns, and standing in the mounds of shredded shantung, crepe, foulard, organza, tulle, and scarlet jersey, scissors in hand, stood Gladys Bradbury.

CHAPTER SEVEN

CHRIS / LAPWING

New Braunfels, Texas

So what do you hear from Dirk?" Chris Brandt asked his friend's father, Ernst Drechsler. The man appeared ten years older since a year ago when Chris had stood at the same bar in the banquet hall of the biergarten and asked his one-time best friend if he was really serious about his decision to go to Germany to join the Nazi Party.

Dirk had raised his beer stein to his lips and regarded Chris over its brimming foam with the stare he believed members of the Abwehr assumed when interrogating prisoners. The Abwehr was the intelligence agency of the German Army, which he planned to join when he returned to "the Fatherland and the Third Reich," as he boasted to all and sundry. All and sundry in New Braunfels, Texas, had been happy to see him go, and those who still had affection for the Drechslers had gathered in the large banquet room of the Frieldholm Biergarten at the end of May 1941 for a combination send-off and graduation party since Dirk, after a struggle academically, had managed to eke out a bachelor's degree from Texas Lutheran College.

"You'll regret not throwing in your lot with us as well, Christoph, when our mother country rules the world," Dirk had told his friend.

"My mother country is America, Dirk, same as yours. As I see it, you'll be sorry you threw in your lot with the Nazis when America enters the war, and you're branded a traitor."

Dirk had set down his beer glass with a smirk. He had begun to grow a mustache and to wear his hair cut and parted in the same slicked-down style as Adolf Hitler. Neither attempt in this early stage to emulate the Third Reich leader appeared successful. Dirk's hair was too bristly to respond to Brylcreem and his upper lip too narrow to support but a thin bushy line that looked like a clinging caterpillar. In time, though, Chris thought that Dirk could pass for another Hermann Göring, head of the Luftwaffe, "the fatty in the dove-gray suit," so his detractors dubbed him.

"We'll see who will be branded a traitor when the

war is over—the Germans in America who remembered the country from which they came, or the Germans who forgot," Dirk said.

"I never knew Germany well enough to remember," Chris said. "Neither did you."

Chris had glanced into the yawning, empty cavern of the vast banquet hall. The tables had been set for guests who had deliberately accepted dinner invitations only to decline them at the last minute to state their rejection of the political leanings of the guest of honor and his family. The Drechslers would have done better to have hosted a backyard barbecue. Chris would have been among the absent guests if the gesture had not been done in poor taste. He had hoped his mother took notice of the price to be paid for being too pro-German in New Braunfels, Texas. Already her luster had faded in the eyes of the townspeople, though they still patronized his father's shoe repair shop, if only because it was the only one in town.

Chris didn't know if Dirk was being stupid or brave to go against the tide of feeling against Adolf Hitler. Misguided was more like it. At the time, he'd wondered if his former best buddy had considered that one day he might face his Texas friends as the enemy. Chris wouldn't be one of them. He still felt shame at being rejected for enlistment into the military services on grounds of "a physical defect." He was as sound as any man and eligible for general duty in every way other than his thumbless right hand that the army held would prevent him from managing a weapon. He was single, young, fit, and educated. He was a teacher and coach at Stephen F. Austin High School in Austin and was earning his master's degree in education at his alma mater, the University of Texas. He'd planned to begin his doctoral program this year, but Japan bombed Pearl Harbor and the Axis powers declared war on America. He'd gone immediately to sign up.

A member of the medical team at his local draft board had told him, "If this war lasts, more manpower will be needed and physical standards will be lowered. Your chance may still come. Meanwhile go back to your teaching and coaching job knowing you're needed there. With so many male teachers being drafted, there will be a dearth of masculine presence in the classroom."

Chris thought that all very high-sounding and noble, even if true, but the medic's counsel did little to assuage the insult at his rejection. The rub now was that he had no idea how long his teaching job might last. That question would be answered in tomorrow's meeting with his principal.

"I've heard nothing at all from Dirk since war was declared," Ernst answered Chris's question, "and I doubt he's received our letters. He wrote in his last letter that he had been assigned to Paris with that German intelligence agency he was so keen to join. We may not have another word from him until the war is over. His mother and I are terribly sad and worried." The man's strained smile betrayed regret that things had come to this miserable pass.

Chris felt a jab of pity for him. Dirk's zeal for Nazi ideology had cost the Drechslers their standing in town, nearly all their friends, and his father's law firm many clients. The "celebration" this evening was on the occasion of Ernst's forced, early retirement. The large group that in 1936 had gathered around the radio in the Drechslers' living room to applaud Germany's stunning reentry into the world community by way of the Olympic games in Berlin now had appalling reason to regret their enthusiasm. Based on the disturbing radio broadcasts and the few letters coming out of Germany to New Braunfels involving Jewish relatives and friends, only a handful of the original celebrants were still enamored with Adolf Hitler. They were the ones in attendance tonight.

The lawyer glanced over his shoulder at the paltry

gathering. "I should never have agreed to this travesty of a party," he announced mournfully. Silently, Chris concurred. Tonight, only one long table was required to accommodate the number of guests. Then, like now, Chris had seen the clothed rectangle as a small island isolated in a sea of darkness, the guests self-exiles huddled together for comfort and safety. He sighed. He might eventually become an exile himself, or rather a castaway for being German, but not willingly, and never for being a Nazi. His loyalty was to America. He could never be a part of the group at the table, no matter that he might live out the war on his own isolated island of the forsaken.

"It does seem unfair that the sins of the son should be visited upon the father," Chris said.

Ernst gave a weak chuckle. "Well quoted. The catfish are biting in the Guadalupe. Why don't you and I go throw in a line early tomorrow morning? I'll pick you up."

Chris heard the wistfulness in his voice, the yearning for the normalcy of the past when he'd take Dirk and Chris fishing on Saturday mornings before the sun was up. Chris's father did not care for rod and reel, and Dirk's father had never taken to Frederik Brandt's passion for golf. They were some of Chris's fondest boyhood memories, the times he and Dirk and his father set off before dawn for a day on the river.

"I'd like to, but I have to get back to Austin early. I have an appointment at my school at nine o'clock."

"Oh," Ernst said, his tone full of regret. "You are indeed dedicated to your profession to give up a Saturday morning of fishing, my boy, but one can't fault that." A wariness in his eye wondered if Chris was making up the excuse to avoid being with him.

Chris remained silent. His appointment was not with parent or student, but an explanation would only make him appear like one of the exiled beginning to take their seats at the table. "Excuse me," Ernst said, somewhat stiffly. "I must see to my other guests."

Chris saw his own father step away from the breaking huddle to come collect him at the bar. Frederik Brandt was the "son" of the sign FREDERIK BRANDT AND SON SHOE REPAIR SHOP, but he and his wife had larger plans for their only child than to add Chris's name to the shoe shop lineage. They had hoped he'd choose a profession more lucrative than teaching, but in time he would earn a PhD, and they could proudly write to their friends in Germany that he was a *Doktor der Padagogik*.

"I believe the Drechslers wish us to sit down, Chris.

Looks like no one else is going to arrive. At least Ernst didn't have to pay for the dinners of those who didn't show up like last year. You couldn't persuade Brenda to come?"

"She despises the Drechslers." Chris did not mention that he and Brenda were no longer seeing each other.

Frederik Brandt shook his head sadly. "Doesn't nearly everybody?"

"Mother doesn't."

"She has an understanding heart."

"She doesn't like to admit she's wrong."

"Ah, yes, well, there's that, too, but we will not disillusion her, huh, Chris, my son?" Frederik directed the plea to him over the tops of his glasses, and Chris turned to the bartender.

"Refill this, please," he said, setting his glass on the bar. "And yours, Dad?"

Frederik thrust out his beer stein. "By all means."

It was a long evening strained by empty sentiment and forced bonhomie to keep at bay the fears that lurked in the outer, unlit environs of the room—fears that had materialized as a result of the country's anti-German feeling, which had arisen last year when the U.S. government penalized the Third Reich for its militant and brutal expansion into most of Europe. In June 1941, President Roosevelt had ordered all German and Italian assets in the United States frozen. Two days later, the State Department had closed all German consulates and Nazi propaganda organizations in the country. What did these actions mean to the naturalized and native-born Germans of New Braunfels? How would they affect their lives, their livelihoods? Then came the surprise attack in December on Pearl Harbor and Germany's declaration of war against the United States. Tonight Chris noticed that some at the table cast anxious looks toward the doors of the biergarten hall, half expecting the police, on the assumption that it was a Nazi gathering, to burst in to arrest them or deport them back to Germany.

At last the evening broke up, and Chris was pleased that it was early enough to return to Austin tonight in preparation for his appointment with his principal. When he told his mother of his plans, she scolded, "But, Christoph, we hardly ever see you anymore!"

"Weekend and after-school sports keep me busy, Mother. You know that."

"I did not think teaching would keep you so occupied. The law, medicine, business, yes, but not teaching."

She had her not-so-subtle ways of expressing her disappointment in his choice of profession, and Chris had come to recognize that, though he loved her still, he liked her less and less. It was another sorrowful situation that the war in Europe had brought about. Tomorrow morning, another would most likely be added to the list.

CHAPTER EIGHT

Chris recognized his principal's black 1938 Chevrolet as he pulled into the parking lot of Stephen F. Austin High School. There were other cars as well, most belonging to the coaches and players of the baseball team who'd come to view the reels of Friday night's playoff game. The Austin A's had won the previous night in a nail-biter that Chris would have preferred to attend rather than Ernst Drechsler's retirement party. His request to be excused from handing out programs at the stadium had incurred the sharp disapproval of Mr. Knowle, the school principal, in a repeat of the conversation they'd had last May in 1941. Bachelor teachers were expected to fill in at home sports events, and last May Mr. Knowle had demanded to know what was important enough to keep Chris from doing his school duty. Chris had told him the event was in farewell to the son of old family friends.

"Where's he going?" the principal had asked.

Reluctant to lie, Chris had said, "To Germany."

Mr. Knowle's pale brow had risen in derision. As principal of the most prestigious public high school in Texas, it was his job to investigate the backgrounds of its teachers, and he had thoroughly examined Chris's.

Chris knew that Mr. Knowle was dying to demand why an American would wish to go to Germany in these treacherous times, but could not in good form push his curiosity further. So he'd said, "Not to become a Nazi, I hope," and when Chris did not reply, his brow had rippled further. "I see," he'd said and from that moment on, Chris knew that he would be under his principal's scrutiny. He was grateful he'd made the decision to drive back to Austin last night. He'd been able to grab eight hours' sleep in his apartment and had time to shower, shave, and eat a sustaining breakfast to prepare for the blow to fall.

He was ten minutes early, so he sat in his car and contemplated how honored and lucky he'd felt when, fresh out of college, he'd landed an ideal job. The Austin Board of Education had hired him to teach math and coach track and field at a fine school that was conveniently located near his apartment. He'd been afraid his youth and missing thumb might be a handicap, but within weeks of his first year of teaching, Chris had established rapport with his students (many the children of university professors), members of the track-and-field team, the other coaches, and the teachers who shared the same conference period as he. Mainly, though, from the minute he'd walked into his assigned room, he'd felt at home behind a teacher's desk, before a blackboard, beside his classroom door as he welcomed his students to class, and on the 340-yard perimeter of a football field, where he coached young men and women in running, jumping, and vaulting events. He'd made no mistake in his choice of careers. He was where he belonged, and he'd never been happier in his life.

But at the beginning of his second year, in the fall of 1941, he'd noticed a slight chill in the faces around him, in his classes, in the teachers' lounge, on the track. Deeply disturbed, he'd understood its source. The growing atrocities perpetrated by Germany were making world news. In September, the Babi Yar Massacre occurred in which German troops, assisted by Ukrainian police and local collaborators, killed 33,771 Jews in Kiev. That slaughter was preceded earlier in the month by German forces laying siege to Leningrad to starve its citizens into surrender. The first of October, the world was shocked to learn that the Nazis had opened an extermination camp in occupied Poland with the capacity to kill 200,000 people, and October 21, German soldiers went on a rampage in Yugoslavia, killing thousands of civilians, including whole classrooms of schoolboys.

It was not comfortable to be a German in America anymore and even more so to work for a man who'd been a prisoner of war in Germany during World War I. Chris understood why Mr. Knowle distrusted him, but he hoped that his own good character might save his job. He opened the door of his car and got out. He would know in a few minutes whether the board of education had decided not to renew his contract, but he had to ask himself if he really wished to continue working in a place where his colleagues and students had begun to consider him one of the enemy.

It was damn unfair. He had created as much emotional, if not physical, distance from his birthplace and heritage as he could. He did not speak or think in German. He had earned money to pay for his graduate studies as a tutor to college students taking courses in German, but in conversation, he had distilled from his speech every trace of the language. He spoke English with a Texas accent. In college he had not fraternized with students of German descent, but had hung out with the sons and daughters of families as purebred as the University of Texas longhorn mascot. But even his longtime girlfriend, Brenda Lane, had gone sour on him after her cousin had been killed by a Luftwaffe bomb in London. "I know you're not one of them, Chris," she'd said, "but I can't look at you without seeing the Nazi pilot that killed my cousin."

He even planned to go through the legal process of getting his first name changed to Christopher during summer vacation. Maybe, after his first year of teaching at Stephen F. Austin, when the direction of the war in Europe had become painfully clear, he should have considered looking into a job out of state where he could better disassociate himself from the stigma of being from a town assumed to be a pocket of Nazis, but he wanted to finish his doctorate at the University of Texas so he could teach and coach one day at the college level. He loved the city of Austin with its youthful, bustling energy, its access to lakes and hills, its festivals and live music offerings. Chris thought it a bit haughty of Austinites to forget that Austin's growing reputation as a mecca for music lovers had begun in the German beer gardens and halls of their city in the late 1800s.

Avery Knowle's office was at the end of the long corridor on the first floor of the three-story building. Chris let the door close loudly to alert the principal of his arrival, its sound reverberating in the Saturday quiet of the building. Halfway down the hall toward his open door, Chris could hear the calm, terse, universally recognized voice of Edward R. Murrow delivering a radio broadcast. Chris stopped and grew cold as he heard that the night before, citizens of a French village near Bastogne, Belgium, were roused from their sleep by rounds of staccato gunfire. Investigating in the light of dawn, they found the bodies of two downed U.S. American pilots along with six members of the family that had hidden them from discovery. They had been brutally tortured then executed by order of the commander of the ruthless and feared German paramilitary organization, the SS—Schutzstaffel—billeted in the area.

Oh, God, Chris thought and forced his steps to the threshold of Mr. Knowle's door. Glancing up from his desk, the gaunt principal turned off the radio with a hard twist of the knob. "You heard?"

"I did. Horrendous news."

"It happened last night while you were at your

party feting your German friend," Mr. Knowle said. "I can only imagine the grief the families of those American boys will have to live with knowing the suffering their sons went through before they died."

"Indeed," Chris agreed, nape hairs rising at the principal's insinuation that he was making merry with the enemy while his countrymen were being tortured and murdered.

Mr. Knowle's eyes burned into Chris with a fire of deep dislike, undoubtedly set off by memories of his own experiences at the hands of the Germans. "If I were the father of one of those boys, I would not rest until I discovered the name of the bastard that ordered my son's execution, and then I would see how brave *he* is."

"Vengeance would be understandable," Chris said, for lack of anything else to say. He wondered if he'd be invited to sit down or forced to stand before the principal's desk like an errant schoolboy.

Mr. Knowle regarded him coolly through rimless spectacles and finally waved him to a seat. "I'll get right to the point, Mr. Brandt," he said, pressing the thin pads of his fingertips together over a folder on his desk. "It has been brought to my attention that some of our parents are uncomfortable with a teacher of German descent instructing their children."

"Really?" Chris said, his apprehension coiling tighter. He would not accept that assertion on Mr. Knowle's word alone. Despite the anti-German sentiment going around, he'd gotten along very well with his students' parents, supposedly because they valued his teaching and coaching ability over the defect of his ancestry. "How many parents and which ones?"

Mr. Knowle looked as if he had to restrain himself from reaching across the desk to slap Chris for his impertinence. "That is of no matter."

"It is to me. None of my kids' parents has expressed that concern to me."

"Well, of course not. That's one of the duties of a principal—to listen to and analyze complaints put forth by parents."

"I'd like to speak with them. I believe I can convince them that I am every bit as much of an American as they."

Mr. Knowle leaned forward, his pallid forehead moving upward at the preposterousness of Chris's presumption. It was rumored that he had been kept in darkness during his long imprisonment, and his skin was never able to take the sun again. Most of the school year, his office blinds stayed drawn against the sunshine, reinforcing the speculation. "I doubt that very much, Mr. Brandt. Many of the families of Stephen F. Austin's pupils are from ancestors who have lived in the area since the land-grant days."

"So have mine," Chris shot back, prepared to defend his point ancestor by ancestor if need be.

Avery Knowle relaxed in his chair, again patting his fingertips together, and smiled in self-satisfaction. "Ah, well now, that's where your family differs from theirs," he said. "Your family has remained loyal to their German roots, whereas the founding families of whom I speak have always remained true to the ancestry of *their* birth, which is America."

Chris's ire rose. "You have *investigated* my family?"

"I have, Mr. Brandt—with the board's permission, of course, given the tenor of the times. The members acted rather hastily in hiring you in the first place without a thorough background check. I believe your employment came about at the behest of one of your former professors, a Dr. Connor Trent, and a man of considerable influence in Austin."

Mr. Knowle moved his head so that Chris had to blink from the light reflected off the principal's rimless lens. The source came from a lance of sunlight allowed in through the opening between the window and edge of the blind. He wondered if the man had discovered the angle as a means to blind the person in the hot seat. Chris adjusted his chair and said, “Professor Trent’s recommendation was valuable, yes, but I’d like to think my academic and athletic credentials were primarily responsible for my employment.”

The principal ignored the rebuttal and extracted a sheet of paper from the folder. “So as not to delay my reason for calling you here this morning, it is my unpleasant duty to inform you that the board has decided not to renew your contract for next year. However—” he slid the sheet of paper toward Chris “—because you’ve proved to be an excellent teacher and coach, I have taken the liberty of researching openings for teaching positions that you might find more comfortable under the circumstances.” Chris gave the paper a quick glance. It was a list of public schools in various towns in the Texas hill country where Germans had settled, each community bringing its individual dialect, customs, and religious doctrines with them.

Mr. Knowle said, “Nearby Fredericksburg, Bergheim, Boerne, Brenham…they will all be happy to have you, Mr. Brandt, especially since many of their able-bodied male teachers have been called up. We will give you a sterling recommendation.”

Chris looked at the man with growing dislike, the

implication of "able-bodied male teachers" not lost on him. "I won't need it, Mr. Knowle. My record will speak for me." He could hire a lawyer and fight for the right to stay, Chris thought, but he would win the battle and lose the war. He'd become a pariah here. This bitter man would see to that. He would turn staff and students and their parents against him, a maneuver already underway. His principal carried unseen but clearly visible scars from his prisoner of war experiences, but Chris would not take the blame for them. He desperately wanted to keep his job, but he would not be a scapegoat for this man's bias. He rose, picking up the list of schools as he stood. "I could poll the board for each member's vote in this matter, but I can see that I would have no better chance of standing against your prejudice than a Jew in Europe now has against the Third Reich."

His remark hit its intended target, and Chris had the pleasure of seeing Avery Knowle's smug face jarred as he wadded up the list of schools and dropped it in the wastebasket by his desk. Back in his apartment, sick at heart, he found among his day-old mail a letter from Washington, D.C. He read it, astounded at the writer's knowledge of the Brandt family and his academic background, college track-and-field records, and his exemption from military duty on grounds of his missing thumb. It also expressed his organization's awareness of Chris's keen desire to serve his country. The Office of Strategic Services could offer him that opportunity. If he wished to learn more, he was to telephone the number listed at any time day or night, any day of the week. Without another moment's delay, Chris picked up the telephone receiver and made the call.

CHAPTER NINE

BRAD / LIMPET

Meeker, Colorado

Brad Hudson cut the lights, turned off the ignition of his Chevrolet pickup outside his house, and pressed his forehead to the steering wheel's cold frame. His gut felt like a bait bucket of writhing worms, but not from the beer at Murphy's Tavern that he'd drunk with the boys after work when they sent off Joe Carlyle to the U.S. Marines. Smoke curled from the chimney, a white plume against the dark sky, and when he'd rolled down the truck window to let in fresh air to clear his head, he could smell the faint waft of sautéed meat. He'd missed supper, and this was the evening his mother had planned to serve Wiener schnitzel, the veal bought on sale at Shreve's grocery. Mr. Shreve had thrown in an extra cutlet when his wife wasn't looking—"so ve have plenty available for family feast in celebration of being together," Joanna Hudson had announced to her family at breakfast in her German-accented English. She'd looked as if she could have swooped them all to her bosom, but only Beata, sitting nearby, received a rough yank to her mother's voluptuous front. "It's a gift so many udders not be enjoying now."

Brad knew she spoke of her relatives and friends either dead or divided from their families throughout Germany and Poland and France, but the last thing he wanted to celebrate was "being together" in wartime, when other men were out doing their bit to keep their families and *his* safe. His draft card designated him as III-D and read "Registrant deferred because of extreme hardship and privation to dependents," a bitter pill to swallow.

Certainly he wanted to see after his family, both his birth and adopted ones. With his father gone, he was the only one to do it, thus the reason for the deferment. But it ate at him that he, hale and hearty, young and perishing to fight the Nazi bastards who'd caused his mother so much grief, would be left behind with the cowards who'd finagled exemptions from service in the armed forces. It turned his stomach to read of men who should be eligible for military draft swelling the priesthood, divinity schools, firemen and police ranks, and labor forces "necessary for the war effort" to avoid defending their country. He was not one of those, but he would be forced to sit out the war in safety and bear the stigma as if he were. God, he'd give anything to take a gun against the arrogant, goose-stepping monsters bent on cleansing the world of the Jewish race.

Bobby cracked open the front door of the house, peered outside, and spotted him in the cab, and after a quick look back over his shoulder, stepped out and quietly closed the door behind him. He pulled his jacket closer and came around to the truck's open window. "You all right, Brad?" he asked, pitching his voice low. His adopted brother had an instinct for knowing when to keep a conversation private.

Brad let out a little sigh before he answered. "I'm all right. You guys finished eating?"

"We saved plenty for you."

"But you ate your share, right?"

"We ate our share. Your ma says she's going to make veal hash tomorrow."

"Sounds good," Brad said, pushing at the door handle, and Bobby stepped back. He was fifteen now and looked as if he'd always be slight of build, but no peer and few grown men were tougher, and what Bobby lacked in brawn, he made up for in brains and will.

"Was my mother worried about me?"

"A little. I told her you were fine."

Not that she'd listen, Brad was sure. His mother did not rest easy now that he was working full days at Cramer's Lumber Yard, where his father had met the accident that had killed him. Brad had been offered the job the night of his high school graduation, and he had snapped it up. It meant steady work and a definite increase in wages with weekends off and a few health benefits thrown in besides. Jared Cramer, son of the man his father had worked for, was a much more competent and fairer employer than his namesake. He had improved safety conditions with the update of facilities and purchase of more modern equipment. Brad had gone on the company payroll three years ago as a member of a sawing crew. He was now to be promoted to lumberyard manager, where he'd be in charge of work assignments, deliveries, lading, and a variety of other responsibilities—his old friend Joe Carlyle's job. Brad had not accepted the promotion with any great pleasure, and he could not think of his increase in pay as anything but blood money. He'd promised the job back to Joe when he returned from the war.

Only because by the time I get back, you'll be running the whole show, and the boss will be living in Florida off the profits you make for the company, Joe had said, good-naturedly.

"Did you forget about the goose?" Bobby asked quietly.

Oh, hell! Yes, he'd forgotten that after work he was supposed to pluck and gut the goose a neighboring farmer had given them for his sister Beata's birthday dinner on Saturday. The send-off party for Joe at Murphy's had been spur-of-the-moment and initiated by his boss. Brad hadn't telephoned his mother that he'd be late because he'd intended to stay for only a short while, but one pint had led to another, and the time had slipped away.

"I'll get to it tonight," Brad said, hoping he stayed drunk enough not to mind the numbing task of picking the feathers from the bird, downward so as not to tear the flesh, then the bloody business of pulling out the innards—heart, gizzard, windpipe, liver—until water ran clean from the stomach cavity. They could have managed a dressed goose from Shreve's grocery, but Joanna Bukowski Hudson was never one to turn down a gift of local game. She believed that money for store-bought meat and fowl could go toward something else, and their neighbors knew Brad couldn't raise a gun against creatures of land or air. Two-legged animals guilty of the atrocities in Europe, yes—he'd have no problem there—but hunting for sport or food was not for him.

"I'll help you clean it," Bobby volunteered as they started toward the house.

"You'll be doing your homework, young man. School's not over yet," Brad said, laying a hand casually on Bobby's neck, as a father would his son, or a big brother a younger sibling. Bobby did not pull away as he would have done when he and his younger sister, Margie, first came to live in the Hudson household. It had all come about when Brad had discovered them alone, starving, and shivering on the banks of the White River in 1938. Orphaned by a house fire that had killed their parents, the kids, then aged eleven and nine, had run away when they learned they were to be placed in an orphanage. The children's uncertainty of their welcome had lasted a month after Brad rescued them. Then gradually, like stray animals eventually coaxed to eat from a human hand, they came to trust the kindness of the people who had taken them in. His mother called them a blessing, a gift dropped unexpectedly into their lives. Yes, they were extra mouths to feed, but Bobby proved an extra hand, seeing to chores Brad could not tend to when he went to work full time at Cramer's, and Margie became company for Beata, who no longer cried herself to sleep from missing her father. Bobby and his little sister were now as integrated into the family as if they'd been born into it with nobody in a town that minded its own business questioning the sudden expansion of the Hudson household.

The cold air hit Brad like a punch in the face. "Oh God!" he said aloud and stopped abruptly.

Bobby halted with him. "What?"

"I just remembered that I forgot something else."

"What?"

"I invited my boss to our house to celebrate his birthday—Saturday, as a matter of fact."

"That's Beata's birthday," Bobby reminded him.

"I know." *God!* Joanna Hudson would have a Bukowski fit. Brad could hear her shriek now: *Jared Cramer in my house for dinner! Whad were you thinkin, Sohn? Whadever led you to offer invitation to Sohn of man responsible for your Vater's death?*

Brad would have to say that in a moment's sympathy for the man, he'd extended the invitation. In actuality it had been offered in the alcoholic glow of the third round of beers when Jared had confided that he was about to hit a milestone birthday. He'd turn fifty next Saturday, May 23. That was the date of his sister's birthday! Brad had exclaimed. What did Mr. Cramer plan to do to celebrate his big day? Why, nothing, his boss had said, sad faced. He had no family and…frankly, he'd not had time to make friends, his being so busy with the lumberyard and all. He'd probably make do with a sandwich at the office catching up on paperwork. Brad had blurted out, "You can't spend your birthday on Saturday at the yard with a sandwich, Mr. Cramer! You're welcome to come share my sister's birthday dinner with us at our house!"

"Well, now, that sounds like a mighty tempting invitation, Brad, and one you're kind to offer. I'll take you up on it," his boss had said.

Brad just now recalled that Jared Cramer hadn't taken a breath before accepting the invitation, and he wondered if his boss hadn't carefully thrown out a line for him to snap up like an unwary trout going for a fly. His mother, busy with house and garden and the family, was not often seen around town, but Mr. Cramer had glimpsed her the rare mornings she'd ridden with Brad to work before taking the truck for the rest of the day to run errands. On one of those early mornings, his boss had spied them from his office window and greeted him with the observation, "Fine-looking woman, your mother." Brad had heard the same admiration in his voice as Mr. Shreve's when the grocer asked after her.

Brad felt his dad would want him to keep an eye on the male attention paid his mother, though Joanna Bukowski Hudson was capable of handling herself. She was indeed a fine-looking woman, still young and... well, nubile, he guessed was the word, and that might give some of the men in town the idea that she missed a man in her bed. He had to be on the lookout for favors men extended her that might not be out of simple kindness to an impoverished widow. Mr. Shreve slipping in extra slices of meat, for example, the automotive garage owner replacing a truck valve for free, the plumber repairing a leaky pipe at no charge. So far their motives had appeared aboveboard, but if his boss held a hope of making time with Joanna Bukowski Hudson, it would be in vain, Brad thought. His mother blamed Jared's father for the faulty equipment that had caused his fatal accident. Brad had tried to get her to see that the son was not responsible for the mistakes of the father. Jared Cramer came onboard only after old man Cramer had died, leaving the business to his son, who lived and worked in California. In his late forties, childless, a widower, Jared had taken a leave of absence from his administrative position with the Southern Pacific and Union Railroad to come back to Meeker and get the lumber company in shape to sell. After a year, he found he couldn't leave the invalid company he'd nurtured back to health and decided to stay.

Bobby asked, "Did you do wrong asking your boss to Beata's birthday dinner?"

"We'll just have to see. I think I'll dress the goose first, then lay the news on my mother."

"You might want to make a telephone call before that. A man called you from Washington, D.C., today and left a number for you. I took the call. He said to call him back no matter the time and said you were to reverse the charges. He sounded…important. I think he wants to hire you."

"Somebody from Washington, D.C., wants to hire me?"

Bobby lifted his shoulders. "It's just a guess. Number and name's by the phone."

"Okay, thanks, Bobby. Let Mom know I'm home and that I'll be seeing to the goose in a minute," Brad instructed as they walked into the house, and Brad saw the piece of paper on which Bobby had scribbled the information. He picked it up and studied the name. Alistair Renault. Beside it, a three-letter, four-digit number. Brad had no reason to be familiar with big-city telephone exchanges. Rural telephone codes were simpler. He felt a small quiver of apprehension when he lifted the receiver to give the operator the number. He would recall the feeling much later when he realized that if he had not returned the call, the rest of his life would not have been the same.

CHAPTER TEN

At eighteen, desperate to earn extra cash, Brad had followed the advice of a friend of his father's who'd loaned him enough money to advertise his intimate knowledge of the White River and Meeker's lakes and trout streams in the classified section of *Field and Stream* magazine. In the month the ad ran, he had garnered three clients, one from as far away as California. After that, his expertise at leading anglers to trout habitats had been spread by word of mouth. He would have made his occasional weekend job his full-time occupation if he could have put some capital behind it and offered the boat, tackle, and amenities of his better-heeled competitors that allowed them to operate for most of the year. Brad's clients had to bring their own fishing gear and special weather attire and make do with his family pickup truck, True Blue, for transportation. He provided only the essentials for survival: tents, food, water, first-aid kit, ponchos, flashlight, and knives, booze if required, but the client had to pay for it. Consequently, the work was not steady and confined only to late spring and fall. Nonetheless, by twenty-two, Brad had talked to a sufficient number of telephone callers inquiring about his services to become quite adept at sizing up each client.

The man who approached Brad at the Glenwood Springs railroad station did not fit the picture Brad had formed of him when he'd telephoned from Washington, D.C., to hire his fishing-guide services for a weekend. *Alistair Renault* had a classy tone to it, unusual for the Toms and Harrys and Charlies who normally gave Brad a jingle. Over the telephone, Alistair Renault had sounded wealthy and important (which Brad's clients weren't) but not full of himself (as some of them were). Brad hated the kind of client who came believing he knew everything about fishing, but didn't know diddly and left knowing less. He got the impression that this man knew a lot about the governing principles of catching trout, but he wondered why he had booked a guide now when a much-publicized sudden spike in temperature had set the heavy mountain snows on their biggest meltdown in years. May runoffs in northwestern Colorado weren't the most comfortable time to be fishing. What puzzled him even more was why the man had hired his services at all when there was great fishing in the streams of Maryland and Virginia, not to mention the Potomac River. Why come to Colorado?

"I have a break in my schedule that I won't have later in the spring and summer. I'll be leaving the country in the fall and not sure when I'll get back, so since I've always wanted to fish the White River, I thought I'd best do it now," the man had explained when Brad posed the question. Brad had thought that sounded rather ominous, as if the man had doubts that he'd return at all. Renault had mentioned the ad in *Field and Stream* he'd read some time ago. "Sounded to me like you have the kind of feel for the place that appeals to me," he'd said. When Brad asked how Washington was these days, his sensitive ear picked up his caller's disinclination to discuss the subject, and so he dropped it. Give it time, and disclosures would come—about home, wife, children, girlfriends, job, colleagues, and other complaints that justified a getaway to the Rockies. They always did.

Brad had drawn a mental image of Alistair Renault

as a distinguished man of stately bearing dressed in finely tailored sports clothes easily recognizable among the other disembarking passengers, so he'd not bothered making a homemade sign stating his client's name. To his surprise and even shock, the man who started toward him by apparent instinct matched nothing of the description he'd envisioned from their phone conversation. He was less than medium height, walked with a sort of shuffling gait, wore a faded brown jacket, and overall looked about as ordinary and common as a bait bucket. Brad felt a moment's disappointment. He'd been looking forward to meeting a client of his grand expectations. "Brad Hudson?" the man called in the rich, well-modulated voice that had conjured up Brad's misperception.

Brad held out his hand. What the hell. The guy was a paying customer. "Yes sir. Welcome to Colorado, Mr. Renault."

"Thank you. Good of you to meet me." He carried the sparse travel luggage of an experienced fisherman—one small suitcase for clothes, not an entire wardrobe, and a well-worn angler's case in sturdy canvas. He set down the small suitcase to return Brad's grip, its force a surprise and his direct gaze even more so. Experiencing another flash of disconcertment, Brad perceived this man was not as he appeared. "You'll want to see some identification, I'm sure," his client said, releasing Brad's hand to reach inside his brown jacket.

"Yes sir," Brad said. It had not occurred to him to ask for identification, but he squinted at the man's driver's license as if the procedure were customary, nodded, then picked up the suitcase. "My truck's in the parking lot over there, if you'll just follow me," he said, feeling his telephone impression somewhat justified. In outward appearance, Alistair Renault might possess all the distinction of a prairie chicken, but unless his instincts were way off base, Brad felt sure there was a lot more to the man than met the eye.

"Meeker's only an hour-and-a-half drive," he said. "I'll drive you straight to the hotel, and we can make an early start in the morning. There's a café next door where you can get a home-cooked meal. We'll leave at sunrise and have all day tomorrow and Sunday to fish. Am I right to understand you'll be leaving early Monday morning?"

"That's correct," Alistair said. "Train leaves at seven."

Outstanding, Brad thought. He'd go directly to the lumberyard from the station in Glenwood Springs in time to get in a full day's work without having to ask his boss for time off to deliver his passenger. Jared Cramer would probably have granted his request without a second's hesitation, but Brad would just as soon not have to ask. He wanted no special favors from an employer romantically interested in his mother that might cause talk from the guys and give the wrong impression to his boss. The combined celebration of his sister's and employer's birthdays the middle of May had not turned out as anticipated. Against all expectations, his mother and Jared Cramer had hit it off, and now they were an item. At the lumberyard, his boss wore a grin so silly, Brad was embarrassed, and his mother hummed while she worked. But Brad would have to see how the cards played out. Given Joanna Bukowski Hudson's devotion to the memory of her husband, things could go south. Brad wasn't particularly worried about losing his job, since the war had left the company short of manpower, but he might be demoted back to sawing and hauling logs. Jared Cramer didn't seem that sort. Brad liked and respected him a lot, but people could surprise and disappoint you in the most unexpected ways, especially when male ego was involved. Meanwhile, the money for this weekend's services would be nestled snugly in the jar with his other savings for emergencies. He demanded payment in cash from his clients, no checks. Greenbacks could not bounce.

As they got underway, Brad put the question to his client he always asked first. "What do you do in Washington, D.C., Mr. Renault?" The inquiry broke the ice, and many times Brad was treated to a passenger's whole life story before he was deposited at his hotel. Brad hoped the question would spark news from Mr. Renault of how the war was going. Would Mexico's declaration of war against the Axis powers make any difference to the Allies? Was there any information of the fate of the twelve thousand prisoners taken captive by the Japanese on Corregidor? Would Canada win the Battle of the St. Lawrence against German U-boats? The one question Brad dreaded to be asked in return was his number in the draft.

"I run a courier service," the client said, but stopped there. Brad sensed a reluctance to talk, period. That impression was reinforced when the man removed an area map from his coat pocket, spread it over his knees, and asked Brad to tell him about the flow and structure of the White River, the hidden creeks and tributaries and enclaves where wild trout thrived. That was Brad's opening to express his concern of the huge snow base that had ripped into spring. They might find the trout nonexistent and the water levels dangerous, he warned. Colorado's flood engineers were predicting the northern part of the state could experience the highest and swiftest flows in years and were urging anglers to take extra precautions on riverbanks and in supercharged currents.

"Warning taken," his client said and went back to the silent study of his maps. Brad shrugged. *Be it on his head what might befall*, he thought, wondering at the man's reticence. He couldn't have cared either way whether the man engaged in conversation, and silence on the river was a virtue of the true fly-fisherman.

They were almost to Meeker's city limits when Brad heard an embarrassing *thump, thump, thump,* and the right front of his truck began to list. Alistair Renault broke his absorption in his map to state the unnecessary: "Er, I believe you have a flat tire, Mr. Hudson."

"*Verdammt!*" Brad swore. He had a spare in True Blue, but the rubber was paper-thin. He'd purchased a good used Michelin with some of the first money from his emergency jar but didn't dare carry it in his truck for fear of theft. Rubber tires were hard to come by now and cost the earth besides. The tire was safely locked in his garage at home. To change the flat, Brad had to trust his threadbare spare to get them to the hotel or take a detour to his house, which wasn't far away.

"Mr. Renault," he asked, "how weary are you?"

Bobby was collecting firewood from the porch when the truck limped up. He spied the problem at once and set down the firewood to offer assistance. Brad said, "You can stay in the truck, sir, unless you'd like to come in by the fire and have a cup of coffee, but this won't take long." He hoped the man declined. His presence would be an intrusion. The girls would be doing their homework and his mother getting supper. Jared Cramer was to come by later in the evening.

Alistair released his voice. "That coffee and fire sound good," he said. "I'll take you up on it."

His mother met them at the door and inquired of her son in German what was going on. Brad replied in her native language that they were to converse in English and introduced her by his father's name, Mrs. Thomas Hudson, as he always did when unavoidable circumstances required him to present her to his male clients. As usual, Brad did not bother to state his customer's name. His mother, who had been preparing the evening meal, wiped her hand on her apron before accepting the one Alistair Renault offered. She lifted her eyes to his, and a small, perplexed frown appeared between her brows. "How do you do?" she said in the slow voice of one struggling to place a face.

It might have been Brad's imagination, but he thought Alistair Renault's height increased by two inches when he squared his shoulders and took his mother's hand in a way that made Brad think he meant to kiss it, and he could have sworn he heard the heels of his brogans click together. *"Mir geht es gut, danke. Wie geht es dir, hoffe ich, Joanna."* (I am well, thank you, as are you, I hope, Joanna.)

His mother emitted a small cry. "*Alistair!*" she exclaimed.

CHAPTER ELEVEN

VICTORIA / LIVERWORT

New York City

The editor in chief at G. P. Putnam's Sons dipped his head to peer over his glasses at the publishing house's French translator sitting before his desk. He stifled a sigh of frustration. This dilemma was what came of hiring inordinately attractive young women. How to present this knotty situation to Victoria without appearing as...well, Beaumont Fournier's *pimp*? There was no other word for it. However, if only an hour or so to sit with Victoria Grayson over a glass of champagne was sufficient to get the illustrious author's name on a contract, then it was his duty as editor in chief to see to it.

"I'm afraid the author has insisted, Victoria. He wishes to spend a little time with the translator of his book before he will agree to the contract," Willard Mason said.

"But I thought the deal was made, that he'd already agreed to let us publish."

"He's... changed his mind. Now Monsieur Fournier has decided that he wants to be sure you are the one for the job."

"I would think my translations of former works would assure him of that."

"You would think so, yes," the editor agreed, feeling his forehead grow damp.

"So what's the problem? What else can be gained by my meeting him for cocktails?"

Willard kept himself from shaking his head. Surely, the brightest of his foreign translators, a woman accustomed to being sought after by men, could figure out the author's motivation without her boss having to explain it. Maybe the man's reputation as a notorious womanizer had not preceded him. The French author of the internationally acclaimed best seller *Cathédrale de Silence* had caught sight of Victoria Grayson on his recent visit to G. P. Putnam's Sons. Willard had been leading Beaumont Fournier and his American agent ahead to his office when he glanced back to find the author had stopped abruptly in the hall before the open door of the reference room, gaze arrested. Willard had muttered an inaudible *Oh, dear*. Victoria Grayson, absorbed over a linguistic matter, sat before a window at a table suffused in the sunshine of the last week of May. The light fell upon her with the deft strokes of a painter's brush, accentuating the glow of her blond head, flawless skin, patrician features, and the luster of her ivory silk blouse.

It was no surprise when the Frenchman had asked as he was seated, "The lovely blond woman at the table by the window in the room we just passed…who is she?"

"One of our translators."

"French, I hope?"

"Ah…yes, she is."

"Then she will be assigned the translation of my novel?"

"Ah…yes. She is our best."

"Her name?"

"Victoria Grayson."

"Is she married?"

"No. Engaged." Willard, father of twin daughters, young, single, and comely and for whom he had to keep a wary eye out for sexual predators like the man before his desk, then launched into attributes of Victoria's betrothed against which not even the internationally famous, rich, and dashing Beaumont Fournier could compete.

"I'd like you to introduce us," the writer interrupted.

Willard poised a finger to push an intercom button. "But of course. I'll ask my secretary to summon her."

"No, not here," the Frenchman said with a smile that looked to Willard like a serpent's smirk. "I'd like her to meet me for a drink this evening in the lobby bar of my hotel. I'm staying at the Plaza. I've found it wise before I sign contracts to…how do you Americans say it?…*unwind* with the person I'm dealing with to judge their capability. You understand what I mean?"

Of course I do, you profligate, Willard raged inwardly. He understood perfectly. Beaumont Fournier had made plain his condition to seal the deal. Whether that extended to Victoria spending the night with him in his hotel room rather than holding her captive over a glass of champagne in the lobby bar, Willard supposed he'd learn in the morning. All he could do was arrange for the latter, but he must make sure his translator understood that neither her job nor the contract was contingent on the former.

But that was proving hard to do since Victoria didn't seem to get it.

"I can meet him only for drinks," she said. "My

brother's in town on leave from the RAF for the evening before he goes to Virginia in the morning to see our parents for one day before he has to get back to the squadron. I'm sure you can understand how important it is that I spend the time with him." The lift of her perfect brow line carried a world of meaning impossible for Willard to misread. Willard was well aware of the high casualty rate for England's Royal Air Force pilots as they fought off Germany's Luftwaffe to remove the last obstacle to Hitler's intention to take over Europe. Victoria's brother, like her fiancé, had been among those at Dunkirk of whom Churchill had made his famous statement: "Never in the field of human conflict was so much owed by so many to so few."

The editor felt a profound sense of relief, not to mention a relaxation of the grip on his conscience. Now he was off the hook to engage in an awkward explanation to Victoria of what was *not* expected of her, while at the same time impress upon her the need to use every feminine artifice at her command to achieve the desired result without compromising her virtue. There was no danger of the author forcing a future engagement. His Vichy-government-issued travel permit was temporary and required him to return to France the following day.

"I will explain that to Monsieur Fournier," Willard said. "How can he possibly not understand? Drinks only, no dinner, in case he should have that in mind once you become acquainted. He'd like you to meet him in the Champagne Bar of the Plaza at six."

"Fine," Victoria said. "I'll have my brother meet us there."

Willard watched her go, then picked up the phone to dial the author at the Plaza. The editor suspected he'd been wasting his paternal concern regarding Victoria Grayson. In contrast to his daughters, pretty but timorous, his lovely French translator could likely handle herself in most challenging situations. The woman was formidable. Every time Willard looked at her, he was reminded of the city fencing competition in which she'd represented the company. He'd been amazed—a bit terrified, really—of her mastery of the sword, her easy but ruthless whip, slice, and thrust of the blade. Victoria Grayson had shown her opponent no mercy. Perhaps Beaumont Fournier should consider himself lucky. Were the evening to extend, she just might serve him his free-wheeling male member upon a silver Plaza platter.

Victoria returned to her office shaking her head. Men. Their subterfuges were as subtle as a broadsword in the hand of a ham-fisted amateur and no match for a woman. She'd known exactly what Beaumont Fournier was after the second she'd glimpsed him staring gaga-eyed at her through the open door of the reference room. She'd checked her watch and allowed ten minutes before she was summoned to the chief's office for introductions. Victoria had done her own homework on Beaumont Fournier before a glance from the corridor had inspired in him a sudden need to investigate Victoria Grayson. She'd learned that he was a scoundrel where women were concerned. Poor Willard Mason. The author had placed him in quite a predicament. Victoria guessed the editor now shared her question of how a writer led around by his gonads could produce a brilliant book of conception like *Cathédrale de Silence*.

But to Victoria's surprise, she had not been bidden to the editor in chief's office until after the author's departure. At her desk she waited a call from Ralph. He was to telephone her at the publishing house the minute he landed at Fort Hamilton in Brooklyn. That would be midafternoon, and then she would tell him of her "flight plan," as he would call it, for their short time together.

The unexpected turn of circumstances had not thrown her plans for the evening off course. Rather than meet her at the Warwick Hotel, where she'd made reservations for the night, Victoria would have Ralph stroll into the Champagne Bar of the Plaza lugging his flight bag to rescue her from the clutches of Beaumont Fournier. After a quick hello, introduction, and good-bye, they'd be off to the Warwick, which was within easy walking distance of the Plaza, saving them from wasting precious time hailing a taxi to thread through the city's congested Friday traffic. Even her attire fell in line with the evening ahead. That morning she had dressed in something that could go from office to a reserved table for dinner at Sardi's, Ralph's favorite restaurant in the city, so she was suitable for cocktails in the Champagne Bar.

Victoria picked up a framed photograph on her desk of Ralph and his best friend posing in their smashing Royal Air Force uniforms. The best friend was Lawrence Grayson, her brother. Ralph DuPont was the man to whom she was engaged to be married. Victoria had lied that the RAF pilot in town for only a night was her brother, but it was true that he'd be leaving for Virginia in the morning. Ralph's father was seriously ill in Williamsburg, the reason he'd been given temporary leave. If Beaumont Fournier had been informed that Ralph was her fiancé, the Frenchman might have—*would* have—waved that consideration aside as of no consequence. So what? But a brother on humanitarian leave from the RAF for such a precious little time...well, that was a different matter entirely. How could the author in good conscience and taste demand her company?

There had been no time for a wedding after Ralph had slipped a ring on her finger in February just before he rejoined his Eagle Squadron. Elopement was out of the question. Their families would have murdered them. "This may not be fair to you, Vicky, tying you down like this, and if you should have reason to change your mind before I get back..." he had said.

"Never," she said. "Never, never, never."

Of that, she would never be surer of anything in her life. She had been in love with Ralph DuPont almost since she could walk. She had simply found no reason not to be. Long before she was old enough to appreciate and respond to him as a man, he had won her heart merely by treating seriously his best friend's little sister through all her stages of growing up. Those had been cherished times, the moments in her childhood and adolescence when he had veered off from Lawrence's company to allow her to introduce him to her doll, her hamster, to show him her new pair of roller skates, the fort she had supervised building out of Christmas trees, the *A* she had made in English composition. He had listened to her and not brushed off her dreams and aspirations as those of a silly schoolgirl. If Lawrence had paid her any mind, he would have seen that there was nothing silly about his younger sister. It had been Ralph who had encouraged her to try her hand at foil when she was still in junior high school. Victoria had found that after stolen moments alone with him, she'd felt suddenly, devastatingly lonely once he had gone.

Her mother had considered it an infatuation only natural to the little sister of an older brother whose best friend was as handsome as Ralph DuPont, but her mother was wrong as time had proved. Three years older than Victoria, Ralph and Lawrence had grown up inseparable, joined at the hip from kindergarten through prep school, through college as fraternity brothers, and in September 1940 as volunteers to join an American fighter squadron of the Royal Air Force during the Battle of Britain. Both had strong family ties to England. Victoria and Lawrence's maternal grandparents and Ralph's divorced mother lived in London. It wasn't until

Victoria was halfway through her studies at William and Mary College that Ralph took her enduring feelings for him seriously, and then it was love at long-last sight.

The darkest hours of her life had occurred the day he told her of his and Lawrence's plans to go help the RAF protect their homeland. They would be defying strict U.S. neutrality laws that threatened imprisonment and the loss of citizenship, but Ralph had said, "We've got to go, Vicky. We're going to be in it anyway when the United States gets pulled into the war, but it won't last forever, then I'll be back for you."

Then I'll be back for you. That was the promise she held on to, her first thought upon waking in the morning, her last when falling asleep at night.

"Your mail, Miss Grayson?" G. P. Putnam's basement clerk hesitated in the doorway before entering to lay a packet of office correspondence and French periodicals on her desk. "There's something there on top that looks more important than the usual stuff."

Victoria saw Washington, D.C., in the return address, and a surge of panic made her tear open the envelope. Oh God. Did the enclosed letter have to do with Ralph or Lawrence?

Dear Miss Grayson,

Your knowledge of and fluency in French, along with your fencing prowess, has come to the attention of this office. Would you be interested in discussing how you might put your language and skills to essential and crucial use in defending the United States against its enemies? Regrettably, for the sake of national security, I cannot tell you more about our need for your assistance at this time. If you are amenable to investigating the request of this office further, please call the listed telephone number at any time of the day or night.

Yours expectantly,
Colonel William J. Donovan
Director of the Office of Strategic Services

Victoria released her breath with a twitch of unease. What was she to make of this? The letter looked official enough, and she had certainly heard of Wild Bill Donovan, World War I war hero, but how had his office heard of her? The signatures of Colonel Donovan and his deputy, Alistair Renault, appeared to be authentic, but was this some sort of hoax?

She glanced uneasily at her watch. It was nearing five o'clock. She'd expected Ralph's call long before now. What if he did not telephone before she had to leave for the Plaza? He had warned her that he couldn't be sure when the plane would land. A delayed flight and weather conditions could affect his arrival, but she'd said it didn't matter. She'd remain in her office until the switchboard shut down a half hour after closing time. After that, he would know to try her apartment.

Victoria decided to cover all bases and dialed the work numbers of her apartment roommates to inform them of the situation and her scheme of rescue. She wanted them to make sure that Ralph understood that he was to introduce himself as her brother, Lawrence, when he met Beaumont Fournier. Victoria gave similar instructions to the switchboard operator, who was also excited to go along with the ruse. Nervously watching the minutes tick by, Victoria finally had no choice but to give herself a final check in her compact mirror before heading out into the fading light of the May afternoon to hail a taxi.

CHAPTER TWELVE

Victoria saw that Beaumont Fournier had chosen a table where she would be sure to see him among the after-work cocktail crowd, or rather, where he would not miss her entrance. You could tell a lot about people from their entrance into an unfamiliar place. Posture, the pause to take stock, the scan of the room spoke much about the person before the mouth could confirm or undo the impression. She advanced toward him, amused. He had chosen the perfect spot in the chandelier-lit lounge for Ralph to see and claim her. She offered her hand. "Monsieur Fournier," she said.

"Please. Beaumont will do, and may I call you Victoria? It is such a...*regal* name. It quite becomes you," he said in French and bowed over her hand to brush her skin lightly with his lips.

"I'd be pleased for you to call me Victoria."

"And *I* was so pleased when I learned that the translator of Robert Desnos's *Deuil pour Deuil* would be assigned my novel," Beaumont said as he drew out her chair. "Accuracy is crucial to avoid the wrong impression of the original, a transgression of which I've never heard it said that you are guilty."

"I'm surprised my name is mentioned in your circles, monsieur," Victoria said.

"Robert is a friend of mine, I'm honored to say. He was very pleased with the quality of your work."

"I'm delighted to hear it. Monsieur Desnos is well?" Victoria had come to know and like the forty-year-old French surrealist poet through her correspondence with him while translating his poem "Mourning for Mourning," but she'd become worried about him. News had filtered across the Atlantic that he had been writing negatively about the Vichy Regime, the pro-Axis government operating in the Free Zone of Nazi-occupied France, and that his opinions had not been warmly received.

"For the moment. I regret that Robert is a bit too outspoken against the current political situation for his own good. It is not healthy for writers of renown to get too involved in the issues of the day in France just now." The Frenchman made a slicing motion across his neck. "Off can come one's head."

"Are you concerned about yours?" Victoria asked, judging that the author would take every precaution to guarantee that his attractively shaggy head remained on his neck. Not for the first time since reading about him, she wondered if he could be a Nazi collaborator. She could see him worrying with her question, considering how best to reply without risking her regard. Willard would have told him her fiancé and brother flew for the RAF. Relief leaped into his eyes at the approach of the wine steward.

"I try not to get involved in politics," Beaumont answered offhandedly before giving an order for a specific champagne to the sommelier. When he bowed away, the author smiled across the table at Victoria and explained, "I've ordered a bottle from the north of France where the distinct taste and purity of the wine is due to the chalky soil and continental growing conditions. You'll like it I'm sure."

She glanced at her watch. "If only I had time to truly enjoy it. My brother will be here at any moment. I'm sure Willard warned you."

"He did. Therefore..." He touched his fingertips to his lips and threw a mock kiss into the air. "Let us make hay while the sun shines, as your imaginative countrymen would say."

"So they do," Victoria agreed and skirted to a subject safer for her temperament by engaging the writer in his favorite topic—himself. As she expected, the Frenchman applied his charm with a trim of humility. Americans were impressed by humility in great men, so the author had expressed in a French interview. Modesty presented an appealing contrast to expectations. While the writer waved aside her obligatory praise of his novel, its salutary reviews, industry awards, and movie deal as embarrassing—"I told them it doesn't matter to me whether Claudette Colbert or Marlena Dietrich plays the lead"—Victoria watched a solitary pigeon, a winged gray blur, settle in the spray of the famed Pulitzer Fountain on Fifth Avenue. She felt a leap of excitement. Ralph should have landed by now.

Her inner glow must have shown on her face. Presuming that it was for him, Beaumont leaned forward and laid his hand warmly over hers. "I have read numerous examples of your English translations of French literary works, Victoria, and know your craftsmanship to be excellent," he said. "Therefore you must forgive my...ploy for luring you here. I know you are engaged, but I simply could not allow the opportunity to go by to enjoy the company of a beautiful woman for even a short while on what will probably be my last visit to America for some time."

Victoria thought she could see how a woman could be taken in if she were not aware of the writer's long history of philandering. A drop or two of honesty introduced at just the right moment was like cream to a dish. It added a little depth and strength to an otherwise false charm.

"You're forgiven, if you'll forgive my running off in a little while when my brother shows up," she said.

He sighed and drew his hand away. "Must you keep reminding me?"

The champagne arrived. "Let's talk about your book," Victoria said.

An hour crawled by. The pigeon on the lip of the fountain flew away. Panic rising, conversation growing as exhausted as the bottle of Bollinger, Victoria nearly leaped from her chair when Beaumont said regretfully with a look at the revolving door, "I do believe I see your brother now. Tall, handsome, wearing a Royal Air Force uniform? I can see the family resemblance."

Victoria thought: *Family resemblance?* Ralph was

dark to her fair; brown-eyed to her gray-green. Beaumont pushed back his chair, irritation tinging his plastered smile. Slowly, Victoria turned around.

"Hello, sis," her blond-haired, gray-green-eyed brother Lawrence said.

There was no need to ask what he was doing here. The weighted features of her brother's face explained why he had come. The room fell into a slow, cream-colored, chandelier-lighted, mahogany spin. Victoria permitted Lawrence to assist her to her feet. Beaumont Fournier, bewildered, swam in a haze of cigarette smoke and the swirl of cocktail chatter. He was an unusually tall man, she noticed, pencil slim, as if he existed on truffles and champagne. "Uh, pardon, please," he said in English, "but I am a bit confused. Is...there anything wrong? Could I be of help?"

"We've lost a family friend in the skies over France," Lawrence said. "We're both in a state of shock. There is nothing anyone can do. Excuse us. I must take my sister home."

"Oh, yes, well, of course," the Frenchman said. "I'm so sorry to hear it, but, uh, Miss Grayson—Victoria—I must ask. Does this mean that you won't be translating my novel?"

Victoria did not answer as she allowed Lawrence to lead her toward the door.

CHAPTER THIRTEEN

JULY 1942
Washington, D.C.

So you believe the team is ready for the next leg?" Colonel Bill Donovan asked his deputy as he tapped his club soda glass to the bartender to request a refill. The men sat in a shadowy corner of an out-of-the-way tavern in Washington, D.C., their private meeting place away from OSS headquarters. Overhead, a lazy ceiling fan minimally relieved the room's trapped heat.

Both men were near teetotalers. The man in brown gloomily watched as their glasses were replenished and waited to answer until the bartender had gone back to his station. "Any further preparation from this end would be gilding the lily," he said.

"Then what's wrong, Alistair? I've never seen you like this before. You're usually raring to go into the final round. This time you seem to be having second thoughts."

"A midnight deluge of them, but never about this team's abilities. Those five kids are the best I've ever hauled in, the smartest and brightest and...nicest."

"Nicest? Since when has niceness ever been desirable for sending an agent into the field?"

"It isn't. The least desirable quality, as a matter of fact."

Colonel Donovan dropped a slice of lime into his glass and studied Alistair closely. He knew what was troubling his trusted right-hand man, but the acknowledgment had to come from him. It was not too late to send another case officer in his place. His spymaster extraordinaire had fallen into the trap that had led many a hard-core member of his trade to turn in his identification badge. Alistair Renault had come to care about his young spies. That chink in his armor could be disastrous for him, the team, and the mission. "Then what is it?" Wild Bill persisted.

Idly, Alistair, an inveterate doodler, drew an oblong shape on a cocktail napkin that metamorphosed into the body of an insect, the thorax larger than the abdomen, the head covered by broadly rounded eyes, the wings spread out flat to the sides of the figure. A dragonfly, his boss recognized, the code name of the team to be dispatched to England in the morning for the final round of training before they would be sent into France. They were the most disparate group of spies in the recorded history of espionage: a civil engineer, a fly-fisherman, a fencer, a dress designer, and a track-and-field coach.

"I have a bad feeling about this mission," his deputy said.

"You have a bad feeling about all of them. What's so different about this one?"

Alistair glanced up from his doodling at his boss, who was sitting back from the table cross-kneed, glass in hand. The colonel's casual attitude irritated him. "Maybe I'm having doubts about risking five young lives on missions that may be pigs in a poke. They're not professionals, Bill. They've had no military experience. They're just kids off the street with more savvy and guts than most who have been given a crash course in espionage."

"All missions are pigs in a poke," Bill Donovan reminded him. "We never know what value will come from them, but we have no choice but to send agents in. What is your worry about this group? You've placed your kids in the most secure situations possible while being in perfect spots to feed us great intel. I think you've put together a brilliant package, Alistair. If your boys and girls land safely in the pickup zone and do not stray beyond their assignments, they should be in no overt danger."

Alistair shook his head. There was no safe ground in Nazi-occupied France. "You've just hit on the source of my worry, Colonel," he said. "The team may stray beyond the safety of their assignments."

Colonel Donovan noticed that his deputy had dropped even more weight during the intense two-month indoctrination of his five-member team. Alistair's sallow skin indicated he'd been living on a diet of caffeine and nicotine. The bowl of Virginia peanuts on the table, Alistair's passion, had remained untouched. "What gives you reason to think so?" Donovan asked.

"Because each of them has their own agenda for wanting to get into France, motives beyond a desire to serve their country, and *that's* what could get them killed—or worse—unless they're fortunate enough to be executed first."

"But those motives are why you recruited them."

"And they are what may come back to bite them and us on the butt."

"The team has been fully apprised of the danger?" the OSS director asked. "Including what they'll be in for if they get caught?"

"Every aspect of it. They'll be issued the L pill, of course, just in case."

Bill Donovan squinted at him. "What else is going on with you besides concern over your charges roving outside their boundaries, Alistair?"

Irritated, Alistair downed half his second glass of club soda. Wiping his mouth with the back of his hand, he said, "All right, if you want me to say it, I will. I don't want to lose these kids. I want them to come home and have a crack at a long life."

"In other words, this time you don't want to be responsible for sending another team of young people to an early and possibly painful death. This is not about them. It's about you."

Alistair extracted a cigarette from the package of Lucky Strikes that was never far from hand and spun a flame to it from his lighter. "It would be hard to live with the deaths of these particular kids, Bill. Not a one that isn't special. I mean really, really special."

"Anybody who willingly risks his life for his country *is* really, really special, Major, and that attitude can get you and those kids killed," Wild Bill said. "Maybe I ought to pull you from this one."

"The hell you will. I'm the captain of this ship. If those kids have a chance of making it back, I'm it, and you know it."

Bill Donovan nodded reluctant agreement and set down his glass. “I have to go,” he said, uncrossing his legs. “I am meeting with the president in an hour. Thank God for air-conditioning in the Oval Office. Eat some peanuts, Alistair. You look like a politician’s hot air could blow you over. And stop worrying. What’s done is done. The rest we leave to Providence. I’ll see you off at the airfield in the morning. What time?”

“Four o’clock.”

“Until then,” the director said and patted Alistair’s shoulder as he left. “Lay off the coffee and cigarettes and get some sleep, buddy.”

As if that were possible, Alistair thought. He took a draw of the cigarette and squinted at his sketch through the stream of expelled smoke. Brad Hudson had suggested Dragonfly to the group as the code name for the team. He’d told them of watching bass leap from the water to snag a hovering dragonfly only to have it dart away before it could become dinner. “They’re almost impossible to snare and have no blind spots,” he’d explained. “Their eyes wrap around their heads like a football helmet to give them a three-hundred-sixty-degree view. Most insects, predators can attack from underneath and behind. Those are their vulnerable areas. Dragonflies don’t have them.”

"That may be so, but dragonflies are also big, making them easy to spot," Alistair had countered. "All you need is a good pair of field glasses."

The son of Joanna Bukowski Hudson had flashed his father's smile at Alistair. "Easy to spot but not to catch. They're natural escape artists."

So the name had carried the vote. Alistair had to admit it fit the group. The boys were strong, the girls quick as darts, all five seemingly tireless and without fear. Dragonflies did not track their prey, following their meal through the air until they caught up with it. They calculated the insect's location, direction, and speed, then lay in wait in their prey's flight path for the chow to fly right into their mouths. That strategy was exactly the scheme the team was to follow in executing their assignments. They would be inserted directly into the enemy's line of sight without the target being aware of their presence or the objective of their mission. Alistair had worked on the scheme from the day Germany had occupied France and perceived it was only a matter of time before America was drawn into the war. While the borders were still open, he had visited the City of Light and set up his network of Parisians willing to resist the Nazis, then returned to search out ideal candidates for the operations he had in mind. The latest intelligence reports indicated his network was still miraculously in place, but what were the odds his contacts would hold, given the French's treacherous wide-scale collaboration with the Germans? If they were betrayed, his young agents could be snared in the net.

At the time, Alistair had not pointed out one characteristic of the dragonfly that Brad had failed to mention: In a pinch, if hungry enough, a dragonfly will eat its own kind. Who could blame it? If one of his dragonflies was caught, it was reasonable to assume the member would break under torture and identify his teammates, and who could blame him—or her? Ideally the team should have been trained separately, never laying eyes on one another, but there had not been the time, instructors, or facilities for individual drill. In fact, "team" was a misnomer for the group, since each member was assigned a different mission and would go into France as a unit but operate alone with a central point of contact—the radio operator who, alone, would report to him.

So to protect the group from one another, Alistair made sure the number one rule of the OSS training camp was rigidly enforced. To break it meant immediate dismissal. Candidates were not to reveal their real names or any details of their personal lives to one another. Unless their accent gave them away, team members were not even to know from what part of the country their mates hailed. For use as names initially, each member was assigned a letter of the alphabet, in Dragonfly's case, A, B, C, D, and E, a cold manner of address designed to discourage intimacy.

But the strategy hadn't worked. Alistair had been daily amazed at how five strangers who knew absolutely nothing about one another could so quickly fit together as a cohesive unit, almost like a pack, not a lone wolf among them. He noticed their budding closeness at meal times, in classrooms, in grueling training sessions, during rare moments of leisure.

When the vetting process had unearthed no sweethearts back home, Alistair had feared the situation presented fertile ground for romance sprouting, never a good thing. They were all single, uncommonly attractive, and eligible for the picking. Had he not been familiar with their backgrounds, Alistair would have wondered why they were still footloose and fancy free. Brad Hudson had been too busy working and caring for his family to get involved with a girl and couldn't afford one anyway. Bridgette Loring had been too career focused to become involved in a serious relationship, and Sam Barton had confessed to a nasty breakup with his girlfriend—bitter for her but sweet for him—just after his twenty-second birthday, Alistair assumed right before his meeting with him in the coffee shop. "Girls! Who needs them with a war on?" he'd declared. Victoria Grayson was feeling the loss of her fighter pilot and Christoph Brandt the rejection of the Texas girl he'd expected to marry, and neither was interested in seeking solace in other arms.

Alistair had thought the girls might be jealous of each other and the boys would square off in competition for their attention, but neither had happened. Their chemistry simply hadn't worked that way. They had settled for friendship, the truest kind, because they had met denuded of their names, families, occupations, backgrounds, level of education, and accomplishments. Shed of embellishments, you were what you were and you got what you saw. The team of Dragonfly had come stripped to the bone and liked what they saw, and that was all there was to it. No further analysis required.

As a case officer, Alistair couldn't be more pleased. He had put together the perfect package for the mission. He simply hadn't counted on his regret at his success. He lifted his hand to signal for another club soda and thought back on how it had all started, the bonding of Dragonfly. It began the morning the potential candidates for induction into the OSS boarded the bus to Station S.

CHAPTER FOURTEEN

Victoria Grayson had been the first to get on and select a seat. It was June 1942. Alistair had sat in the back row of the vehicle, from where he could observe his new recruits' behavior. They were headed to a country estate not far from Washington, D.C., known as Station S. The country house and grounds had been commandeered to be used as a facility where candidates were evaluated for their psychological soundness to work as covert operatives in enemy territory. Alistair suspected that half of the group on this morning's bus would be returning to OSS headquarters at week's end, having failed the first leg of the weeding-out process. But Alistair was sure that the five he planned to keep a special eye on would not be on that bus. Victoria Grayson in particular.

Though he possessed a little black book thick with details that had led to his interest in her, Alistair had first laid eyes on Victoria Grayson in the gymnasium at William and Mary College, where he watched her participate in the one and only fencing match that he had ever witnessed. It was May 20, 1940, and the bout was not a competition of record, but a farewell occasion for students and members of faculty to witness, for the final time on the piste, the amazing skill and footwork of their acclaimed fencing star.

"She would have won gold in foil at the Olympics, you know, if the Games hadn't been canceled because of that stupid war," said a student to his male companion as they trooped over Alistair's feet to sit down next to him in the last seats close to the sidelines. Except to mumble an apology without a glance at him, they paid him no mind. Alistair took pride in being about as noticeable as a pigeon on a rooftop. In his line of work, his invisibility was an asset.

Alistair felt in a maze of ignorance as he tried to follow the twirls, ducks, thrusts, feints, ripostes, lunges, parries, and explosive attacks of play. Watching the two young women compete, he was in awe of the expertise required and felt sure his fellow audience members were right—that Victoria would have made a name for herself even on an Olympic stage. He at least knew that points were scored by the player touching the opponent's torso with the tip of the sword coated in a black substance that left a dot designating a "hit." By the end of the match, Victoria Grayson's form-fitting jacket showed four black marks to her competitor's five. She had won the bout. Applause grew louder as, after the opponents' final salutes, mask under her arm, face glowing with perspiration, Victoria turned and raised her foil to the audience who'd given up their Saturday morning to pay tribute to a school champion.

Her grayish-green eyes lit on Alistair, of all people, and he felt a chill brush his skin. It was as if she'd heard him call her name. Her glance passed on, but he was left with the traitorous urge to throw away his little black book and forget he'd ever seen her. To think of all that beauty, strength, and poise possibly destroyed...He put the thought from his mind as he rose and slipped out in the hubbub of spectators that surged down to the floor to congratulate the girl, wondering if she'd remember him when their paths crossed again.

From his back seat in the bus to Station S that June morning of the candidates' departure to hell, Alistair had watched the rest of the thirteen candidates board, none speaking for fear of breaking the rule that would get them expelled from the program. At the estate, they would be assigned cover names by which to communicate. Alistair noticed that the candidates spread out with no obvious intent to sit next to a particular person, but the fisherman, track coach, and civil engineer chose to sit together. By the time the blond head of Bridgette Loring appeared above the boarding rail, only two seats were available. One was next to Victoria Grayson; the other beside a mousy young woman with lank hair and owlish spectacles worn low on her nose. Alistair had observed that everyone had bypassed the seat next to the fencer. All others had seemed intimidated by her glacial beauty and patrician reserve, but not Bridgette Loring. Without another second's hesitation, Bridgette took her seat next to Victoria, smiled, and said, "Hi."

CHAPTER FIFTEEN

Indeed, there was nothing tentative about Bridgette Loring. Alistair, still doodling, sipping on his third club soda under the twirl of the tavern ceiling fan, shook his head. Of the five, she was the most amazing for the simple reason that no one expected such physical strength and pure guts from a five-foot, blond, doe-eyed, dainty young woman who looked about as threatening as a lace glove. Alistair figured she'd had to spend most of her young life so far trying to prove herself to overcome other people's presumptions based on her size and delicate appearance. Her school records bore out his perception. Among her numerous accomplishments, she'd graduated valedictorian of her class, won the title of state champion of Michigan's junior chess tournament, earned the crown as winner of the state's high school debate competition, had been elected school class president each of her years in high school, and served as captain of the school's softball team, on which she played shortstop. Her coach noted that she'd been called "Slugger," a nickname he felt she resented because it "diminished her femininity."

Her recently deceased French grandmother, an emigrant from France, had reared her and supported them as a much-in-demand seamstress. Angelique Duvalier had lived from girlhood through her young adult years in Berlin and preferred to converse in French and German, rather than English, with her granddaughter. Alistair had gathered that the woman had a fear of intruders, stemming from her and her husband's arrest in Berlin at the beginning of the Great War when they were charged with spying for the French government. Her husband was executed and Angelique tortured, a never-forgotten ordeal that had left her crippled and harboring an abiding hatred for police organizations. Bridgette's mother was fifteen years old at the time. Relatives spirited her out of Germany back to Paris, where she remained until after the war when Angelique was released and joined her there. Bridgette never lived in France. Her American father brought her mother to Maryland in 1920, the year Bridgette was born. It was a difficult delivery, and Bridgette's mother died of complications four months later. Her father sent for Angelique to care for the baby, but he was never able to forgive the child for the death of his wife and took to traveling extensively on behalf of his company. On one such business trip in 1924, he was among thirty passengers killed when a passenger train fell through a bridge washaway near Glenrock, Wyoming. The will provided for Bridgette a small trust fund and a modest house in Traverse City, Michigan.

In one of her Station S interviews, Bridgette was asked if she remembered her father, and the psychologist wrote in his assessment report that "a shadow crossed her face. His memory was painful to her. The candidate may have an innate distrust of men."

During their five-day session at Station S, Alistair observed that the candidates were already drawn together as if by a magnetic pull, clearly feeling a kinship even without a clue of his plans to bring them together as an intelligence-gathering team. Birds of a feather, no doubt—bright, emotionally stable, positive, confident, easily the best of the bunch. It was no surprise to him that they passed each phase of the tests with hardly a negative comment on the candidate rating board.

But it was petite Bridgette, most unlikely of all the assembly, who scored the highest points on all the tests, especially the stress interview, the make-or-break segment of the elimination process. This part of the program simulated a Gestapo interrogation, a trial to gauge a candidate's capacity to tolerate severe emotional and intellectual strain. With amazing aplomb, sitting on a hard chair with hands bound for hours in an airless room under a blazing light, she concocted a plausible story that successfully fielded her interrogators' demand that she explain what she was doing going through secret papers in a government office building in the middle of the night.

"To prove to you people that you have a security break, that you are sloppy in securing classified material, and that your means of locking down this building wouldn't keep out a blind man," she stunned them by answering, her tone scathing.

"What do you mean? How did you get into the building?"

"I simply crawled through the coal chute."

It was also Bridgette who may have saved the eventual team of Dragonfly from being on the bus back to Washington at the end of the assessment program. Those still in the running were to be treated to a graduation party. The candidates were to relax, let their hair down, have fun, get drunk if they liked. They deserved it. Bridgette was reported to have said to her group of friends, "I am suspicious about the objective of this party. The program isn't over until midnight. We're still being evaluated. I think they want to get us snockered so that we will let our guards down and reveal our cover stories. It will be all over for us if we do."

The others allowed that she had a point. They were all tired, sleep deprived, anxious, and vulnerable to the balm of alcohol, but heeding Bridgette's gut warning, their names were not among those scratched from the rating board the next morning.

The next phase of training took place in a remote, wooded area known as Camp X, where the remaining candidates were drilled in field- and tradecraft, weaponry, and intelligence gathering and reporting; given instruction in how to translate data into code, pick locks, and break into buildings to steal and photograph documents; and subjected to grueling physical exercises that tested the limits of stamina and nerve. By the end of the six-week period, Alistair had settled on the name of the alpha dog upon whose shoulders the whole Paris operation would depend—Bridgette Loring. She would become his radio operator.

CHAPTER SIXTEEN

Brad Hudson had been the last reeled in or, rather, the last to jump willingly into the Dragonfly boat. As May drew to an end, all had been recruited except for the young fly-fisherman Alistair reluctantly had in mind to complete his specially picked network. Sam Barton, aka Bucky, had signed the OSS applicant form in Kelly's Coffee Shop in Oklahoma City the Monday after his twenty-second birthday. Chris Brandt, christened Christoph, of New Braunfels, Texas, had scrawled his signature on the dotted line within twenty-four hours of his call to Washington asking for an interview. Victoria and Bridgette had already contacted him and were as good as signed up when Alistair left for Meeker, Colorado, and returned relieved that he'd failed in an objective he'd had little hope and desire of accomplishing in the first place. He'd given in to the temptation of a chance to see Joanna again with the added bonus of a weekend of fishing that might ease some of the stress chronic to his life.

He'd found Brad Hudson a carbon copy of his dad and Joanna as desirable as he remembered. How she'd managed to stay the woman of his memories considering the tough life she'd lived was beyond him. It had been twenty-three years since he had last seen her. When he first laid eyes on Joanna Bukowski, she was wearing a threadbare coat, standing in freezing weather in a soup line in Koblenz, where he and his army buddy, Thomas Hudson, were billeted as part of the Allied force occupying Germany at the tail end of World War I. A ruckus broke out in the line that required military authority to restore order. A man had grabbed Joanna's ration of bread and soup and run away, leaving her without a bowl for a second serving. She had spun around with a cry of appeal to the American soldiers butting in, and Alistair had never seen a look so desperate or a face so beautiful despite it being gaunt from malnutrition. It was a moment he'd never forgotten. "Let us help you," he'd said. And Thomas, already extending his arm, had added, "Yes, let us help you, Fräulein. There's a café close by where you can get warm, and we can get you a hot meal."

She'd taken Thomas's arm, and just like that, Joanna Bukowski was whisked out of Alistair's reach. Alistair served as best man at their wedding in January 1919. Upon his friend's discharge from the army that year, Thomas had brought his bride to Meeker, Colorado, land of the mountains and rivers he loved. Alistair had thought it best not to see them again.

She had naturally been shocked to see him, but Alistair had been gratified that she recognized him after only a few seconds' stunned stare. "It was your voice," she explained. "I've never forgotten the sound of your voice."

Of course.

After the initial shock, Brad had hovered in the background, curious, inquisitive. He had wanted to know about the history that his client and father had shared. Alistair, for his part, had gotten the economic lay of the land at once. Financially, the boy was needed at home. He could not be spared for the Paris mission, so the man in brown would concentrate only on the fishing while he was here and forgo the purpose he'd had in mind, but when Joanna asked if he were still in the army, he'd answered truthfully and said yes, that he was a major now assigned to a civilian agency.

Her son's eyes had filled with doubt and suspicion. "Running a courier service?"

"For want of a better description," Alistair had replied and said no more. He had planned to get back to Meeker when he returned from France. Who knew? Joanna might accept *his* arm this time, but then she had confided to him as he'd said good-bye, "I'm getting married again, Alistair. Brad doesn't know yet."

"Who to?" he had asked, his hopes once again falling like a rock.

"To Brad's boss, the owner of the lumberyard where he works. It's been quick, but I care for him. He's a good man and wants to take care of us."

So, having heard the boy express his dissatisfaction with his military deferment while they had waited for the fish to bite, Alistair had not been surprised at Brad's telephone call shortly after his return to Washington to ask if there was a spot for him at the OSS.

"Does your mother approve?" he had asked.

"She knows I want to join up to do my part. What else she doesn't know can't hurt her," Brad had said.

Oh, yes, it could, young man, Alistair had thought, but he'd given the lad the go-ahead to come to Washington, D.C.

He'd tried to discourage the boy as much as the necessity for secrecy allowed. He'd pulled no punches about the business of the OSS. The agency could do without the son of Joanna Bukowski Hudson. She had suffered enough. But Alistair had been unable to dissuade him. Brad Hudson would not be put off because, as he'd correctly guessed, Alistair wished to protect the son of a woman he still desired. The boy had a sharp ear and keen eye for the indiscernible.

Now he and the others were ready to go. Alistair had chosen the French and German cover names they would use in living their false identities in Paris. They would go by these working names in Paris but would remain unknown to one another, even after their missions were complete. Alistair had informed the team of their cover names separately and ordered them not to divulge them to one another. Secrecy would be their greatest protection against betrayal. He kept the process simple. He selected noms de plumes beginning with the first letter of their real names. Sam Barton would become Stephane Beaulieu. Brad Hudson was to go by Barnard Wagner, and Chris was to answer to

Claus Bauer. Bridgette was Bernadette Dufor, and Victoria, Veronique Colbert.

But as a group they'd chosen and had fun selecting their field code names, or call signals, to identify themselves in radio transmissions and by which they would communicate with each other from now on. Alistair had steered them away from tags suggesting gender, occupation, or physical size—any clue that would tip off the enemy to their identity. They had consulted a dictionary and agreed to select names from under whichever letter Webster's Dictionary fell open to. The book parted to L, so Bridgette selected Labrador, a good choice for a woman as even-tempered and dependable as she. Victoria's finger had lighted on Liverwort, the godawful name of a flowerless green pancake of a plant, in ludicrous contrast to her beauty. Brad had favored Limpet, a marine mollusk with a muscular foot that could cling powerfully to wave-swept rocks. Alistair thought that an excellent fit for the young man he had come to know.

The other two men also chose words descriptive of Alistair's perception of them. Sam picked Lodestar, the guiding star of a ship; and Chris, Lapwing, a bird noted for its slow, irregular flapping flight and shrill, wailing cry. Alistair had to laugh at his selection. He wondered if Chris had made the connection to his singing voice, overheard when he belted out a tune in the camp shower of Station S, or to his own slow, swinging way of moving contrary to the smooth grace of his lightning-fast running speed.

At his table in the tavern, Alistair stubbed out his final cigarette among the other butts in the ashtray. If the group stuck *strictly* to the mission they were trained for—to gain and report intelligence—they had every chance of survival. At this point, the contacts he'd lined up in Paris were ready and waiting to receive them. None had been blown. Sam Barton—Stephane—would go to work in a French firm of consultant engineers doing business with companies taken over by the Nazis. Bridgette—Bernadette—had been hired as an assistant to Madame Jeanne Boucher, couturier of one of Paris's top fashion houses, and Victoria—Veronique—as a fencing instructor in the famous fencing school L'Ecole d' Escrime Français, whose students were officers in the German Army. Chris—Claus—had been assigned a job as a physical education instructor in a school formed to educate the sons of high-ranking Vichy and Nazi officials, and Brad—Barnard—was to ingratiate himself with an Abwehr general passionate about fly-fishing. None would know their specific assignment until they arrived for final training at Milton Hall, located sixty miles north of London, a large estate used as the espionage headquarters of Britain's Special Operations Executive, the SOE.

Stop worrying, Alistair! Bill Donovan kept telling him, but Alistair could not calm a deep-seated unease that each member had cause to strike out on secret missions of their own. He had yet to determine Sam Barton's and Victoria Grayson's hidden agendas, but the others were plain enough. Brad Hudson and Bridgette Loring each had big scores to settle with the Nazis and might not be satisfied with merely gathering and reporting information on the enemy. Chris Brandt, son of German parents still with a foot in the old country, was out to prove that he was every bit as American as hot dogs and Coca-Cola.

As far as Alistair knew, no member of the team was aware of any other member's motive for volunteering. Other than their own impressions gleaned in the eight weeks they'd trained together, they knew nothing at all about one another. What they didn't know of their teammates' histories, assignments, targets, work locations, and cover names could not be spilled in a Gestapo or an SS torture chamber.

Lights were coming on in the tavern. The cocktail crowd was beginning to filter in. Time to go.

Returning the pack of Lucky Strikes to the pocket of his brown jacket, Alistair swallowed the last of his club soda, set his glass on the napkin, and left before the moisture from the melting ice obliterated his inked drawing of the dragonfly.

THE MISSIONS

CHAPTER SEVENTEEN

SEPTEMBER 1942
Milton Hall, England

Their orders were simple and could not be deviated from. They were intelligence-gathering spies only, Alistair continued to drill into them. They were not to engage in sabotage, armed or peaceful resistance, politics, or propaganda. They were to live their cover stories quiet as shadows in the glare of the spotlights that would be upon them and report their intel to the man in brown, who would be hovering over his radio receiver in his assumed role as station chief of French Affairs in the city of Bern, three hundred miles away just over the French border. They would possess no weapons. They would be issued self-defense devices developed in the research labs of the OSS and the SOE to look like everyday items generally carried by hand, in pockets, and in purses. These were umbrellas with handles that could release a stiletto at the push of a disguised button, pencil fuses designed to explode after a set time to provide a chance for escape, cigarette cases that detonated upon opening, and pipe pistols that could fire off a round of .22-caliber bullets through their stems. Cigarette lighters, matchboxes, compacts, lipsticks, buttons, belt buckles would serve to conceal cameras, maps, and compasses. They had to have their L pills handy at all times. Alistair hoped—prayed—that the Gestapo, the SS, and the Abwehr, which were growing more savvy by the day to the deceptive gadgetry used by the Allies' saboteurs and spies, had not yet caught on to these latest inventions.

Once in Paris, only Bridgette would be able to make contact with him. As his radio operator, she was essential to the success of every mission. By now he thought of her as the head of Dragonfly, and the others as the wings. The living and working environments of the wings placed them under the constant eye of their German associates and suspected French collaborators, making it too risky for them to conceal and activate the Type B Mk 11 wireless radio designed to fit in a suitcase.

Bridgette's accommodations, attic rooms in a fifteenth-century convent, offered the most safety from discovery, since the thick convent walls provided protection from the street-cruising Gestapo vans that could rapidly pinpoint wireless transmissions. Time on the air was the greatest danger to the radio operator in enemy territory, but Alistair's hope was that the labyrinthine location of the Convent of the Sisters of Charity made radio detection almost impossible.

But a serious problem loomed, the source of his worry. Alistair had partially solved it by first housing Dragonfly apart but in proximity of one another. They were to be lodged in the Latin Quarter, located on the left bank of the River Seine. Paris was a city of quartiers, in ancient days called hamlets, today called arrondissements, another name for the city's twenty government administrative districts. These districts are like villages made up of close neighborhoods. Residents seen talking together, passing on the street, taking the same streetcars, waiting on the same corner, frequenting the same cafés and markets should not rouse suspicion.

To convey their intel to Bridgette for transmission to Bern, Alistair with great reservations had assigned the other four a mutual dead-letter box, a secret hiding place to leave messages. It was a mail slot in the door of an OSS rented house connected to the courtyard wall of the convent next door. There had been no way around using a single collection point. If their dead boxes were scattered around the Latin Quarter, Bridgette would be limited to only one pickup daily sandwiched between her departure from work and the evening curfew. Inevitable problems like heavy traffic, transportation snafus, weather conditions, especially in winter, and delays at work would make it impossible for her to do her job in timely fashion.

Alistair had made clear the danger of a common drop to the team. If one member was caught and made to talk, the others could be rounded up when they dropped off their intel, and Bridgette when she collected the material, but with their usual verve, all had seen the sense of his reasoning and agreed that the convenience of a mutual location outweighed the risks involved. The team did not know that behind the convent wall was their radio operator's lodgings. Bridgette would check the floor beneath the mail slot in the morning before leaving for La Maison de Boucher and in the evening after her return to the convent.

Only Bridgette possessed a key to the door. The property was empty except for bolts of fabrics, design sketches, drawing materials, a sewing machine, wire dress forms, a cutting table, and several chairs, all subterfuge to explain the reason for her visits. The house was simply an additional workroom for the House of Boucher, where Bridgette, a newly hired designer, sometimes did sewing for customers after working hours. The callus on her right index finger bore out her claim.

What Alistair had *not* figured out was a way for the head to communicate with the wings. As another safeguard to protect Bridgette's identity and theirs, the others were to have no overt contact with her. If her cover was blown, without radio connection to Bern, the whole operation would naturally fall apart. It was critical that Labrador's identity, address, and workplace be kept secret. But various situations were bound to jump up that would require her to contact her teammates individually.

This dilemma was unique to his professional experience, and Alistair had racked his brain trying to come up with a way out of it, but nothing had clicked, and he was running out of time. As the date neared to release them to their fates, he decided to lay the problem before the sharp minds of his young charges.

Brad—Limpet—suggested a central location to leave coded chalk marks. Cutting on wood would require too much time and attract attention, and the French were banned from carrying knives. Alistair immediately rejected the proposal as too obvious. A collection of chalk marks on a wall, doorstep, tree, or telephone pole was a dead giveaway to Nazi patrols and the collaborationist French police, and they'd lie in wait for the next operative to show himself. There was also the new danger of arrest by the Gestapo if a Parisian was found with any sort of marking medium other than pencils and fountain pens in pockets or purses, especially chalk. The discovery automatically stamped the owner as a member of the Resistance.

It was Bridgette who suggested a mural as the solution.

At this point, the group was aware that they would be living in the Latin Quarter of Paris, though Alistair had informed each of them of their accommodations privately with the stern admonition that they were to keep their addresses secret from the others. He had little expectation of his orders holding, however. The group members could bump into one another at the mail chute, or discover the locations of one another's abodes by the simple act of catching their teammates entering and leaving their residences.

"Explain, Labrador," he said.

"How can the Germans object to decorating a drab wall with a beautiful piece of art during wartime?"

Bridgette replied. "If you can arrange it with the convent, Major, I propose that I paint a mural on the outside of their courtyard wall as a means to communicate in code."

They had been shown a picture of the house with its attached courtyard wall and convent behind. "You mean use a wall painting as a code pad?" Alistair said. *Yes!* he thought jubilantly and said, "It can be arranged."

"I have in mind a water landscape inspired by Lapwing," Bridgette said with a smile at Chris. "Here's how it will work. I'll start by painting a dragonfly flitting about a lily pad. I will then fill in the objects representing our field names. Four are natural to a seaside scene. Labradors are retrievers of waterfowl. Liverworts are water-loving plants. Lapwings are plovers that live in watery habitats, and limpets are mollusks that must reside in bodies of water to survive."

"And Lodestar?" Bucky asked.

"The North Star that looks over all," she said. "I can leave messages to all of you in the form of some feature typical to your symbol without the enemy ever being aware that it is a code mark."

Victoria spoke up. "In other words, your encryption would be disguised as some part of the artwork."

Bridgette smiled at her understanding. "That's right, Liverwort."

Victoria looked impressed. "Sounds good to me."

"Or put another way, our symbols would serve as our individual code pads for you to leave messages to us," Bucky said.

"Right again, Lodestar. If you see a new detail on your star, you'll know the message came from me and what it means. All we have to do as a group is come up with code markings suitable to your symbols and memorize their significance."

Bucky said, "It could work since we'll all be living in the same neighborhood and could make a point of walking by the wall every day. As residents of the area, our interest would be natural."

"I agree with Lodestar, but haven't the Nazis already caught on to the French Resistance's use of graffiti as a propaganda tool and a means to send coded messages?" Brad asked.

"Good point, Limpet, but I don't think they'll mistake the mural for that," Bridgette answered. "I believe they'll look upon it as a perfectly harmless pursuit meant to lighten the atmosphere of the neighborhood. They may even welcome it as a way to prove they're not the monsters everybody knows them to be."

"I thought the Germans hated art," Victoria said.

"They burned about five thousand paintings in Berlin in 1939." The Nazi plunder of priceless works of art from German museums and their wholesale destruction was another atrocity ordered by Hitler that had made it to American newspapers.

"Those paintings represented *modern* art, Liverwort," Bridgette explained. "My mural won't have a stroke of expressionism in it. The Germans might even contribute their own touches, and if I know the artistic French, so will they, since the painting will be seen as a public display. It's not a perfect plan, but at least it gives me a way of making contact with reasonable hope that it works. And like Lodestar pointed out, all of us have reason to have a natural interest in the wall."

"What if street urchins—vandals—get at it just for the orneriness of it?" Bucky asked.

Bridgette shrugged. "It could happen, Lodestar, but most likely not in daylight with the German patrols about and certainly not after curfew. I expect street contributions. You can bet some other artists won't be able to resist adding their own touches, and I wouldn't doubt but that some children's marking in *crayon de couleur* will show up, but they shouldn't interfere with my renderings regarding you, not if you know what to look for."

Bucky nodded, satisfied.

Alistair had sat back and allowed the group to toss the plan back and forth, looking for holes and sticking points without butting in. The team would have gathered that Bridgette must be an artist of some sort working in a capacity that required her talent. Logic would also tell them that the courtyard wall would be close to her lodging to allow her ready and fast access to it. It was a brilliant plan if it worked. "A ray of light in a city gone dark. I like it," he said.

Victoria stuck up her hand. "Well, if we're voting, Liverwort here casts her vote for giving the mural a go. I see no reason why we shouldn't try the plan, and I like the idea of putting one over on the Germans right under their noses."

Bucky held up his palm as if swearing an oath. "And I, Lodestar, cast my vote to try it as well. Nice going, Labrador."

Brad gave a rainbow wave. "Count Limpet in."

Chris raised his thumbless right hand and smiled at Bridgette. "Ditto for Lapwing."

A duplicate of the painting Bridgette had in mind went up on a wall, and in the next few days, the group memorized and developed a secret language made up of the features common to aquatic landscapes. Shadings, vertical and squiggly lines, circles, light and dark brushstrokes assumed meaning. Certain markings warned, notified, informed, and confirmed. Every emergency situation that could crop up were impossible to anticipate or address. The team concentrated only on the ones likely to occur. For example, a need might arise for a member to speak with Bridgette in person—what if the mail slot was compromised? That person should draw a diagonal line through his or her own symbol. It was an emergency summons to meet with Bridgette at the tea and book shop at four o'clock the day of the mark's appearance. By the same token, a diagonal line drawn across the mural's central dragonfly—Bridgette's symbol—called for the entire group to meet.

Brad posed a question. How would Labrador notify the team that she'd been blown?

Bridgette pursed her lips while they looked at her expectantly. "I'll leave a V in the dog's ear if I am able. Then you'll know to head for your safe houses."

"And if you're not able?" Victoria asked.

"I am afraid I don't have an answer to that question," Bridgette said.

CHAPTER EIGHTEEN

It was to be their last time to meet as a complete group on safe ground. Alistair had surprised the Dragonfly team with permission to gather for a last night of freedom and celebration before they were dispatched at staggered times within the next two days to Tempsford. There pilots of the secret "Moon" squadron, a unit of the RAF whose mission was to deliver and pick up agents behind enemy lines on nights when the moon was full, would airlift the team off individually to various improvised landing strips in the French countryside. Bridgette would be the first to leave. Her pickup call was for 0400 hours: four o'clock a.m.

"There's a good pub in the village where you can kick up your heels," Alistair had told them. "The Crown and Scepter. Go and have a good time, but don't kick up your heels too high. I'll send a driver to bring you home."

Though the group understood that this night was different from the last night at Station S—the major really did mean for them to relax together—he needn't have worried about the height of the heels. Packed around a pub table, shoulders touching, the group was drinking little and saying less. The deadly seriousness of their assignments had sunk in. The moment of truth had arrived. They had willingly volunteered to risk their lives for missions from which they had no way of knowing when—or if—they might return. But palpable also, thick as the fog pressing against the pub's windows, was their reluctance to part company, separate from this congenial and safe cadre of mutual respect and deep affection they'd formed in four months of training. In Paris, they would meet up at a tea and book shop to count heads, their gathering point should the diagonal mark appear on one of their symbols. But for that mark on the wall and perhaps glimpses of one another in the neighborhood, they would part company at that time and never again be together as the team of Dragonfly.

"Do you suppose Major Renault will reveal our true identities to us once this is over so that we can make contact when we're back home?" Victoria asked. "Since we'll be extracted at different times, it's not likely we'll run into one another again once our missions are over."

Gloom pulled at her finely modeled features. Early on, Bridgette would have been surprised at the depth of Liverwort's sadness at parting. Liverwort was not a girl who wore her emotions like face pancake, but as they'd become friends, Bridgette had discovered that warm and intense feelings were going on behind that cool exterior. In their sleepless late-night sessions, they had gone against the rules and revealed their motives in signing on with the OSS. Bridgette told Liverwort about the loss of her grandmother, her only living relative, who had been tortured by the Germans, and Liverwort shared with her that she had joined the agency to find her fiancé, who had been shot down close to Paris. No parachute had been seen, but she was convinced that he could still be alive and hiding out somewhere in the city or the French countryside. Bridgette had gone cold at the danger her friend was letting herself in for, but she knew better than to try talking her out of it. Instead, she'd offered gently, "Would that not be like looking for the proverbial needle in a field of haystacks?"

Liverwort's lovely, gray-green eyes had filled with determination. "Yes, but I must try," she'd said.

As for "the boys," as they called the rest of the team, neither had discovered a clue to explain their personal motives for being here. From careful observation, though, Bridgette had been able to pick up some hints of their interests and backgrounds. Apparently, Limpet liked fishing—fly-fishing, specifically. Bridgette overheard him discussing the sport with one of the staff members at Milton Hall, and several times she had seen him about the estate casting out a line with practiced ease. A few days ago, the major had asked him if he'd made sure to pack his "special gear," which Bridgette felt certain referred to the rod and reel. Somehow Limpet's angling expertise figured into his assignment. Thereafter, she and Liverwort referred to Limpet as "the fisherman."

Lodestar's métier remained a mystery, but the ease with which he'd mastered Bridgette's art lessons suggested a familiarity with drawing board and pencil—"an architect or something on that order," Liverwort speculated, but his practical approach to matters indicated the mind-set of an engineer. They had laughed over Liverwort's relation of the joke about the engineer sentenced to death by guillotine. "He watches the device malfunction, studies it, then calls out, 'Hold on! I see the problem.'" Victoria had overheard Lodestar questioning Moon pilots about an antifascist military leader they might have picked up in France to join French General Charles de Gaulle, who was forming an army in exile in London. Lodestar asked if they'd heard the name Nicholas Cravois. Sure, said the pilot, only he wasn't with General de Gaulle. He was an important French Resistance leader living in the hills around Paris. The Nazis called him the Black Ghost. Victoria had described their teammate's face as "lighting up like a neon sign," and the women agreed that the name had something to do with Lodestar signing on for the Paris mission. His soft drawl and pronunciation of *Saturday* as "Sa'erdee," like Bridgette's college classmate from Duncan, Oklahoma, pegged him as an Okie.

Bridgette would guess Lapwing to be from Texas. He spoke with a twang except when speaking German. His passion was long-distance running. He'd been allowed to get in a daily run during training sessions, even though their instructors had every minute mercilessly and crucially packed. But soon the team came to deduce that running was part of Lapwing's cover and the laps were necessary to stay in shape. Bridgette wondered if he was aware that

Milton Hall's females were ogling him from an upstairs window as he ran along the estate's service road shirtless, long legs golden and sinewy, chewing up the dirt track with effortless ease.

At the pub table, brought back from her ruminations, Bridgette heard Lapwing say, "Let's ask the major tonight. I'm for a reunion when we get back home."

They all chimed in: *"I second that." "Name the date and place, and I'll be there." "Me, too." "Anywhere, anytime."* They spoke confidently, as if without question—without a dreamer's doubt—they would make the date. Bridgette became aware of Liverwort's gaze turned upon her. "And you, Labrador? What do you say?"

"I'll send the invitations," she said, "but what if the major refuses to reveal the information? We're like classified documents, you know, and he plays that card by the book. Our identities could be sealed in top secret files for years."

Silence fell. Eyes dropped to their half-imbibed pints, fingers toyed with glasses. The unspoken question they were forbidden even to contemplate spread around the table like spilled beer: *What's to keep us from sharing the information now?*

Bucky shook his head. "We can't, gang. As much

as we'd like to, for everybody's safety, you know we can't." Sheepish expressions signaled agreement. The major's warning, first heard in their initial briefing in Washington, D.C., and repeated many times with bone-chilling examples of the penalties for disregarding the order, must be heeded. *You may think it's safe to exchange names, addresses, information of your civilian life, but let me tell you a story...*

The major had then told them many terrifying tales. One OSS agent had been caught, tortured, and subjected to a horrible death because she'd shared details of her private life with a fellow agent who'd fallen into the hands of the Gestapo. German intelligence had managed to track her identity through their network in the United States that had led to her capture in Berlin during the early stages of the war. The poor woman had been bound, gagged, and cremated alive.

"Do not for a moment think your identities cannot be traced in the United States," he'd said. "I'm ordering you to keep your mouths shut about who you are, your families, where you live, where you were educated, and what you do for work and pleasure. If you want to stay alive, you'll obey. Understood?"

They had understood.

Victoria now said, "Well, then, to be on the safe

side, I suggest we set a place, time, and date to meet once the war is over."

"Excellent idea," Bucky said. "Suggestions, anyone?"

All eyes turned to Bridgette. Over the past four months they had begun to look to her as their leader. "Well, I've never been to New York City and promised myself I'd go someday," she offered. "My first visit there would be even more special if it was to meet you guys."

"Lovely idea," Victoria said. "I can suggest a place that I went on my first visit there. How about the Rose Main Reading Room of the New York Public Library on Fifth Avenue as a rendezvous point?"

"Why not?" Bucky said. "Does everybody agree?"

Everyone raised a glass to concur.

"Now let's decide when," Chris said.

Bridgette spoke up instantly. "Tomorrow's date is September twenty-third, the day our group breaks up. If we lose contact with one another, I suggest we meet at two o'clock in the Rose Main Reading Room of the New York Public Library the twenty-third of the first September after the war is over. Is everybody okay with that?"

"Done," Brad answered.

There was a merry pounding of the table, interrupted when a British Army sergeant from the training staff appeared before them. "Party's over, lads and lassies," he announced. "Time to go."

Bucky lifted his pint and thrust it out to the middle of the table. "To Dragonfly," he said.

"To Dragonfly," they all chorused, tapping glasses, and Victoria added tipsily for good measure, "God save the king and bless America."

And all you wee lambs, the sergeant thought.

CHAPTER NINETEEN

Are you all tucked in, miss?" the pilot of the Lysander asked the sweet-faced young agent he was about to drop off in occupied France, a regular Kewpie doll. It took all kinds to do what she'd been trained for, but bejesus... a pretty little thing like her?

Bridgette nodded and wriggled into a more comfortable position in the small aircraft's cramped quarters, grateful that she did not have a parachute strapped to her back. She was to be set down in a farmer's field ten miles from Paris, which would be signaled only by short bursts of light, quickly extinguished. She'd scramble down a fixed ladder on the port side of the fuselage and head toward a signal she hoped would be flashed by her contact and not a cadre of Gestapo agents. A vehicle was supposed to be waiting to spirit her away to assume her new life as

Bernadette Dufor, newly hired assistant to Madame Jeanne Boucher, owner of the couture fashion house La Maison de Boucher—the House of Boucher.

The flight plan had called for an approximate two o'clock touchdown. They were taking off at midnight—plenty of time to calm her nerves, Bridgette reckoned. She mustn't panic. Whatever happened, she must not panic. She must trust the pilot to get her to the drop-off point safely, though her confidence would have been considerably bolstered if she hadn't been told that the Lysander would be flying without its usual defense, communication, and protection equipment. The aircraft's belly had been painted matte black to be invisible to searchlights, and its upper surface had been camouflaged in dark green and pale gray colors to conceal it from enemy night fliers. If those tricks failed, they would be at the mercy of ground fire and the German Luftwaffe.

"Not trying to scare you, miss," the Special Operations Executive officer in charge had said. "Just giving you a chance to back out while you can. It's my job."

Alistair, a cigarette between his lips, doodled at a table in a far corner, not allowed to offer comment. Each member of Dragonfly was to be given this spiel in individual briefings to allow them the opportunity to withdraw from their missions in private. She was the first to be offered the chance, since she was the first to be dispatched. The understanding was that she could simply get up and leave the premises—"fold your tents like the Arabs and silently steal away," the SOE officer had quoted Henry Wadsworth Longfellow. A driver would take her back to Milton Hall and from there to London, where she could hop a flight back to the United States. Bridgette had glanced at her case officer and caught a look that made her think he hoped she'd bail out. As time had gone on during training, the whole team had begun to suspect that he regretted getting them into this mess.

But what was there to go home to? A job as a women's buyer for the J. L. Hudson department stores in Detroit, Michigan? An empty house within spitting distance of the best friend who'd betrayed her? A tombstone engraved with the birth and death dates of Angelique Duvalier? Bridgette had arrived too late to celebrate her college graduation and twenty-second birthday with her grandmother. When the Greyhound bus had finally pulled into Traverse City and a taxi deposited her before the little house on Elmwood Street, a neighbor informed her that Angelique had been taken to the hospital because of chest pains. She lived two days after Bridgette made it home, the letter from the Office of Strategic Services still in her purse.

Disregarding her case officer's look, Bridgette said to the SOE captain, "I'm in."

The captain had then instructed, "Now go grab some sleep. You'll need it. You'll be taking off at twenty-four hundred—midnight."

In the Lysander, Bridgette found space to stretch out her legs. The racket from the single engine was deafening but somehow lulling. She forced herself to relax in the roar and let her mind wander back to how it was that she came to be "in." By now, September 24, 1942, the first night of the full moon, she'd expected to be on the payroll of Paramount Pictures as an intern of Hollywood's most famous costume designer, but Gladys Bradbury's scissors and sick possessiveness had altered that direction in her life. Bridgette still grew numb from the shock of seeing Gladys standing in the shimmering wasteland of slashed fabrics among the troupe of naked dress forms, the rhinestone-studded shoulder of her scarlet jersey toga all that was rescuable of her design. The girl hadn't gone directly to the Pennant Hotel that day when she left the lunchroom. She'd gone back to the design department to steal the key to the exhibit room the aide had left in the chairman's door box. The day after the small burial service of her grandmother, Bridgette had contacted the Office of Strategic Services.

Did Bridgette miss her best friend of nearly all her lifetime? Not a jot. But she would miss the friends she'd made in Dragonfly. As she was leaving in the predawn darkness, she'd cast a look back at the windows of their upstairs quarters, and her throat still tightened at the memory of their heads gathered at the sash to see her off. The boys peered from their room and Liverwort from the one next door, their faces pale in the glow of the lamps. They'd given her the thumbs-up, and Bridgette had waved and mouthed *See you soon!*, doubting they could see her in the dark. She'd climbed aboard the jeep with her heart heavy and her throat throbbing, feeling as they drove off like a tethered boat breaking away from shore.

On the jeep ride to Tempsford, headlights cutting eerily through the damp fog and thick darkness, Major Renault recited in his typical, terse style the litany of instructions already inexpungable in her mind, more a sign of his nerves than hers. Prior to meeting the others in ten days' time, she was to check out the memorized list of safe houses and establishments deemed secure to make sure they were still viable. And of course she was to begin preparing the wall for her mural. The major wanted her presence noted in the neighborhood before the others arrived. Whatever happened, she was not to be captured, he warned her once again. Despite her impressive performance during training, nobody, but *nobody*, held out under a Gestapo interrogation. She was the head of the dragonfly, the others her wings. In time she would undoubtedly learn from her teammates' intel where they lived and worked—in other words, the nature of their missions. She alone would possess the information the Gestapo would be after to throw a net around the lot.

"At the first sign of trouble, get out of there," he'd said. "That's an order. You know where to go, what to do. And remember to leave that V in the dog's ear."

"I won't forget," Bridgette said, but at the takeoff point, before she boarded, he'd seemed incapable of further words and simply pulled her into a tight embrace that lasted long enough for her to hear the rapid thump of his heart.

"Be safe," he'd rasped as he let her go, this time the huskiness in his voice not due to his predawn pack of cigarettes.

It was ludicrous when she thought about it, feeling

so attached to four people whose real names she didn't even know and thinking of a bossy, chain-smoking, corn husk of an old soldier with tobacco- and coffee-stained teeth as a father figure, but there it was. It was all a new feeling for her. She'd found that she wasn't such a love 'em and leave 'em sort of person after all, but then these were the first people she'd ever met who she wanted to remain in her life always.

The major had turned them down last night when Liverwort, nothing if not audacious, a little potted, had led the march to his room and rapped on the door.

He'd opened it smelling of tobacco. "Yes?" he inquired mildly.

Liverwort had demanded that after their missions were complete he pass on their real names and addresses so that they could make contact back in the States. "Sorry," he'd said. He wasn't allowed to do that. Her lovely face had darkened. Why not? she'd wanted to know. "National security," he'd answered. They knew the rules of the Official Secrets Service Act. Why not set up a place and time to meet when the war was over? They could exchange names and addresses then.

"We already have," Lodestar said and related the plan.

"Good for you," he'd said as if they were children come up with blueprints for a spacecraft to fly to the moon. Did that hint of patronage mean he expected they would forget about the meeting once the war was over or that they would not make it home?

"You are invited," Liverwort announced.

"I am? Well, then I'm honored."

"That's why we'll need your address," she said.

"Sorry. No can do. When is this proposed date and where?"

"The first September twenty-third after peace is officially declared. Rose Main Reading Room of the New York Public Library, two o'clock," Limpet answered.

"We won't start without you," Lodestar said.

"In that case, I'll try to make it."

As they'd started for their rooms, Liverwort had whispered, "He doesn't think the meeting will come off."

"O he of little faith."

"We'll show him though, won't we?" Liverwort said, and they had bumped elbows on it.

The mural...from now on her only lifeline to them. What if it did not work as a means to communicate? For the first time, in the glaring light of the plane's chilly and utter darkness as it began its descent to the drop-off point, its drone now a deafening taunt of the danger into which she was headed, Bridgette could clearly see how all sorts of problems could render the painting useless as a communication pad. Why hadn't she thought of them before? Why hadn't the team? And why had the major gone along with her insane idea?

"*Get ready!*" she heard the pilot yell, and Bridgette, flesh tingling, heart galumphing, took hold of the suitcase radio. She would have one minute in the three-minute operation to climb out and clear the aircraft before the pilot took to the air again in a blast of slipstream. Peering out the canopy, she saw a small fiery light appear on the ground, then more flamed in a line that defined the landing area. God help her, she hoped the hands that held those torches were friendly. Before she could catch a full breath, the Lysander had landed with a jolting bump, made a hard U-turn, and returned to the first light, quickly snuffed.

"*Go!*" the pilot commanded, and Bridgette quickly shoved back the canopy. Her foot felt for the yellow-painted step to better guide her down the ladder in the now cloud-shrouded moonlight, and she was suddenly on the ground as he threw the throttle into place for an immediate liftoff. "Good luck!" she heard him yell as the plane taxied for departure, and she was alone with her radio in an empty, silent field shrill with the sudden desertion of human life. She waited, motionless, and listened for a man-made stir, someone to claim her and take her to safety. Whoever the shadows were that had laid out the landing strip had disappeared into the deeper darkness of the forest beyond the field. If Gestapo, they would have made themselves known by now.

Bridgette turned toward a hedgerow of hawthorn in full pink bloom, surreal in the filtered glow of the moon, their blossoms looking like bodiless heads. Beyond it must lay a road, she conjectured, her guess confirmed when a car engine suddenly hummed to life and two quick bursts of a flashlight pierced the darkness. She walked cautiously toward the hedgerow and heard the soft opening of a vehicle door. Her heart in her mouth, she could have fainted from relief when she heard a female voice say in crisp French, "Mademoiselle Bernadette Dufor, I presume? Welcome to France."

CHAPTER TWENTY

Victoria—Veronique Colbert—was the first to arrive at the meeting place. It was Saturday, October 3. La Petite Madeleine was a narrow little book-and-tea establishment tucked away on a back street in the quiet and sleepy charm of Montparnasse, a residential district adjoining the Latin Quarter. Less prosperous than others of its kind located closer to the renowned tourist attractions of the Montparnasse Cemetery and the Paris Catacombs, the shop was not often visited by guidebook-carrying German soldiers. Equally unenticing were the shop's watery tea and dry madeleines that food shortages had forced La Petite Madeleine to serve in lieu of its once delicious tisane tea, buttery pastries, and rich *boursin* sandwiches. The back room of an establishment of no distinction with instant egress to a maze of alleys and winding streets was an ideal meeting place for a group not wishing to be seen congregating around a café table in their own neighborhood.

The book section of the shop was located at the entrance. Patrons passed through it to reach the tearoom. Victoria had dressed with careful downplay of any detail about her person that might invite notice. In the six days she'd been in Paris, she had already attracted too much attention, a desired effect in L'Ecole d'Escrime Français, the most celebrated fencing academy in France. As calculated, from the first day of her employment as an instructor of foil, the young German military officers enrolled as students had swarmed about her, and now the docket under Mademoiselle Veronique Colbert was filled.

But here, and on the street, it was wise to be invisible, so today she wore a prewar trench coat over a dowdy dress, down-at-the-heels oxfords, and a scarf that concealed the severe bun at the nape of her neck, in contrast to the French chignon that had drawn admiring gazes from her jackbooted students. A pair of thin, wire-framed sunglasses sat on her nose, and she carried a market basket with a week's ration of bread and cheese. Here was a woman no more remarkable than a weary housewife of the lower classes stepping into the shop for a cup of tea after a day of waiting in grocery lines with the hope food was still left to buy when she reached the head of the queue.

"Tea," she said in French to the aproned man wiping the counter to indicate that she was not here for reading material. The shop smelled dankly of old books and spent tea leaves.

"One?" he asked.

Victoria shook her head. "Five. I'm meeting friends."

The man slung his polishing towel over his shoulder, eyes lighting up at the prospect of customers. "Very good, madame. Follow me," he said.

Employee or proprietor? Victoria wondered. *Proprietor*, she thought. He led with the right-of-way of ownership. Was he working with the SOE or OSS? Would the major have chosen this spot if it wasn't a safe location? Had the proprietor been expecting her and the rest of the team? Was he one of them?

Only one table was occupied at this, the tea hour, in Paris. A lone customer, a Frenchman by the looks of him, sat reading in a corner by the light of the October afternoon that filtered through a dirty window. As trained, Victoria memorized his features in case she should see him again. Thick in the neck, broad in the shoulder, florid-faced, he wore the traditional black beret, turtleneck, black leather jacket, and inevitable scarf of his countrymen. A Gauloises cigarette drooped from his lips. Absorbed in his book, he did not glance up at her entrance. The proprietor paid him no more mind than if he'd been the shop's house cat curled up in a corner, and Victoria guessed him to be a regular at his usual table. Okay, then.

She removed her sunglasses to better make out her surroundings in the gloom and said, "Over there, *s'il vous plaît*," pointing to the table farthest away. The team would push two tables together to make room for five. The proprietor drew out a chair facing sideways to the Frenchman and asked in a courtly manner if madame wished him to take her coat.

She answered, "*Non, merci.*"

"You will wait to order?"

"*Oui*. My friends will be here shortly."

"May I bring you something while you wait, madame?"

"*Non, merci.*"

"You have only to ask," the man said, giving the table a vigorous swipe with the towel before he bowed away.

Victoria sensed the Frenchman glance over at them, as if he, too, were surprised by all the bowing and scraping in an establishment where ceremony was not expected. She rejected her impulse to pull her scarf forward to obscure her profile, in case the gesture seemed furtive. In this city, it paid to be extremely careful of one's smallest movements and to suspect every stranger a potential enemy. The Frenchman went back to his book, and Victoria set the basket on the floor and her purse in her lap—she had already marked the exit door—and laced her hands together on the edge of the table to wait, a frump of a woman, bowed down with the weight of misery wrought by the German occupation.

Actually, she did feel bowed from the weight of misery. For all she knew, Labrador might have already been arrested by the Gestapo. If her teammates did not show today, she would know that their radio operator had been made to talk and the others picked up at the dead-letter box within their first days in Paris. Victoria had escaped only because of a chance glance down an alley near the drop's location. The team had been instructed to go to the mailbox as soon as possible to alert Labrador of their successful insertions. Dressed as she was today, she'd been on her way to the house next to the convent wall when she spotted a black Mercedes 260D sedan parked facing the street from a narrow alley. The car was the preferred choice of the Gestapo and

SS—the "death mobile," Parisians called it. Seeing such a car on the street struck terror into hearts. It meant serious trouble for some poor soul, and this one looked ready to pounce.

Panicked, she'd wondered if it was waiting to pounce on her. She'd hurried away from the street like a woman late for work, her coded note to Labrador tucked deep into her coat pocket. The Mercedes windows had been too dark to see whether the car was occupied, but she'd expected to hear it roar into life any minute and tear after her. She had torn up the note and strewn the pieces in the litter on the street, and not dared return to the drop.

Once out of danger and her panic under control, Victoria took stock. If Labrador had been taken, the major would learn of it and alert her through her facilitator, Jacques Vogel, fencing master of the school. Labrador could give up no information about her working name, her address, or place of employment, thanks to the shrewd design of Major Renault. So for the moment, she was safe. She would not abort her mission and give up her only chance to find Ralph, not until word came that Labrador had been compromised.

The rest of the week, while waiting to hear from the major, Victoria had gone about her assignment as planned, gathering fragments and pieces of intel dropped carelessly by students without giving a thought to the possibility that their foil instructor could understand every word of German they spoke. As of this morning, when she had still heard no bad news from Jacques Vogel, she'd felt justified in risking an appearance in the tea shop this afternoon. She'd chance it that she'd have time to slip out the exit door before the Gestapo crashed into the tearoom.

The surface of the table felt gummy with the film of a half century of use despite the proprietor's earnest arm grease, and she would have removed her hands at first touch, but that, too, might attract attention from the man by the window. What did a Frenchwoman of her station have to be so persnickety about in the sort of shop she was accustomed to patronizing, especially in these times of rationed soap?

She knew that informers were everywhere, their treachery fueled by desperation for food, medicine, travel permits, the release of a loved one from prison, or simply out of petty jealousy or a personal desire for revenge. No place and no one was safe. The most innocent actions could be reported as suspicious to the Gestapo and French police. A resident on her street was taken in for questioning because a neighbor had reported that each morning she rearranged the pots of herbs on her windowsill, a code used by the Resistance. For the same reason, a Catholic priest in the neighborhood had been arrested on the notion that his homilies conveyed clandestine messages. The butcher's son had been denounced for allegedly relaying information of German activity in meat wrappings, and the corner newsstand operator was not seen again after being taken off on the false charge of distributing underground newspapers. Such was the atmosphere in Nazi-occupied Paris.

Victoria took a deep breath and relaxed. There was time yet. She'd arrived ten minutes early, even after taking the roundabout route to make sure she wasn't followed. One of her students, a young lieutenant in the Wehrmacht and a novice to foil but confident of its mastery, had taken a pesky shine to her. Victoria suspected he was nothing more than a file clerk in the organization, but he had access to information that he spilled willy-nilly, trying to impress her. She'd refused his offers to escort her home, but he wasn't one to take no for an answer, and she half expected to find him waiting outside the school at the end of her workdays, a serious concern on days like today.

Minutes passed. Three...five...seven...nine. Victoria checked the lining of her coat to make sure of her L pill, and her purse for her pencil explosive. Apprehension swelled in her chest, dried her throat. Her friends were not coming. They were lost. Every horror that she'd imagined had come to pass. She glanced at the exit door and was about to pick up her market basket when her peripheral vision caught the Frenchman lift his gaze from his book. Chatter in the bookshop penetrated her plugged hearing, voices growing familiar as they came closer. Were her ears deceiving her? The door to the tea shop opened and the proprietor entered, the smile of Limpet beaming over his head. Following him were Lodestar and Lapwing, but where was Labrador? Where was their little pixie?

Then Labrador's blond head poked out from behind the wide shoulders of Lapwing. "*Bonjour, notre ami*," she said smiling.

Victoria rose from the table, her fencer's legs trembling. "*Bonjour, mes chers amis*," she whispered, her voice lost in a flood of relief.

The proprietor swept a hand toward them. "Your friends, madame?" he asked with a flourish.

"Yes, indeed they are. *Merci*, monsieur," Victoria said.

The Frenchman snuffed out his Gauloises and stood, tucking the unsmoked half of the cigarette into his pocket and his book under his arm, presumably because the newcomers had interrupted his reading or perhaps to allow old friends their privacy. So engaged were the young people in their enthusiastic greetings that they did not notice him watching them with heightened interest as he passed out of the room.

CHAPTER TWENTY-ONE

It had been a long wait for Bridgette to learn if the team was still in operation. She'd not found a scrap of intel on the floor beneath the mail slot all week. She had begun to worry they'd been rolled up, and on the fifth day radioed the major to ask if she should close up shop. He'd last heard of them from their contacts who had confirmed that they had landed safely, but not a word since.

"Remain until the date of the meeting at the café," he'd said. "You're to keep the appointment, but if you see a red flag in the window, get the hell out of there and head for your safe house immediately. Copy that?"

She copied. The stone wall, freshly cleaned and primed, still waiting for the first stroke of her brush, glowed in the afternoon sunlight when she set off for the meeting, an eye out for surveillance, but her nerves were so tightly strung after a week of worry that she could imagine shadows waltzing with lampposts. She was sure the major was as nerve-racked as she. It was no wonder then that when she approached the café—no red flag in the window—she thought she was hallucinating when she saw Limpet and Lapwing and Lodestar jump out smiling from behind a bell tower across the street, where they'd obviously been hiding. "Well, you're a sight for sore eyes," Chris said, sweeping her into a crushing hug. "We thought you'd been arrested!"

After each had had a turn at hugging her, Bridgette said with the annoyance of a mother overjoyed to be reunited with her lost chicks but angry enough to give them a good swat for wandering off, "What? Really? Well I thought the same of you!" She swiped the tears of relief from her eyes and said, "I thought you'd all been rounded up when I didn't hear a peep from any of you. The major and I have been worried sick. You were supposed to let me know when you were in place."

"I'm sorry, Labrador," Brad said, "but we couldn't contact you because the drop box has been compromised."

"So we stayed out of sight until you turned up," Bucky explained.

Bridgette stared at them. "You *all* think the drop box is compromised? Why?"

"We'll tell you in the café," Chris said. "Have you heard from Liverwort?"

"Not a word."

But there she was when they walked in, looking like a hausfrau on washing day, plain as a scrub board, but she didn't fool them. They would have recognized that profile anywhere. She stared at them as if they were genies materializing out of the room's smoke, and Bridgette recognized that Liverwort, too, had spent the week thinking they'd all been blown.

After exuberant greetings, they pulled out chairs, drew close, and Victoria, speaking in a low tone that did not carry beyond the tearoom, recounted her story first. "I saw a Mercedes, a Gestapo car, parked in an alley up the street from the house with the mail slot the day I went to report to you. The car was pointed forward as if lying in wait to snag somebody, so I kept on walking. The next day, I circled back behind the passageway and found the same car parked there and the day afterward. I could only conclude that you'd been arrested, Labrador, and...well, you know...so I stayed away."

Bucky said, “I saw the car you described the day I went to report in, too, and made the same deduction.”

Chris said, “And that goes for me, too.”

“That makes four of us,” Brad said to Bridgette. “I spotted the car of the same type and assumed you’d been taken.”

Bridgette looked around at the drawn faces showing the strain of their worry and anxiety of the last week. Her own stomach muscles had yet to relax. But rather than head off to their safe houses, they had stuck it out and taken the risk to attend this meeting to see if she’d made it. Amazing. But her fear and anxiety, mixed with a surge of affection for the team, was now also flooded with relief. Bridgette knew the car that had spooked them and what it was doing in the alley, but only after the fact, and what could she have done about it if she’d known earlier?

“You don’t have to worry about the Mercedes, guys,” she said. “It wasn’t parked there because of you. It belongs to the Gestapo lover of a prostitute who lived in the building by the alley. She’s since been arrested on charges of being a spy and the car is no longer there.”

“How in the world do you know that?” Victoria asked.

“I have my sources,” Bridgette replied archly. In fact,

the plight of the poor prostitute had been discussed at the supper table at the convent. Sister Mary Frances, mother superior of the Sisters of Charity convent, got the news from the concierge of the apartment complex where the prostitute lived. Bridgette had not connected the dots between the Mercedes and the bare floor under the mail slot. All along, for the team's safety, she had not been comfortable with the major's decision to assign Dragonfly a mutual drop box. Last week's situation called for revisiting the issue. She sat forward and folded her hands on the table. "For your own peace of mind, and mine, maybe it's time we question the wisdom of a central location for a drop. All our angst this week could have been avoided if you each had your own dead-letter box," she said.

She stopped talking as tea was brought in. *Just as well*, Bridgette thought. The lull would give them time to think about an alternative to the mail slot, but when the proprietor had gone, Chris spoke up. "Speaking for myself, I see the logic of a single collection point. As the major pointed out, Labrador, I don't see how you could possibly do the footwork your job would require."

"I could manage it," Bridgette said.

"Really?" Victoria challenged, eyebrow perked. "How?"

"Well, I thought I'd look for places within close proximity to one another near the metro stop where we get on and off the train each day..."

"The Saint-Michel station and surrounding areas are heavily guarded, crawling with Gestapo and SS and guard dogs," Bucky interrupted. "The shops and apartments have eyes, and informers on the lookout for escaping Jews are thick around every lamppost. How long do you think you'd stay safe in an environment like that?"

Before Bridgette could reply, Brad butted in. "I agree. Somebody is bound to notice you visiting our hiding places each day, Labrador, even if we're lucky to escape going undetected. Your comings and goings would establish a pattern."

Victoria said flatly, "The drop box we have now is ideal. I see no need to change it."

"I don't, either," Chris said. "I think convenience trumps all arguments for separate collection points. The mail slot is right by the mural that we pass every day, which makes it easy for us to check our coded messages at the same time we drop off our intel."

"I was thinking of it for your sakes," Bridgette said.

"And we are thinking of yours, *ma chère amie*," Victoria said.

Bridgette swallowed at the tightness in her throat,

but numbers won. "Very well, then," she said. "Then let's get on with the business at hand."

Drinking flavorless tea and nibbling at something scalloped that passed for madeleines, Bridgette apprised the team of the revised list of shopkeepers in the Latin Quarter to trust and those to be wary of, churches to avoid, cafés under surveillance by the Gestapo. The safe house off the Place Saint-Michel has been rolled up, and Pierre Durant, the greengrocer, has been betrayed. As instructed by the major, she inquired about their jobs and living conditions. Were they settling in well enough? Would there be a problem getting enough to eat, keeping warm? These questions were necessary to ask in a country occupied by an enemy that had willingly left the French population to starve and freeze through a winter without energy sources to heat their homes.

Finally all had been said that could be said. Time for the team to break up. Bridgette rose, a signal that brought the others to their feet in the awkward silence of pending good-byes. This meeting would be their last together unless a diagonal mark appeared across the central dragonfly. From now on each dragonfly was to fly alone.

CHAPTER TWENTY-TWO

Bucky was the first to leave. At ten-minute intervals, the others would follow suit. They had each been trained in how to make an immediate and accurate reconnaissance of an area. Bucky would check the street to see if a window browser, a maintenance worker, a shopkeeper plying a broom on his sidewalk, a cyclist working on his bike, or a pedestrian tying his shoe broke away to walk in his direction. He'd take a few steps, then, as if he'd forgotten something, return to the tea shop to warn the others, and they would escape by the exit door. A Gestapo tail would be easy to spot. The men in the black leather overcoats were not known for their streetcraft.

He saw only a lone deliveryman straining to lift a heavy box from a van. At the corner, Bucky glanced back to see that another man wearing a butcher's apron had come out to give him a hand, their voices loud and voluble in the empty, quiet street. He walked on. Dusk was beginning to fall, and an early October chill gripped the air. Soon, because of the blackout and nine o'clock curfew, Paris would go completely dark and fall eerily silent, the only illumination the dim glow of blue-shrouded lampposts and house lights filtering from behind draped and shuttered windows.

He had arrived in a Paris nothing like the city his mother had described. She would be heartbroken to see the city of her birth and youth now. "You have never heard Schubert's *Ave Maria* performed until you've heard a Paris street violinist play it on the banks of the Seine," she'd told him. "The notes float across the water like airborne feathers."

But those performers and their violins were gone now, and Paris's street magic was no more. Gone were the verdant open-air markets and the vibrant stalls of the flower sellers. Balconies once draped with riotous roses and ablaze with geraniums and begonias, petunias and lobelias—the botanical pride of Paris—had been displaced to hold rabbit hutches and vegetable bins.

Bucky was especially disappointed at the absence of the food vendors and their stands. He'd looked forward to buying a meal on the fly—light-as-air crepes and savory kebabs and sizzling sausages, roasted potatoes and cheese puffs and caramelized onions on a stick. His mouth had watered at his mother's description of the smell of freshly baked croissants and baguettes drifting from open doors of bakeries, locked and shuttered now, FERMÉ signs in their windows.

The authoritative roar of a German motorcade cruising down Edgar Quinet Boulevard was another desecration that Monique Barton would find appalling. The famous boulevards were now thoroughfares for gray-uniformed men driving loud military vehicles flaunting the Nazi flag and parade grounds to show off Germany's martial might. Venerable tower clocks had been reset to Berlin time, and signs in German defiled the stately splendor of the famed plane trees lining the streets. Most of all, though, she would have loathed the cruising radio trucks that blared German music and Nazi propaganda on streets in quiet neighborhoods. The music, culinary delights, color, gaiety, and light of Paris were gone. In all this darkness, where was his father?

Bucky had left for La Petite Madeleine hours early to allow time for a metro ride to the sixteenth arrondissement and the chic neighborhood of Passy-

Auteuil, where his aunt lived. Before he left Oklahoma, he'd made a note of his aunt's address, which he'd learned during training was in the area most occupied by high-ranking German officers, especially the Schutzstaffel, better known as the SS, the most vicious, anti-Semitic, and feared organization of the Third Reich. Its members considered themselves not only the elite of the Nazi Party, but of all mankind.

The hissing sound of the initials SS and the lightning bolts symbol reminded him of venomous snakes. Bucky feared for his widowed aunt, who had chosen not to flee with her wealthy neighbors when it became clear that a German invasion was imminent. He knew Aunt Claire would have been disgusted by the cowardly, self-serving exodus of her privileged French countrymen to safer ground in Switzerland, Spain, or America. In one of her last letters to his mother before Germany declared war against the United States, Aunt Claire had described how the Nazi military mucky-mucks had moved in to occupy the vacated houses of her neighbors, freely helping themselves to their beds and larders and wine cellars. Her next-door neighbor was an SS colonel charged with the duty of the deportation of Jews to concentration camps.

On his morning sortie, Bucky had located Aunt

Claire's house, an impressive eighteenth-century villa set back in an enclave shaded by ancient trees and enclosed by a vine-covered courtyard wall. From a park bench across the road, he looked for a sign of life in the one Palladian window visible and wrestled with a decision. Should he contact his aunt to learn information about his father? He wouldn't for the world put her in danger. His parents did not know that he was in Paris. As ordered, he'd informed them by telephone from Washington that he would be secluded for a while working on a special assignment for the government, and he tried not to imagine Horace Barton worrying that he was skipping out on his military duty. They were not to be concerned, Bucky had told them. He would contact them when he could. Now he had to consider the risk that Aunt Claire might somehow get word to his parents that their son was in Nazi-occupied Paris on an undercover mission.

He'd seen several German staff vehicles parked on various leafy lanes as he'd passed on his walk from the metro, but none occupied the cobblestoned entry to his aunt's house. If he was to move, now was the perfect time. He could simply walk across the road and ring the bell to her house. He had his story and his papers ready if he were intercepted. The men on his team had been given covers that would explain why they were not among the young and single Parisian males rounded up to work in Germany's factories. Stephane Beaulieu worked for a French firm of consulting engineers in a position essential to the German war effort. He had simply come to call on a friend of his mother's.

Bucky made up his mind. Aunt Claire was his only hope of finding Nicholas Cravois. There was no reason for anybody to question his identity. She would recognize him from his mother's yearly pictures. Bucky could only hope he had time to intercept her surprise to see her American nephew in France before her reaction betrayed him to the staff or a possible visitor.

His decision made, Bucky struck off across the street. All was quiet on this chilly Saturday morning. Smoke rising from the chimney told him someone was at home. He swallowed, prepared to deliver to the maid who answered the bell the little speech he'd rehearsed to explain his connection to the mistress of the house. The door opened. A woman stood there, still beautiful, slim, and elegant these eight years later. Her clear hazel eyes widened. Bucky snatched off his fedora.

"My God! Is that you, Bucky?" Claire Bellerose said.

CHAPTER TWENTY-THREE

Brad left next, glad to be out of the stuffy tea shop. He drew in a breath of fresh, bracing air and set his beret firmer while surreptitiously scanning the street. Lodestar would have come back if anything had roused his suspicion, but it paid to be extra cautious in a city where an enemy shadow could melt into dark doorways and honeycombed passageways. Satisfied that the coast was clear, Brad drew on his peacoat and set off. He would walk to the Latin Quarter. The metro would have taken him within a block of his accommodations, but the few times he'd ridden it, he'd been unable to abide the close breathing space in the overcrowded compartments. A great number of trains had been taken off rail lines because of the petroleum shortage, and metro cars were jammed with German soldiers and gaunt, vacant-eyed Parisians giving off the body odors of a population deprived of nutrition and hot water and soap. Now that an unusually cold October had arrived, the mothball smell of woolen coats added to the foul air.

Seeing the team of Dragonfly alive and well, at least so far, had been a lift to Brad's spirits. God, what a miserable city. Earlier he'd seen six ragtag school-age children moving like a pack of abandoned animals down an alley in search of garbage cans. They'd ventured into the Latin Quarter from the poorer area of Paris in hope of finding food. They'd reminded Brad of his first sight of the orphaned Bobby and Margie on the banks of the White River, hungry and destitute, and a shaft of homesickness had rammed right through him. His family would be wondering where he was, missing him, worrying about him, little Margie with bent head and clasped hands saying her prayers on her knees by her bed—*Please, God, keep Brad safe.*

Brad had left the family with the notion that he'd been called to Washington, D.C., as a consultant for a government fishing project. It was all highly secret stuff, and he couldn't tell them more than that. During training, the team had been allowed to write one letter a week to their families, carefully scripted, censored at times, but the group had been permitted unlimited mail from home, sent to an anonymous post office box. Joanna Bukowski Hudson had written that Jared had begun to build them a fine new house with five bedrooms, a master for her and her husband, three for the children, one reserved for guests—"and one for you, Brad, when you come home." There would be four—*four!*—bathrooms. "No more sharing one tub and sink," his mother had written, and there would be a proper dining room and a screened porch to sit in summer. The exchange of letters had been designed to weed out members of the team whose homesickness was too powerful to overcome. None of them had fallen for the ploy, even when they were allowed to call home one last time the day before they left for England. They were told to say they would be secluded for a while on business crucial to the nation's interest and unable to be reached, but a government official would contact the families from time to time to assure them that all was well. They were not to worry.

Beata had asked Brad to bring her a present when he came home. His mother had posed the usual maternal questions of concern, but Brad had sensed a deeper worry that he was involved in something more perilous than the discussion of fish. She did not press him. She understood that her son was engaged in what he believed he must do. "Will you be home to serve as Jared's best man?" she had asked. Probably not, Brad told her. They were not to delay the wedding for his sake.

Bobby had said, "You're going somewhere dangerous, aren't you?" in a voice as quiet and level as his gaze when aiming a question.

"Yes," Brad had said, "but let's keep that between us men."

Worn though they were, Brad reflected he'd not had much time to break in his river-plying duds of peacoat and Breton top, set off with a red scarf. He'd been in Paris only five days. After his successful drop, his contact had escorted him to the arranged spot on the River Seine where he'd been picked up by a transport barge and taken as the sun rose to meet Claude Allard, a wizened riverboat captain and owner of a fishing-tour company. They'd gone to a nearby café for what passed as breakfast and a private chat. The captain had explained to his other two fishing guides that Brad's addition to the payroll was necessary to his business. Barnard Wagner was German, spoke passable French, and was an experienced fishing guide, he'd told them. He'd been hired part-time mainly as an interpreter to assist in communicating with the company's growing customer base in the German military. Brad's papers supported his cover name and import from Austria where he had worked as a "fish finder" for a large cannery. His forged *Ausweispapiere*—identity papers—also served to exempt him, a German, from the current conscription of able-bodied Frenchmen hauled to Germany to replenish its diminished labor ranks.

"Do not trust my other two guides," Captain Allard had warned him in a voice barnacled from age, gray head drawn close to Brad's over the table, hard seaman's hands warmed by a cup of toasted barley mixed with chicory that served as coffee. "They have proved to be *collabos*, both of them. They are generally good men. I've known them since they were babies, but these are very desperate times, monsieur. They'll do anything to feed their families, and one of them, Desmond Martine, has a brother in the French police. You'd be quite the prize if either discovers you. Neither would hesitate to turn you over to the Gestapo in exchange for a goose for their table." The captain held up a hand to add one final admonition before Brad spoke. "And do not tell me why you've been sent. I don't want to know. I have my wife and children and grandchildren to consider. Your employment is all I can risk."

Brad said he understood. The captain sat back and released a sigh of relief. Brad figured that Claude Allard would assume his new guide had been placed with him to gather intelligence from his German clients as well as to report river transports of military troops and equipment. However, the real purpose of Brad's mission was to ingratiate himself to Major General Konrad March, an avid angler like himself and chief of the Abwehr in Paris. The general had forgone living in the luxurious Hotel Lutetia in the heart of Saint-Germain-des-Prés, the Abwehr's headquarters, to reside in an imposing house seized from a wealthy Jewish family. The house's attractions were that it was located within a line's cast of the River Seine and was more suitable for raising a seven-year-old son. Just over the hedge separating the general's confiscated quarters from the mansion next door, Brad lived above the stables in a small apartment rented from the property owner, a widow who had fallen on bad times. He had been briefed on the weekend pattern of the general's visits to the riverbank, and he planned to use the information to introduce himself as soon as possible.

Brad's thoughts were halted by a small, middle-aged man hurrying toward him. A yellow star on the left breast of his flapping jacket identified him as a Jew. The poor guy was obviously trying to make it home to beat the Nazi-imposed six o'clock deadline. Rage flared in Brad at the insult forced upon people like his aunt's husband. He hoped the man made it. Infractions of the curfew carried harsh penalties, like the beatings he'd witnessed inflicted in the Latin Quarter. More to his disgust was that some Parisians carried whistles to alert the police that a Jew had broken curfew. Apprehension meant a reward for the betrayer—a loaf of bread, wedge of cheese, piece of meat.

Suddenly the man darted into an alley. Seconds later, Brad saw an SS officer emerge from a stationery shop, hand patting his pocket, presumably to locate a light for the unlit cigarette between his lips. Soon, two other SS men stepped from the shop, packages under their arms. Brad could not imagine how the Jew had known to jump out of sight. Possibly a sixth sense had warned of the presence of evil. Brad was not completely familiar with the nomenclature of SS ranks, but he recognized the piping, silver pips, and single oak leaves on the first man's collar as indicative of a *Standartenführer*, or colonel. The others were junior officers to their taller regiment leader. All wore the skull and crossbones emblem of the Schutzstaffel above their hat visors and the dreaded earth-gray uniforms with the eagle-and-swastika patch on their left sleeves. Men of their notoriety were accustomed to Parisians hurrying to the other side of the street, but as Brad made his move to do so, the colonel called out in halting French, "Pardon me, seaman!"

Brad halted. He turned toward the three men and said in German, "*Ich spreche Deutsch.*" (I speak German.)

The three men visibly relaxed. They started toward him, heels of their jackboots striking the cobblestones, and the colonel held up the cigarette. "*Hast du ein Streichholz?*" (Do you have a match?)

"*Nein,*" Brad said, shaking his head. Too late, he stuck his hand into the slanted outer pocket of his pea jacket to cover the exposed tip of his French briar pipe with its contraband concealments. The pipe could be smoked, but it was really a pistol that could fire .22-caliber bullets through its stem.

"I see you smoke a pipe," the regiment leader said.

"*Ja,*" Brad answered.

"Well, how do you light it?" one of the junior officers snapped impatiently.

"With a lighter," Brad said.

"Let's see." The colonel held out his palm and motioned with his fingers to hand it over.

Heart racing, Brad fished in his trousers pocket and produced his OSS-designed camera lighter that could also spark a flame. Only a few days in Paris and he was already done for. Besides the pipe, his pocket weapon of choice was a cigarette case that exploded once the lid was removed. The colonel meant to confiscate his lighter. Cigarettes were so scarce that Brad could offer a full case in exchange for his lighter's return and be gone, and the Nazis blown to damnation before they learned the Gauloises were fake. He carried the case for just such situations as this predicament, but the device was useless to him. There were too many innocent civilians nearby, some of them children, and the killing or wounding of three SS officers would result in brutal reprisals against the French.

The colonel spun the wheel and a flame shot up. The cigarette lighted, he inhaled, then inspected the lighter. The stainless steel case was German manufactured but the inner workings were American made. "German?" he asked Brad.

Was he asking his nationality or manufacturer of the lighter? Panic rising, Brad said, "*Ja,*" and offered nothing more. In his ear he could hear Major Renault's voice: *Never volunteer information your interrogator has not asked for.*

"Shall I buy it from you, *freund*, say for...thirty francs?"

Friend, he'd called him. Brad stared the regiment leader straight in the eye. He calculated that an abject appeal would not move this man. "It was a present from my grandfather," he said in a firm voice that made clear the lighter had great sentimental value to him. "It's not for sale at any price."

The junior officers looked at their superior to assess what he made of this seaman's brazen refusal of his offer. The colonel reflected upon Brad for a moment, then handed back the lighter. "Then of course you must not sell it," he said. He clicked his heels together and thrust out his arm in the Nazi salute. "Heil Hitler!"

Brad repeated the gesture. "Heil Hitler!"

"Auf wiedersehen, Seemann."

"Auf wiedersehen, Standartenführer," Brad said. *Until we meet again.* God, he hoped not. He turned at the next corner and leaned trembling against a shop wall, thankful to the OSS designer for the meticulous deception of the camera as a functioning lighter. A close one, that. From now on Barnard Wagner would carry matches.

CHAPTER TWENTY-FOUR

For Chris, known in Paris as Claus Bauer, the Saturday meeting at La Petite Madeleine was the second of the day. That morning, he had met with his contact, a school administrator who held the position of *directeur du personnel* at the Sorbonne, France's most prestigious university. Come Monday, Chris would assume his cover as a physical education instructor there. Having agreed with his contact that it was wisest to meet openly to avoid suspicion, he had shown up ahead of time at the appointed place, a favorite hangout of the university staff. Before sitting down, he had peered with a newcomer's curiosity at the display of artwork, posters, letters, cards, and other memorabilia of the Sorbonne's famous and illustrious alumni tacked to the tobacco-hennaed walls. In reality, his interest was an excuse to check for quick exits and to be on his feet should the man show up with company. He was then to excuse himself to go to the toilettes, where he would make a fast exit through the back door. *Jules knows to come alone. If someone's with him, assume he's Gestapo*, the major had told him.

Thus it was with relief that Chris spotted a man of short stature and bent shoulders enter the bistro alone and look about him with the air of the proverbial absentminded professor. Chris raised a hand, and Jules Garnier spied him over the scholarly rims of his spectacles, his expression clearing of its myopic confusion to beam a look of relief. He seized Chris heartily by the shoulders and cheek-kissed him in the customary manner of a French greeting, a perfect display of welcome to a new staff member. "I am most happy to see that you made it," Jules whispered after they were seated in a far corner and ordered croissants and coffee. They had agreed to converse in French. "I was very concerned when I was told that you were not at the rendezvous point."

"I was dropped off course," Chris explained and told him of the farmer and his wife and teenaged son who had discovered him hidden in the grain of their loft and had not betrayed him to the German soldiers who banged on their door in the middle of the night and demanded to search their house and outbuildings for an Allied agent they believed had parachuted down near their farm. Not even when the Germans had made off with all the precious eggs and chickens in the henhouse had the family given him up. They had even arranged transportation for him into Paris. After the war, Chris vowed that he would find his way back to the farmhouse to express his gratitude. "They were very brave, like you, Herr Garnier," he said.

With a grimace and shrug of his shoulders, the director dismissed his own efforts as nothing. "All I've done is perform some small measure of resistance against this tide of gray rats that have invaded my country."

The man's efforts were hardly nothing. Before the United States and Germany were at war, Alistair Renault had made a trip across the water and learned of the formation of a special school for the young sons of the Nazi elite that would be housed in the Sorbonne. The Vichy regime had begun to expel Jewish professors and students from the Sorbonne and supplant them with teachers and apostles of Nazi ideology. The goal was to convert the hallowed liberal arts school into an institution that excluded all non-Aryans and offer only disciplines that furthered the nationalist swill of the Third Reich. In Germany, Hitler had ordered public schools to increase their compulsory physical education requirement for students from two hours a week to two hours a day. The major had rightly conjectured that the same directive would apply to the special school formed in the Sorbonne, which would then necessitate the need for more physical education instructors.

On that trip, the spymaster had slipped into the office of the *directeur du personnel* while the man's secretary was on a coffee break and found the director crying quietly into a cup of café au lait. A colleague had been executed for objecting to the Sorbonne's becoming a Nazi indoctrination center. Jules had been easy to recruit. The Sorbonne, owing to the Vichy French and German student enrollment and the new teachers' connections to the occupiers, had quickly become a boiling pot of Nazi gossip, rumors, and secrets. For several years now Jules had kept his ears perked for information he deemed important to the Allies and passed it to an OSS cutout for transmission to Milton Hall. Alistair Renault had returned to Washington with Jules's promise to let him know of a physical education opening and begun to seek the perfect candidate to fill it. The *directeur du personnel* could now turn over his valiantly assumed duties to his new young instructor and get on with his life, such as it was in occupied Paris, perhaps to live out his remaining years in relative safety.

"Tell me about my students," Chris said.

They were an elitist bunch, Jules informed him, the sons of top-ranking officers in the German High Command, higher-up Gestapo thugs, and Vichy officials, but superior in their mean little minds only because of their fathers' elevated statuses. In peacetime, the little monsters would *never* have placed at the Sorbonne.

"How old are these boys?"

"Between seven and eighteen. All are members of the Hitler Youth, the Hitlerjugend. Membership in the organization has been compulsory for school-age children in Germany since 1936. Its aim is to target young people as a special audience for the Nazi Party's propaganda messages, so your students have been thoroughly indoctrinated into Third Reich ideology and the glorification of Hitler."

Herr Bauer would find them a great source of information, Jules said. The boys tried to outdo one another in their boasts of their fathers' exploits and dropped secrets right and left that would have had their *Vaters* shot if their sons' carelessness became known. "Listen carefully on playing fields and in locker and classrooms, and you'll see what I mean," Jules said. "Also, the fathers like to ask the boys' instructors to dinner with the idea of winning academic favors to boost their sons' school records to impress officials when they report to the army at eighteen. Don't be surprised to receive such invitations." Behind his glasses, Jules's nearsighted gaze glinted meaningfully. "If you go to their houses, you might have a chance to use your Minox, no?"

Chris's flesh crawled as Jules described the teaching environment. Adolf Hitler's system of education, described in *Mein Kampf*, was inscribed on a poster displayed beside the portrait of the Führer that hung in every classroom. It stated Hitler's aim to stamp out weakness by producing "a violent, masterful, dauntless, cruel younger generation," Jules recited with a disgusted quiver of his upper lip.

"The Führer"—Jules spat out the word as if it were a piece of spoiled meat—"is fanatical about the importance of physical education for German youth. He wants a student to be 'swift as a greyhound, tough as leather, and hard as Krupp's steel,' to quote the student handbook." Jules leaned forward with his elbows on the table. "As repulsive as you will find it, Herr Bauer, you will be expected to achieve those goals. You will be responsible primarily for field and track events within an arduous program that includes gymnastics, swimming, boxing, fencing, and warfare tactics and drills. These fill much of the school day. True academic studies take last place."

"What kind of warfare tactics and drills?"

Jules's mouth turned down. "The children are taught hand-to-hand combat and how to throw a grenade, use a bayonet, dig a trench and dugout, shoot a pistol—insanities of that sort, all instructed as competitive games and sports but certainly not with the aim of teaching the participants fair play. The students are divided into teams and work as one unit. The entire team has to pass every course. One fails, they all do. There are no individuals. Peer pressure, sanctioned and encouraged by the instructors, is the tool that keeps everyone striving to do their best." Jules leaned back as if exhausted and added bitterly, "You can see how such a program can lead to horrible bullying of the weakest link."

Chris had listened, appalled, thinking how well Dirk Drechsler would have fit into the Hitlerjugend. "I assume there's someone in charge of this mad program?"

"You assume right. Louis Mueller, the sports director. A snake. Handpicked for the job and a nasty bastard through and through. You'll have to be on your guard around him, especially watchful on a personal level. The instructor you're replacing resigned because he simply could not stomach subjecting seven- and eight-year-olds to such an unconscionable regimen. Mueller had hoped to tap a friend for the job, but your—how do you say?—bona fides beat his qualifications. He'll despise you from the start. Also you must be very careful of the regular teaching staff. I don't know who is to be trusted. There are spies even among the janitorial crew."

"Does this school have a name?" Chris asked.

Jules laughed scornfully. "Academy for the Young Warriors of the Third Reich."

Chris had left the meeting feeling queasy. The academy sounded like a whirlpool of water moccasins, the pit vipers you had to look out for when you fished the rivers of Texas. He'd once seen a man wade into what appeared to be a simple disturbance of water stirred up by a current, only to realize too late it was a school of one of the deadliest snakes in the state. The ghastly scene and the man's screams had haunted Brad's sleep for years. He would have to be very, very careful of his steps in the snake pit of the Academy for the Young Warriors of the Third Reich.

CHAPTER TWENTY-FIVE

The following morning, Sunday, October 4, the members of Dragonfly met their enemy. Dressed in a painter's smock, drawing materials in her pockets, palette in hand, Bridgette applied the first strokes of her mural to the peal of cathedral bells ringing throughout the city. Those coming to lauds in the convent's small chapel paused before the courtyard wall to view the figure of a dragonfly come to life from under the hand of the petite newcomer to the area. Onlookers gazed and commented until something on the street prompted a sudden scurry to the chapel door.

Bridgette, standing on the top rung of a short ladder, glanced toward the cause of the hasty dispersion. The French police had come to be despised by their countrymen for their collaboration with the

German authorities against their own people, and swaggering down the street swinging a truncheon was a blue-suited figure of slight build and short stature who apparently represented the sort they hated. The single chevron on his uniform sleeve declared him one year out of police training, a *gardien de la paix stagiaire*, an intern; *in other words, a rookie*, Bridgette thought.

He halted before the painting, mulling over the drawing with the arrogance of one greatly empowered to judge such irregularities for malicious intent and the authority to administer the appropriate penalty. *Oh dear*, thought Bridgette. *One of those*.

"What is the meaning of this?" he demanded with a flourish of his baton toward the wall.

Bridgette climbed down from the ladder and gave him a friendly smile. "Well, as you can see," she explained cheerfully, "it is a dragonfly. It is to be part of an aquatic mural to lighten the mood of the street."

"Who gave you permission to disfigure this wall?"

"The reverend mother of the Sisters of Charity."

"We'll see."

Off he hurried in an officious stride to confront the head of the community of nuns, and Bridgette calmly returned to her painting. Less than ten minutes later he was back, red-faced, tight-jawed, replacing his hat with an angry set of the bill, and marched past Bridgette and her mural without another word or glance.

Bridgette smiled. No one messed with Sister Mary Frances. But after lauds, the mother superior delivered a warning: "You have made an enemy of that jackanapes, *ma petite chérie*. You must be careful of the overzealous, puffed-up ones like him looking to make a name for themselves. Their noses make up for what our Father denied him in brains, and somehow he sniffed out something about you. He wanted to know where you came from, what you are doing here. I had to tell him your name and where you work. His name is Achim Fleischer. He grew up in this district, attended Saint Stephen's, where I taught. He was an abysmal student. That is why I could set him straight without retaliation, but my position will not prevent him from keeping an eye on you."

Bridgette took the warning seriously. The short little creeps in uniforms of authority were the worst. They were as insignificant as road dust but, once stirred up, capable of choking an engine. She thought suddenly of Steve Hammett and his watchful eye back in Traverse City High School. There wouldn't have been a grease spot left of Achim Fleischer if Steve had gotten hold of him, but here in Paris, there would be no Steve Hammett keeping watch over her from afar. Achim Fleischer would be back, and she must be her own guardian angel.

CHAPTER TWENTY-SIX

Early that Sunday morning Brad had been at his surveillance post on the riverbank since dawn, a pattern he planned to establish every Sunday until his quarry spotted him. He had caught several good-sized perch to explain his presence should Major General Konrad March ever show himself and feel suspicious enough to inquire. If nothing else, at least Brad had caught another meal for Madame Gastain's table. His dignified landlady would be starving if it weren't for him, even though tonight would mark the fifth evening they'd had perch for dinner, but she'd be pleased at the potatoes he'd bought yesterday from a farmer who lived by the Loire and the bunch of wild asparagus he'd picked from a patch growing by a riverbank.

Brad heard his neighbor's back door open and

shut, the sound carrying over the low boxwood hedge. He stepped away from his casting spot to be seen and to give the corner of his eye a better view. His heart leaped. Finally, at last, the general! Brad moved farther back to offer his mark a better field of vision, winding his reel as if to call it a morning. *Come on! Come on!* he urged. *Investigate the stranger who has come to fish on this private stretch of the Seine.* Anyone posing as an innocent fisherman could be an Allied agent or a member of the Nazi Party sent to spy on one of its senior military officers.

For a few minutes, Brad thought his ploy had failed. The general returned to his house but appeared again with a short, squat man in tow, most likely an aide, summoned to question the strapping young fisherman who had recently shown up on his neighbor's property. Brad pretended total absorption in removing a streamer lure from his hook, but he had the eyes of a dragonfly and was keenly aware of the scene going on on the other side of the hedge.

As he approached, the aide called in French with a German accent, "You there, Frenchman! Who are you and what are you doing on Madame Gastain's property?"

Brad, pretending surprise, said, "*Ich bin Deutscher.*" (I am German.)

The aide seemed taken aback and repeated the question in their mutual language.

Brad appeared flustered. "Why, I am...just fishing. Madame gave me permission. I've rented the rooms above her stable." He gestured toward the upper story of a handsome structure whose purebred occupants had long been sold for meat.

"What do you do?" the aide asked.

"I am a fishing guide for a riverboat company in the fifteenth arrondissement."

"The name of the company?"

"Claude Allard Fishing Tours."

"And your name?"

"Barnard Wagner."

The aide motioned toward Brad's fly rod and his open tackle box with its assortment of artificial bait. "A fly-fisherman?"

"*Ja.*"

"*Ach so*," the man said in apparent satisfaction and set off to report to the general. They conversed a few minutes, then Brad's mark dismissed his aide and, as Brad had hoped, started toward him. Fly-fishermen were a breed apart. They belonged to an exclusive club—a cult—that paid no heed to social rank or other boundaries. Brad watched the general's approach. Even out of uniform, in casual, everyday wear, Major General Konrad March's military stride left little question of his profession and rank. He was middle-aged and carried a small paunch, but he walked with an air of authority and the agility of a strong and fit younger man.

At the hedge, he paused without a smile, but the lack of it told Brad nothing. Men in his position had a face trained to remain neutral, but Brad thought he saw a trace of sadness far back in his eyes, no meanness, which was surprising, given the man's line of work. He understood the general had lost his wife a few years back. The loss of a spouse…human eyes had a certain bareness to them when a mate died. He'd seen it in his mother's every day.

"Konrad March," his neighbor said and extended his hand across the hedge. Brad was surprised at the courtesy and lack of mention of his rank. He wiped his right hand on his pants and shook the one the general offered as the man nodded toward an upper window of his own home. "I've observed your fishing techniques," he said straightforwardly, as if his admission of something akin to window peeping was no issue. He might have been pointing out that Madame Gastain's roof needed repairing. "You use handtied flies for catching black bass and have had considerable luck, whereas I have had none with the bait I've been using. Where in Germany are you from?"

"I am from Hamburg," Brad answered. It was the region where his mother had been born and raised, and its dialect the one they spoke at home.

"My aide tells me that you are a fishing guide for Captain Claude Allard."

"That is correct."

"I've heard of him. Some of my colleagues have availed themselves of his services and say there's none better to know the rivers around here. I understand there's good fishing on the Loire."

"The best."

Suddenly there was a bit of an uproar behind the general. A little boy—the general's seven-year-old son, Brad presumed—ran out of the house with the squatty aide chasing after him clutching a white towel. "Wilhelm! Don't run! You'll make it bleed more!" the man yelled.

The general turned to see the boy running across the green space toward him. "Papa! Look! Look!" the boy cried, showing a bloodstained smile.

When his son reached him, the general took the boy by the shoulders and said, "Slow down, my *Sohn*. What is it?"

The child held out a small palm on which lay a

bloody molar and spoke breathlessly. "A tooth, the one that was bothering me. I pulled it all by myself."

"What a brave lad you are! I am proud of you, but you must let Hans have it to wash and put under your pillow or *die Zahnfee* will not come in the night and leave a gold coin under your pillow. Now open your mouth and let's have a look." The boy obeyed and his father peered inside the open cavity. "The bleeding's stopped, but you mustn't run." He took the towel from his aide and cleaned the child's mouth, then turned to Brad. "My son, Wilhelm March," he introduced him. "Ordinarily he would shake your hand, but it's unpresentable at the moment. Also, my aide, Sergeant Hans Falk."

"Barnard Wagner," Brad said with a smile at the boy and a nod at the aide. The child was slight for his age and seemed not to have yet grown out of belief in tooth fairies.

"How do you do?" Wilhelm said politely.

"I am very well, thank you."

"And I as well."

"Go with Hans, *Sohn*," the general said. "I'll be in shortly."

"*Auf wiedersehen*, Herr Wagner," Wilhelm said, waving a small hand rather than giving the Nazi salute.

"*Auf wiedersehen*, Wilhelm," Brad responded.

As they walked away, the general said, "I'd like to give your touring company a try. Make a reservation for me next Saturday, will you? As early in the day as possible with hope you will consent to be my guide. The name is Major General Konrad March, chief of the German intelligence agency in France." He added with a rueful lift of his lip at Brad's pretended look of surprise, "I am aware that Captain Allard most often has a full tour roster, but perhaps that title will carry enough weight to secure a spot on his reservation list."

"I'm sure it will, Herr Major General," Brad said.

"Good. Now show me some of your flies, if you please."

"Of course," Barnard Wagner said, inviting the general to step through the hedge to his tackle box, and thought: *Fly into my mouth, said the dragonfly to the moth.*

CHAPTER TWENTY-SEVEN

Jules Garnier had made arrangements for Chris to be admitted that Sunday morning into the wing of the Sorbonne allocated for the sons of the Nazi and Vichy elite. Nazi flags and posters showing Hitler's picture and stating the objectives of the curriculum were hung as Jules had described, further increasing the atmosphere of evil Chris felt the moment he unlocked the door and walked into the chill of a school closed on a cold fall weekend. Physical education instructor Claus Bauer had wanted to acquaint himself with its sports equipment and facilities and to organize his office before meeting his classes the next day. The required reading texts, lesson plans, class roster, and desk materials that Jules had promised would be waiting for him were on his desk. He found that his office was no more than a partitioned area situated between two others obviously thrown together to accommodate additional staff. The makeshift units were windowless and the walls paper-thin. No privacy, then, and no handy exit. Chris sighed.

He had been at his desk an hour when a man filled the open door of his cubicle. "You must be the new math and field sports instructor," he said.

"I am," Chris responded, rising, and held out his right hand. "Claus Bauer. And you must be?" He did not have to ask the man's name. He fit the description Jules Garnier had given: shaved head, small, merciless eyes, thick, brutish body inevitably doomed to flab in time.

The man noted the missing thumb of Chris's hand with a curl of his lip. "Louis Mueller, director of the sports program of the academy," he said in German, giving Chris's four fingers a quick, crushing squeeze. "I assume you were informed that classes start promptly at seven o'clock around here. Instructors are to be at their posts thirty minutes after morning curfew." The implication was that the early reporting time was out of the realm of Chris's coaching experience. "I do not tolerate tardiness."

"Of course not," Chris said equably.

"Also, you need to know that we do not coddle our students. We push them to their physical limits. Any slack from that duty by one of my instructors, and I have the authority to dismiss him and report him to my superiors. Is that understood?"

Chris acquiesced with an understanding nod. "Perfectly."

Mueller's glance fell to Chris's thumbless right hand. "I must tell you frankly, Herr Bauer, that I was surprised, if not shocked, that with your handicap, you were even considered for a position here."

Chris sat back down. "I have never found it to be a handicap, Herr Mueller."

"It better not be."

It was as Jules Garnier had warned him. Claus Bauer had been put on notice. Louis Mueller would be watching his new physical education instructor. The slightest slipup, and he would be out.

"Very well, then," the man said when Chris did not respond. "Now I see that you have your students' roster on your desk. I must point out to you the names of several boys in the school that you must give...special attention to." Louis Mueller glanced at him sharply. "You do know what I mean?"

"I am afraid that I must ask for enlightenment."

The director sighed as if he should have expected such ignorance from the likes of his new instructor. With exaggerated patience, he explained, "As I have said and apparently must repeat, we do not tolerate slack from the students for any reason. There are no allowances made for those who are undersized and immature for their ages. You have three of those sort assigned to your class." He came around the desk to run a sausage-sized finger down the student roster and jabbed at three names. "Him, him, and him," he said. "You are to see that they measure up to the demands of the curriculum. If they do not, they will be severely disciplined. A sheet is attached to the roster that describes the forms of correction allowed, which you will administer."

Chris turned the page to read a list of approved methods to "correct" a student's failure to live up to the physical expectations decreed by Adolf Hitler. The methods were no less than torture. To prevent telltale bruising, some of the acceptable measures suggested were water dunking, beatings with cotton sacks filled with potatoes, and requiring a student to stand on his toes with his arms outstretched for an unendurable length of time.

"I'm sure these forms of persuasion for the boys to strive harder are most effective," Chris commented approvingly, "but I see here that these boys are the sons of high-ranking Vichy officials and German officers. Aren't you afraid of repercussions from their fathers for the harsh treatment of their children?" Chris could not resist referring to the students' age. "This boy, Wilhelm March, for instance"—he pointed to the name—"is the only child of the chief of the Abwehr in France. I would think the general would not look favorably upon what he might consider abuse to his son."

Louis Mueller snorted. "You are to have no fear of the consequences for doing your job. The boys know not to carry tales to their fathers. They know what will happen to them if they do."

"The boys or their fathers?"

"The boys, but the fathers, as well."

"And that is?"

"Any interference from the fathers and they will be reported to Berlin as unsupportive of the Führer's mandated curriculum whose disciplines are designed to form their sons into ideal German males. That would not be good for their careers, and the boys know it. In trouble at school, in trouble at home."

"Yes, of course, and there is also the boy's affection and respect for his father that would prevent him from saying anything about his mistreatment that would jeopardize the man's career," Chris said smoothly, his expression full of understanding.

The director blinked as if Chris had spoken in a foreign language. "Well, yes, I suppose there is that benefit as well, so you needn't worry about any complaint of…mishandling."

"That is good to know. I am most relieved."

Louis Mueller continued to eye his new physical education instructor warily. Chris returned a benign gaze. "Any other information of which I should be apprised?" he asked.

The director emitted another testy sigh. "I had hoped that Herr Garnier had fully briefed you on the rest of what we do here, but since he did not do his job, you will have to figure it out on your own, and immediately. Remember that you are on trial here, Herr Bauer. Your position is in no way secure. I have very strict expectations from members of my department. One deviation from them, and you will be on your way to the Russian front, from which you have been exempted because of your appointment here, I understand. I can assure you that the Wehrmacht will have no issue with your infirmity. Have I made myself clear?"

"Most abundantly, but have no fear, Herr Mueller. I will not disappoint you," Chris said cheerfully.

"Oh, I have no fear, Herr Bauer. Fear should be your concern. Now I will leave you to go and enjoy what is left of my Sunday." Louis stuck out a stiff arm. "Heil Hitler!"

Chris stood and repeated the salute. "Heil Hitler!"

The director drew back from the proximity of Chris's missing thumb, and said, "Make sure to lock up when you leave and remember to be on time in the morning."

"*Jawohl*, Herr Mueller!"

Chris heard the heavy tread of the director's footsteps heading for the exit and a minute later the slam of the outer door. Louis Mueller had made a special trip to the school this frosty Sunday morning to deliver his warning. Chris now knew exactly who he was dealing with—no surprise there. The surprise would be for the loathsome Herr Louis Mueller when he learned exactly who he was dealing with in Herr Claus Bauer.

CHAPTER TWENTY-EIGHT

At six o'clock that same Sunday morning, his landlady's soft knock on his door roused Bucky from a deep sleep that not even the loud and incessant ringing of the steeple bells from the church on the corner had pierced. He had fallen into bed at two, fully clothed, craving sleep after having spent much of the night in his landlady's parlor playing the French card game Barbu. Bucky had joined the game with his fellow French boarders to divert the unanswered questions thrashing about in his head after Madame Dupree handed him a note upon his return from La Petite Madeleine. "I have spoken with Uncle Emille about a visit," Aunt Claire had written. "Come for tea at four o'clock next Sunday."

Bucky had read the note in a state of shock. *Holy Moses! Aunt Claire had made contact with his father! He wanted to see him!* "Who brought the note, Madame Dupree?" he had asked.

"An elderly gentleman. He arrived on a bicycle."

His aunt's old butler, Bucky guessed. He had suddenly felt giddy. After all these years, he was finally to meet his father!

"Are you all right, Monsieur Beaulieu?"

"*Absolument!*" he said. He had read the note again. When Aunt Claire had told him about his son, what had been the reaction of the man whose color and shape of eyes he had inherited? A price was on the head of Nicholas Cravois. Would it be too dangerous for him to show himself in Paris? Could Bucky be sure that Aunt Claire had even told him of his son's existence? Her wording might have meant that his father had agreed to discuss a visit with *someone*. Bucky had learned from Aunt Claire that his father was still unmarried. Mistresses, yes, but no children by them that she knew of. Samuel Barton was his only legitimate child. Had his aunt told him how much his son wished to meet him—wanted to get to know him?

Somehow he had to curb his impatience until tomorrow at four o'clock. Would his father be waiting for him in her parlor? Or would he have decided that he couldn't possibly risk seeing him? Bucky had felt a crushing squeeze of his heart. Tomorrows in France were so uncertain. If he missed this chance to see his birth father, the opportunity might never come again.

"Monsieur Beaulieu, it is Madame Dupree. You must get up—now!" his landlady's hushed voice implored urgently through his bedroom door.

Groggily, Bucky staggered to open it. "It's all right, Madame Dupree. I didn't intend to go down for breakfast."

"It is not about breakfast, monsieur," she said, pushing her way in, her glance quickly taking in his disheveled shirt and pants. "I have news. I am informing you first in case you must do... whatever you must do. We are about to receive new occupants."

Bucky came alert. "Who?"

His landlady kept her voice low. "Three of my tenants were quietly evicted before daybreak and their rooms requisitioned as quarters for three members of the Abwehr. Bella is cleaning them now. The men will be arriving this morning. I came to warn you so that you can make sure your papers are in order and that nothing compromising can be found in your room. The pigs will probably have it searched for contraband." Indignation dissolved into stricken sadness. "Esme, Dashiell, and Farrin have been with me for years. They are old. Winter is coming. Where will they go? Where will they live?"

Bucky was helpless to answer. There was also another concern so obvious as not to merit mention. In her years of cooperation with the Allied intelligence services, the enemy had been out of sight and far removed from Madame Dupree's activities. Now they had taken residence under her roof, which put her in danger of discovery. If Bucky was discovered, she would be taken, too.

Madame Gabrielle Dupree was a facilitator for the OSS. Her role did not involve clandestine activities. She offered assistance by making her *pension de famille*, or boardinghouse, available as a trusted abode for the agency's covert operatives. She had come to Alistair's attention in early June 1942, when he learned that her boardinghouse had offered sanctuary to several RAF pilots shot down close to Paris during a bombing raid. Her husband was a casualty of the First World War and her son a victim of the Second, both at the hands of the Germans. Gabrielle Dupree did not loudly parade the depth of her hatred for "the pigs in gray" but quietly put her grief and rage to effective use by holding vacant a few rooms to rent to Allied agents requiring walls without ears.

Booted footsteps and voices speaking imperiously in German drifted up from downstairs. Madame Dupree's face whitened. "Oh, my God. They're here," she said.

Bucky laid a hand on her shoulder. "Hold tight to your courage, Madame Dupree. You are a brave and resourceful woman. You will handle this."

She straightened her shoulders. "Yes, I will," she said. "I was told they'll want to interview the residents. I'm to ring the dinner bell to summon everyone downstairs. Meanwhile I'd get into pajamas, if I were you. The pigs might wonder what you've been up to."

The dinner bell rang fifteen minutes later. Bucky had changed out of street clothes and further tousled his hair. His aunt's note was now ashes mixed with the smoked remains from the bowl of his French briar. His umbrella with its concealed stiletto was tucked in his closet, his pencil fuse lay inconspicuously among other writing materials in his desk drawer, and his L pill was hidden in his belt buckle. His other clandestine materials were in his office at the consulting firm where he'd expected they most likely would be needed. He had not anticipated this turn of events.

When Bucky descended the stairs in robe, pajamas,

and house slippers, he found the other three tenants in similar attire and the members of the house staff forming a line. The new boarders—a captain, a first lieutenant, and a sergeant holding a clipboard—were in full Wehrmacht uniform. Bucky made a quick assessment. The captain appeared pleasant enough. He had just heard him compliment Madame Dupree's collection of Lalique figurines, but the mannerly, courteous ones could be the worst kind. The lieutenant, tall, slim, and straight-backed, looked fresh out of the Prussian Military Academy, Hitler's trolling ground for the elite of the elite. By contrast the sergeant with the clipboard was lacking the polish and presence of his superiors. His uniform, designed for the physique of the typically fit German soldier, was ill suited for his pudgy frame, a drawback to his military appearance that his slicked-down Hitler haircut and thin mustache failed to offset.

Also, Bucky couldn't say why he sensed that, aside from the difference in their ranks, the sergeant was not held in high esteem by his superiors.

The captain turned to Madame Dupree, standing nervously nearby, and addressed her in impeccable French. "Is this everyone?"

"*Oui*, Capitaine," she said. "Monsieur Beaulieu is the last one."

"Splendid." He smiled and greeted the group in French with a small bow. "Messieurs and mesdames, I will ask that you kindly turn over your papers to me and give your names, room numbers, duties, and places of employment to my lieutenant, who will translate them for the sergeant to write down. But first, allow me to introduce myself. I am Captain Edmund Achterberg, and these are Oberleutnant Fredrik Dahl and Unterfeldwebel Dirk Drechsler."

CHAPTER TWENTY-NINE

That same Sunday, to her chagrin, Victoria was summoned early on her day of rest to report to the L'Ecole d'Escrime Français. It happened that she was already up, having planned to catch the metro deeper into the Latin Quarter to interview a woman who might have knowledge of her fiancé's fate. Victoria was following the only lead her brother had been able to give her. Though no one had seen Ralph's parachute after he was shot down over Gennevilliers, a municipality about nine miles northwest of the center of Paris, a report suggested that several pilots had made it to a boardinghouse in the Latin Quarter whose proprietor, Madame Gabrielle Dupree, had offered shelter and safety. The failure of the RAF bombing raid over the aircraft engine factory in May was still being gleefully recounted by her German students. The plant had hardly been damaged, but thirty-four French civilians were killed and 167 injured. The citizens of Gennevilliers, therefore, had not been inclined to help downed Allied airmen. Victoria had managed to locate the address of the boardinghouse and was hoping to meet Madame Dupree to learn if one of the surviving airmen was Ralph DuPont.

"I am sorry, Mademoiselle Colbert, but you were specifically requested," Jacques Vogel, the school's director and fencing master, apologized over the phone at the registration desk of Victoria's lodging, a small residential hotel.

"Who asked for me?"

A pause. "Derrick Albrecht. You may have heard of him?"

"Should I have?"

"Perhaps. In the thirties, he was Germany's top fencing champion in foil."

Vaguely, the name emerged from the list of international fencing stars Victoria had read about. "What does he want with me?"

"He requires a fencing bout today to stay in form and wishes to set up a regular schedule with you."

"Why not with you? You're the best."

"He has heard of you and...feels that you will

provide a suitable challenge." It went unsaid that Victoria had no choice in the matter.

Victoria sighed and closed her eyes. *Oh, damn!* She got the picture. The man must be important for her employer, the OSS facilitator responsible for her insertion into L'Ecole d'Escrime Français, to yank her out of bed on Sunday when the school was closed. She figured he was some pompous high Nazi official who'd heard of the attractive foil instructor and thought to make a little time with her when Monsieur Vogel, certified in all three weapons of fencing—a *prévôt d'armes*—was perfectly "suitable" to serve as his bout partner.

"Well, what do you know about him?" she asked. "What's he doing in France? I need to know who I am dealing with."

A pause followed that told Victoria the news would not be welcome, to her or to the fencing master whose assistance to the OSS had exposed him to more danger than he'd bargained for. "What is it you are not telling me, Monsieur Vogel?"

Another weighty pause, then, apologetically: "He is a *Standartenführer* in the SS, mademoiselle."

Victoria drew a sharp breath. Oh God. A colonel in the Schutzstaffel—the dreaded SS. "What...does he do? What are his duties?" There were two branches of the Schutzstaffel, administration and combat, both vile.

Victoria could hear the fencing master let out a sigh. "He is the chief of the counterintelligence division of the Sicherheitsdienst here in Paris, mademoiselle."

The news got worse. The Sicherheitsdienst, better known as the SD, was the security service of the Reichsführer, a police unit as brutal as its equally vicious brother organization, the Gestapo. Its role was "to discover the enemies of the Nazi Party and to initiate countermeasures through official police authorities." Those countermeasures involved unspeakable crimes against those deemed enemies of the Third Reich.

That would be Victoria Grayson, also known as Liverwort and Veronique Colbert.

"Have you ever met him?" she asked.

"Yes, but only once, years ago when we engaged in an international fencing competition. He was a formidable opponent. I bested him, but barely. I don't believe he ever lost another bout. His request came by telephone."

"How old is he?"

"I would estimate about thirty."

Victoria imagined him older, closer to Jacques Vogel's age, trim, still fast on his feet, but pushing past his prime. "That's awfully young to be in charge of an organization like the SD," she remarked.

"They rise quickly in German military ranks, but he would have soared up the SS ladder in any case. Colonel Albrecht comes from a very wealthy and influential family, members of the top hierarchy of German aristocracy. His forebears once ruled a powerful duchy until the unification of Germany in 1871, but his lineage and connections are not responsible for his rank and position, mademoiselle. You will see, so you must be very, very careful." A faint trace of cheer entered his voice. "A good source of information, no?"

Not likely, Victoria thought. The SD boys were too well trained to let drop a crumb of intelligence. On the other hand, there were none within the ranks of the Nazi police organizations better at detection than the monsters in the Sicherheitsdienst.

"Now, I beg you not to be late. The colonel will arrive within the hour," Jacques said. "Oh, and one other thing. Colonel Albrecht prefers his officer's rank to his monarchic title of duke."

Oh brother, thought Victoria.

Actually, she was late by half an hour and the man already getting into his fencing gear in the men's dressing room when she arrived. Monsieur Vogel greeted her nervously. "The metro I usually take was jammed, and I had to wait for another one," Victoria forestalled his rebuke when she saw his look. She'd be damned if she'd apologize to the colonel, or duke, for missing the hour of an appointment he'd arbitrarily imposed on her and disrupted her critical plans for the day.

Stepping into the changing area, by the men's dressing room, Victoria saw the colonel's SS uniform on a hanger topped with its chillingly recognizable peaked hat set with the death's-head insignia, the skull and crossbones. The Iron Cross, the highest German military decoration for bravery, hung from a ribbon suspended from the same peg. At the start of the war, but for a few elite groups within the organization, the SS had dropped their infamous red armbands and all-black uniform for a more suitable field gray. In combat, the original choice had made the wearer an easy target for the enemy to spot. The SD must be one of the elite groups still authorized to wear the former color. The uniform hanging from the peg was pure black.

The colonel stepped out from the dressing room in full fencing gear as she appeared, wire mask tucked under his arm. He bowed. "Mademoiselle Colbert, I believe," he said in perfect boarding-school French.

"I am Derrick Albrecht. Thank you so much for meeting me on such short notice. I am quite sure my request must have inconvenienced you greatly."

They were all so infernally polite and correct, the members of the SD, even in their interrogation rooms, so it was said. A spike of irritation at his courteousness—he didn't give a damn that he had put her out—sharpened Victoria's already thin-edged temper. "You are quite correct in your assumption, Colonel," she said. The uniform and the fact that he fenced had given her some idea of his physical size, so his trim form and considerable height were not unexpected nor, considering his background, his pedigreed air. But his Ivy League crew cut, friendly eyes, and Gary Cooper "aw shucks" smile were at odds with her mental image of the man she'd expected to meet. One would never know that behind that boyishly handsome façade lay the face of evil.

Behind him, Jacques Vogel widened his eyes warningly and made a little sound in his throat correspondent to slicing a finger across his neck.

"Then I must find a way to make it up to you," the colonel said, the eyes still friendly. "*Sprichst du Deutsch?*" (Do you speak German?)

"*Nein.*"

"Then after the bout, we shall discuss in French

how I should make amends. Perhaps you will allow me to take you for a meal?"

Behind the colonel, Jacques Vogel nodded vigorously. *Say yes!*

"That won't be necessary," Victoria said and stepped aside to move to the women's dressing room.

"It is necessary to me," he said, putting out a hand to bar her way. "Otherwise, I shall feel like a heartless lout."

Which is exactly what you are, Victoria thought, understanding that the invitation was not to be refused, and said coldly, "Very well then, since you insist, Colonel. I will meet you at the piste." Beneath her jacket, her silk blouse clung to her clammy skin. She felt she'd just come eye to eye with a swaying cobra.

CHAPTER THIRTY

"You want me to do *what*?" Achim Fleischer's commander demanded, staring up at the newest recruit in his department from a desk piled with the never-ending paperwork. "As short as we are of personnel and as busy as I am, you want me to investigate a *mural* going up on the courtyard wall of the Sisters of Charity? What the hell for?"

"There's something suspicious about it. It's a gut feeling I have. The drawing's being done by a fashion designer new to the neighborhood. She could pass for a teenage girl, but she possesses the eyes of a woman, no matter her attempt to seduce me to believe otherwise."

Seduce you, you little weasel, you with a penis the size of a shrimp! his chief thought uncharitably, his temper short-fused from his having to work on

Sunday, his day off. The commander, head of a unit in a police force now as ostracized as the Jews, was already so weary of this meddling prick's suspicions against neighbors and friends based on nothing but gut feelings.

"And that's *all*? What is its subject?"

Undeterred, Achim Fleischer answered, "The subject quite escapes me, but there's a dragonfly in it and some…seaweed, I think, and various other water plants, I believe they would be called."

"Are they objectionable to look at?"

"Uh, no."

"Then what do you find suspicious about them?"

"I don't know. It's…just this feeling I have that they have a clandestine purpose."

"Ah, yes, that talking gut of yours again." The commander continued writing. "Check with the mother superior of the convent. I'm sure she's not unaware of somebody splashing paint on her courtyard wall. Find out where the girl came from, if she has her permission to do…whatever she's doing."

"I already have," Achim Fleischer said.

The pen arrested, the commander glanced up. "And?"

"She…sees it as a painting of beauty to enliven the mood of the street."

"Well, then, Achim, how can we disagree with Sister Mary Frances? Do you wish to spend eternity in hell?"

"Of course not, but I am sure the drawing is more than it appears and bears investigating. There's the paint, for one thing. Where did she get it? My sister is an artist, and she can't find the acrylic medium the woman is using. It's a new artist compound just developed and is scarce even in peacetime. I think it's smuggled contraband."

"May the Almighty save us from such danger."

"Nonetheless, I request that you take a look at it. I'm sure your superiors would agree."

The commander glared at the lowest-ranked member of his squad. *You sheep shit*, he thought. He was now sure that this twat was an informant to the higher-ups who were in bed with the Gestapo and Vichy government. Now that America had entered the war, an Allied invasion was coming that would liberate France and all of Europe from under the Nazi boot heel. Who knew where and when, but it was whispered about on every corner, in every household by those not deaf to reality. Come that blessed day, he would see that Achim Fleischer got his just due.

It was late in the day and unusually cold for the eleventh day of October. As commander he would soon be able to go home to his meager supper and skimpy fire that would at least be shared in the warm lap of family. He had no desire to go traipsing off in the falling night and cold to view a harmless painting on a wall, much less with a *flic* on the eager lookout for curfew offenders that would mean an arrest and a trip back to the station for an interrogation. He swallowed his chagrin, sour as cheap wine, and growled, "All right, Fleischer. Let's go see what has got a stick up your rump."

His mouth dropped open the moment he saw the object of his intern's suspicions. Awe flashed across Achim's face as well. Neither man paid attention to the small knot of people who had dared to risk breaking curfew to admire the unfinished aquatic scene developing on the convent wall. They scattered before they could be noticed, but the policemen paid them no mind as they approached the wall. The artist was nowhere in sight this close to curfew.

"It's…beautiful," the commander said softly, face filled with admiration. "And you have a problem with this, Fleischer?" he asked incredulously.

"The artist has…added more to the drawing since I was here Friday," his intern defended his report. "She must have worked on it this weekend. It…gives a larger picture."

The painting was far from finished, but there were enough details and background for the street viewer to feel as if he had only to step forward to enter a magical garden where lily pads floated over clear blue water, and dragonflies darted among bright tropical flowers and flora under fluffy clouds and serene skies. Though partially formed, a golden Labrador with yearning eyes dominated the scene, its gaze on a wading bird oblivious to the dog's presence.

The commander said, "Well, I've seen enough. There is not a single stroke on this mural to raise doubt that it is anything but what it clearly is to the rest of us—a peaceful scene on a convent wall to suggest that somewhere in the world there is calm and order and people aren't shooting at one another. You're to do nothing to get in the way of its completion. As a matter of fact, I order you to stand guard to make sure nobody does. This street is your beat from now on. Understood!"

Achim opened his mouth to protest, but then the awareness of this unexpected gift hit him. His commander's order gave him the excuse to keep a constant eye on the artist. She wasn't working alone, although he believed he could rule out Sister Mary Frances as a fellow conspirator. The old harridan had her nuns to think of. Sooner or later, the artist would betray herself and the others working with her, then he'd have her. Give him an hour with her in an interrogation room, and she'd spill her guts like a split sack of peas, and then they'd round up her accomplices. That coup ought to get him a place in the French Milice, the new paramilitary police organization that the Vichy government was organizing. Then his commander would see what was what and who was boss.

"Oh, but I—" he started to argue to make it look good.

"No buts, Fleischer. Do as you're told, and don't you dare take your suspicions to my *superiors*, as you say! Do you want to cause a riot on this street? Run afoul of Sister Mary Frances, who has obviously sanctioned this painting? This neighborhood will revolt and blame you if this mural is destroyed and the artist arrested. Parisians may knuckle down before the Boche, but they'll stand up against anyone who challenges the Catholic Church. Got that?" The commander jabbed a finger into Achim's chest.

"*Oui*, Commander," Achim said, sighing and feigning a face of disappointment. "I will follow your orders to the utmost of my ability."

CHAPTER THIRTY-ONE

On his balcony, Major General Konrad March gazed across the boxwood hedge for sight of his unlikely new fishing buddy, disappointed not to find him on the riverbank this second Sunday morning of their acquaintance. Church bells were ringing, but Konrad did not think the boy was a churchgoer. Madame Gastain, yes. Never came a Sunday but that his binoculars did not pick up his neighbor walking to mass in her widow's weeds, slim and willowy. He would like to know what the face looked like beneath the black veil. Very pretty, despite her age, but sad and lost, Barnard had told him when he asked.

"Why sad and lost?"

It was an inane question. All Parisians looked sad and lost over the foreign occupation of their city, especially those who had fallen from the social and financial pinnacles of their former prosperity, as had Madame Gastain, but Konrad had wanted to know the other specifics. Barnard had answered his questions straight, without giving a hint that he perceived the reason for his neighbor's curiosity. "Her husband lost their fortune in the financial crash of 1929 and never recovered from the disgrace of it. He committed suicide a few years ago, and she has not recovered from his death. There were no children, so Madame Gastain has been alone ever since but for two elderly retainers."

"How old?"

"Who? Madame Gastain or her retainers?"

"Madame Gastain."

"Around her middle forties, I'd guess."

"And she's still wearing widow's weeds for her husband?"

"Well…not entirely just for him."

Of course not. She wore them for all of France, like a lot of Parisian women. "What does she do to occupy her time, shut away in her house?"

"I've only known her a short while, but I gather she listens to the phonograph, reads—she has a huge library—and plays the piano. Perhaps you've heard her? I know nothing about music, but she sounds very accomplished. I bring her the fish I catch, and she invites me to share it at her table, which is very pleasant for me."

"I've heard her play. You are right. She is very accomplished."

This conversation had taken place the day before in Normandy waters on Captain Claude Allard's fishing boat. The presence of the general had displeased the captain, and Konrad hoped it had not jeopardized Barnard's job. The general's ears were trained to hear through walls, and when the captain ordered Barnard to join him in the wheelhouse, Konrad, packing up his rod and tackle just outside it, had caught faint snatches of their conversation but clear enough to be understood. They had spoken in French, Konrad's second language.

Do you know what you're doing hobnobbing with the chief of German intelligence in France? I don't like it that you've brought him onto my boat, and now he'll be around every Saturday through November. His presence intimidates my other customers.

We're neighbors and met last Sunday over my tackle box. The man's an avid fisherman. He'd heard of you as the best boatman on the Seine and when I told him that I worked for you…

That wouldn't have been by design, would it?

The less you know, Captain.

Major General March was still mulling over that last bit of dialogue between the boat captain and his fishing guide: *That wouldn't be by design, would it?* And Barnard's reply: *The less you know, Captain.*

It was probably harmless. The captain might have been implying that Barnard was taking a risk ingratiating himself to the chief of German intelligence with hope of securing favors from him—extra ration cards, coal, petrol, foodstuffs—items impossible for Parisians to come by since the occupation. The general had already sent a canned ham with his compliments to the widow next door.

But he would keep alert to the remote possibility that Barnard Wagner was not who he declared himself to be. The general had learned to trust no one, not even his closest and dearest friends, as some had discovered to their sorrow, more was the sad pity of things because of this damned war. He would be especially disappointed to discover that Barnard Wagner, who reminded him of his younger brother in their innocent days before a deer hunter's bullet caught him in the chest, had appeared by design in the lives of him and his son.

For Wilhelm had taken to their neighbor, too. A shy lad, lonely, still missing his mother, finding no solace in school, he had found in the fisherman the promise of a friend. The general had returned home last Monday evening to hear that his son and Herr Wagner had played kickball after school, after Wilhelm had inadvertently kicked his soccer ball over the hedge into Madame Gastain's yard. The following evening, Hans had reported that Wilhelm had climbed the steps to the fisherman's garage apartment that afternoon to ask Barnard if he wanted to come out and play. Barnard, whose workday finished early because Captain Allard liked to dock his boat before dusk, had readily agreed, and the two had been playing kickball on the back lawn every afternoon all week.

"You mustn't let my son impose on you, Herr Wagner," the general had told him the day before. "Do not feel under the least obligation to allow Wilhelm to intrude on your free time."

"It is no imposition, General. It is good exercise for us both and gives Wilhelm a chance to practice for his soccer games."

"Well, it is very kind of you. The boy has no friends, and Hans is too stiff and gimpy to run around outside kicking a ball."

Barnard had suddenly looked uncomfortable, as if he were working up the courage to tell him something. "Uh, General, it is none of my business, but your son says he is not too happy at that school he attends."

"I am aware of that. Did he say why not?"

"His classmates bully him, and all but one of his teachers encourage it."

Konrad had felt his neck grow warm. "Do they now? Why didn't my son share this news with me, or at least with my aide?"

Herr Wagner had hesitated, then answered, "Because he admires you, sir, and he's too brave to tattle."

Konrad had felt a surge of pride, laced by a slow anger. "I knew something was bothering him beyond grief for his mother. I will question him and get to the bottom of this."

"But, please, General, don't tell the boy that I betrayed his confidence. He will never trust me again. I just thought you ought to know. If he were my son, I would want to be informed."

Konrad had found himself moved by this young man's concern and compassion for a child he barely knew, the son of a dangerous man. These days people could not risk caring for anyone but themselves, often ensuring their safety by betraying even those they loved. He had laid a hand on the fisherman's shoulder and said from heartfelt gratitude,

"You have my word and appreciation, Herr Wagner. Wilhelm will believe that his father suspected things were not going well at school and investigated. He will never learn that it was you who whispered in my ear. Did he happen to mention the name of the one teacher who does not encourage the bullying?"

"Yes, his name is Herr Claus Bauer. Wilhelm talks fondly of him. The teacher allows him to stay in his classroom during lunchtime to avoid eating with his tormentors."

"Which means that my son goes without a midday meal," Konrad said, the rage that could strike like a whip beginning to uncoil. "Herr Claus Bauer. I shall remember the name."

So this afternoon, he had an appointment to pay a visit to the sports director of his son's special school in the Sorbonne, one Louis Mueller. Meanwhile, he was nonplussed at his own inertia. His desk was stacked with reports that needed his attention, but he was in no mood to settle down to them. His concentration was on this latest revelation concerning his son and the young man from whom it had come as well as a consuming interest in the widow next door. He had hoped to spot Barnard Wagner down at the riverbank today to ask if he knew what Madame Gastain had thought of the tinned ham

Hans had delivered. His aide had put it in the hands of the old housekeeper. Would madame reject his offer of friendship?

He turned from the balcony to go inside. The truth was that Konrad March, Major General in the German Army, holder of the Iron Cross, World War I hero, head of the Abwehr in France, was lonely, too. He desired more in his life. He yearned for human contact beyond Wilhelm and Hans, for conversation with a refined, educated woman like the mysterious widow who hid her face from the world. Barnard Wagner was a breath of fresh air beyond the stifling stench of German intelligence headquarters, but now, in that overheard conversation, he'd caught a whiff of something possibly off about him. It was a shame. He'd become fond of the young fisherman who shared his love of the greatest sport in the world.

CHAPTER THIRTY-TWO

Dirk Drechsler heard the church bells, and a swell of homesickness filled him with such pain that he drew his knees tight to his chest and turned his face into his pillow to stifle a moan. The bells, deep throated and mellow, reminded him of those that rang in the First Lutheran Church back in New Braunfels, Texas. His mother and father and little sister would be attending morning services today and sitting in the same pews they'd laid claim to every Sunday since Dirk had been alive. Saturday, his father would have stopped by Naegelin's Bakery to pick up lebkuchen to take home for dessert to follow the Wiener schnitzel and potatoes and peas his mother always prepared for Sunday dinner. God, what he wouldn't give for a plate of his mother's sautéed veal and buttered paprika potatoes and a taste of that brown cookie with the pink icing that were his favorite foods in the whole world.

His taste buds watering, Dirk swung his legs to the floor and clasped his head in his hands. His decision to cut ties with America to join the German Army was the worst mistake he would ever make in his life, if he survived long enough to have a life. What in God's name had he been thinking to chuck his family, home, country, and friends to live in a miserably cold, paranoid, unfriendly country run by a crazed dictator like Adolf Hitler? It hadn't taken Dirk but a month of Abwehr training in Berlin to realize that he was first, foremost, and would ever be an American, fractionally a German, but never a Nazi. Obviously, the members of his intelligence unit believed the same about him. Rather than welcome him with open arms as Dirk had expected (he'd figured that an American would be quite a catch for the Abwehr), he was shunned by the other enlistees and treated with near contempt by the officers. They did not trust him. Disloyalty to a man's country, even a foe's, was foreign to the German chromosome system.

But to stay alive, he had borne his disillusionment with Hitler, the Abwehr, the government's anti-Semitism policies, and the diabolical goals of the

Third Reich without giving away the bitter regret of his decision and revulsion for his job. He had even risen to the grade of sergeant and been posted to the plum location of Paris, but he had no doubt that he would have already been transferred to the Russian front had he not possessed a special skill needed by the intelligence-gathering branch of the German Army. The Abwehr needed him as an English interpreter.

That job he could have tolerated. The Abwehr respected the rules of the Geneva Convention and treated the enemy and suspicious persons with relatively decent human conduct during interrogations. But no sooner had he arrived in Paris than he was loaned out part-time to the anti-Jewish section of the Gestapo. They were short of English-speaking staff.

Now he would live with the eternal shame and horror of what he'd been forced to do and witness. A steely eye, threatening pose, and menacing tone were not the techniques he'd expected would be employed to pry information from the poor sucker strapped in the chair of an interrogation room. *Pry* was not the word, either. *Extract* was more accurate. God, the deplorable acts of inhumanity those Gestapo bastards were capable of. The worst were the times he entered a cell to find an American in restraints, the look he received when Dirk was ordered to inform him that his interpreter was a fellow countryman. The Gestapo interrogators took great pleasure in that directive. "Sergeant Drechsler is from Texas in America," they would say, bending down to speak into the anguished face of the downed U.S. pilot or the American OSS liaison to the French Resistance. He would then repeat loudly as if his American captive was deaf, "*America! Texas!*"

At such times, Dirk's entrails would twist in self-revilement and another layer would be added to the hatred he felt for the whole German war machine and the country he'd volunteered to serve.

If only he'd listened to Chris, his best friend, who had not bought into the crap of a thousand-year reign of the Third Reich. Lucky Chris, to have been born with a missing thumb that guaranteed a military deferment. He was now safe in the land of the free, cozy in his Austin apartment, enjoying his teaching job and living in the city that he loved. He could work on his PhD, attend music festivals and rodeos, date girls, see his family, and eat Mexican food whenever the mood struck him—all without a clue of the loneliness, danger, cold, and deprivation his buddy was enduring over in German-occupied Paris.

If only he could find a way to get home. He had thought and thought about it. There ought to be a way to get across the border into Switzerland or Spain or across the English Channel into England. He had money hidden away—U.S. dollars—that the Abwehr didn't know about. At least he'd not been dumb enough to leave home without funds on hand. He was growing desperate. He couldn't sleep at night for fantasizing what it would be like to walk up to the front door of his house in New Braunfels and ring the bell. *"Mater! Vater! I'm home!"*

Although now he would say *Mother* and *Father*, maybe even *Daddy*, like everybody else's son in Texas. He would be through with all things German if he should ever get out of Europe. If he ever made it home, he would take whatever was coming to him, like the prodigal son, willing to eat pig swill, not expecting the fatted calf.

But for now he had his hopes pinned on a new rumor that not only would the war not last forever, but that Germany would lose it. The German Army was losing ground on both the eastern and western fronts. German citizens were losing faith in their raving moron of a Führer. The French Resistance was growing, and rumors were flying that an Allied invasion of the continent was being planned for the near future. If he could hang on, Dirk Drechsler just might be able to make it home again.

Hurriedly, he dressed in his army shirt and pants, forgoing the jacket, since German soldiers were not required to dress in full uniform in their quarters on Sundays. It was so damn cold and only October 11. His floor heater did little to warm the room beyond a three-inch radius, but he was lucky that he could leave the pilot light continuously burning. The French boarders were rationed to the use of four hours of gas a night in their rooms, none during the day.

He heard his neighbor next door—Stephane Beaulieu—lock his room door. The French engineer puzzled him. He couldn't put his finger on it, but he didn't seem...well, as much French as the other frogs. French people, unless with friends and family, had struck Dirk as very posture and gesture conscious. They were formal in their conventions: how they dressed, how they spoke to one another, how they presented themselves at the dinner table, and how they greeted one another. They did not hug. They did not shout unless in anger. Neighbors calling to each other across the street in Texas would be taboo in France, and they never ate while walking down the street. The French were unbending around strangers, but Stephane Beaulieu seemed looser somehow, his mannerisms less stiff. He was polite and reserved without being aloof, proper without being prudish, but Dirk had noticed that he seemed inordinately careful and watchful, and once he had seen the engineer bite into an apple (onc of a bag given to the boarders courtesy of Captain Achterberg on one of his more generous days) while setting off to catch the metro, but who wouldn't break convention if there was no breakfast and you were hungry enough? Dirk noticed such anomalies, an asset in his job that had won from Captain Achterberg his only praise. He called him "sharp-eyed," using American slang.

Stephane Beaulieu was the only one of the French boarders with whom Dirk had felt he could develop a cordial relationship. He took French lessons daily so that he could converse and had become fairly comprehensible, but the engineer had side-stepped his attempts to be friendly—not exactly *shunned* him as the other Frenchmen had, but *avoided* him. Dirk had noticed that difference, too.

He heard his neighbor pass his room and quickly

stepped out, catching him at the head of the stairs. The Frenchman was dressed for the weather and in finer clothes than he wore to work. "Headed for church?" Dirk called in broken French.

His neighbor's back stiffened as if he'd suddenly been caught with a hand in the till, and Dirk indeed caught a deer-in-the-the headlights expression when he glanced around.

"*Oui,*" he said.

"Well, then, say one for me."

"Excusez-moi?"

"A prayer. Say a prayer for me."

"*D'accord,*" his neighbor said and hurried on down the stairs.

Dirk went back to his room and grabbed his army overcoat. For something to do this Sunday, he'd go to church, too. He'd follow Stephane Beaulieu to whichever one he attended, probably the Catholic church on the corner. It would be nice to sit in a pew again and listen to organ music in a quiet, candlelit sanctuary with people not wearing Nazi uniforms, never mind that the church wasn't Lutheran. Maybe he could entice the engineer to go to lunch with him, his treat. He knew a café that treated German soldiers especially well. But to Dirk's disappointment and discomfort—he was shivering to his gonads even in his overcoat—Stephane Beaulieu did not enter the church on the corner. He hurried past it toward the metro as if late for an appointment.

Dirk never knew the source of the nudge that prompted him to follow Stephane Beaulieu. The engineer's reaction when he hailed him at the stairs was definitely enough to rouse suspicions, but Dirk preferred to believe that the push came from the hand of God. He had not deserted him, after all, for when he successfully managed to tail the French engineer to his destination, he saw a way to get back home to America again.

Stephane Beaulieu's metro ride took him to the port village of Honfleur, where he walked to a tall, narrow town house wedged between an automotive shop and fish market. Mingling among churchgoers attending services in the church opposite, Dirk saw a woman open the door to the engineer's knock, and Dirk's pulse raced when the Frenchman threw a furtive glance over his shoulder down the street. When Stephane stepped inside, Dirk had turned into the church's walled cemetery, where he could keep an eye on the house through a chink in the ancient stone. After a couple of endless hours the door opened again, and Dirk beheld a scene that stunned his eyes unless they had deceived him: Stephane Beaulieu embraced by the most wanted man in France, the bearded leader of the Resistance, the former French Army general and Resistance leader Nicholas Cravois.

CHAPTER THIRTY-THREE

Sunday afternoon, fuming, Louis Mueller unlocked the door of his school office and threw his heavy set of keys onto his desk. The ring should have held only the keys to the doors of his domain, but this one clanked with the means to enter the offices of department heads in the Sorbonne. Louis had taken the university president's spinster secretary to Maxim's and wooed an invitation afterward to her apartment for a nightcap. Leaving her drugged, he'd stolen her office key and met a locksmith at the Sorbonne who'd made paste imprints of select keys right on the site. The secretary woke at six o'clock the next morning with a headache but fully clothed and tucked cozily in her bed, the key safe in her purse, and a note from Louis apologizing for having overdined and overwined her but with the hope she'd allow him the pleasure again. Of course, the invitation was never extended.

Louis was a snooper, and he liked to know all about not only his staff but the people in authority over him. A man never knew to what use he might put the information. Usually, he carried the full ring to the school only on Saturday afternoons, when he ostensibly read students' progress reports, checked sports equipment, and caught up on paperwork. The maintenance crew was gone by then, and unless Louis saw lights in some overzealous professor's office, he had free access to other doors in the greater Sorbonne to examine at will personnel files, business papers, private correspondence, address and appointment books, cabinets and drawers and closets. Louis Mueller, lowly physical education director of a school created to instruct "the mongrels of Nazi bastards" so a private memo referred to the students, had collected enough incriminating material to hold over the heads of a goodly number of the senior Sorbonne staff.

But yesterday, he'd received a call from the father of one of his students, Major General Konrad March, requesting an interview on Sunday—today, October 11, the only day to spend time with his lover in Lyon. He had tried to beg off—his mother was ill—but the general had insisted. One did not say no to the head of the Abwehr in France, although that lofty position would gain the general little footing if he'd come to protest his son's education. Louis Mueller's physical education program had the full support and endorsement of the Führer, but still, he'd prefer not to cross swords with a man of Major General March's authority and connections. He and Admiral Wilhelm Canaris, chief of the entire Abwehr, a man of immense power and influence, were best friends. The general's son, Wilhelm, was named after him.

Wilhelm March was the type of student Louis made his mission to weed out from the program. The boy was weak, timid, *verweichlicht*! His arm was like a limp *nudel* when he gave the Nazi salute. The other boys in his pod despised him because he was their weakest link. There was no toughening him up, no igniting of German pride. The extra laps, cold-water dunks, ridicule, and taunts had no effect. He was a disgrace to the program and to the Hitlerjugend organization. Louis would not have the *verzogenes Gör*—spoiled brat—screw up his record of producing physically fit, race-conscious, obedient, self-sacrificing Germans willing to die for their Führer and Fatherland.

"Has your son complained?" Louis had asked the general and could have bitten off his tongue. Now he had given the general grounds to think his son had reason to whine. It could be the man had called simply to ask how he might help to build a fire under his whelp.

But the general had answered, "No, he has not. I heard the complaints from another source."

"And that would be?"

"The name is of no consequence, Herr Mueller. Three o'clock sharp tomorrow. Give my aide the directions he'll require to drive us to your office."

After Louis had hung up, he'd sat a while considering who of Wilhelm's instructors could have tattled to the boy's father. The only member of his staff sympathetic to the little wimp was the newcomer Claus Bauer, but he had been here only a week. Would he have dared such a risk when Louis had made clear to him that he had him in his crosshairs?

The instructors' cubicles were an open field for Louis's Saturday rummaging. Today he would take a peek in Claus Bauer's office to see what he could find before Major General March arrived. Ten minutes later, nothing, except some notes that Herr Bauer had written to himself in his day book. "Monday, bring an extra sandwich for W, so he won't go hungry, poor kid." *Kid*? Not *kind*? *Kid* was American slang for "child." Obviously, the *W* stood for Wilhelm. Why would Herr Bauer feel he must bring an extra sandwich for the boy? The students were well-fed at the academy.

Louis studied the jottings. The handwriting was distinctly German, but the overall syntax pattern struck him as odd. A couple of *I*'s and *O*'s were missing their diagonal marks. There was no cross through *7* and the letter *Z*. Some nouns were not capitalized. He pondered the page. The oversights could have been the result of hurried scribbling, but the rules of penmanship were second nature to Germans, automatically followed, and the arrangement of words and structure of several of Herr Bauer's sentences were definitely unconventional to German. There was an informality about them, like the pattern of American English. Had Claus Bauer spent time in America? Was he learning English on the sly? Why? German would eventually become the world language. Nowhere in the personnel file of the department's most recently hired instructor was there a mention of his having been in America or of his learning the English language. After his meeting with Major General March, he would check the files in the office of Jules Garnier, the personnel director, and perhaps they'd tell him more. One scrap of information Louis had learned: Claus Bauer was coddling Wilhelm March.

He rose quickly in answer to the pounding of a balled fist on the outer door. He rushed to open it to two stern-faced men in German Wehrmacht overcoats, one an army sergeant, the other unmistakably Major General Konrad March. "Heil Hitler," Louis said as he raised an arm in the Nazi greeting and stepped respectfully back to allow their entrance. Major General Konrad March returned a careless military salute and a murmured "Heil Hitler" as he and his aide passed by Louis into the room, his gaze going at once to the portrait of Hitler, then sweeping to the anti-Jewish posters and Nazi flags displayed about the room. The man drew off his gloves, and his aide assisted in removing his overcoat, revealing the full regalia of his rank and military honors. Impressive as they were, the medals, soutache piping, knotted gold braid shoulder boards weren't necessary to substantiate his authority. If sheer power were of human shape, it would take the form of Major General Konrad March.

Turning his attention back to Louis, the general said, "I am here in the capacity of a parent to discuss your physical education program, Herr Mueller."

Louis felt a jab of alarm. The man's face and tone expressed no emotion by which he could judge his mood. Had he come to praise or upbraid? "Of course,

Herr Major General," he said. "Shall we go into my office?"

The general nodded to his aide, who took a visitor's seat, then paused to study the department's mission statement posted on a wall. "So your aim here is to graduate a product 'swift as a greyhound, tough as leather, and hard as Krupp's steel'?"

"Yes, Herr Major General, by orders of the Führer."

"I see."

After a discussion of the school's curriculum and his son's daily schedule, the general asked to see the physical training facilities, the shower and locker room, and the arsenal of weaponry used in preparing the student for the military, his only expression of judgment an occasional "I see." The one possibly negative observation was his comment, "Not much time for science, math, literature, and languages, is there?"

"The Führer believes a fit, disciplined body is more important," Louis said.

"That he does."

Walking him and his aide to the door after the interview and tour, Louis itched to ask the general what he thought of the place and the program. Was he impressed? Did he approve? To whom had his son run to complain? Would the little weakling be in trouble with his father when he returned home? But the general betrayed nothing of his opinion at his departure, and Louis had the uneasy feeling that a technique used in an Abwehr interrogation chamber had been applied to him. A soft-spoken interrogator questions the victim quietly, with no overt intention to do him harm until he leaves and sends in the goon squad.

But Louis Mueller should have no fear of a backlash. He was following the Führer's orders, and at the moment he must deal with another issue. Locking the door after the general, he hurried off to the personnel director's office. Louis would never forgive Jules Garnier for turning down his chosen candidate for the job in favor of Claus Bauer. The position would have meant that his lover would move to Paris. The Lyon prostitute was a myth Louis had invented to cover his real sexual preference. Babette was really Aristide, the love of his life. Now that information was a secret he must make sure never came to light to the authorities.

Half an hour later he found a note that again raised his suspicions of a serpent in the grass, not in Claus Bauer's personnel file, but in the recordings of Jules Garnier's private datebook: *Friday, October 2: CB in Paris. Safe landing. Saturday, October 3: Met with CB. Monday, October 5: CB in place.*

In place? That sounded like spy terminology. Safe landing? That suggested a clandestine arrival in France. Why would Herr Garnier use those terms? Herr Bauer had crossed into France from Emmendingen, across the French-German border. Nothing covert about that. He had been vouched for by Harriet Straub, a well-known German doctor and author from the area.

Louis nibbled at a fleshy lip in thought. Did that note explain why Aristide, thoroughly qualified, was denied the job? There could be nothing to the personnel director's choice of phrases, but the worm of doubt had been lured from its hole and would remain aboveground until Louis could prove one way or the other that Herr Bauer and Jules Garnier were not who they professed to be.

CHAPTER THIRTY-FOUR

From a window in the *salle*, the upstairs fencing hall of the L'Ecole d'Escrime Français, Colonel Derrick Albrecht watched Veronique Colbert walk up the street to keep their Sunday appointment. He had spent time in many of the notable countries of the world, and nowhere had he found a population with as many stunning women as in France. Slim, graceful, poised, so many of these women walked with a purposeful stride, shoulders back, head held high, gaze forward with never a glance downward, an amazing feat of smooth navigation in a city known for its uneven cobbled pathways.

So it was that Veronique Colbert strode now, the most stunning of the lot, certainly of the women he'd ever known, though *known* was not exactly the correct word he'd ascribe to her. Today would mark only his second time in her company, and since last Sunday, when they'd first met, he had learned much about his new bout partner without feeling that he knew her. Some of his information had been dredged from her own mouth, in answer to his questions over a truffle quiche in the dining room of the Ritz Hotel after their match. She was unmarried, had been educated at the Sorbonne, and had lived in Paris all her life but for a couple of years in Spain after college, where she instructed foil to the children of the ambassador and staff of the American Embassy. Upon the ambassador's recall to the United States, she had treated herself to a year's travel, then returned to Paris and her employment at L'Ecole d'Escrime Français. She had no family. She never knew her grandparents from either side, and her parents were deceased. She had no siblings. Her childhood home and the street where she'd lived had been destroyed by fire while she was in college, the neighbors long since relocated beyond reach to be questioned about the blond-haired little girl who had grown up among them. Her natural skill on the piste had been sharpened by a moonlighting instructor whose coaching came to an end when he emigrated to England in 1939.

It appeared that all roads to confirm the veracity of

Mademoiselle Veronique Colbert's background led to dead ends. Well, he would see.

Her uncommunicative responses and unwillingness to engage in conversation would have made her boring company at the Ritz had it not been for the pleasure of looking at her. He talked and sipped wine, a lightly oaked chardonnay, while she ate. She was pleasant to watch even then. Many women were ugly when they chewed. Champing jaws and bouncing facial muscles could distort the loveliest of faces. While she cut into the delicious flaky tart with the restraint one did not often see among hungry Parisians these days, he imagined her hair released from its luxurious chignon and the feel of her skin and curves of her body beneath the black suit and silk blouse. Of course she was fully aware of his admiration, but she met it with the cool disregard with which she ate the custard-filled pastry made with the most expensive ingredient in the world. However, her patent disinterest in him—or antipathy—would not discourage him from learning more about Mademoiselle Veronique Colbert. It was his job.

To that end, the following morning he'd dispatched his most competent wolfhound to dig up whatever information on his aloof fencing partner was available. His detection dog reported that according to her college records, she had been a good student, majoring in Franco studies and graduating at twenty, but he was able to sniff out little else from that quarter. Her professors had been Jews and political dissidents who had fallen under the Nazi ax and had either been deported, disappeared, or sent to extermination camps. Without an intensive search of student files, he could locate no one who could tell him who her classmates were these two years after her graduation. School officials referred him to the director of personnel, one Jules Garnier, because of his long tenure at the Sorbonne. Yes, indeed, the director remembered seeing a young woman of that name about the halls of the university, but he'd had no personal contact with her. His position did not call for him to deal directly with students. He remembered Mademoiselle Colbert because of her great beauty.

Surprisingly, she appeared to have no boyfriend. Since she'd only recently returned to Paris, her fellow instructors at the fencing school and her neighbors in the quiet residential hotel knew little about her except to mention that Mademoiselle Colbert kept to herself and did not invite personal interchange.

So it would seem that hardly anybody knew anything about Veronique Colbert except SS Colonel Derrick Albrecht. He had gleaned much from his short acquaintance with the beautiful instructor of foil.

For one, she was highly bred. Good breeding meant more to him than sex appeal, though she had plenty of that—an unbeatable and irresistible combination to whet the desire of a man of his tastes. For another, French was not her native language. It required a quick ear, for which he was well-known, to detect a certain inflection not of the romance language of the Indo-European family. Also, her control of the blade, her attacks by prise de fer to lure him into committing to a parry, and her brilliant feints to provoke a specific reaction that she skillfully managed to counteract were not learned in after-school sessions at the hand of a conventional instructor, as she'd claimed. Natural ability played the essential part in producing a great fencer, but the development of it could only be achieved by years of coaching and training under the tutelage of a master.

He had won the previous Sunday's bout but only by the rule of priority. They had each landed a hit simultaneously, but he'd been first to initiate a correctly executed attack. Derrick believed he would have won by points if he had not been so distracted by her skill and grace and his own lust. Veronique Colbert, on the other hand, seemed invincible to distraction. He knew from the moment she'd set foot on the strip, salutes over, that she had come to win. She was like a matador facing a bull, aggressive and combative, perhaps angry at the change in her plans for the day or her revulsion of him, but she did not allow emotion to obstruct her play. He saw immediately that she did not plan to win by overpowering him with physical speed. She was no match for him there, though her fast footwork astounded him. She'd determined to best him with guile. He saw how she watched the movement of his hands and feet and the shift of his weight for the slightest opportunity to move in for the kill. Over and over she pressed the attack, fearless and indefatigable. Never had he been so happy at the conclusion of a fifteen-point match to see Monsieur Jacques Vogel, who'd served as referee, straighten his arm with palm toward him to declare him victor.

"I would like to walk a bit," she had said in response to his assumption that he would see her to her hotel at the conclusion of their meal at the Ritz. "It has been a while since I've strolled about the Place Vendôme. I'll take the metro later."

Her point was clear. It was not to keep her address private that she declined his offer of transportation to her lodging. She would know that information was easy enough to find, but that she did not wish to arrive seated in the staff car of a colonel in the SS.

He had acquiesced with warm understanding, expressed his hope to see her the next Sunday, and left her standing before one of the most elegant hotels in the world, a fitting backdrop for a woman of her regality. He had ordered his driver to make a U-turn on Rue Saint-Honoré and headed back to 84 Avenue Foch, headquarters of the Sicherheitsdienst, where his office had a view of the Arc de Triomphe. He had work to do. Mademoiselle Colbert had not asked him a single question about himself. Under the circumstances of her forced presence, even the most impeccable manners did not require her to do so. It had amused him to hold back information that would have tripped her up and exposed her as the fraud she was right on the spot, but he preferred to wait to discover what she was up to. It could be that she was an innocent sojourner caught in Paris at the German invasion of France and had assumed a false identity as her only form of protection. Why would she not? But if she had been of the mood to make the inquiries usual to two strangers sharing a luncheon table, he might have told her that he, SS Standartenführer Derrick Albrecht of the Sicherheitsdienst, had enjoyed the privilege of spending a year in her country as a graduate student at Harvard University in Cambridge, Massachusetts, and knew an American when he met one.

CHAPTER THIRTY-FIVE

By the following Sunday, October 18, working on her mural before reporting to the fashion house and after returning to the convent, Bridgette's canvas of stone came to life with all the details that mattered. The broad head of a Golden Labrador with its chiseled features peered nobly through a stand of rushes at a dragonfly hovering over a lily pad afloat in a pond of blue water. A number of pencil-thin liverworts sprawled along its watery edge close to where a black-and-white wading bird, crowned with its species's splendid crest, stood surveying its domain. The cup-shaped shell of a limpet clung to an algae-covered rock buried among fronds, and a faint impression of the North Star still showed in the early morning sky. Against a background of subtle corals and various greens, soft blues, and luscious hues of purple and aqua, the code symbols of Labrador, Liverwort, Lapwing, Limpet, and Lodestar were in place.

Under the eye of the French *flic* lurking close by, passersby all through the week had stopped to wonder, and some to ask the artist, what the painting was meant to state. "Whatever you wish it to," Bridgette had answered with a smile.

The day before, again under the watchful gaze of the beat cop, her work had drawn a crowd in overcoats and scarves to watch reeds and flora and tiny aquatic denizens along the pond's bank come into being. Today, they had gathered to watch her, standing on her ladder, put the finishing touches on trees and clouds and tall grasses with her magic brush. When she stroked in the final detail of the North Star and started to descend the ladder, the crowd applauded. One Frenchman declared, "The mural represents hope. The star is us—the French. Our light has dimmed, but it has not gone out!"

The ladder wobbled, and Achim Fleischer rushed to steady it. To his amazement, he had gained an unexpected status in the neighborhood as the protector of the mural. Earlier in the week, two Wehrmacht officers had stopped to view and discuss it in German. Achim's heart had turned over. They did not look pleased. They saw him and beckoned him over. "Who is the artist that did this?" one of them inquired in French and motioned toward the wall.

Achim had suppressed a gulp, surprised by his reluctance to provide a name. In the course of the days that the artist had worked on her painting, she had introduced herself as Bernadette Dufor and tried to disarm his cold manner by engaging him in warm conversation. He had resisted her attempts, still suspicious of both her and her mural, but as a male, he could not help but appreciate her winsome face and energetic little body, so perfectly formed and feminine and of the perfect height.

"A young French woman, a fashion designer," he'd answered. "The mother superior of the Sisters of Charity"—he pointed toward the convent—"gave her permission to...to bring beauty to the street."

"Well, that she has done," the officer said. "Remarkable. I'm sure her efforts will result in quite a work of art when it is finished. See that you protect it."

A woman from the neighborhood had witnessed the exchange but not heard it. After the army officers had moved on, she crossed the street to ask him, "Did the Boche wish to have the mural removed?"

"I believe that was their intent, madame."

"But you talked them out of it?"

"It would appear so."

"Bless you, monsieur."

Thus word had gotten around that the painting was under Achim's personal protection. Recently, a customer in a shop had pointed him out as the "guardian of the wall," and he preened from the title and recognition. Familiar faces now passed him on guard duty with expressions of approval rather than scowls of contempt, and German soldiers on patrol nodded in friendly acknowledgment of his assignment. The seascape going up on the convent wall of the Sisters of Charity was drawing more traffic to the Rue des Soeurs de Charité, and visitors, willing to part with a shot's worth of their rationed film, had begun to take his picture posing beside the mural. The attention required he take extra care with his appearance to project the appropriate image of a police presence, but more important, and quite unconsciously, to present a favorable impression to the artist.

Safe off the ladder, Mademoiselle Dufor turned toward him, her tender face warm with gratitude. "*Merci beaucoup*," she said with a smile, and Achim was unprepared for the feeling that swept him from head to toe.

CHAPTER THIRTY-SIX

That Sunday afternoon, Chris was in his hostel room when two long buzzes from a wall unit alerted him that a guest was waiting for him in the living room downstairs. The signal gave him a start. He could think of no one who would be visiting him, since he had made no friends among his colleagues and had only a nodding acquaintance with the other tenants, all of them young Germans who'd been imported to fill clerical positions for the Nazi authorities. Major Renault had chosen his quarters as another hotbed of intel to pass on to Labrador. No member of Dragonfly knew where he lived, and he could rule out Jules Garnier and Louis Mueller. The personnel director would not risk meeting him at his lodging, and he had heard the director brag that he would be spending all day Sunday in bed with his Lyon prostitute. Chris pushed the button twice to let the clerk manning the desk know he'd be down, then tucked a pencil fuse into an inner pocket of his jacket. The L pill he carried in the casing of his German-manufactured wristwatch.

At the reception desk the French clerk, a collaborator whom Chris had loathed since checking in, jerked his head toward the living room with a smirk that implied he was in trouble. Chris's heart kicked. Staring out the window in a pose of meditation, his arms crossed behind him, stood a German officer in an overcoat whose collar insignia identified him as a major general. Chris made the instant connection of the rank to Wilhelm March, whose father was the head of the Abwehr.

The major general turned, and a fractional smile relaxed the ruminative lines of a ruggedly attractive, middle-aged face. "Herr Bauer, Konrad March, Wilhelm's father. You instruct Wilhelm in field sports and mathematics," he said, approaching Chris with outstretched hand.

"That is correct, Herr Major General," Chris said.

"I've come to discuss a matter with you regarding him."

"I am most happy to be of service."

Immediately, the German residents who had gathered to read and listen to the phonograph this

Sunday afternoon snapped shut their books, folded their newspapers, turned off the record player, and quietly left the room. General March drew the tails of his overcoat about him and sat down in one of the vacated chairs without appearing to take notice. It seemed generally understood that men of his rank and power were to be granted privacy.

The general indicated that Chris take a seat and began without preliminaries. "Last Sunday afternoon, I met with Herr Louis Mueller, director of the physical education program at your academy," he said, "and I did not like what I heard or saw. I've decided it's best to withdraw Wilhelm from the school and put his education into the hands of private tutors."

"I will miss him, sir."

"Not if you undertake to tutor my son in mathematics at my home three days a week after completion of your school duties. The thirty minutes the school allots to the study of mathematics are simply not enough. Wilhelm likes and trusts you. I hope you will consider it. I would pay you well."

Chris maintained a polite, mildly surprised expression. Before a man trained in reading facial expressions and body language, he must not betray his elated shock over this intelligence plum to fall into his lap.

He would like to be a fly on the wall when Major Renault received the message that Lapwing—Claus Bauer—had gained access to the home of the head of the Abwehr in France. His case officer would not believe his luck.

"Should I give you time to think about it, Herr Bauer?"

Chris was aware that the question was asked out of courtesy. Unless he had a very good excuse to refuse the general's offer, he was expected to accept it. "I do not believe that is necessary, Herr Major General," he said. "I would be honored to undertake the tutoring of mathematics to your son. I shall look forward to it."

The general rose. "Excellent. Here is my address card." Chris got to his feet to accept it and the offer of the general's hand. "Tomorrow afternoon, then?"

Chris nodded. "Tomorrow afternoon."

CHAPTER THIRTY-SEVEN

Finally, a Sunday had opened up that allowed Victoria to make a trip to the boardinghouse where Ralph might have found refuge. The previous Sundays, the only day in the week that permitted sufficient time for her mission, had been tied up by Colonel Derrick Albrecht. To her bitter chagrin, he had scheduled their bouts at an hour that did not allow time for a metro ride to visit Madame Dupree at her boardinghouse. Yesterday, however, Colonel Albrecht had called to ask if mademoiselle would consider changing their two o'clock bout to four o'clock. Victoria had readily agreed.

She would be springing her visit on Madame Dupree without prior notice. She would have preferred to telephone first, but Victoria's consideration for the woman's safety as well as her own prohibited making contact by phone. Switchboard operators were notorious for reporting suspicious conversations to Nazi police officials, and the boardinghouse telephone might not be in a safe spot for the owner to take the call. Notes delivered by hand were risky and uncertain as well. Licensed couriers on bicycles were subject to interceptions and searches by German patrols, and Victoria could trust no one to deliver unread a message of the necessary length to explain the purpose of her visit to Madame Dupree.

So she had no recourse but to arrive unannounced with the hope of finding the brave *propriétaire* at home and willing to talk to her this cold, nose-nipping Sunday. Parisians were understandably afraid to trust one another, and it could be that the woman who might have saved Ralph's life would deny having done so. Victoria could think of no convincing cover story to explain why she had come, so she would have to risk trusting Madame Dupree with the truth.

Her heart was knocking by the time she rang the bell to the boardinghouse. It drummed harder when it was answered by a young, heavyset man wearing the rolled-sleeved shirt and loosened tie of an off-duty sergeant in the Wehrmacht. She had not expected the boardinghouse to have been requisitioned as quarters for German soldiers. At seeing her, the man's gaze widened and his jaw sagged slightly. Victoria smiled at him. She would use his starstruck fascination to her advantage. Hoping he understood French, she said, "*Bonjour*, monsieur. I am here to see Madame Dupree. Is she in?"

He stepped back like a mesmerized mute to allow her entrance into the hall and waved a copy of a German-language newspaper, the *Pariser Zeitung*, toward the rear of the house. "*Cuisine*," he managed to say, indicating the kitchen. Victoria heard male voices speaking German in a room with its door open a few paces down the hall.

"*Merci*," she said, and struck off through the dining area rather than expose her presence to the men in the room. Stepping into the kitchen, she said softly to the back of the woman at the stove, "Madame Dupree?" Thankfully, no one else was in the kitchen, but through a window, Victoria could see several men, one a German Army captain, another a civilian, bent over a garden row cutting cabbages.

Gabrielle Dupree whirled from the stove and blinked. "Who are you?"

Veronique took a step forward and in her most imploring tone spoke softly in French. "My name doesn't matter, Madame Dupree. You must trust me that I mean you no harm. I am the fiancée of an

RAF pilot, an American to whom I believe you gave sanctuary in May of this year. He was shot down over Gennevilliers—"

"Sssh!" Madame Dupree hissed sharply, pressing a finger to her lips. She turned to switch off a burner flame and motioned Victoria toward a pantry. Squeezed between shelves of the previous summer's canned bounty, she whispered, "Are you an American?"

"Yes."

"Prove it."

"What?"

"Speak to me in English. No, tell me why you are here in the *American* tongue. I will be able to distinguish the difference."

With emphasis on the prolonged vowels of a Virginia accent, Victoria spoke a few sentences of nonsense about the weather. "Ah," said Madame Dupree, apparently convinced of her nationality. She wrapped her hands around Victoria's and said softly, "Leave, mademoiselle. Walk south one block. You will find a cemetery park next to a church. I will meet you there in twenty minutes."

They heard the kitchen door open, and quickly Madame Dupree snatched down a jar of canned turnips. "I am sorry, *mon amie*," she said loud enough for the intruder to hear, "but this is all I can spare from our meager larder. Times...they are so hard."

"*Oui*," Victoria said and took the jar. Madame Dupree stepped out and Victoria followed. Standing at stiff attention in the kitchen was the sergeant who had admitted her into the foyer. He had donned his uniform jacket and tightened his tie.

"May I help you, Sergeant?" Madame Dupree asked crisply.

"Uh, yes, well—" The sergeant stepped uncertainly forward, the bluster of his military uniform failing the impression he had meant to establish. "As a member of the Abwehr, it...it is my duty to...to interrogate all unknown visitors to this house," he stammered.

"Is that so? You've never done so before."

The sergeant seemed to shrink inside his jacket. "Uh, well, that is so, but it is policy now—"

"Mademoiselle is *not* an unknown visitor to this house," Madame Dupree interrupted him. "She is merely unknown to *you*, and I shall take this matter up with Captain Achterberg. Here he comes now."

Eyes turned to the men from the garden heading toward the house with their sacks of cabbage, breaths frosting the air. The sergeant's plump face blushed splotches of pink. "That won't be necessary, madame," he said quickly, snapping to attention with a click of his heels. "I have made a mistake."

Victoria's heart grabbed the minute he'd opened his mouth. He spoke garbled French with a Texas twang. The man was an American and in the German intelligence agency. Another shock almost made her drop the jar of canned turnips. Coming through the outside door behind the German officer, stamping his shoes free of frost on the doormat, cheeks red from the cold, was Lodestar. Absorbed, he did not see her until he lifted his head and saw her staring motionless at him. The other man, Captain Achterberg, merely looked surprised at the presence of such a woman in his landlady's kitchen.

Victoria broke her stare, aware that their mutually stunned gazes had caught the sergeant's attention. She was grateful that Madame Dupree, tall as she, stepped in front of her and kissed Victoria's cheeks in the French fashion. "Good-bye, *mon amie*. We will visit again soon."

"*Oui*," Victoria said again and turned toward the door.

The sergeant stepped out of her way with a stiff bob of his head. "Mademoiselle."

Twenty minutes later, Madame Dupree joined her on the park bench where she sat, still numb from her discovery of Lodestar's address and the knowledge that he shared it with an American.

"I assume from your start at seeing my young boarder that you are acquainted with him and were surprised to find him in my *pension de famille*," the boardinghouse owner stated. Victoria, for both their safety, offered no comment. Madame Dupree's establishment was a safe house. She was working for the OSS.

"*Oui*, I thought so," the woman said. "I will speak no more on the matter and trust in God that you will never have reason to divulge my name or that of my boarder. Do not worry, mademoiselle. He is aware that bumbling oaf is an American. He knows to be very careful. Now to reply to your inquiries. *Oui*, I gave sanctuary to two RAF airmen who were shot down over Gennevilliers in May. One, an American, was badly wounded and died before he could be turned over to the underground. The other, English, must have made it to England for you to have knowledge of me."

Her heart holding, Victoria said, "And... the name of... the pilot who died?"

"Peter Billings. He was from... Idaho, I believe you say it. Is that the name of your fiancé?"

Victoria's eyes closed briefly in relief. "No," she said.

"However, I have something more..." Madame Dupree reached within a coat pocket to pull out an object that Victoria recognized as the RAF version of an American dog tag. "I found this in Peter Billings's possession before we buried him," she said and held it out. "Would this be the identity tag of your fiancé, mademoiselle?"

Victoria took the single brown disc threaded with a cord and stared at the inscription that stated the name, service number, and religious affiliation of Lieutenant Ralph W. DuPont. Slowly, her eyes stinging, she nodded.

"I assume Monsieur Billings removed it to give to the pilot's family, but died himself before he could deliver it," Madame Dupree said. She stood and addressed Victoria's bent head. "Remember the name Group Captain Gavin Longworth. He was from Lewes in East Sussex. After the war, you may wish to visit him to learn more about the death of your loved one."

She had walked away before Victoria knew she was gone. Tears forming, Victoria ran her fingers over the back of the engraved disc that had lain against the chest of the man she loved. She brought it to her lips and held it there. The RAF identification tags came in pairs, the octagonal green one to be left on the body and the circular brown one to be taken to record the death. Where was he buried, her beloved? In what field, what village, what churchyard? She would not leave him there. After the war, she would track down Group Captain Gavin Longworth to find Ralph's burial place and bring her love home.

Church bells were announcing that Sunday services were over. She must go. She slid the leather piece deep into her pocket, tears rolling down her cheeks. She could go home now. She'd gotten the answer she'd come to Paris to find, and now her discoveries of Lodestar's address and Madame Dupree's association with the OSS put them in danger if she were caught and made to talk. It was her duty to report her discoveries to the major and remove herself from Dragonfly.

But how could she go home and leave to the others the work that might help the Allies win the war, the reason that Ralph had joined the RAF?

No. Her duty was here, where her beloved had died. She would leave it to Lodestar to report their chance meeting to the major.

CHAPTER THIRTY-EIGHT

At his desk in Bern, enveloped in a thick cloud of smoke from the dozen Lucky Strikes he'd chain-lit since receiving Bridgette's coded messages from Paris, Major Alistair Renault was the picture of despair. Information from the OSS's investigation into Colonel Derrick Albrecht, born a duke in Bavaria, had come in. The man in brown already had some knowledge of him, but only who he was and what he did as the chief of the SS counterintelligence division in Paris. He had not known that the man was one of Germany's former champions of foil and that he had studied a year at Harvard. Those details had not been in the file.

Dirk Drechsler was from New Braunfels, Texas, which happened to be the fleet-footed Chris Brandt's hometown, and lived in the same boardinghouse as Sam Barton, otherwise known as Dragonfly's Lodestar. Chris was now tutoring the son of the head of the Abwehr in France, who lived next door to *his* Dragonfly teammate, the fly-fishing Brad Hudson, who had become friendly with the same lad, the general's son. Could there be a greater muddle of his carefully laid plans to keep his operatives separate and safe?

Within the week had come other encrypted messages that threatened to produce the cardiac stroke his boss had predicted for him for years. Victoria had stumbled across Sam at his boardinghouse when she somehow tracked down Gabrielle Dupree for information about her missing fiancé, shot down in a bombing raid over a target near Paris. How Victoria had come by word that the proprietor had sheltered him—Alistair's sources had not identified the RAF pilots—might never come to light, but her visit explained her ulterior motive for joining the OSS. Madame Dupree was able to confirm her fiancé's death—this learned from his man in Paris after Gabrielle contacted him, not from Victoria or Sam, who had yet to inform Labrador of the chance encounter. Alistair would bet those two had decided to sit on that information because they knew he'd pull them out. The accidental meeting had put Gabrielle in danger and Sam in double jeopardy, first from the American traitor living under the same roof and the other from Victoria, now privy to his address.

It was Friday, October 30, thirty-seven days into the operation. Alistair's design to protect each member of Dragonfly by keeping them ignorant of one another's identities, cover names, addresses, and missions, their paths never to cross but in the natural flow of foot traffic in the Latin Quarter, had blown up in his face. His notion to assign the team the same dead drop and collection point hadn't been so sterling, either—sheer idiocy, in fact. According to his man in Paris, the mural was drawing so much attention that a French policeman with fascist leanings had been assigned to guard it. The situation had put Bridgette under his constant eye and increased the likelihood of the man noticing the same four faces passing regularly by the mail drop.

Bloody hell!

Alistair told himself that he could not have anticipated these latest developments. There were always cock-ups. The unexpected was the bane of every mission. But in this case, he couldn't help but blame himself, irrational though his thinking may be. He'd been delusional to think that a team of young, inexperienced, marginally trained, sheltered Americans set in a foreign country blatantly cooperative with their Nazi occupiers could escape detection. Dragonflies got eaten all the time.

That is, if they were caught.

So there was only one solution. He must get them out of Paris.

"Alistair, are you crazy?" Wild Bill Donovan exploded with rare anger at his top spymaster when Alistair called to state his proposal. "You will *not* jerk Dragonfly out of Paris on a notion that they are in imminent danger. So what? Every agent we send behind enemy lines is in *imminent* danger. Those kids are in prime locations to keep feeding us invaluable intel. My God, what more could we wish for? Lodestar hobnobbing with the Abwehr in the boardinghouse and Liverwort with the head of the CI division in Paris, Lapwing tutoring the son of the head of the Abwehr in France, Limpet the man's fly-fishing guide, and Labrador in a position to transmit it all back! They're in the perfect spots you trained and sent them to Paris for! Rather than flagellating yourself, you ought to be patting yourself on the back. You've managed one of the biggest coups in intelligence history, just based on their results so far. Why in hell would you want to bring them home?"

"Because their arrest is inevitable, Bill."

"How do you know? Nothing may come of these new revelations the kids have stumbled onto. Give them credit for the courage and resourcefulness to deal with them. They don't seem the type to turn tail and run at the first sign of trouble anyway."

That was what Alistair was afraid of. "I thought we agreed that at the first sign of danger to any of them, the decision was mine about when and if to exfiltrate them," he said.

"*We* agreed on no such thing. That was *your* idea hatched out of your emotional attachment to those kids, an involvement that I warned you to steer away from. No sir, you will *not* indulge your personal feelings at the forfeit of years of planning and the taxpayers' bill. Already that team has supplied us with some of the best intel we've had out of France so far. You can warn them of their danger, but they're to be given the chance to sink or swim on their own. It will be *their* decision to stay or go. Copy that?"

"I copy it, Colonel, but warning them of their individual threats by radio transmission is out of the question. I don't have time to work out a code anybody could make sense of, and the volume of information would keep my radio operator on the air too long. If you won't allow Dragonfly to come to me, I'll have to go to them. If you'll authorize transport, I can fly in and out of Paris within thirty-six hours, and—"

"Alistair, now I know you've lost your mind!" Wild Bill's voice rose to a roar. "I do not authorize you to do any such fool-crazy thing. Have you forgotten that you are well known to the German and Vichy police authorities? If you're snagged, God help us. Contact your boy in Paris by the usual channels. Let him be the bearer of your news. If they decide to get out, *then* and *only* then are you authorized to make arrangements for their exfiltration. Is that clear?" When Alistair did not at once respond, Wild Bill's tone softened. "Comfort yourself with the knowledge those kids knew what they were getting into when they signed up, Alistair. God knows you drilled it into their heads often enough."

"Doesn't make it any easier."

"Now you're being childish. Easy is not a player in this game, Major, as you well know. Those boys and girls are to stay in place unless they decide otherwise. That's an order."

The line went dead. Furious, Alistair slammed the

receiver into its cradle. Never in his career had he felt the urge to disobey orders until now. He didn't give a damn about the consequences, but his boss was right. It was too much of a risk to the OSS and SOE for him to show up in France, and Dragonfly was even better placed now to feed them the most reliable and accurate intel they would ever get out of Paris. Resistance groups and the military had already acted upon information the team had provided. A Gestapo general had been disposed of—quietly, to avoid reprisals—because his mistress, in being fitted for a new gown, had made no secret of the private party she was to attend with her lover. The RAF had taken out a secret Nazi facility in Norway on word leaked in Sam's engineering consulting firm that it contained a bomb under construction that could wipe out a small country. Sam had also managed to photograph blueprints of a Nazi laboratory under development to create chemicals of mass destruction and had made copies of drawings for a plant to produce gliders designed to carry a warhead capable of destroying a city.

Brad had reported information of a crucial store of naval mines hidden in a cove on Le Mont-Saint-Michel, an island commune off the northwestern coast of Normandy, to be buried along the region's shoreline in anticipation of an Allied invasion. A party of Maquis had swum ashore under cover of night, overtaken the guards, dismantled the fuses, and dumped the whole lot into the Couesnon River. Acting on Brad's intel, Norwegian partisans had successfully blown up a ship carrying armaments bound for the Russian front to relieve the German troops' dwindling supply.

Chris, living and working in hotbeds of gossip, had passed on a tip of an officer in the German High Command who picked up bed partners in bars catering to his gender, a penchant the Third Reich considered punishable by death but which made him ripe for blackmailing into working for the Allies. And Victoria had put the major onto a high-ranking German official furious with Hitler for bungling the war on the Russian front that had led to his son's death. When Alistair's man in Paris had approached the father to betray his country, he had readily agreed. So far, Dragonfly's intel had netted gold, and other nuggets had come in that might pan out.

Reluctantly, Alistair reached again for the phone. His man in Paris, Henri Burrell, was a longtime friend with whom he'd worked in the last war, a trusted associate of the French Vichy government with unlimited travel restrictions. Once contacted, his friend could be across the Swiss border into Bern and at their rendezvous point by lunchtime, then back in Paris by the dinner hour. Alistair would set up Henri's meeting with Dragonfly tomorrow at the café.

But Wild Bill Donovan's deputy would make one alteration to his boss's order. He would go ahead and arrange for a couple of Lysanders to be fueled up and ready to extract his operatives from Paris once Henri gave him the green light for takeoff.

CHAPTER THIRTY-NINE

That evening at eight o'clock on the dot, Bridgette faithfully withdrew her suitcase radio from a spacious recess hidden behind a panel concealed by an armoire in her attic room. The space had been built during the French Revolution to hide aristocrats on the run from the guillotine. She waited with no expectation that the wireless instrument, volume turned low, would speak to her. It seldom had, and then only briefly, in all the nights she'd sat before the box with pen and paper in hand. When she sent transmissions, the response was merely *Copy that. Great work.*

But this evening, the long and short sounds of *dit* and *dah* cracked the silence. Bridgette wrote hurriedly, for the transmission was brief. The decrypted message read: *D meet 1600/31.* Further transcribed, the text ordered Dragonfly to gather at four o'clock the following day, Saturday, October 31, at the tea and book shop. Bridgette stared at the summons in alarm. It meant that an emergency had flared up.

Bridgette tapped a reply: *Copy that. Awaiting further instructions.* An answer came back after several anxious minutes, as if the major was considering a reply: *Nothing more.*

She had no idea what times her teammates checked the wall during the weekdays or weekends. Her working hours were long. She was required to report to La Maison de Boucher by eight and did not return to the convent until six, and weekends her appearances to paint were irregular. So far no member of the team had left a code mark on their symbols, nor had she been called upon to leave messages for them. She had not seen a dragonfly since the operation began. Their intel appeared on the other side of the door of the mail drop as if deposited by ghosts. Bridgette guessed they melted in with the increased foot traffic taking the Rue des Soeurs de Charité on their way to and from work. Achim had spoken of no one suspicious, and Bridgette was sure that he would have bragged of accosting someone he even slightly suspected of mischief.

So, tomorrow, a few minutes prior to the lift of the

morning curfew, she would slip down to the mural before Achim Fleischer planted himself before the wall. He had told her proudly that he planned to stand his watch earlier than usual on Saturday mornings, when he calculated vandals would be most likely to strike between shifts of the German street patrols.

The policeman had surprised her. Bridgette had expected him to become bored with his sentry detail by now, but he basked in the attention he received as "guardian of the wall" and took great pride in his diligence that so far, he believed, had protected the mural from defacement. One day a small park bench, hand carpentered, had appeared beside the painting to give his legs a break. Residents dropped off cups of tea and occasionally, at the bidding of parents barely able to feed them, children slipped a sweet or item of fruit into Achim's hand. Daily, he was asked to pose for snapshots and sign autographs.

Bridgette's amazement at the neighborhood's reception of the mural was surprising as well. As word of the painting grew, it had gained an even broader audience. Residents from other districts had begun visiting it. German soldiers and their girlfriends sought it out on weekend strolls. Art students studied it as an exhibit. Flowers were left at the foot of the wall. At first, to explain her presence and allay suspicion should she have to stroke in a code mark, Bridgette made a point to appear with palette and brush to add more depth and color to a stargazer, a lily pad, a cloud. For Bridgette, her palette and brush provided escape from days of catering to the demands of revolting wives and mistresses whose illusions of superiority were based solely on the authority their husbands and lovers wielded over a subjected people. At times she almost forgot the purpose of the mural.

Afraid that she would oversleep, that night Bridgette hardly closed an eye. The penetrating cold made a good night's rest impossible anyway. A few days before, the farmer who had supplied wood for the convent had been shot for harboring a family of Jews. Fifteen minutes before six o'clock, Bridgette grabbed her brushes and paints and slipped down the flight of narrow stairs to the courtyard, creaked open the ancient door bolted during the night, and poked her head out. The street was empty and quiet but for the forlorn barking of a dog far off in the Latin Quarter. Quickly, under the murky glow of the blue-shrouded streetlamps, she drew a thin diagonal line through the mural's central dragonfly and added a few strokes of shadows to the other symbols as a warning to beware of a trap.

Minutes later, precisely at six o'clock, Achim Fleischer, beside himself, pounded on the bolted courtyard door until a little nun, dispatched from morning prayers, came running to see what the hammering was all about. She slid open the pocket door of the small window, and inquired, out of breath, how she might be of help to monsieur.

"You can unlock this damned door, for one!" Achim shouted into the wide eyes peering through the grillwork. Once the bolt was thrown, he pushed by the black-robed figure to march down the walk, fling open the convent door, and stomp into the nuns' communal living quarters demanding to see Sister Mary Frances. The mother superior appeared a few minutes later.

"What is this all about, Achim?"

"You must summon Mademoiselle Dufor, immediately!" he ordered.

"She is in bed."

"Wake her *up*!"

"May she be told why?"

"Somebody has desecrated the mural! And on my watch, too." Achim's vocal rage thinned to a whine like a sail suddenly depleted of wind power. "She's got to do something to repair it immediately before the Saturday crowd starts coming."

"She will be in her nightgown."

"I don't give a fiddler's...bow if she's wearing her birthday suit. Get her down here right now."

Sister Mary Frances turned calmly to one of her charges. "Pray be good enough to summon Mademoiselle Dufor, Sister."

"And tell her to bring a paint cleaner!" Achim shouted to the nun's retreating back.

Bridgette, shivering in her night-robe, considered the "desecrated" dragonfly and Achim's assertion that "something different" had also been done to the painting that he couldn't figure out.

"Achim, the only change I see is a thin white line of a medium I can't identify drawn through a dragonfly, not enough to disfigure the mural. The stone is porous, so I must determine the correct cleaning product to remove it. Mineral spirits and turpentine will only smear it."

"No they won't. You primed the wall. I saw you. The mark should come off easily. Give me that turpentine and I'll show you!" Achim reached to snatch the bottle of paint remover from Bridgette's hand.

Bridgette whipped the container behind her back, heart pounding. The diagonal line must stay untouched. "No!" she said. "You'll ruin the dragonfly. I will not be able to restore it as it once was. The mural is *my* work of art, not yours, Achim. You're just upset because you think the mark is somebody's way of thumbing their nose at you, but it's just a tweak, *mon ami*, barely noticeable." She put a hand on his arm and said quietly, "Be thankful it wasn't worse. The fact that it wasn't shows respect for the mural and for you. It was just a small prank done without malice, not likely to happen again."

The fire dimmed in Achim's eyes. He enjoyed the gentle touch of Mademoiselle Dufor's hand on his arm, and he had just noticed the outline of her body through her flowing night-robe. "My sister had trouble correcting her artwork with turpentine, now that I remember," he acquiesced. "All right. I'll let it stand. You are shivering. Forgive me. You must go inside, but if I ever catch the person who did this…"

"I'm sure that person will be in serious trouble," Bridgette said.

CHAPTER FORTY

Dirk Drechsler studied Stephane Beaulieu over his coffee cup on this last morning of October. Dirk was drinking a *noisette*—an espresso with just a splash of milk. Stephane was sipping barley roasted with chicory. Privately, Dirk had invited him to share his ration—he really didn't care for the dark French coffee as he did not like the milder-roasted stuff the Germans swilled—but the engineer had politely declined, as Dirk had expected. Stephane was not the type to partake of food or drink that the other French boarders were not offered. Dirk wondered if the Frenchman was aware of his scrutiny. He ate his eggless pancakes with a dab of jam at one end of Madame Dupree's breakfast table with the French boarders while Dirk chowed down on sausage and fried eggs with the captain and lieutenant at the other, each group speaking in their native language.

Dirk wondered if Stephane Beaulieu was aware of his increased interest in him, period. During this past week during the few occasions they had been in the same room, Dirk could not seem to tear his attention away from the engineer's every word. Dirk had been busy with a huge roundup of Jews whose interviews, transport to concentration camps, and executions he'd had to document and file. Nazis were obsessively meticulous record keepers no matter how abominable the acts they felt it necessary to chronicle for posterity. At the end of every long day, Dirk had trudged back to the boardinghouse more determined than ever to get out of France and back to his homeland, and Stephane Beaulieu was his ticket to get there.

After last Sunday, Dirk was fully convinced that the man was more than just a civil engineer who reported to his consulting firm every day and came home to eat stewed cabbage and potatoes. That stunning girl who'd appeared at the boardinghouse last Sunday was from somewhere in his past. The girl was enough to knock the socks off any man, which would explain Stephane's reaction to her, but not her reaction to Stephane. She'd recognized him, but not as someone who reminded her of a deceased acquaintance, despite the story Madame Dupree had taken pains to tell at supper. The look in the girl's eyes was not from seeing a ghost. There was no mistaking that she and Stephane knew each other, as there was no doubt of their mutual decision to remain quiet about it. Madame Dupree had hustled her out before a word could be exchanged between them, a cause for Dirk to wonder about his landlady. Of course the scene in the kitchen could have meant nothing. Maybe Stephane and the girl had once had a thing going and decided not to make a deal of it in front of everybody, and Madame Dupree had sensed the tension. She was an intuitive old bag. Dirk would have questioned Stephane about it, but he'd not wanted to alert the engineer that he was onto him. For the time being, the guy's relationship with the girl must remain a mystery.

What wasn't a mystery was the fact that Stephane Beaulieu was apparently well acquainted with General Nicholas Cravois. Unless Dirk had mistaken the identity of the man, the embrace and Beaulieu's knowledge of the most secret address in Paris proved a special association between them, a point that would work in Dirk's favor when it came time to bargain with the Black Ghost. Dirk could have reported his information and Stephane to the captain and earned credit for the biggest catch in the history of German intelligence, but to hell with that. He intended to use Stephane to get General Cravois to help him. Among other crimes against the Third Reich for which the Black Ghost was wanted, the general ran a well-organized network of escape lines that helped Allied personnel, Jews, and political dissidents get to freedom. Dirk planned to grab that ride out of France. And if possible, he wanted to do it without involving Stephane Beaulieu more than he had to. He seemed decent, and Dirk wasn't too keen on having the Frenchman arrested and interrogated by the monsters he worked with, but that would be up to him.

But he must be careful not to move too fast. He would curb his impatience until he'd collected enough information too indisputable for the Frenchman to refuse him. Today was Dirk's first off-duty Saturday in a month. The captain and the lieutenant were leaving shortly to attend a company soccer game, then spend the rest of the evening partying with the players. Of course, he'd not been invited to go along. To hell with them. He had better things to do. The Frenchman's coat hung on a peg in the hallway. He had brought it with him when he came down to breakfast. Dirk had immediately hurried upstairs and slipped back down with a bag containing a civilian coat, hat, and muffler as a disguise to wear over his uniform when he followed him, explaining the sack as containing old clothes he would be donating to the corner Catholic church for their rummage sale. Maybe the Frenchman would lead him back to Nicholas Cravois.

While waiting for his luncheon guests to arrive, Major General Konrad March opened the diplomatic pouch the courier had just delivered. The sealed bag held a dispatch from his direct superior and mentor, Admiral Wilhelm Canaris, commander in chief of the Abwehr, headquartered in Berlin. Konrad read with a sinking heart that the admiral was planning to pay him a visit the following Saturday, November 7. That was the date Konrad had tickets to the much-anticipated premiere of *Les Visiteurs du Soir*. Only a select few had been invited, and today he planned to ask Madame Gastain to be his guest. Since she had agreed to come to his luncheon, he hoped she would accept his invitation to the evening affair and perhaps dinner afterward. Perhaps Konrad could induce the admiral to retire early.

Konrad shook his head as he read the encrypted message. Wilhelm should be more careful with the content he dispatched in his diplomatic pouches. In spite of diplomatic custom, no messages were safe coming out of Germany these days. The admiral's dispatch purportedly alerted Konrad to his forthcoming visit, but evident between the encrypted lines was his superior's disgust at the needless carnage resulting from Hitler's running of the war. The dispatch reported that on October 29, on Hitler's orders, sixteen thousand Jews were murdered at Pinsk in the Soviet Union. In October alone, ninety-four German U-boats had been sunk due to the growing superiority of Allied sea and air power.

Konrad was continually surprised that the Führer hadn't yet caught on to the admiral's sedition. As early as 1935, his appointed head of the intelligence branch of the German Army had been behind some of the subversive tactics to undermine him. In September 1939, having already witnessed the German Army's savagery against Polish civilians, the admiral lost all stomach for the Third Reich when SS troops locked two hundred Polish Jews into a synagogue in Będzin, Poland, and set it afire. Fearing for the future of his country, his friend had then attempted and failed to negotiate a separate peace with Allied officials to prevent further slaughter. Under the ever-alert noses of the SS, the Abwehr's archenemy, Wilhelm had arranged for the rescue of a number of Jews doomed to the concentration camps, sent reports to the Vatican detailing Nazi atrocities with the hope that the pope would intervene, and prevented the killing of nineteen captured French officers in Tunisia. Konrad wouldn't have been surprised if his commander in chief had been involved in the unsuccessful coup attempts to assassinate the leader he had come to despise. How these acts of rebellion had not been detected, Konrad didn't know, but his luck was bound to run out, and with it, perhaps that of his protégé in France as well—guilty of treason by friendship.

His mentor's visit meant trouble, and for the first time in a long while—not since before the war, actually—Konrad had entered a period of relative peace and contentment in his life. He'd drawn an impenetrable line between his home and workplace, where he was devoting less and less time. He was tired of war, having fought in two, and weary of his duties that so often involved the basest actions against his fellow man—and all for the sake of an ideology and a Führer he no longer believed in.

The fisherman next door and the tutor he'd hired

had made the difference. Konrad now came home to a happy child who did not take off to his room after a silent supper he barely ate. Now Wilhelm could not wait to tell his *Vater* of his day, of the things he'd learned, the fish he'd caught, the games he'd played. His little boy had filled out in appetite, muscle, and mind, and Konrad owed it all to the two young men who had entered their lives.

It was primarily for Barnard and Claus that he was giving this luncheon today. That Madame Gastain would be coming was extra sugar on the cake. Konrad had thought it a stretch to think it only appropriate to invite Madame Gastain, since he invited her tenant, but to his amazement and delight she had accepted. Perhaps the woman was hungry, or tired of fish.

But he had thought it most certainly fitting to do something to express his gratitude to the two young men who had breathed new life into his son. When Konrad had brought home a large leg of lamb confiscated from the stash of an arrested French black marketeer, his immediate thought was to share it with Barnard and Claus. It was time the two young men met anyway, since Konrad was sure they'd heard so much of each other from his son.

Hans appeared at the door of his study. "Your

guests are arriving, Herr General, and young Wilhelm cannot contain his excitement."

"Madame Gastain as well?"

"Yes, Herr General."

"I will be right there." The dispatch was still in his hand. No time to destroy it. The closest fire burned in the drawing room grate, a matter of forced firewood conservation, even for the head of the Abwehr in France. The admiral's message would be safe on his desk until he could destroy it later with others reserved for his study's fireplace. His concern that Barnard Wagner might be some sort of spy was almost shameful now that he'd become better acquainted with the boy.

CHAPTER FORTY-ONE

In the Saturday morning quiet of the relatively empty headquarters of the Sicherheitsdienst, the security service of the SS and the Nazi Party, Colonel Derrick Albrecht finished reading the report of Veronique Colbert's real identity. The information had come from a German-born naturalized American citizen transmitting to the Sicherheitsdienst on a secret shortwave radio on Long Island in New York. Not a single fact in the report surprised him. Having spent only a short time in Mademoiselle Colbert's company and without a shred of information about her true background, he could have written the dossier himself. Victoria Grayson came from a line of titled paternal and maternal English ancestors stretching back to the barons who forced King John of England to sign the Magna Carta, and as American aristocracy went, both sides could claim a seat. Victoria Grayson's family tree seated a number of important political figures, high-placed judges, eminent physicians, inventors, educators, and Wall Street financiers from both branches who had done their part to do their progenitors proud. There wasn't a black sheep among the generations apparently.

He ran his eye down the page. Education: William and Mary, Phi Beta Kappa, with a degree in Franco studies. And her fencing instructor had been none other than the college's acclaimed master of foil, Tucker Jones.

Well, well, well. Colonel Albrecht reached forward on his desk and lifted the lid of a humidor that bore his family's heraldic crest. He removed a Montecristo #2, withdrew a cigar cutter and butane lighter from a drawer, and sat back to perform the ritual required to enjoy the finest "smoke"—as the Americans would call it—in the world while he contemplated what to think about Victoria Grayson. To prepare a Cuban cigar properly for smoking required patience and tranquility, the perfect occupation to induce clear thinking.

Once the smoke of woody, leathery flavors were afloat in the air, and he felt the light, pleasant burn at the back of his palate, he reached a conclusion about the deceptive Victoria Grayson. His first assumption, that she'd been too late to leave Paris after Germany declared war against the United States, had been almost correct. The report stated that in late September of this year, Victoria Grayson had disappeared from her country. Her parents were under the impression that she was doing some secret government work for the U.S. State Department. Rubbish! After reading in the dossier of her engagement to an American RAF pilot feared dead after his plane went down near Paris during a bombing raid, Derrick Albrecht had no trouble believing their daughter had somehow found a way to smuggle herself into France to learn what had happened to him. It was something a girl of her spunk would do.

He was almost certain she'd discovered that the pilot had not survived. The previous Sunday, he'd had her followed to a boardinghouse in the Latin Quarter, owned by a Madame Dupree. His trusted wolfhound had reported that Mademoiselle Colbert had entered, then left a half hour later to walk to a church park several blocks away, where she had been joined not long afterward by a middle-aged woman who handed the girl something. After a brief conversation, she bent her head as if she were crying. Then the woman returned to the boardinghouse, and mademoiselle walked to the train station. His man reported that Mademoiselle Colbert had looked out the window of her metro seat the entire way to L'Ecole d'Escrime Français, and in the light of the passing trains he could see tears on her face.

The report explained her distress when she'd walked into the fencing hall later that same Sunday. She had insisted that nothing was wrong, but her play had been so distracted that he'd called a halt minutes into the bout. She'd been grateful and confessed, "I am not well today." He had expressed his concern—genuine, as it happened—and offered to drive her home, but she'd refused. He had not insisted, but he'd had her followed to make sure she arrived at her hotel safely. The next day, he'd sent her flowers that probably ended up in a wastebasket. He could have Madame Dupree brought in for questioning, but he did not want Victoria Grayson alerted to his inquiries nor did he want to risk alienating her until he learned all about her. But he would keep the name of the proprietress of the boardinghouse in his files. He had become…taken with Mademoiselle Veronique Colbert. Thinking of her beauty shone a light in the darkest corners of his life, and she was among the most challenging bout partners he'd ever met on the piste.

"Herr Colonel?" Karl, his aide-de-camp and man-of-all-purposes, interrupted his thoughts from the doorway of his office. "There is a Monsieur Beaumont Fournier to see you."

"The author?"

"Yes. He says it's urgent."

"It must be for him to appear at Sicherheitsdienst headquarters on a Saturday morning. I would think he'd be sleeping off last night's coitus activities with his latest paramour."

His aide smirked. "I don't like his writing."

"Neither do I, almost as much as I don't like him. Send him in, Karl."

To avert a French greeting, the colonel stood when his guest entered, but did not move from behind his desk. The author took the hint and, ever his unctuous, effusive self, approached Derrick with a large smile and outstretched hand. "Your Grace," he said with a dip of his head. Inwardly, Derrick winced. "Your Grace" applied to ducal lords of England. "So good to see you."

"Yes, well, this is where I am most usually seen," the colonel said, shaking his visitor's hand.

"Ah, yes, most, but not always, no? Your manservant told me I'd find you here this Saturday morning." He shivered in his overcoat. "Let us hope this last day of October is not a precursor of the winter to come. May I?" He gestured toward a chair before the desk.

Warily, Derrick nodded. "By all means. What can I do for you?"

"Oh no, no—not what *you* can do for me, Duke, but what *I* can do for you. Is that a Montecristo I smell?" The author's glance skewed toward the humidor.

"It is," Derrick said, ignoring his visitor's hint to be offered one of the treasures in the box. "How may you be of help to me?"

The author settled for fitting a Gauloises into a slender cigarette holder. "I've information about a young woman that I know to be an American living in Paris under an assumed name and pretending to be French. She goes by the name Veronique Colbert, but her name is really Victoria Grayson, and she is employed as a fencing instructor at L'Ecole d'Escrime Français here in Paris. I believe you fence there?"

Derrick felt his shoulder muscles tighten. Casually, he drew on the Montecristo. "That is so. How do you know her?"

"I met her in New York. She was working as a French translator at the publishing house that acquired the rights to my international best seller,

Cathédrale de Silence. Perhaps you've read it?" Beaumont held a lighter to the tip of his cigarette.

The colonel inclined his head. "I have." *With all due haste*, he thought. "Do you fence?"

"Not at all."

"Then how did you come across Mademoiselle Colbert?"

The author blew out a stream of smoke and chuckled. "Oh, come now, Your Grace. You can't pretend you don't know her. Your association with her, whatever it is, is safe with me. I know the importance of discretion. I saw Victoria Grayson dining with you at the Ritz one Sunday not a month ago. It did not take much checking to learn of her employment and your association at the fencing school. That's why I am here. I wanted to warn you to be careful of what you say around her. I believe she could have been sent here to spy. I can't imagine any other reason for her to be in Paris in a time of war with her country, can you?"

"For the moment I can't think of any, no."

Beaumont turned his head to one side to expel another casual stream of smoke. "I hope the colonel can appreciate that I am sensitive to his embarrassment should the Gestapo learn that the head of its brother organization was unaware of the danger

Mademoiselle Colbert poses to the security service of the Reichsführer."

The colonel's brow rose a fraction. "You plan to take this information to the Gestapo?"

"That is my plan, yes. Again, my reason is plain. I wish to spare the duke the... unpleasantness of interrogating a beautiful woman in whom it would be understandable if he had more than a casual interest. She has a distinctive regal manner. I wouldn't doubt but that there is royal blood from somewhere back in her lineage. It takes a European to see it."

"It does indeed. You seem to know a lot about... this young woman. Did you spend time with her in New York?"

"Only a brief few hours. There wasn't much time to... get to know her. My visa was soon to expire."

"An annoying interference to the objective you had in mind and most certainly would have achieved, I've no doubt."

A flicker in the author's eyes confirmed to Derrick that all the time in the world would not have achieved what he had in mind for Victoria Grayson. Beaumont Fournier had come to betray her for her rejection of him. "Yes, most annoying," he said smoothly.

"Well then, Monsieur Fournier, it is most kind of you to be concerned for my welfare," Derrick said.

"You must tell me how I can express my gratitude." He glanced at the wall clock. "But before you do, it is my habit to have a cup of coffee this time of morning. Perhaps you'd care to join me?" He nodded toward a sideboard. "There are fresh croissants, as well."

"No croissants, *s'il vous plaît*, but I would very much appreciate a cup of coffee. I am recovering from…an arduous night."

The colonel returned his visitor's man-to-man smile. "But none too stressful to be enjoyed, I hope." He punched a button on his desk. "Karl," he said into the intercom, "bring us two cups of coffee, the kind we serve to special visitors."

"Yes, Herr Colonel," came the reply.

Ten minutes later, the author of *Cathédrale de Silence* lay sprawled in his chair awaiting disposal by the usual means. His eyes were staring and mouth gawping in horrified realization of his immediate death, and the duke was not disposed to close them. The author had died of cyanide poisoning.

CHAPTER FORTY-TWO

After giving Dirk Drechsler sufficient time to be off, Bucky headed for the metro that would deposit him within a few blocks of the site of the mural. He had delayed his departure until the sergeant had left the boardinghouse. Bucky had not wanted to risk the man foisting his company on him, or worse, following him. The traitor—a *Texan*, no less! There was no mistaking that accent—had taken a disturbing interest in him.

At first he'd thought the attraction had to do with his longing for a friend. The guy was pathetically lonely. If Bucky hadn't despised him, he'd have felt sorry for him. His Nazi cohorts treated him like a stray dog cowering up to the back porch looking for handouts and wanted no part of him. Bucky had thought at first that the sergeant, desperate for companionship, had singled him out for no reason other than he needed a buddy, but he had given him no opening for friendship. It had been a strain to avoid him, but Bucky thought he'd successfully prevented any chance of the guy picking up a trace of behavior or speech that would betray him as a fellow American. Now, though, he wasn't so sure.

Doubt had set in the morning following his meeting with his father in Honfleur almost three weeks before. At breakfast, Bucky had felt a definite change in the sergeant's notice of him, heightened last Sunday after he witnessed Bucky's shocked reaction at seeing Liverwort in Madame Dupree's kitchen. Drechsler had thrown him a look as plain to read as the Nazi ACHTUNG signs set on every street corner. Drechsler impressed him as short on intelligence but long on instinct, and the knowing glance he'd flashed him as he left the kitchen two Sundays ago told Bucky that he *knew* he and Liverwort recognized each other and had kept silent, the question of *why* clear in Drechsler's eyes. To cover the moment, Madame Dupree had casually mentioned at the supper table that monsieur had made her friend think she was seeing a ghost, he looked so much like someone now dead that she'd once known. Drechsler had looked as if he wasn't buying it, and fear had coiled in Bucky's gut that the turncoat might begin to sniff around the engineer's job at a firm handling sensitive Nazi construction projects. Whether that flash of instinct included suspicion that Stephane Beaulieu was as American as he was, Bucky had no idea.

Of course there might be another explanation for the sergeant's sharper attention. It was a stretch, but maybe the guy felt a romantic attraction to him. That was hardly attention he'd welcome, but a safer possibility than the others. Maybe he'd seen the beautiful Liverwort as competition. Whatever was behind the drill of those small, narrowed eyes, it was one more situation that Bucky knew he should report to the major, but he had held off. The other was his kitchen encounter with Liverwort. Their case officer would judge both as grounds for extractions, but Bucky wasn't ready to abort his mission, not now that he was firmly in place. He was sure that Liverwort felt the same. Until he received orders from headquarters, he'd say nothing and do nothing, and he'd bet that Liverwort wouldn't, either. He'd just have to be extra careful around Drechsler. Given time, the guy was bound to reveal his hand, and then Bucky would decide his next move.

The smell and crush of passengers on the metro to the Place Saint-Michel to check the mural made

Bucky recall his trip to Honfleur and the reunion with his father. It had been a time of both pain and joy, a space of a few hours locked forever in his memory. An old woman showed him into the room where the legend sat cross-legged in a chair, a heavily draped window behind him. Never would Bucky forget the moment that he first laid eyes upon Nicholas Cravois, the storied Black Ghost—his father. He wore a beard and was bonier than Bucky had expected. The hardships of war and guerilla life had worn his tall frame to a razor sharpness. It took a son to detect his own likeness, and he could see it in his father's body structure and eyes with their chameleon irises and thick lashes. They had stared at each other in a moment of breath-held silence, and then the legend had risen and spread wide his arms. "You have your mother's shy smile," he'd said in French. "The rest I can claim. Hello, my son."

"You were brave to come over here to do what you are doing," his father told him later, even though he'd ordered Bucky not to tell him his exact mission and place of work. It was dangerous enough that he knew his son's address.

"Not really. I came solely to find you. The rest is...incidental."

"But equally as perilous and risky."

"Like father, like son."

"A pity," he'd said with a smile that expressed both regret and pride. His father had questioned him about his home, his education, the sports he liked. "Tell me about your life," he'd invited.

So, while hardened men strapped with guns had stood lookout at doors and windows, and the old woman in her faded kerchief and apron had slipped in silently to serve them a bitter tea, Bucky had covered the missing years in Oklahoma.

"You learned the truth of your mother and me when you were fourteen, so I understand from your aunt."

"Yes sir. By accident."

"Does your mother know that...you know?"

"No sir, and Aunt Claire has vowed never to tell her."

His father had wanted to know if his mother was happy. "Content, I'd say," Bucky had replied.

"Ah," he'd said, nodding in approval. "That is good. Happiness is most often short-lived. Contentment is more durable."

His father asked if his family knew where he was and what he was doing in France, and Bucky had said they'd been told only that he was secluded in a highly secret job for the War Department and could not be contacted. Aunt Claire had promised not to reveal to them that he was in France.

"Aunt Claire possesses information not safe for us or her. I have made arrangements to get her out of Paris tonight. If you ever need to contact me—but only in case of extreme emergency," his father warned, "leave word in the cavity of the plane tree in the park across from her chateau. It is the one that shades the bench by the stream. Should I need to contact you, you will find a black mark on the right underside of the first step of your boardinghouse. Couriers are too risky. Go to the tree."

"Yes sir," Bucky said.

Otherwise, they were not to meet again until the war was over. It was too perilous for them both. The house in Honfleur was to be closed, and his aunt's chateau vacated but for a caretaker. Nicholas Cravois would disappear into the mountains, and Bucky would not see him again until France was liberated. Then he would contact him and they would reunite. "However," he'd said, holding his son's gaze with eyes the changeable hues of Bucky's own, "if I do not survive, promise me that your American father will never learn the truth of your birth."

"I promise," Bucky had said.

Bucky had been thankful that Aunt Claire would

be out of Paris. One more door closed to his discovery, he'd thought, until another had opened up with the unexpected appearance of Liverwort at the boardinghouse. Captain Achterberg had not noticed her start at seeing him, only her beauty. "Amazing," he'd said. "I wonder who she is."

"I haven't the faintest idea," Bucky said.

He was approaching the convent wall. Despite the biting cold, since houses and apartments were no warmer anyway, a small group had gathered around the mural and others were approaching. Even on this freezing Saturday the usual policeman was standing about, puffed up with self-importance, mouth clamped tight and eyes steely beneath his billed cap. Bucky drew up behind a man whose height and size blocked him from the sweep of the cop's surveillance and spotted the diagonal mark drawn through the central dragonfly. His heart did a little somersault when he noted the slightly deeper clouding of the tip of the North Star and the subtly darker shadings on the other code symbols.

Coat collar up and head drawn into his shoulders ostensibly for warmth, Bucky walked away quickly. He saw no sign of the others. He would not know which or if any member of Dragonfly had gotten Labrador's message until they showed up in the tearoom today at four o'clock. No code had been devised for "message received."

The engineer had not seen him, Dirk assured himself in satisfaction as he settled down at his observation post to await the Frenchman's next move. He'd have liked the Nazi jerks who'd jeered at him in surveillance-training classes to have witnessed his street skills in avoiding detection after one hell of a long and boring day tailing his mark. Dirk could remember his instructor saying, "Herr Drechsler, in a yard of beehives, you would be about as undetectable as a bear in a beekeeper's veil." Well, he wished that horse's butt could have observed his tradecraft management today. It wasn't as if shadowing Beaulieu had been a walk in the park. As a matter of fact, the engineer seemed to have knowledge of a few tradecraft tricks himself. Every now and then he'd glance back over his shoulder or stop before a shop window, his gaze not on the display of goods but on the reflection in the glass of the street activity behind him. Now why was that? To see if he was being followed? It was another question mark to chalk up in the Stephane Beaulieu column.

It was now fifteen minutes until four o'clock. Dirk had tailed the engineer from the boardinghouse to the metro through the Latin Quarter in the opposite direction of Honfleur. There he'd walked aimlessly with no apparent destination in mind. He'd taken a gander at a painting on the wall of a convent with a lot of other people standing around admiring it. It was a thing of beauty dabbled on stone by somebody who must have wanted to bring a little sunshine to the street—the saints bless 'em, as his Lutheran mother would say. Then on the Frenchman had sauntered to the shops and bistros in the twisting streets of the fourteenth arrondissement. He had remained nowhere long. Then the engineer had checked his watch and set off with more purpose until just a few minutes ago, when he'd entered a little out-of-the-way tea and book shop up from the Catacombs. Dirk's heart had begun to thump. The spot showed promise. Was Stephane meeting Nicholas Cravois there?

The street offered no protected site for street surveillance, but up ahead was a bell tower that looked older than his great-grandfather's hay barn and as much in need of repair. The minute Stephane disappeared into the bookshop, Dirk hurried to it and found a joke of a rusted lock on the door. He picked it easily and creaked the door open on a small entryway. A flight of narrow stairs led to the belfry, which looked too rickety to hold his weight. Several loopholes were strategically placed around the chamber that allowed in air and afforded an outside view. Birds had built nests in them. Dirk cleared the one that gave him an unobstructed view of the street and shop across the way. If he could endure the cold and rat droppings under his feet and the squeaks and scurry of little feet in the belfry overhead, the opening offered an ideal lookout point.

CHAPTER FORTY-THREE

Nothing seemed to have changed in the last weeks. The dim light and smell of old books, stale tea leaves, and acrid cigarette smoke were the same but for the deeper damp and cold, and a sputter of heat emanating from a floor heater. The same proprietor swiped a towel over the counter in the book room, the same patron sat reading and smoking at the corner table by the window of the tea shop. No one else was present. Bucky took a seat at the same table in the same chair he'd occupied before, his apprehension growing. He was early, but he'd expected at least Labrador to be here ahead of him—that is, if she were still alive and this meeting was not a trap. As a precaution for a quick exit and an inducement for the Frenchman to leave, Bucky got up and approached his table.

The stub ends of half a dozen Gauloises filled the ashtray of his chair arm.

"Pardon, monsieur," Bucky said. "Do you mind if I open the door?"

The Frenchman took a deep drag of his cigarette and did not look up from his reading. "*Non,*" he said.

As Bucky opened the door to the outside court, a clatter of voices filtered into the room, dear and familiar, and he turned to see Labrador entering, the others behind her, all accounted for. They fanned around him, and after the joyful embraces and handshakes, Bucky asked Bridgette in French, keeping his voice low for the sake of the customer in the corner, "What is this all about?"

"I don't have a clue," Bridgette answered. "All I know is that the major told me to summon you."

The Frenchman closed his book, stubbed out his cigarette, and maneuvered his substantial girth from the tight squeeze between table and chair. "I can answer your question," he said in English, accented by French, and reclosed the exit door. "No one is here but us, and the OUVRIR sign has been turned to FERMÉ in the window. We are alone."

The Dragonfly team stiffened and stared at him.

The Frenchman held up his large hands in surrender. "I am Major Alistair Renault's contact in Paris. He has asked that I meet with you to give you crucial information that cannot be related over the wireless. There have been unexpected developments that jeopardize your covers and increase the risk to your lives. After you hear what I've been dispatched to report, you are to make a decision, but individually, not as a committee. Your decisions are not to be put to...how do you say in America?...a vote."

"How do we know we can trust you?" Bridgette demanded.

"You don't, my dear, but I would strongly advise you to do so."

"How do we know that Major Renault sent you?" Victoria asked.

The Frenchman handed over a sheet from a notepad filled with Alistair Renault's characteristic doodles, one of which was a dragonfly. "That is how. Also, the major has a particular fondness for Lucky Strike cigarettes. I can't stand them myself, far too mild, but then each man to his own vices. Shall we sit down?"

The team pulled out chairs, eyes glued to the Frenchman, and Brad got right to the point. "Okay, let's hear it. What's the information?"

The Frenchman sat forward and laced his broad

fingers together on the table. "I shall try to recite it as clearly and thoroughly as Major Renault related it to me. I believe I am speaking to Labrador, Liverwort, Limpet, Lodestar, and Lapwing, yes?" At no affirmation of this statement, the Frenchman continued. "Of course, for your security's sake, I am not to know the face that belongs to each code name, so I shall simply lay out the details of each individual's situation as if they were cards on a table, and you pick which one applies to you. I would suggest that neither by comment nor facial expression nor glance are you to reveal to me who is who or which card pertains to you."

The Frenchman noted that their healthy, rosy, American faces had begun to show signs of stress and the austerity of their living conditions. A shame. They had arrived as such a winsome group. "We will begin with the code name Liverwort. You have made the acquaintance of one of the most dangerous Nazis in Paris, who appears to have taken an interest in you. You need to know that he spent a year in graduate school at Harvard University in the United States, where he honed an already facile command of English. He is a master linguist with fluency in numerous languages and is known for his extraordinary ability to detect dialects and accents—a great asset in his job, Major Renault asked that I stress."

All faces remained rigidly focused on him and none paled, but if the Frenchman was called upon to guess, he would venture that the card belonged to the tall, stately beauty who seemed the most changed of all in her time in Paris. A light had gone out behind her reserved exterior, somewhat like a lamp usually seen aglow through the curtains of an elegant abode now extinguished, leaving one to wonder about the occupant inside. Colonel Albrecht came from among the oldest lines of aristocrats in Europe. Of the group, she was the only one who would be of interest to him.

He moved on to the other code names, his listeners' eyes on him still as stones. "Lodestar, this card is for you. You have several problems that threaten your safety. By a fluke of chance, Liverwort has made the discovery of your address, and as I assume you are only too aware, a sergeant in the German Army, born and reared in America, is a boarder under your roof. He works for the Abwehr here in Paris, and his job is to serve as an interpreter for the interrogations of Allied prisoners. Needless to point out, that situation creates a grave danger for you and the others."

No one moved a muscle, but the Frenchman could feel the room fill with tension. He'd have liked another cigarette, but the distraction might break their attention. "There is more," he said. "Not only is the Abwehr sergeant sharing quarters with Lodestar, but he happens to be from Lapwing's hometown in America. They grew up together as neighbors. His name is Dirk Drechsler."

The group met this information with the mute astonishment of board members watching a grenade roll into the conference room. The Frenchman had expected a rise from one of them at the name of the American, but none bit. A well-trained bunch. "I am afraid there is even more," he said. "The major general in charge of the Abwehr has become friendly with Limpet, who lives next door to him. As happenstance would have it, the general has engaged Lapwing in a capacity that is likely to put him in the path of Limpet. Major Renault instructed me to say that the two to whom the information applies will understand the ramifications of this unexpected turn of events."

The Frenchman avoided looking at Bridgette, who he would have bet his last pack of Gauloises was Labrador, Alistair's favorite. "One last item pertains to Labrador," he said. "A French policeman is glued to your side. The man has been accepted into the Vichy Milice when it goes into operation in January. Major Renault felt that was enough information to make you aware of the danger the policeman poses to you and your assignment."

Henri unlaced his hands and sat back. "Now, mademoiselles and messieurs," he said with the satisfied air of a messenger having safely delivered the goods, "I have put all the cards on the table, as you would say. It is up to you to do what you will with them."

Now he could smoke. He drew out a pack of Gauloises. He loathed the evil-tasting things, but they were an addiction. The light at the window had vanished and the room was filling with dusk. The cold had seeped in, forcing the group to draw their coats closer around them. Before lighting up, he held a match to the wick of a table candle stuck in a wine bottle encrusted with years of molten wax drippings, then to the tip of the Gauloises, sat back, and waited. The silence was as thick as the smoke clouding the room.

Bridgette spoke. "What do we call you?"

The Frenchman blew out a spiral of smoke and answered blandly, "No name."

"Fair enough. 'No Name' it is. So what is the decision we're to make, No Name?"

"Whether or not to leave France. You can all go to your safe houses, wait for your pickups, and be airlifted out of the country before dawn. A couple of Lysanders are standing by in England, fueled and ready for me to send word to Major Renault. I was instructed to tell you that by tomorrow evening, you can be enjoying a pint at the…Crown and Scepter, I believe your major called it. By midweek, you will be back in your hometowns, reunited with your families in time for the feast day Thanksgiving." Alistair had expressly told him to emphasize that last item. It was the carrot he was to wiggle before their noses, and indeed a few of their expressions flared briefly at the mention of it.

There was a shifting in seats, a cough, a clearing of a throat. Even now, released from their orders, the team did not speak or look at one another. Finally, the well-muscled, dark-haired young man the Frenchman took to be Limpet lifted his hand. "A question."

"By all means," Henri Burrell said.

"Has our intel proved valuable?"

Alistair's man in Paris hesitated, then answered reluctantly, "Yes."

"How valuable?"

"Invaluable."

Another hand went up, that of the petite Labrador. Henri nodded at her. "Does the major have replacements for us?"

Another hesitancy. Then, unwillingly: "No."

After a moment, Bridgette surveyed the group. "Well, what do you say, troops?"

No immediate response. The Frenchman was also adroit at interpreting body gestures and movements. The fellow with the familiar brow line and eyes that reminded him of somebody he couldn't place rubbed the bridge of his nose, the petite spokeswoman had pursed her lips, and Lapwing, the sleek-lined lad missing a thumb, drummed the table with four fingertips—all indications of deep reflection. Only the reserved Liverwort remained still as a bust, a message in itself. The Frenchman felt his hopes drop for his friend Alistair. *Those kids are tight as a pride of lions*, Alistair had said. *You and I know, Henri, about the strength and durability of human bonds forged in times of war. I'm afraid that if one stays, they all stay, out of some misguided feeling of loyalty to one another. You've got to talk them out of that foolishness, Henri. You've got to convince them that united they fall. Divided, they stand.*

Poetically put, but perfectly true, and Henri was indeed aware of graveyards on two continents strewn with the dead from two wars who'd belonged to the one-for-all-and-all-for-one club. "Well, my friends?" he prompted.

Bridgette lifted a brow at the others. Their answer was a unified silence. She turned to the Frenchman. "Give us a little time to think about it and discuss, monsieur?"

Henri shook his head. "I must repeat: Discussion is against the rules. Each of you is to decide for yourselves what you wish to do. Besides, what is there to think about and discuss?"

"You've given us a lot to digest," Bucky said.

Henri whirled a hand as if directing a plane in for a risky landing. "What is there to digest?" he asked incredulously. "You are all in danger of discovery!"

"Actually, I'm not so sure that's true of me," Brad said.

"Or of me, either," Chris remarked.

"What difference does that make?" Henri looked thunderstruck. "Do you not see the grocer's pyramid of lemons you have here? You all know too much about the others. Pull one from the stack, and all come tumbling down." He demonstrated his point with a downward motion of his hands and leaned forward with the earnestness of an attorney urging his clients to take a plea bargain. "I beg you to consider no other choice but to leave Paris. Major

Renault instructed me to tell you that this may be your only opportunity to get out. You are young. You have your full lives ahead of you, and you've already served your country valiantly and well. There would be no shame in pulling out. And—" Henri drew in a breath "—may I remind you what will happen to you if you are caught? How will you feel if you're made to betray the others?"

Another solemn silence met this very real horror. When none spoke, Bridgette made a polite sound in her throat to indicate she'd speak for all of them. "A little time to think about it—in private?" she said quietly.

Henri shook his head and pushed back his chair. *Ah,* moi*!* he thought. *This is not good, not good at all.* "As you wish. I will wait in the other room, but don't take too long. I must report to Major Renault in regard to the Lysanders."

CHAPTER FORTY-FOUR

A tense silence gripped the room. Eyes were down, no one looking at any other. The candle burned ominously, throwing the circle of faces around the table into the cast of a group assembled for a séance. Finally Bridgette gathered a breath and spoke. "Like the man said, guys, we don't have much time. Who wants to go first?"

"I suggest it be you, Labrador," Bucky said. "Without you, the rest of us have to pack our bags."

All nodded agreement, even Victoria, who had sat through the whole proceedings like a figure cast in marble.

"Same goes for you guys," Bridgette said. "My mission here is over once you leave, but if only one of you stays, then I do, too."

They remained silent, keeping their attention on

her as if expecting her to take the lead. "Okay," she said, accepting her cue. "We've heard some very disturbing news, so may I suggest we take a vote by a show of hands? Who, without discussion, right now at this moment, wants to head for the door?"

No hand went up.

"Well," she said, as they continued to stare at her, "should we begin there, keeping in mind that pyramid of lemons and possibly one-time offer? I am sure you'd agree that any sane person would be opting for a pint at the Crown and Scepter." Bridgette emphasized *sane*, looking at Victoria, who sat beside her. Besides Lodestar, she was in the greatest danger of them all. A single dropped American inflection into the acute ear of one of the most dangerous Nazis in the SS, and it would be all over for her.

Everyone murmured their approval.

"In that case, let's not hesitate to play the devil's advocate as we discuss," Bridgette said with another quick glance at Victoria. "Somebody might point out something we can't see that could affect our decisions. Liverwort, we should start with you, since you and Lodestar are in the most threatening situations."

Victoria shot a look across the table at Lodestar, who returned a wink and small smile. Obviously, he had not reported their chance meeting to the major, either, and for the same reason. It must have been Madame Dupree who had reported them. Who could blame her? "Like Lapwing and Limpet," she said, "I don't believe that I am in as much danger of exposure as it appears. The mentioned Nazi and I don't converse much. He comes for a couple of hours weekly where I work, and that's all I see of him. I speak impeccable French that I doubt even his ear can detect for a trace of English. If it's so infallible, why hasn't he had me arrested already? A far greater reason for me to go is the possible danger I present to Lodestar." She addressed Bucky. "Lodestar, if you want me to leave, I will."

Bucky shook his head. "Don't leave the party on my account. You're no more a threat to me than anybody else in this room. That turncoat Texan is a greater problem."

Bridgette leaned in close to Victoria and in a lowered voice said, "You'll never find him. Like I said, you'd have a better chance of finding a needle in a field of haystacks."

"I found the needle," Victoria said quietly.

Bridgette pulled away, comprehension flooding her face. "Oh, Liverwort, I am so sorry."

"So you see that I have to stay to do what I can to make sure that needle wasn't buried in vain. Don't worry about me, *chère amie*. Now that I've been warned about the man, I'll take extra care to watch my step." Victoria squeezed Bridgette's hand and turned back to Bucky, her voice rising to include the rest of the group. "It's Lodestar that we should be worried about."

"I agree," Brad said, turning to Bucky. "You're boarding with an American traitor. It must be like sleeping with a live grenade under your bed."

"It is, but so far the sergeant hasn't been inclined to pull the pin."

Chris, still shocked by the news that Dirk Drechsler was actually living in Paris, spoke up. "What does that mean—that Dirk hasn't been in the mood to turn you over to his buddies or that he hasn't had reason to? God—" He shook his head in incredulous wonder. "I just can't believe the meathead went through with it…join the enemy. I knew he left home with the intent to sign up with the German intelligence agency, but I thought he was just shooting his mouth off—being his usual all-thunder-but-no-rain self. I expected him to chicken out and lie low somewhere in the States until the war was over rather than come home to face his family and community. I would never have believed that he could actually be part of an organization that interrogates…tortures American prisoners…"

"You can believe it," Bucky said, "but if it's a comfort, I think he regrets it and would jump at the chance to turn around and go home." He readjusted his seating position. "But I have to come clean with you guys and tell you that I believe I *have* roused the sergeant's suspicions, so if anybody should head for the door, it's me."

"Because of me?" Victoria asked.

"No, Liverwort. You may have added to his suspicions, but Drechsler was onto me before you showed up. I don't think he suspects me of being an American. It's not anything he's heard in my speech. His ear isn't that finely tuned to French. It's something else, but I can't figure out what. I just know he's done nothing about it, and I'm willing to take the risk that he doesn't intend to, but if you guys think it's too dangerous to your security for me to chance it…well, then, I'll head for the door."

"Why do you think he won't turn you in?" Brad asked.

"Because I believe he's lost heart for the job. It's clear he's become totally disillusioned with the Nazi Party and regrets joining the German Army. He's downright miserable and lonely as hell. His superiors treat him like a mud hen in a muster of peacocks, and I gather that everybody he works with does, too. He's an outcast. You'd think he'd hand me over just to get into their good graces, but I've gotten the impression he no longer gives a piss whether he's in their good graces or not. He just wants out."

"That's Dirk all over," Chris said. "I've known him his entire life. Leaps without looking, like the time on a class picnic he tried to impress us with a high dive into a creek without checking its depth and knocked himself out cold. It took our school bus to haul him out."

The image prompted a brief burst of nervous laughter around the table. "So what are we hearing from you, Lodestar?" Bridgette said to Bucky. "Are you electing to stay?"

"Only if no one disapproves. It's not just my hide in question here. Should we take a vote?"

"Before we consider that," Brad said, looking at Chris, "I think we should hear from you, Lapwing. You know the guy. If you were in Lodestar's situation, would you take the risk that he wouldn't turn you over?"

"I can't see him doing it," Chris said. "Dirk's one of those guys who, once he loses faith in who he thought you were, it's over. He was never one to pretend otherwise. If he's disenchanted with the Nazi setup, he wouldn't want to throw Lodestar to the wolves, especially if it doesn't gain him anything he wants and especially if he suspects Lodestar of being an American. I'd say Lodestar is safe taking the risk."

Bridgette consulted the table. "Is a vote necessary?"

Heads shook no.

Bridgette's eye lighted on Chris and Brad. "Okay, boys, looks like the mike is yours. Tell us why you believe you're in the least danger. Aren't you bound to interface with each other in your capacities for the general?"

"We already have," Brad answered. "We met today on the way to a luncheon he hosted in his home. I nearly fell off the stoop when I saw Lapwing saunter up, but by the time his aide opened the door, we were just two strangers who'd met as guests and got the introductions over with. The general didn't suspect a thing." Brad flashed his slow grin. "His attention was too much on my buxom landlady, who I was escorting, to pay much mind to us anyway."

Chris added, "We can't see how our discovery of each other's cover names and jobs place us in greater jeopardy than we were before. In our simple occupations, we're not liable to draw the interest of the police organizations. Our danger would come from the general should we rouse his suspicions that we're not who we say we are, and I don't believe there's a danger of that."

"How can you be so sure?" Victoria asked.

"Because he has no reason to look."

"In other words, he trusts us," Brad chimed in. "We're just two guys who in our separate capacities have become a part of his son's life. We're accepted like trusted members of the staff. There's nothing about us to suspect."

"Which means that we have access to his house, which means that we have lots of opportunities to use our Minoxes," Chris said.

"Which reminds me that I need you to ask the major to arrange a cutout for me. I have a roll of film to get to him," Brad said to Bridgette.

"I'll see to it," she said. "So all those *which*es mean that you boys are staying?"

"We're staying," Chris said, and Brad nodded.

"Okay, then." Bridgette raised her shoulders and spread her palms. "Now that we've heard from everyone and decided that the risks in remaining are no worse than those we came prepared to take, should we call in the Frenchman?"

"Not yet, Labrador." The interruption came from

Victoria. "We haven't heard from you. What about the threat of the policeman?"

"Oh, him." Bridgette flipped a hand to discount her concern. "He's harmless. He's just a young recruit too busy reveling in the attention he's getting as the guardian of the mural to be a threat. Once he's in the Vichy Milice, he'll be gone from the scene anyway. Besides, he's sweet on me. I can handle him." Her gaze swept the table again. "Well, guys, it's now or never. Let's make it official. All in favor of sticking it out, raise your hands."

All hands went up.

"Okay, unless there's anything else to discuss..." She glanced at Bucky. "Lodestar, will you call in the Frenchman?"

CHAPTER FORTY-FIVE

In the bell tower, at the peephole, Dirk came alert. The door to the tea and book shop was opening. At the window, a man in an apron, presumably the proprietor, was turning the sign back to its original position. The shop was now open for business. A big, heavy-shouldered man, middle-aged, obviously French, stepped out. He lit a cigarette, cupping his hand around it, but not as protection against the nonexistent wind. His large hand provided a screen for his eyes to pan the street left to right. An age-old covert maneuver. Seemingly satisfied that the street gave no cause for concern, he turned to walk away, then suddenly stopped and cast his attention directly at the peephole. Startled, Dirk jerked his head aside and almost landed among the rat droppings. A quick grab of the rotten baluster saved him from falling but at the cost of some racket. Had the Frenchman heard it? Had he spotted his eye peering through the cutout in the masonry? Dirk inched his eye back to it. He could see the man's gaze travel to the belfry and hold steady. After a while, apparently convinced that no unseen eye was upon him, he strolled on. If ever Dirk needed proof that something of a clandestine nature was going on in La Petite Madeleine involving Stephane Beaulieu, the window sign and the Frenchman's behavior cinched it.

Certain that the man had moved on, Dirk planted his eye back at his peephole, and his mouth popped open at the appearance of the blond knockout from Madame Dupree's boardinghouse. With her was a girl about her age, a midget in comparison to the blonde's height but pretty as a peach, while the knockout was downright gorgeous. After a glance up and down the street and a quick embrace, they set off in opposite directions.

His breath trapped in his lungs, Dirk kept his eye on the café door for the exit of Stephane Beaulieu and was rewarded with sight of him a few minutes later. Like the others, he gave the street the same once-over, now coming to life with people hurrying home before dark. His eye also lit on the bell tower. This time Dirk simply moved his head to one side and remained perfectly still, his heart knocking so loudly that temporarily he went deaf to outside sound. *Steady*, he told himself. The first Frenchman to enter could simply be a customer; Beaulieu and the blonde could be secret lovers and the café their meeting place. It was smart in France these days to keep your private life to yourself, and it wasn't unusual for people to look over their shoulders for watching eyes in this country where everybody had become afraid of their own shadow.

Stephane had taken off toward the metro. Dirk would give him time to put distance between them, then, glad to get out of this literal rat hole, head that way himself to consider what he would do with his newly gained windfall of information. Just to make sure he'd seen all there was to see, he placed his eye once more at his observation post and instantly lost his restored breath. Coming out the café and pausing to survey the street was his best friend in all the world, his neighborhood pal he'd known his entire life, Christoph Brandt of New Braunfels, Texas.

Major General Konrad March wondered if he were imagining that there had been a slight shift of

Admiral Canaris's letter on his desk. Was he becoming paranoid like so many of his comrades? His eye and mind were trained to detect the most minuscule details that could give away clandestine activity, but only if he'd committed their original order to memory. He had to confess that at Hans's announcement of Madame Gastain's arrival, his mind had not been committed to any order but the voluptuous arrangement of his neighbor's figure. Also, unless someone had entered through the windows, which were locked against the cold, the only persons who had been in his house after he received the letter were Hans, Wilhelm, and his guests. Hans would never have touched it. He understood that to remain deaf, dumb, and blind to his superior's business was safer for them both. Besides, during the luncheon, his aide had never left the kitchen but to serve. Madame Gastain had never been out of his sight, not even to visit the toilettes. The same for the others. Their only opportunity to read the letter was in the time he walked Madame Gastain to her house and back. He had felt a little light-headed because the luncheon had gone so well and she had agreed to be his guest at the premiere the following Saturday. She had invited him in to enjoy a cup of the tin of coffee he'd sent along with the invitation to join him for luncheon. One cup was all. Propriety demanded that he not overstay his welcome, despite his urge to ask her to play a number on the Steinway set grandly against a wall of priceless paintings in the salon. He had left the fisherman and tutor on the back lawn playing kickball with Wilhelm, and there he found them finishing the game when he returned. Both young men had left immediately. It seemed his guests had late Saturday appointments.

It would require the most paranoid of minds to suspect his son's tutor of having read Admiral Canaris's letter. Konrad had him checked out before engaging him. The boy lived almost a Trappist's existence in Paris. He had no family or friends in the city, had no social interactions with colleagues (not that Konrad could blame him there), and as of yet had acquired no girlfriend, which was surprising, given how handsome he was. The missing thumb must put women off. Herr Bauer took the same route to and from the school each day with no deviation from his daily routine except for the days he traveled to the general's house. He couldn't be a plant, because Herr Bauer could not have known he'd be hired to tutor the son of the head of the Abwehr when he took his position at the boys' school.

The fisherman, maybe. There had been that

moment's doubt about him, but it had long passed. Barnard Wagner had given him no further reason to suspect him of being anything more than what he was—a simple young man whose ambition was to fish and earn his living on the water. Nonetheless—Konrad sighed at his memories—he had uncovered treachery behind the unlikeliest exteriors, and gratitude for the kindnesses shown a man's son could blind him to the motives behind them. Best that he investigate.

Hans took a nap this time of afternoon, and he'd outdone himself with the luncheon, so Konrad left him undisturbed and went in search of Wilhelm. He found him reading a book Claus Bauer had brought him, one of the numerous entertainments he'd provided to fill his son's solitary hours. To round out the boy's study, Konrad had engaged another tutor, a middle-aged, brisk, businesslike woman who came in the mornings, but his son was alone for the rest of the day. Wilhelm liked the woman well enough, but he absolutely adored Herr Bauer.

Konrad sat down on the chair's footstool. "Wilhelm, I have something to ask you. After luncheon, when you and our guests were playing kickball, did Herr Wagner leave to come back into the house?"

His nose still in the book, Wilhelm replied without apparently having to think about his answer, "No sir."

"Well, then." Konrad rose, satisfied. He ruffled the boy's hair. "Continue with your reading."

Konrad was almost out the door when Wilhelm said, "Herr Bauer did."

Louis Mueller locked his set of master keys to the Sorbonne in his desk drawer, feeling his usual frustration at his empty-handedness. He had finished his rounds of Saturday snooping and once again found nothing of report in either the office of Jules Garnier or in the cubicle of Claus Bauer. Both had been under his special scrutiny for almost a month after the October 2 search of their desks had jiggled his suspicions, but Claus Bauer's peculiar language pattern had never appeared again in his notes. His penmanship followed the rules of proper German syntax. No more references to Claus Bauer had shown up in Jules Garnier's datebook, nor any notation of a clandestine nature in his personal papers. Still, Herr Bauer's reminder in his lesson planner to bring a sandwich for Wilhelm March and the personnel director's cloaked phrase *CB in place* continued to nag him. They meant something. He was sure of it.

He would love to find evidence sufficient to report the two to the Gestapo, who'd have no qualms getting the truth out of them, but without a stronger case against them, Louis ran the risk of getting in trouble himself. Claus Bauer, disfigured as he was, had become the most popular instructor on his staff. Parents—the fathers, the most powerful Nazi and Vichy officials in Paris—had begun requesting Herr Bauer as their sons' field and mathematics instructor. Also, Louis had discovered that Major General Konrad March had hired him to tutor his son, a move that had outraged him, since it could reflect badly on himself and the program.

Nor did Louis dare to point a finger at a man in Jules Garnier's position based on a mere hunch that might turn out to be a waste of the Gestapo's time. Garnier had been nothing but cooperative with the Nazi authorities in establishing the special school for their children, and the Gestapo had their hands full tracking down and interrogating persons of real interest. The organization had begun taking a dark view of informers who turned in suspects out of vengeance, jealousy, and personal gain. And in his secret heart, Louis had to admit to all three.

Absorbed in his thoughts, Louis did not at first hear the sound of someone knocking on his department's outer door. By the time it registered, the knocking had increased in tempo and volume, demanding entrance. *Who in hell—?*

Louis set his teeth angrily and grabbed a truncheon. What idiot would come pounding on his door at six o'clock on a Saturday evening in the cold and dark? He'd make him sorry he ever had the notion. He stomped to the door and threw it open. "Oh, my God!" he let out, hiding the truncheon behind his back and snapping up a Nazi salute at the presence of his visitor on his doorstep.

"Your landlady said I might find you here," Major General Konrad March announced himself.

CHAPTER FORTY-SIX

Holy mackerel! Dirk mouthed silently. Christoph Brandt in Paris? Not a chance. Impossible. The guy might *look* like Chris Brandt, but he couldn't be. His friend was living in Austin, Texas, enjoying safety and peace and comfort in the land of barbecue and Western swing. He fixed his eye to the opening in the tower wall again and peered harder. The blood pounded in his head. Dear God, it *was* Chris. Despite the French clothes, the turned-up collar and high-standing scarf, and the bill of his cap pulled down to obstruct his face, no one else stood with the loose-limbed joints particular to his buddy, the New Braunfels High School's track-and-field star. When he pulled his hands from his pockets to draw on his gloves, Dirk knew for sure. A chill, sharp as a Texas hill country wind, passed through him. What the hell was Christoph Brandt doing halfway round the world in German-occupied France?

His hometown friend also checked both directions of the street, his gaze lighting on the bell tower across from the café. Dirk kept his eye to the peephole, halfway hoping Chris would spot it and walk across the street to investigate. He'd see the jimmied lock on the door and poke his head in to investigate and then…

Dirk didn't know. Would they embrace, pound each other on the back, cry, and Dirk apologize for his crazy, stupid, ridiculous belief in Hitler and the whole damn, crappy Nazi war machine, and tell him that he wanted to go home? *Home, Chris, you hear me? Back to New Braunfels, Texas, baby! You've got to find a way to get me outta here, buddy, before I go crazy—or get sent to the Russian front and be killed.* Because Dirk *knew*, he just knew that Chris was up to some covert work for the Allies, probably an American intelligence organization. It didn't take much of a leap of logic to figure out that once the army rejected him, Chris, desperate to serve, would have turned to the secret services, and they would have snapped him up. They wouldn't give a damn about his thumb. He was fluent in German, hale as a lumberjack, and smart as a whip. And somehow he was in league with the blond girl and Stephane Beaulieu, who seemed tight with Nicholas Cravois. They were all in it together.

Or...would Chris back away from him, want nothing to do with him, call him a traitor, a disgrace to his family and friends, and refuse to help him? Dirk drilled him with his eye, hoping to beam a message. *Look at me, Chris. Look at your old buddy! I'm over here in the bell tower, Chris, boy!*

But his buddy started to walk away, the sight of that familiar flapdoodle stride of his like a dart to Dirk's homesick heart. What to do? In minutes he'd lose him in the dark. He ached to run after him and call his name: *Chris, Chris, it's me!* But that could be a bad move for both of them. If Chris was undercover—what was he doing here if he wasn't?—his buddy wouldn't welcome being recognized, especially by one he thought of as the enemy. He'd take off like a rocket and be lost to him in this city of millions. Dirk would never find the best friend he'd ever had to make things right between them. He settled for following him. Chris was probably heading to his living quarters because of the curfew. Learning where his friend could be contacted, his link to home, would be enough for now.

The call from his man in Paris came through for Alistair at six o'clock that evening. Alistair's mouth felt like a tobacco bin, his stomach a coffee grinder. A full wastebasket of empty cigarette packs and coffee rings on his desk explained the kind of day he'd had waiting for the phone to ring. "You're not going to like my report," Henri warned him.

"I wasn't expecting to," Alistair said.

"They're staying. To a man and a woman, they elected to remain in Paris. I tried my best to persuade them to leave, Alistair."

Alistair thought first of the son of Joanna Bukowski Hudson. She would never forgive him. Then of the little ball of fire, Bridgette Loring. The others' faces, every one dear to him, swam in, and Alistair closed his eyes with a sigh of resignation. "I'm sure you did, Henri," he said. "I suspected your mission was futile, but it was worth a shot. Please tell me, though, that they made their decisions based on what was best for them individually, not as a team."

"I wasn't allowed the privilege of hearing their conversation, so I can't say. All I can tell you is that they wished me to assure you that each had a valid reason for remaining. They all agreed that they had invested too much, that their missions were too important to abandon now. They thought the advantage of being forewarned was protection enough."

Alistair rubbed his forehead wearily. "What naivete. One loose thread can unravel the whole ball of twine. How many times did I tell them that?" He reached to extract another cigarette from its wrapping, reconsidered, and sent the package flying across the room with an angry swipe of his hand. "How did they look?" he asked, swiveling his chair around to a window that offered a distant view of the snow-covered Swiss alps.

"They would all benefit from more food in their bellies, but overall, your team seems to be in good health. The tall blonde looks to have had the worst of it so far, not necessarily from lack of food. She seemed quite... hollow inside."

"She has suffered a loss. I hope to God it doesn't make her careless," Alistair said. "She's in the most vulnerable spot of all."

"It would certainly seem so," Henri concurred. "I am to let you know that you'll need to arrange a cutout for Lapwing. Your boy photographed an important letter found on Major General March's desk this afternoon. The film is stored in the barrel of a fountain pen."

"I'll get right to it," Alistair said. "Anything else?"

"Well, there is one other thing..."

Alistair tensed at Henri's pause. "What is it?"

"This may mean nothing, but I thought my observation worth reporting. One of the young men... well, they were subtle, but a couple of his features reminded me of somebody I couldn't place at the meeting, but now I recall the name."

"Who?"

"Nicholas Cravois."

Alistair swung back to his desk, instincts jumping as he recalled a poster of Nicholas Cravois in the files. Alistair had never met the Maquis leader known as the Black Ghost, but he had dispatched numerous OSS teams to liaise with him in the mountainous regions of southern France. Of all the Resistance commanders and underground groups operating in the German-occupied countries and territories in Europe, the general and his growing band of Maquis were the biggest and most dangerous threat to the Nazi war machine. A bounty of a million German marks was on his head.

"Alistair?"

Hauled back to the conversation, Alistair asked, "What features?"

"The structure of his forehead, but mainly his eyes.

I knew the general before he grew the beard that obscures the face you see on his wanted posters."

"If you're right, you've provided the missing piece of a puzzle."

"Could he be a nephew, related through a sibling of one of the parents? Perhaps…even a son, *mon ami*?"

"His father is American. His mother, French." Sam Barton looked nothing like his rough, heavy-jowled father, Alistair recalled. He had checked out the boy's home and seen Horace Barton leave for work the Monday he had met Sam at the coffee shop in Oklahoma City, but his French mother…

"My immeasurable thanks as usual, Henri," Alistair said abruptly. He'd kept his friend on the phone long enough. It was unsafe for his man in Paris to talk longer. "Stay safe, my friend," he urged and rang off.

Alistair went immediately to a cabinet and pulled the file that contained the poster of Nicholas Cravois. If he looked hard enough, beyond the beard, he could see the faint similarities that had prompted Henri's observation. Alistair put in a call to OSS headquarters and requested a clerk to read the items pertaining to Samuel Barton's parents and relatives. There was no information to indicate that he was anything other than the son of Horace Barton. The mother had only one sibling, a sister, who was childless and still lived in Paris, where Samuel's mother, Monique, had lived until her marriage to Horace Barton. Sergeant Barton had been stationed in Paris in 1919 as a member of the American Expeditionary Forces, the year he married Monique. Alistair felt the chill of instant comprehension. That timing explained it. Whether her American husband was aware of her pregnancy when he married her was irrelevant. It was clear now that Samuel Barton had volunteered to serve in the OSS as a means to come to Paris to find Nicholas Cravois—his father.

Now was the perfect time, Achim Fleischer thought. The sisters had just left for the chapel and five o'clock vespers, and the convent was practically empty. Mademoiselle Dufor—Bernadette, he'd begun to call her—had gone to meet friends for tea at four o'clock and would probably not be back until six. An hour's break from his guard duties was all he needed to search Mademoiselle—Bernadette's—room. It was located in the attic, she'd told him.

His desire to see where she slept and ate and dressed and bathed had become an obsession. He seemed unable to control his need to touch her personal things, to see the books she read, to look at photographs and fashion drawings, to rummage through drawers and cabinets and closets to discover more about her. Would he find her attic room in order or disappointingly untidy? Would he see the dishes washed and neatly put away or piled uncleaned in the sink, the bed made, floors swept, lavatory and commode spotless? Would the ice box stink of rotting leftovers and the stove be grimed with grease and food spills, though there was precious little food these days to go bad or spill and no fuel to cook it. Would he have the pleasure of discovering private and feminine items washed and hung on a line in the toilettes? Her nightgown and robe that carried her scent hung from a peg in her closet? These were questions he had asked himself in his fantasies as his affection for her had grown—and as hers had increased for him, he was sure.

However, before he pursued her further, he must see how she lived. He was a tidy man himself, some would say excessively so, and no matter the depth of his admiration for a woman (not that he'd had contact with many—none, as a matter of fact), he would find it impossible to commit himself to her if she did not possess his passion for cleanliness and order.

The convent was virtually empty. Now was the time to put his questions to the test about Mademoiselle Bernadette Dufor. He crept up the stairs without being seen and let himself into her attic room.

She passed the exam. All was as Achim had hoped, dreamed. His affection and desire for the adorable, petite Bernadette Dufor grew by the minute. Perhaps if they should marry, the convent would consider the antique armoire against the wall as a wedding present. It was a fine piece—fifteenth century, he guessed. A corner stuck out a bit, a distraction to the eye. He would line it up properly before making for the fire escape.

He spotted the floor-to-ceiling hairline crack in the wall behind the armoire and thought at first that the chest had been placed there to conceal an eyesore. Then he looked more closely, remembering what he had read of the secret nooks the English called "priest holes," built in old monasteries and convents throughout France to hide members of the aristocracy seeking to escape the guillotine during the French Revolution. Today, they were used to hide Jews on the run. He had time to spare. He had better look. He moved the armoire farther away from the wall and gave the hairline fissure a push. A door swung back.

Holy Mother of Christ!

It was indeed a cleverly concealed entrance to a priest hole. No smell of human occupancy drifted out. Curious, Achim stepped inside and saw in the darkness an object on a table that froze him stiff as a stick. He was standing thus when voices reached him from downstairs. Quickly, hardly able to tear his gaze away from the evidence of Mademoiselle Bernadette Dufor's betrayal of all his fantasies and hopes, Achim backed out, closed the door, and returned the armoire to the exact position in which he'd found it before dashing out by the attic's fire escape.

CHAPTER FORTY-SEVEN

The following afternoon, Colonel Derrick Albrecht allowed his valet to finish securing the red, white, and black armband displaying the thunderbolt rune of the Schutzstaffel, the last item of his uniform to be donned before leaving for his trip to L'Ecole d'Escrime Français and his Sunday bout with Mademoiselle Colbert. The elderly family retainer who'd looked after him since he was a boy stood back and surveyed him admiringly. Designed to project authority and foster terror, the SS uniform was often enough to shake information out of someone brought to SD headquarters before the luckless soul even had to be escorted to the cells on the top floor. "The uniform was designed for you, Herr Colonel."

"Pardon?"

The valet handed him his uniform hat and repeated, "The uniform. It becomes you." The old servant's wrinkled lips stretched into a grin. "Your mind is on the beautiful mademoiselle you were with last night, *ja*?"

"You are most observant, Eduard. As a matter of fact, my thoughts were indeed on a beautiful woman."

"So, who is my competition?" Celeste had asked in her matter-of-fact way without rancor the previous night after Derrick's distracted performance. "Your mind is elsewhere other than in my bed, *mon ami*." She'd set a cigarette between her teeth and clicked a gold Cartier lighter to its tip.

Derrick had pulled up against the satin-padded back of the headboard monogrammed with the logo of the Ritz Hotel and took the draw she offered. Celeste was his mistress. She had no designs on him other than as a friend as well as a lover. She lived in the hotel. "Someone I must protect," he'd said.

She'd tousled his hair. "Protect? Do I detect a man in love? You—the man I suspect would give his life for someone, but never his heart."

"Love is an irrational emotion that runs contrary to human nature, Celeste."

"Against self-preservation, you mean."

"I admit to holding with Kipling's view of relationships to let all men count with you, but none too much. I include women in that philosophy."

She'd laughed, taking back the cigarette. "Until one comes along that means everything."

"You cannot be in love with a person who loathes you, Celeste. You can only admire her for her good taste." He'd leaned over and kissed her bare shoulder. "Have no fear, my sweet. I shall be returning to your bed often."

Now, Derrick accepted a fresh white handkerchief from his valet and slipped it into his pocket. Handkerchiefs were sometimes needed in interrogations of women. Lastly, he drew on a pair of black leather gloves. A final look in the mirror confirmed that he was indeed a figure to inspire terror.

Not that the trappings of his authority had much effect on Mademoiselle Colbert, or so she would have him believe. Of course she feared him. A woman in her situation would be foolish not to fear a man of his position and power, but she would die before betraying a flicker of fright. Her remote indifference was a mask molded by years on the piste and the notion, inherent to members of her lofty bloodline, that people of her status did not reveal their terror to thugs.

Which was the American epithet Mademoiselle Colbert—Victoria Grayson—would ascribe to him. A regret, but such were the consequences of his work. His duty was to protect his country from its enemies, and he made no apologies and offered no excuses for doing it as he saw fit. He did not relish the methods his job sometimes required, but someone had to do it, and he had the faculties, temperament, and skill to perform it well. However, it was not his duty to arrest people he knew to be innocent. He had, therefore, decided what to do with Victoria Grayson.

He would simply do nothing.

Mademoiselle Colbert had committed no crime against the Third Reich. Self-preservation was not a criminal offense. She was guilty of nothing more than being in the wrong place at the wrong time, and that was why it had been necessary to rid her of the threat of the dissolute Beaumont Fournier, that cur of the literary world. How could the French literati be so beguiled by his writing? His death would be no loss to readers of taste, and he'd had to keep Mademoiselle Colbert—Victoria Grayson—out of the interrogation cells of the Gestapo.

How that profligate Beaumont Fournier could believe Victoria Grayson guilty of being a spy was laughable. Derrick now wished he had relieved the man of his delusion before killing him. Victoria Grayson was no more a spy than he was Mickey Mouse. She had risked her life and sacrificed the substantial comforts of her home to come to an enemy country to search for the man she loved, a brave RAF pilot, who himself had risked loss of his American citizenship by joining the British air force. Derrick would further say to the author that a man like him could not possibly understand nor appreciate—most certainly had never inspired—the selflessness that had motivated mademoiselle's courage, so it was no wonder that he would make such an absurd accusation against her. Well, too bad. His misconception had cost him his life.

Derrick intended to protect Victoria Grayson. He liked Americans. He liked the United States. Some of his fondest memories had been made and friendships formed on its shores, and he regretted that Hitler, typically, had seen fit to declare war against the only world power that did not sign the Treaty of Versailles because its leaders recognized the severity of its unfair terms. Without the treaty that had been designed to punish and cripple Germany for the First World War, the second war would never have come. The Third Reich would never have risen from the ashes incurred by the document's penalties. *Mein Kampf* and Adolf Hitler and his common herd would be names lost to history had the signers been more gracious in victory. Denying Germany a voice in the negotiations, the victors had drafted a document that had destroyed its economy and starved its people, allocated land to France and Britain for their own empire building, reduced its army to a size that left it defenseless and vulnerable for takeover, and then added insult to injury by not allowing Germany to join the League of Nations. As a result, Adolf Hitler, Austrian born, school dropout, failed watercolor painter, a nobody, was now Führer of the Nazi Party and chancellor of Germany, and the country once exalted for its culture, literature, music, and art was now the most feared and despised nation on earth.

"The car is here, Mein Herr."

"*Danke*, Eduard," Derrick said. "Go enjoy the rest of your Sunday. A new film is showing at the corner cinema. I won't need you tonight."

The old retainer bowed away. "Yes, Mein Herr."

As the staff car pulled from his hotel into the Sunday quiet of the deserted avenue, Derrick sighed. Every week, he looked forward to his fencing bouts with Mademoiselle Colbert, but today he wished they could lay aside their foils and talk—in English. He imagined Victoria Grayson would enjoy the pleasure of speaking in her native tongue, and he would have the opportunity to practice her language. He longed to tell her that he knew the truth of her identity and nationality but that she had nothing to fear from him. He was not her enemy. He understood her reason for being in France, and he admired her for it. He should be so fortunate to win the affection of a woman willing to sacrifice so much on his behalf. He would invite her to tell him about her home, her family, her life in Virginia, and he would tell her about his time in America, the experiences he'd had, the states he'd visited, the friends he'd made. Was she by any chance familiar with the works of two of his Harvard classmates—the film critic James Agee, who wrote for *The Nation*, and Elliott Carter, who was making a name for himself as a brilliant teacher and composer at Julliard? Jim was a very gifted writer who had aspired to become a novelist. Derrick hoped to visit him and Elliott in the United States when the war was over.

Mademoiselle Colbert would no doubt scoff at this idiocy. Did he really believe a reunion possible with his American friends—him, a Nazi? He would be a pariah to them.

And so he probably would be. Another regret, one almost as searing as his remorse that he would always be a pariah to Victoria Grayson. Another time, another place, and he might have had a chance with her. "An image," Celeste had called her last night, having reminded him that he hardly knew the girl. "You're in love with an *image* of the perfect woman for you."

Love? Maybe. Image? No. He did not have to get into the mind and heart of Victoria Grayson to know that she was the woman of his hopes. She possessed it all—every quality he desired in a wife, a mother for his children, a companion, a lover. He had known it the moment he laid eyes on her.

But alas…

The car drew before the door of its destination. Derrick saw a prick of light in the far reach of the school salle. Mademoiselle had arrived. Monsieur Vogel, the director, was visiting his daughter today and would not be with them this Sunday, so they would fence without a referee and chaperone. Derrick took hold of his fencing bag, leaving Karl to read behind the wheel of the staff car, and stepped through the unlocked entrance of the school. Off to the right, the basement door stood ajar, and he could hear voices coming from below that he recognized as Mademoiselle Colbert's and a man's, too young to belong to the janitor. The man was speaking broken French in a harsh tone. Then came a bellow of anguish. Derrick dropped his bag and rushed for the basement door.

CHAPTER FORTY-EIGHT

Victoria had arrived at the salle early. Her apartment held no inducements for sleeping late and doing the usual domestic chores reserved for Sundays. The hotel's meager coal ration was barely enough to warm half her bedroom. There was no hot water or soap for washing her clothes, no tea and little food in the larder. The residence hotel had once boasted a small, high-scale restaurant that had closed permanently the week she moved in. The mostly elderly residents were now forced to eat their meals out, a difficult situation to manage in inclement weather, or to cook their scarce food in their apartments' small galley kitchens. Her neighbors' black market sources had dried up, and Victoria worried that the old dears found themselves in her set of circumstances this morning, cold to their knickers and feeling the dull ache of hunger.

She'd also awakened feeling brutalized by nightmares of capture and torture interspersed with equally cruel dreams of happy bygone Thanksgiving holidays celebrated in the security and bounty of family. She could still taste their old cook's turkey and pumpkin pie, see her father ceremonially sharpening the carving knife and Lawrence pouring the wine. She'd needed warmth and a place to shake free of the dreams, and the boiler room in the basement of L'Ecole d'Escrime Français offered both. For use by the staff, the room came equipped with a washroom, hot water, and soap and a line for hanging laundry to dry in the heat. Along with her weekly wear, a set of her whites needed washing, and while there, she'd carry down the school's swords to sand off the rust they'd collected when their protective coatings wore off.

At the washing sink in the boiler room, so warm that she could do her laundry divested of coat and jacket, the flotsam of last night's turbulence continued to lap at the edge of her consciousness. Victoria wondered if the rest of the team was also flirting with regrets about their decisions of yesterday afternoon. Had they also awakened from nightmares of Gestapo interrogations and dreams of food-laden tables and warm beds in the good old USA? In the morning light, being hungry and cold in comfortless surroundings in a destitute and dangerous country with no end yet in sight, the last plane out having departed, made for the kind of harsh realities that invited doubts.

She must not entertain them. She'd made her decision yesterday fully conscious of the danger and discomforts it entailed. She had no regrets. Her place was here, doing her indispensable part. The war would not last forever, and the Allies would win. Underground newspapers reported that a British victory appeared imminent in North Africa. That would crush Hitler's plan to gain control of the Suez Canal with its access to the Mideast oilfields and raw materials from Asia. Allied air power was taking control of the sky, and the vast supply of American armaments was outstripping Germany's shrinking armories. She was bound to go through these occasional tunnels of depression, but she would live to keep that date in the Rose Main Reading Room of the New York Public Library.

Her wash was hung, and a finished stack of sanded and oiled blades rested on their pommels against the wall of the staircase when Victoria heard the basement door creak open. The wall blocked the landing and half the stairs, so she was unable to see who had entered, but the door remained open and the visitor paused as if having a moment's indecision about coming down. A thread of apprehension purled through her. Colonel Albrecht? He was early—unusual for him, as he was always punctual to the minute for their appointment, so German of him. Also, the colonel would announce his presence from the head of the stairs before coming down. *Mademoiselle Colbert? Are you there? It is I, Derrick Albrecht.* It must be the late-shift janitor, arriving early to get out of the cold. He was a kind, jolly old fellow, and Victoria liked him. She'd appreciate his company and hearing again the tales of his rip-roaring youth—anything to take her mind off her own thoughts.

"Monsieur Dubois?" she called.

"*Non!*" came the answer. "Oberleutnant Peter Janssen."

Victoria stiffened. He was the student who'd pestered her and tried to make time with her when she first arrived at the school. He'd quit taking lessons after the fencing master was ordered to remove his name from her roster to open a spot for another German student of greater skill and more promise for improvement. The lieutenant had accepted the put-down poorly and believed her responsible for his removal.

She heard him begin his descent, arrogance in every deliberate step on the cement stairs. Victoria felt her mouth go dry. Colonel Albrecht was not due to arrive for another fifteen minutes. For the first time, Victoria would be relieved to see him. The lieutenant bent his head to leer around the edge of the stairwell at her, and Victoria demanded in her most imperious tone, "What are you doing here?"

The lieutenant stepped down into the light of the basement. He looked more official in his military uniform and shiny jackboots than in fencing clothes, more in charge. He carried a swagger stick, a wooden dowel covered with leather that Victoria saw as a pathetic attempt to augment his lowly status. "I saw lights on in the fencing hall and thought that odd since the school is closed on Sunday," he said in patchy French. "I decided to investigate."

He was lying, Victoria thought. He'd decided to call on her at her hotel and frightened the hotel concierge into telling him her whereabouts. "Well, as you can see, there is nothing to investigate here."

"Oh, I wouldn't say that." His gaze lit on the bras and panties strung along the line, prurient menace in his eyes, then flicked to the swords set against the stairwell. Slowly and deliberately, he laid his swagger stick and hat on a laundry table and pulled off his gloves. "This is where you do your clothes washing?"

"I did today." It was time to drop names. "I came early before my appointment with Colonel Derrick Albrecht. The salle is open because he meets me here on Sunday afternoons for private fencing sessions. Sunday is the only day in the week he is free for such activity. Perhaps you know him? The chief of the counterintelligence division of the SD? I am expecting him at any moment."

The lieutenant began removing his overcoat, and Victoria's pulse pounded at the base of her throat. Next would come his jacket. She would make short work of him if she could get to the swords, but he stood between her and the stack propped against the staircase behind him. "Colonel Derrick Albrecht? Germany's famous champion of foil?" he said. "I know *of* him, of course. What would *you*, as skilled as you are, have to teach *him*?"

"I didn't say he was a student. The colonel required a bout partner experienced in foil to maintain his skills. He will be here any moment. I was just on my way upstairs to get dressed to meet him, so if you will excuse me..."

His overcoat shed, the lieutenant stepped in front of her, eyes glittering, full of hate. "I don't think so, mademoiselle. Not this time. I happen to know that a member of the colonel's staff also serves as his fencing partner. They've been a team for years and bout in the basement of his hotel."

Victoria managed to keep from showing her surprise. She should have suspected it. The colonel had used the ploy of requiring a bout partner to meet her.

"You caused me much humiliation, Mademoiselle Colbert, and you will pay for it," the lieutenant continued. Swiftly, he stepped behind him and reached for one of the dueling swords, protective sheaths and rubber tips removed. He brought the naked point of a rapier to Victoria's throat. "Remove your clothes—now!"

"What?"

"I will not repeat myself again, Mademoiselle Colbert. *Remove your clothes!*"

"I most certainly will not."

He pressed the point of the blade harder, and Victoria could feel a hot sting and a trickle of warm blood. "I believe you will."

Victoria backed up. He had her trapped in the narrow space between washing machines, laundry tables, and equipment, the stairs behind him. She allowed him the satisfaction of seeing her shoot an anxious glance over her shoulder at the wall of the furnace. He grinned. "Yes, I see you've determined your three choices: my blade at your throat, hot metal at your back, or a delightful afternoon pleasing me on the janitor's couch. I'm sure you won't disappoint." He began to unbutton his jacket.

Victoria tried to draw her neck out of reach of the rapier and could feel the fiery heat from the furnace. "Ah, so this is the only way of getting a woman into your bed—by the use of force!"

Anger, compounded by the embarrassing truth, reddened his face. "*Undress*, I say!"

"How do you expect me to undress with a rapier at my throat?"

The lieutenant stepped back, creating space for Victoria, who with seductive slowness, began with one hand to thread the top button of her blouse through its opening, then the second and third, while keeping her eyes riveted on his face. As expected, his fascination at the revelations to come was so intense that she had space and time to grab her fencing jacket hanging within reach and swipe it with all her force across the limply held blade. It bounced, clattering over the top of a washing machine and out of rescue range before the startled lieutenant could even register it missing, seconds too late to avoid

Victoria's vicious kick between his legs. Cradling his crotch, the lieutenant dropped to his knees with the bellow of a cow giving birth. "You bitch!" he screamed at her, lifting a face contorted with pain and rage, and offered a perfect target for Victoria to land another kick under his jaw.

"Take that, you nasty little worm!" she said as the lieutenant crumpled forward. Victoria dashed by him, reaching the stairs just as Colonel Derrick Albrecht appeared on the landing by the basement door.

CHAPTER FORTY-NINE

Major General Konrad March sat at his dining room table, ruminating, having barely eaten a bite of the succulent chicken Hans had prepared with a savory stuffing of rye bread and mushrooms and onions and walnuts. A bowl of stewed sweet apples sat untouched as well, and a custard was expected for dessert. The general dined alone. He had denied his son's request to invite Herr Bauer and Herr Wagner to join them, and in a fit of petulance against his father's refusal, Wilhelm had spurned the meal and stomped upstairs to his room, where he now sat sulking and no doubt hungry.

The general and Hans had observed the boy's unprecedented act of rebellion with astonishment. "I've never seen him like this, Herr General," his aide said. "I don't know what's gotten into him."

"I do," Konrad said thoughtfully.

"Will you...punish him, Mein General?" Hans asked, sounding worried.

Konrad gave him a look of understanding. His aide's affection for his son knew no bounds. "No, Hans. Let's let him be for a while, then take him up a plate."

Of course he wouldn't have punished his son. How could a father discipline a child for the infraction of expressing a wish to share his food with the hungry? Wilhelm was now at an age when he noticed the desperate want of others around him. He saw it in the hollow faces of the children and their mothers on the playground where Hans took him to ride the carousel, and on the metro when he and his aide went to the cinema, on the occasions when he caught his morning tutor slip tea pastries into her pockets—"for my grandchildren," she would explain with an embarrassed smile. For now, Wilhelm accepted that Herr Bauer and Herr Wagner were underfed because they were poor. The poverty that Germany had inflicted on the French people was a daily shame to Konrad, and he wished to keep Wilhelm ignorant from his people's role in it as long as possible. He was proud of his son's empathy for the misfortunate and of his desire to share with them the bounty that he enjoyed every day. He had inherited that quality from his mother.

Konrad had explained that he must not monopolize Herr Wagner's and Herr Bauer's time. Their Sundays were sacred to them, and as fond as they were of Wilhelm, they did not wish to spend their one unobligated day with the boy and old man with whom they had dined only yesterday and would see later in the week. His tutor and soccer partner were young men, handsome and single, and perhaps they wished to spend their Sunday in the company of a lady companion. Wilhelm understood that, no?

He did not. "But they are hungry," he declared. "I know it. I hear their stomachs rumbling when we're together. Food is more important than a *girl*!"

"Well then, the next time they come, you must ask Hans to serve them tea and sandwiches. Now let's say no more about it," Konrad ordered, sterner than he wished.

The main reason that he had refused his son's request was that he did not want to include Herr Bauer in the invitation. Wilhelm thought of his tutor and soccer mate in pairs, and to exclude one would have resulted in another tantrum, but Konrad had become unsure of Herr Bauer.

He had been in the business of intelligence too long

to ignore the smell of smoke, no matter how faint. Even a whiff signaled fire somewhere or at least one that had been present. His trip to Wilhelm's former school yesterday had netted him a couple of puzzling tidbits worth reflecting upon, but he had regrettably set Herr Bauer more firmly in the crosshairs of that pig, Louis Mueller. He had gone to the school to request a harmless look at Herr Claus's employment file on the pretense of locating the address of the young man's parents to arrange a surprise visit from them as a gift to their son at Christmas.

But unfortunately for Herr Bauer, Konrad's request had opened the door for Louis Mueller to infer slyly that his recently hired instructor was up to something more than teaching math and track-and-field sports. Exactly what, he couldn't say, but the general best be on guard. Since Mueller appeared a man suspicious by nature and his dislike for Herr Bauer blatantly obvious, Konrad would have disregarded his insinuations had he himself not had doubts of his own.

"On what grounds do you base your suspicions?" he'd asked, and Herr Mueller had unlocked the door of Claus Bauer's cube of an office and without compunction riffled through his lesson planner until he came to the page he was looking for. It was missing.

The man's pink face blanched to the shade of boiled meat, undoubtedly thinking that General Konrad March would think he'd been blowing smoke up his anus.

"I—I swear that it was here," he cried, without realizing that the missing page was more damning than what was written upon it. "Look, there's a gap in the dates!"

"I see," Konrad had said.

Some color was restored to the director's face when a page was similarly discovered missing from the Sorbonne's personnel director's daily diary that Mueller claimed to have stated *CB in place*. "Do you not see the oddity of the coincidence, eh, Herr General?" he'd asked, a spark of triumph lighting his porcine eyes.

"Yes, I see," said Konrad. "I ask that you keep this visit confidential between ourselves, understand?"

"Most certainly, Herr General," Louis had said with a conspiratorial wink that almost earned a slap across one of his portly cheeks.

"And now perhaps you can tell me how you happened to come across the personal writings in the private diaries of your instructor and the Sorbonne's personnel director?" Konrad had asked just to watch those cheeks blanch again.

At his dining room table, Konrad rang the table bell.

Hans appeared. "Mein General?"

"As a peace offering to Wilhelm, let's have Herr Bauer stay for dinner tomorrow night after their tutoring session."

"Very good, sir. I shall serve roast beef with potatoes, brussels sprouts, and much gravy. That should fill Herr Bauer's stomach. And...Herr Wagner as well?" Hans suggested, a note of hope in his voice.

"Of course. Let's invite him, too. Why not?"

"The young master will be very pleased. I will tell him when I take up a plate."

Konrad's heartfelt desire was that he, too, would be pleased at the end of the evening tomorrow night, for he intended to set a trap for Herr Bauer that would establish beyond all doubt the tutor's innocence or guilt.

Sunday afternoons Brad spent tying flies and repairing and cleaning the parts of fishing rods for Captain Allard's customers. It enabled him to pick up extra money that he'd not have to add to the stash provided by the OSS, should there be enough left to turn in at war's end. Once it was all over, he hoped to convert his French francs to dollars to set aside for the kids' college funds. By "kids," he meant Bobby and Margie. By the time he made it home, Bobby would be college age, and he couldn't expect Jared Cramer, his mother's new husband, to pick up the tab for his adopted siblings. Beata, yes. As Joanna's daughter, she now belonged to Jared Cramer as part of his family, but the others...they were his responsibility.

He tried not to think too much about his home and family, the glory of the White River at the end of fall before the mountains slept beneath their snow caps and the rainbows settled down in their winter habitats. That was fruitless thinking. There was critical work specific to his assignment to be done here in Paris, and he was the only one in place to do it. It was essential to keep his pole in the water while the fishing was good. Rumors were flying about an Allied invasion coming by way of the coast, and that had made the captain's customers nervous and edgy. They'd become careless about dropping classified secrets before a German fishing guide, one of their own countrymen, who gave no mind to anything but his fish business. Friday, he'd heard of a shipment of tungsten coming from Spain headed for a Nazi weapons manufacturing plant, but he had not yet learned the name of the ship or port where it would be unloaded. With more time, he believed he could wheedle the information out of the man who'd been hired to guide the ship into harbor. Tungsten was essential for the manufacture of military arms, and the delivery would be the perfect target for the French Resistance or RAF.

Brad heard light footsteps on the stairs to his apartment and smiled to himself. He knew who they belonged to. The boy's father and Hans would chastise him for bothering the fisherman, but Brad welcomed the company. He got up and opened the door before the boy could knock. "Wilhelm, my friend! What brings you up to my lair?"

The boy thrust forth a tray covered in a table napkin. "For you," he said, large blue eyes filled with a giver's hope that his gift would be well received. Brad removed the napkin. The tray contained a plate going cold of slices of roasted chicken with servings of a mushroom concoction and apples smelling of cinnamon and sugar. A bowl of custard sat alongside.

"Food," the boy said in case Brad needed an explanation.

"I see that," he said. "It looks and smells delicious."

"But don't tell Papa or Hans. I was to eat it myself, but I know you are more hungry."

Brad's heart moved at the boy's selflessness. It resurrected a memory of Bobby in the days he'd brought him and his sister home. *Here, sister, take part of my share. You're younger than me and still growing.*

"I promise not to tell," Brad said. "You are very nice to do this."

"And I'm to invite you to dinner tomorrow night with Herr Bauer." The boy's face lit up. "We'll have a party!"

"I will look forward to it. Thank you very much."

"Good-bye now. I'm not to pester you," the boy said, and scampered down the stairs before Brad could invite him to stay.

At an upstairs window, Konrad watched his son sprint across the adjoining lawns back to the house before he could be discovered missing. He had taken the fisherman his own dinner, and now he would go to bed hungry. Pain and pride filled his chest. The boy would never make it in the army. He was too loving and kind, but to no regret of his father. Konrad regretted only the world in which his son was too tender to live, a world that he and his kind had helped to create that would cause him to be suspicious of young men like Claus Bauer and Barnard Wagner. But his professional detectors were now on full alert. He had caught those whiffs of smoke, and the fisherman as well as the tutor was not beyond their scope. He hoped with all his heart that tomorrow's trap would prove his suspicions absurd, but God help those young men if it revealed either of them to have befriended his son only to spy on his father.

CHAPTER FIFTY

At the head of the stairs Colonel Derrick Albrecht demanded, "What is going on down there?" but a narrowed glance at Victoria's unbuttoned blouse, the trickle of blood on its collar, and the bleeding nick in her neck gave him a quick answer. She stared up at him, adrenaline spent, with no breath, strength, or will to explain.

Hearing a voice and footsteps, Oberleutnant Peter Janssen scrambled, panting, to his feet, surprise overtaking his fury as a figure wearing the black leather overcoat of the SS and the rank of *Standartenführer* descended the stairs. His eyes widened further when the SS colonel reached the basement floor and he recognized that indeed the officer was Colonel Derrick Albrecht.

Instantly, the lieutenant pointed a finger at Victoria

and screamed in German, "She attacked me, Colonel! That French bitch lured me down here on the pretense of requiring assistance with a washing machine, but her intent was to kill me—rid France of one more Wehrmacht officer, she said. She came at me with a rapier from one of those swords!" He swung his finger to the stack of cleaned and sanded blades. "I would be dead if I hadn't knocked the rapier from her hand. It's over there!" He directed the finger at the area where the sword had fallen. "Thank God for your arrival."

"Yes, indeed. It appears that I arrived just in time," Derrick agreed. "I can see what the death of an officer like you would have meant to the German Wehrmacht." His gaze swept to Victoria's lingerie hanging on the line, then settled on the sergeant's half-unbuttoned jacket.

The lieutenant hastened to rebutton it, growing pink in the face. "I—I, it was so warm in here, I had to—to—"

"—remove your jacket. Just so. I quite understand." He switched his attention to Victoria. "You are bleeding, Mademoiselle Colbert," he observed calmly, reverting from German to French, and handed her his white handkerchief.

Victoria pressed it to her neck. The colonel could

not have mistaken what had almost occurred, but would he take the word of a Wehrmacht officer over hers? She had followed the lieutenant and colonel's dialogue in German, but she said in French, "I don't understand what he said, Colonel, but it doesn't sound like the truth."

Derrick turned again to the lieutenant and spoke in German. "What is your name, Oberleutnant?"

The lieutenant snapped to attention and threw up a smart Nazi salute. "Oberleutnant Peter Janssen on the staff of Major Hartmann in the office of Wehrmacht communications, Herr Colonel!"

"How did you happen to be at L'Ecole d'Escrime Français on Sunday, Oberleutnant Peter Janssen?"

"I—I saw a light on in the salle. I tried the door and found it unlocked. I—I thought I might find one of the instructors or students at practice who would give me a bout."

"Ah, so you fence?"

"I...uh, yes. Foil." The lieutenant glanced quickly at Victoria to see if by chance she'd interpreted his claim and would dispute it.

Derrick smiled. "Is that so? Good."

Relief flashed across the lieutenant's face at the colonel's friendliness, taking it as evidence that his story had been accepted. His expression turned to horror when the colonel stepped to the swords stacked against the stairwell and took two foils by their pommels.

"Mademoiselle Colbert," Derrick said softly, his eyes on the lieutenant, "perhaps it would be best that you go upstairs. We will not engage today, but I would appreciate your waiting for me. Also, may I impose upon you to ask my driver to join me in the basement?"

Victoria complied without a word, but at the top of the stairs she heard the whip of a foil tested in the air and the colonel say, "*En guarde!*"

Less than fifteen minutes later, unruffled, showing no effects of the deed Victoria was certain had been committed in the basement, Colonel Derrick Albrecht reappeared in the salle's small conference room, where she waited shivering in her bloodied silk blouse, still shaken. The colonel was without his gloves but was wearing his overcoat, which she'd guessed the contest in the boiler room did not call for him to remove. He carried her jacket and coat over his arm. She stared up at him accusingly. "There were no protective rubber tips on the points of those foils," she said.

"So Oberleutnant Peter Janssen discovered."

Despite her loathing for the lieutenant, Victoria demanded, "What did you do to him?"

"I did not relieve France of one more Wehrmacht officer, if that is your concern," he said. He held open her jacket. "I merely taught him a lesson in manners. Come, you must be freezing, and did I hear a murmur of hunger earlier? When did you eat last?"

"It is no matter," Victoria said, slipping into the blissful warmth of her jacket and then her coat. "I am fine. My gratitude for your assistance. Now all I require is to get to my hotel."

"Without your laundry? I assume those were your delicates hanging on the line?"

"Oh, yes, there are those. I'll just go get them..."

"That is not necessary. Karl is folding them now. They're dry. He's married and therefore knows the finesse required to handle such items. He'll take them to the car."

"No—no, really, Colonel," she said, understanding his meaning. "You are kind to offer a ride, and again I am so grateful for your appearing when you did, but I am quite all right now. The metro is not far, and the walk will do me good. I can get to my hotel on my own."

The colonel took hold of her elbow. "You are in no condition at the moment to entertain any such delusions, Victoria. Are all the members of the Grayson family so pigheaded, or is the trait restricted only to you? You may answer that question on the way to the car."

For the stretch of a few arrested heartbeats, Victoria thought she'd only imagined, filtered through the wooly residue of last night's nightmares, her fatigue, hunger, insomnia, and attempted rape, a voice addressing her in English by her own name. Then the fog lifted. There was no point in trying to bluff her way out of this. Colonel Albrecht was not a man to be deceived. She'd been a fool to think that she could escape his infallible ear. She breathed deeply. Right now, knowing what she faced, death did not seem like a bad option. Her cyanide pill was in the lining of her coat. If her hands were left free, a quick pull of the seam's thread, and she would be dead before they left the salle. Her friends in Dragonfly would remain safe.

But he would expect her denial. As he led her away, she spoke in French. "What are you talking about? I am Mademoiselle Veronique Colbert."

"I am afraid not. You are Victoria Grayson from Williamsburg, Virginia, in the United States of America. You graduated with a degree in Franco studies from William and Mary College, where you were America's hope to win the gold in foil in the

1940 Olympics. Your brother, Lieutenant Lawrence Grayson, is a pilot in the RAF."

At her speechless silence, he said, "You must of course be wondering how I am aware of that information. The Sicherheitsdienst has sources in America, but I have known since the moment I heard you speak that you are an American, Victoria." He tendered a small smile. "At the risk of appearing boastful, I have an unerring ear for languages, but I admit mine for English was boosted by the year I spent at Harvard University. A great country, America. I thoroughly enjoyed my time there. Now watch your step," he said when they were at the door. "I am quite alarmed by your condition. You've paled even further."

"Where are you taking me?" Victoria demanded. "To your interrogation cells at Sicherheitsdienst headquarters, I presume?"

He halted to stare at her, genuinely shocked. "Now why would you presume such a thing? I know all that I need to know about you already, including why you are in France."

"Which is?"

"To discover the fate of your fiancé, Ralph DuPont, an American pilot also flying for the RAF until he was shot down near Paris in May of last year.

You've now discovered to your deep sorrow that he is indeed lost."

Alarmed for Madame Dupree, she asked, "And how did you learn that information? It couldn't have come from your source in America."

He opened the salle door and steered her outside. "I didn't know for sure of your sad discovery until you just confirmed it. So why would I wish to arrest a woman who came to the country of her enemy only to search in vain for the man she loved? Do you think me that much of a fiend?"

He paused, brow raised, to await Victoria's answer. When she remained silent, he sighed disappointedly. "I can only extend my condolences to such a woman and envy the man who had earned such courage and devotion. Now shall we?" He indicated the door that Karl held open to the back seat of the staff car. Victoria slipped in and the colonel settled beside her. In the whirling reel of her emotions was the relief that for the moment, she and her cover were safe. She could assume that the colonel's dig into her personal life had missed her undergraduate studies in German and the detail of her sabbatical from G. P. Putnam's Sons in New York—information that in any intelligence organization in the world would have raised a red flag. So for the time being, she was unsuspected of being a spy. The Nazis shot spies. They did not send them off to concentration facilities or labor camps; they lined them up against a wall and shot them. Victoria forced back a surge of hysterical laughter over the irony of it. Ralph's failed flight over Paris had saved her mission, and his death, her life from the firing squad.

CHAPTER FIFTY-ONE

Sundays, Achim Fleischer took a break from his guard duty, but on Saturdays he stayed until the Jewish curfew, when he was relieved by the presence of German patrols in the area. Bridgette was therefore surprised when she returned to the convent Saturday after the meeting at La Petite Madeleine and did not find him at his post, nor was he there this Monday morning of November 2 as she set off for La Maison de Boucher. The day had broken foggy and rain was forecast, but, like the American mailman, Achim Fleischer had so far allowed neither snow nor rain nor heat nor gloom of night to stay him from his appointed rounds. Had he become ill?

With a nick of concern, Bridgette looked up and down the street for a glimpse of his rain gear, the white cap and cape worn by municipal policemen, but the Rue des Soeurs de Charité offered no sign of him. Bridgette stood a moment in the thick fog and silence. His absence was unsettling. The street seemed eerily empty without him. He had become a fixed feature of her morning. When no one was about who raised suspicions of imminent mischief, he would walk with her to the corner and see her off to the metro with a wish that she enjoy her day.

Bridgette was now more convinced than ever that Achim Fleischer was no threat to the clandestine activity going on behind his back. The focus of the street's watchdog was on the protection of the mural—and on her. If he'd noticed the Dragonfly foursome at all, Victoria especially, he took them for ordinary residents of the neighborhood whose jobs took them daily past the house next door. No danger on that score.

Bridgette recognized her hollow feeling as having little to do with Achim Fleischer. He was just another question mark on a cold, dreary morning when she was wondering when or if she'd ever see her friends again. Her first thought after the alarm clock went off was that if they'd elected to catch those Lysanders, they'd all be waking up in the safety and warmth of Milton Hall, a little hungover after an evening at the Crown and Scepter, their stomachs still full of the pub's crunchy fish and chips. In a few days, they'd be heading home, addresses exchanged and plans in place to meet earlier than the date in New York.

The Frenchman plainly believed—as did the major—that they would not survive. The poor man had been horrified at their unanimous vote to remain. His face had drooped longer than a basset hound's at their decisions. As they got up to leave, he'd heard the scrape of their chairs as cell doors slamming and coffin lids closing. "Your case officer is not going to like this," he'd said, to which Liverwort had replied in her serene way, "We know."

Achim Fleischer, while an irritating pebble in her shoe, represented familiarity and stability. His absence simply increased her feeling of being alone and lonely on a day that offered no salvation from her gloomy mood. She missed her friends terribly. Seeing them for such a short while yesterday was like a drop of water on a thirsty tongue, and today Frau Helga Richter, the reigning witch from hell, was to come in for a fitting. She was the wife of Sturmbannführer Gottlob Richter, the SS major in charge of the notorious Nazi transit facility in

Drancy, a suburb northeast of Paris. The camp was a holding tank to house Jews until they could be transferred to concentration camps like Auschwitz-Birkenau and Treblinka, where it was rumored they would be gassed. Horror stories had leaked out about the brutality of the guards and inhumane living conditions under the whip of Major Richter that, at the risk of their jobs, the staff of the House of Boucher had been warned not to bring up to his wife.

Meeting the woman would discourage even the bravest from ignoring the warning. Flat where she should have been round, round where she should have been flat, possessing the taste of a Parisian streetwalker and the disposition of a killer shark, the woman expected fashion miracles to atone for nature's cruel injustices to her figure. It was Bridgette to whom she looked to wave her magic wand or, in this case, to apply her drawing pencils.

Having heard the horror stories about Frau Richter, Bridgette had expected the woman to greet her in the haughty manner of other customers who would look her up and down, then say contemptuously to Madame Boucher, "I want an accomplished dress designer to attend me, not a child apprentice." But surprisingly, Frau Richter had taken one look at her and said simply, "Stick me with a pin, midget, and I will slap you." So, no problem with acceptance there.

That was the word—*acceptance*—that Bridgette had been looking for to explain her connection to the team of Dragonfly and Major Renault. Right from the start, they'd all accepted her as she was. She had not had to prove her right to the spot she'd earned. She had not been judged instantly and treated as younger than her age or as delicate as her size suggested. None had addressed her irritatingly, indulgently with asinine tags like *little bit*, *short stuff*, or *Pee Wee*. They had not kindly rushed to her aid during training to offer an unsolicited hand where taller, stronger, smarter people prevailed. They had cut her no slack, given no quarter, nor set the tee box forward. They had trusted her to be their equal in strength and intelligence and capability. How could she not feel connected to people like that? How could she not feel as if...well, it was like being among family?

But the realist in her could not help but anticipate the obstacles that got in the way of the staunchest friendships enduring. As she'd tried to point out to Gladys, time corroded bonds, memories faded, loyalties fossilized. They were the facts of life. Bridgette supposed the weight of that eventuality was responsible for the particular depression she was feeling this morning, so much so that she'd even looked forward to Achim Fleischer's smiling face and friendly greeting.

CHAPTER FIFTY-TWO

You have a letter, Herr Bauer," Louis Mueller said when Chris arrived at the academy that Monday morning and handed over a note-sized envelope of heavy vellum. The man's smirk and the unsealed flap told Chris that he had already read its contents.

"The letter appears to have been opened," Chris said.

"It came that way. Perhaps the Abwehr courier who delivered it is responsible."

"Hmm," said Chris. He took the note to his cubicle, aware that the narrowed eyes of the sports director remained on him until he had shut the door. A shiver of unease ran between his shoulder blades. Herr Mueller's suspicion seemed intensified this Monday morning. Chris was well aware that he had been under the man's microscope since his arrival, so he'd taken the precaution of removing certain carelessly written pages from his lesson planner and had warned Jules Garnier to do the same. They were both convinced that someone employed at the school went on the prowl after hours, and Chris was sure it was the sports director. Chris had left a small trap for him, a note concerning one of the students that the boy was to deliver to his father. Instructors were forbidden to make direct contact with the parents. Sure enough, that afternoon, Louis called a meeting to remind his staff that they were *not* to interact with the students' parents. It was his job, and his alone, he made clear, directing a blistering look at Chris.

The courier-delivered note was from Major General Konrad March. *Please do my son and me the honor of joining us for dinner after your tutoring session today. Herr Wagner will also give us the pleasure of his company.*

My goodness, thought Chris. The note was just short of a formal invitation. Maybe the general had expected Louis to read it and the language was for his benefit. But why a written invitation at all? Why not have Hans extend it when he arrived at the general's this afternoon? Was it to make sure of the presence of his son's tutor in case he had other plans? Maybe he and Limpet had been invited at the behest of Wilhelm, and the invitation extended this early in the day was simply the general's way to make sure the boy would not be disappointed.

Yet something about the invitation nibbled at him. It was this sort of subtle gnawing to which the major had urged them to pay particular attention. *If the aura of something doesn't smell right* (Major Renault was a good one for the word *aura*), *be alert to it. There's liable to be something dead in the woodpile somewhere. Use your own judgment and beware.*

He'd given the general no reason to be onto him, and he was sure that Limpet hadn't, either. The general couldn't possibly know that Herr Bauer had photographed Admiral Canaris's letter. But he would beware, and he would warn Limpet to be on guard, too.

He'd gotten out of bed yesterday without a trace of regret for his decision to stay in Paris, and he'd not been surprised at the other dragonflies' votes to remain as well. That was just who they were—all guts and with no expectation of glory. He wished they'd gone home, though. It would have been a comfort knowing they were safe. He'd come up with an idea that he hoped they'd all go for if they made it to New York. He would suggest that they visit a tattoo studio. Chris was sure that any tattoo artist was bound to have a drawing of a dragonfly in his stock.

Anyway, Chris could not in good conscience have left Paris at this time on any account. He was in a place that amounted to a fox set free in a henhouse, and he couldn't walk away from the intel opportunities that access to the March house afforded him. His only regret was having to take advantage of the trust of a father and son that he and Limpet had both come to care about. But, he reminded himself, in this job trust was a tool that opened locked safes. It made people careless, like the general leaving Admiral Canaris's letter on his desk for anyone to read. And what a shocker it was! If Chris had interpreted it correctly, the chief of the German Abwehr was a traitor to the Nazi regime.

As Bucky shivered through a cold-water shave, a glance out the window of his upstairs room warned him that today deserved the description of "blue Monday." Skies were overcast, and a heavy fog clung to the air. Bucky thought of this time of year in Oklahoma City, when the weather was at its best—crisp, dry days, blue skies, a golden cast over everything, perfect football weather. He pushed the image from his mind. No good going there. There would be other years to enjoy fall for real in his home state, and then he would recall this time in Paris in November 1942.

He'd had to cast his vote to remain in Paris, no question about it. The firm had received a consulting contract for the construction of a secret mountain facility in the French Alps, where the Nazis planned to build guns with barrels capable of launching bombs across the English Channel. Work was to begin in January. If he could get his hands on the blueprints, he could make sure that plant never got off the ground.

Since Saturday's meeting, Bucky had been paying extra attention to Dirk Drechsler. On the surface, he could certainly be considered an undetonated grenade. The major had that much cause for alarm. It was possible that the sergeant was waiting to turn him in until he had more on him, but it was clear to Bucky that the guy wanted something from him first, and whatever it was would determine his decision to expose him. Bucky could almost hear those wheels grinding in his fat head. As long as the sergeant did not suspect him of being an American, then he did not suspect him of being a spy. If he were arrested on that score, Bucky had his story ready, and his boss would back him up. Yes, he was an American who had been hired by a French engineering firm before the war and didn't get out before the borders were locked tight. Being a smart guy, why wouldn't he have on him a false set of documents made up to protect himself?

The team trusted him to stay out of trouble, and he would. Forewarned was forearmed. Horace Barton was one to say that if you could see it coming, you could ward it off or get out of the way. The major seemed to have forgotten they had their escape hatches. Unless their safe houses had been rolled up, a point the Frenchman would have mentioned, Lodestar would carry on until those blueprints were in Allied hands. Meanwhile he had more reason to worry about the safety of the others. Good God! Little Labrador under the eye of that collaborationist policeman, the beautiful Liverwort tap-dancing with the chief of the counterintelligence division of the SD, and Limpet and Lapwing wining and dining with the head of the Abwehr in France. And they were worried about *him*? Christ!

Dirk Drechsler was just getting into his overcoat as Bucky came downstairs. A look about him gave Bucky the feeling that the sergeant had been hanging around waiting for him. "*Bonjour*, Monsieur

Beaulieu," he said. "I see you, too, are just now leaving. Shall we walk to the metro together?"

His Monday just got bluer. "Of course. Why not?" Bucky said. It was only a ten-minute walk. He'd avoided the guy all day Sunday by perusing the stalls of the *bouquinistes*, Paris's famed booksellers lined in their green boxes along the Seine, one of the few charms of Paris still in operation.

"How did you spend your weekend?" Dirk asked in his sketchy French as they set out. "We saw nothing of you on Saturday."

"That's because you were at the rummage sale." An alarm went off in Bucky's head. *Why only Saturday? Why not Sunday as well?*

"What? Oh, yes, the rummage sale."

"You had success, no?"

"Success about what?"

"The rummage sale."

"Oh, yes, very. My old clothes went right away."

"Where did they go?"

"Where did what go?"

"Your clothes. When they went away."

"Oh, that's just my American way of putting things. I meant that they were picked up right away."

"Picked up? From where? Did they fall to the floor, perhaps?"

"No, what I meant was...oh, forget it. What did you do Saturday?"

"What did I do? First, I rose from my bed, then I went to the toilettes—"

"No! No!" Dirk interrupted impatiently. "I meant what did you *do*, where did you *go* to occupy your time for the day?"

Bucky assumed an indignant tone. "Why do you ask, monsieur? Are you interrogating me?"

"No! No!" Dirk threw up his hands, his face flushed with apology. "Not at all. I...was just curious is all. It's...just always interesting for us Americans to know how Frenchmen enjoy their leisure time."

"Us? You mean *all* of you?"

"No, uh, just me, actually. I mean, just me...as your friend...your *ami*!"

They had arrived at the station. "Monsieur, my train is here. I must bid you adieu or I should be late for work. I wish a good morning to you. *Au revoir*."

Squashed between passengers, more alarm bells went off at the sergeant's interest in his whereabouts Saturday, but Bucky felt the release of at least one source of tension. Dirk Drechsler hadn't the faintest suspicion that he was an American.

CHAPTER FIFTY-THREE

The glaring Monday morning headline of *Le Temps*' November 2 edition, Paris's most important daily newspaper, read: FAMOUS AUTHOR FOUND DROWNED IN THE SEINE! Victoria saw the newspaper on the concierge's counter as she passed through the reception lobby on her way to work and on a sudden hunch paused for a quick glance at the deceased's name in the page-long article. Beaumont Fournier. A fisherman had drawn up his seaweed-draped body in his net. A sick feeling crept through her. She'd forgotten that the author was in Paris until his name had come up last evening in the dubious company of Colonel Derrick Albrecht. No preliminary examination of the corpse suggested foul play, but an investigation was underway to determine the exact cause of his mysterious death.

An autopsy was expected to reveal an aneurysm, but a family member of the deceased had reported having no idea why the author was on the bank of the Seine close enough to fall in, since he disliked the smell of the river and could not swim.

Victoria continued slowly, thoughtfully, to the door. Beaumont Fournier...She should not feel relieved at his death, but she could not deny breathing easier knowing that he was not a threat to her identity as she had reason to fear from her conversation with the colonel the previous night. Going by the list of names expressing shock at the author's untimely death, Victoria would guess that his social acquaintances were among the ranks of Derrick Albrecht's associates, and she knew only too well how the networking of the small world of the wealthy and well-connected operated. It would have been only a matter of time before Mademoiselle Veronique Colbert, aka Victoria Grayson, came face-to-face with Beaumont Fournier. Even if she'd remembered that he lived in Paris, it would have been unlikely that she'd have run into him unless he caught a chance glimpse of her on the street, but last night, over veal marsala, she had willingly submitted to a proposal that would have eventually put her into his path.

Once in the staff car, she had no idea where the

colonel was taking her or what he planned to do. He'd met her silence with silence, and she'd been ready to expect anything. The place was a small café, its posted hours stating that it was closed on Sundays. When they arrived, a fire blazed in the great stone fireplace, and a table before it was laid with glassware and cutlery, a basket of fresh bread, and small crocks of cheese and butter. A stand holding a wine bucket and a bottle of burgundy with a napkin-wrapped neck stood beside it. The French proprietor hurried out of the shadows to take Derrick's gloves and overcoat. "And yours as well, mademoiselle?" he offered.

"No," Victoria answered, more forcefully than she intended. She never wanted to be but fingers away from the capsule lightly sewn in the lining of her coat.

"Very well. Soup to begin, I think, monsieur?" he said to Derrick as he pulled out Victoria's chair.

"Something rich and hearty, I hope, Emile?"

"As you requested, Colonel." The restaurateur unfolded a napkin to lay in Victoria's lap, and she risked a longing look at the bread smelling fresh from the oven. The colonel passed her the basket, and with feigned indifference, she took a slice of the warm loaf, refusing to give in to her stomach rumblings or to give the colonel cause to pity her hunger.

But he was not deceived. Immediately, he pushed the crocks of cheese and butter within her reach and said in English once the proprietor had left them, “Really, Miss Grayson, let us not stand on ceremony. You are going hungry, a situation that pains me greatly. I cannot bear to think it. You must allow me to alleviate my pain and correct the most unfortunate grievance I hold against Hitler.”

They were the only ones in the room, but Victoria automatically glanced around to make sure they were alone. He’d said “Hitler,” not “Mein Führer,” as Nazi officials unctuously referred to the dictator, and *most* implied other grievances the colonel held against the dictator. The statement, spoken with contempt, came close to being seditious and would be dangerous for him if overheard. Had it been a careless slip of the tongue, or a deliberate ploy to lead her to believe he shared her view of the crazy man who had led the world into war? Members of the SD were not known to err in careless slips of the tongue.

“I’m afraid I cannot allow you that comfort, Colonel.”

“Well, then, if not for my comfort, for my sense of fair play. We must keep your strength up.”

“For what?” she asked sharply.

With a small chuckle, he plucked the bottle of burgundy from the bucket and poured wine into her glass, the bloodred stream catching the firelight. "Not for the reason you surmise, I assure you. Come now, Mademoiselle Colbert, after the quick dispatch you made of the lieutenant, do you think I'd be so foolish to tempt the fate you had in mind for him if you could have gotten to the swords?"

"For what, then?

"I would not feel right winning against a fencing opponent on the brink of starvation."

"I appreciate your concern, Colonel, but I could not possibly fill my stomach knowing that those of my fellow lodgers were empty."

"Well, we must rectify that, too."

So early that morning, she and the nine residents of her hotel had awakened to find boxes of food deposited before their doors. A voucher for meat, cheese, eggs, and milk with information on a number to call for home delivery was attached. Her neighbors, in response to the unusual sounds heard before daylight in the hall, had stood on their thresholds in their nightwear with mouths agape at the piled boxes of fruit and vegetables, bread and coffee and tea and canned goods apparently meant for their consumption. When Victoria opened her door, all heads turned to her in unison, amazement melting to sad awareness of the cost for such bounty. Last evening, she had been noticed arriving back at the hotel in a German staff car seated beside a handsome young colonel recognized as a member of the security service of the Reichsführer.

As the evening had progressed at the café, the colonel had regaled her with stories of his days at Harvard and his trips around America, speaking English almost like a born native and coaxing a laugh from her at his mimic of a Texas drawl. "Ah even got down to Texas way and spent a spell in Foat Wurth. Found it hot as blazes and dry as a creek bed in drought," he said.

She found it surreal sitting with a senior officer in the black uniform of the SS, dragged into discussing the latest movies and novels released in the United States, the likelihood of the Washington Redskins playing the Chicago Bears in the National Football League championship game, and, of all things, the pros and cons of hot dogs versus hamburgers. The colonel asked questions about her family and region of the country, which she answered sparingly, and he freely told her about his. He spoke with worshipful respect of his parents, both still living but unwell, a worry to him, and dotingly of a younger sister—

"a gifted cellist"—and Victoria disclosed her anxiety over her mother's dicey heart. It was like sitting in a coffee shop at William and Mary swapping family stories and current news with a foreign exchange student.

The name of Beaumont Fournier came up when the colonel asked her about her work as a French translator. Did she enjoy it?

Only when she did not have to translate works by French authors that she did not like, she'd said.

"Such as?" he'd asked.

"Beaumont Fournier, the writer of *Cathédrale de Silence*. I hope he's not a friend of yours," she'd said.

"An acquaintance only," he'd said and shifted to another subject.

Looking back on that brief moment of exchange this Monday morning, Victoria felt certain that she'd seen a slight change in the colonel's expression when she'd mentioned the author's name, then chided herself. Derrick Albrecht was guilty of enough crimes without suspecting him of having something to do with the author's drowning. The afternoon had waned to evening and table candles lit the café's deepening shadows when Victoria, her stomach filled, drowsy from the wine, decided to dance with the cobra.

"*Les Visiteurs du Soir* is premiering at the Madeleine Cinema Saturday night," he'd said. "It's been greatly anticipated as one of the best films of the year. Would you care to go?"

Victoria had read of the coming premiere, open only to members of the German High Command and important officials of the Vichy government. She had been on the verge of refusing when suddenly she realized that literally staring her in the face was a source of intelligence equal to a vault of gold—and now she no longer had to worry about a dropped American syllable tripping her up. The colonel socialized with the Nazi war planners, had entry into their salons and soirees and dinner parties, where a high-level exchange of rumors and gossip were as normal within a trusted fraternity as the flow of champagne. Moving among the gatherings on the arm of Colonel Derrick Albrecht, she was bound to pick up information that could be of incalculable value to the Allies. Alistair Renault must not learn of her plan. *Absolutely not! Sleeping with the enemy goes beyond the bounds of your mission!* He would order her exfiltration, but how could she turn away from an opportunity to pick the lock of such a treasure chest?

But she would have to play her hand well. The

colonel would expect stiff resistance. "Do I have a choice?" she'd asked.

He'd appeared sincerely mortified. "Why, Miss Grayson, have I given the impression that I would use my position to coerce you into doing anything that you would find objectionable?"

She'd said coolly, "Haven't you?"

"I thought you rather enjoyed our Sunday bouts, but under the circumstances, I suppose I can understand your mistaken notion about my intentions. However, let me assure you that while I find you immensely—incomparably—attractive, your suspicions are unjustified. I ask only that you allow me to prove it."

"And exactly how am I to do that?"

"Perhaps you would permit me the pleasure of practicing my English on occasion? I would not wish to impose on your time, but I would like to share a meal with you now and then, go to a film, perhaps escort you to a party. Surely you as well as I can use a pleasant diversion outside the four walls of our workplaces and cheerless abodes."

"You would become bored soon enough."

"I doubt it. Shall we begin our little exercise in proving who is right on that point Saturday night?"

"If you like."

His brow arched hopefully. “Does…that mean you accept my invitation?”

“Yes, I should like very much to see the film.”

“Mademoiselle Colbert…Miss Grayson…Victoria!” He took her hand and raised it to his lips. “I am delighted.”

“Don’t be. I don’t promise to be good company.”

“Completely unnecessary. I shall simply take great pleasure in the enjoyment of your beauty and the opportunities to converse privately in English.”

Of course it had been coercion, simply a different sort than men in his position were at liberty to wield to get an unwilling woman into their bed. Oberleutnant Peter Janssen passed through her mind, but she believed she could trust that Colonel Derrick Albrecht had no intent to force her. He would exercise charm and civility and his considerable male appeal to win her over, but he would be disappointed. She would not be sleeping with the enemy, but she would be judged as if she were. Even the most harmless interaction with him would make her appear at best a French woman willing to share her bed with a high-ranking officer of the despised SS, at worst a collaborator. From the look the concierge gave her as she passed out of the hotel door, the residents were already murmuring among themselves.

CHAPTER FIFTY-FOUR

So Wilhelm will not be joining us for dinner tonight," Chris said, having arrived for the boy's tutoring session to find that Hans had taken him to a soccer game.

Major General March explained that the dinner was to be a surprise for his son, that he'd invited Barnard as well, but he'd come by the tickets unexpectedly and could not refuse his son's pleas to go when he learned he had them. The general apologized for tying up his and Brad's time when he and Wilhelm had enjoyed their company only two days earlier, but he'd thought it too late to cancel the evening's dinner. Hans had left them a cold but most appetizing spread on the sideboard. They were to help themselves.

Chris heard the news uneasily. "And Madame Gastain? Is she not to join us as well?"

"Just us men tonight, though I will pop over to see her after dinner. She's invited me for a nightcap."

When Brad learned of this, his brow rose. Chris, catching Brad's puzzled look, asked softly after their host left them to go to the wine cellar, "What's up? You seem perplexed by what the general said."

"It's just that I don't think Madame Gastain is expecting him," Brad answered in the same lowered tone and explained that his landlady had not mentioned the nightcap when he spoke with her as he was leaving for the general's house. She'd been in her garden dressed thickly, her hair sticking out from beneath a stocking cap, as she prepared to cover her plants against the heavy frost expected that night. "She'd have had a lot of repair work to do to get herself ready for the general's visit," Brad said. "Her butler says that Madame Gastain spends countless hours at her toilette when expecting guests."

Chris said, "You think she forgot?"

"Wouldn't she have remembered when I told her that I was on the way to dine with the general?"

Chris slipped the general's invitation from his pants pocket. "I'm thinking something is fishy about tonight, too. This was delivered by courier today." He handed the note to Brad. "I gather it was sent to me before March got the tickets."

Brad frowned. "Otherwise, why not have Hans

invite you to stay for dinner when you showed up for Wilhelm's tutoring lesson this afternoon?"

"Exactly," Chris said. "So I'm thinking something smells about tonight. Wilhelm suddenly not here. Madame not knowing, or forgetting, about her nightcap date. Of course we could be boxing at shadows, easy enough to do when you expect the bad guys to jump out of the bushes at any second."

Brad nodded. "Hans told me that Wilhelm got in trouble with his papa yesterday. The sweet kid threw a fit when the general refused to invite us to share his chicken supper. Our invitations might be to make up to him for last night. I don't think it could be more than that, unless somehow we've given him reason to be suspicious of us."

"I don't see how that would be possible, unless the Abwehr has a mole inside the Bern station."

"We'd have been intercepted by now," Brad said. "But to be on the safe side, we better keep a sharp eye out tonight."

After dinner, the general glanced at his wristwatch and said, "Madame Gastain is expecting me shortly. I must leave before the soccer game is over." Apologetically, he looked at Brad and Chris. "Gentlemen, could I impose upon you to wait here until Hans and Wilhelm arrive? Since my wife has been gone…I'd rather my son not come into an empty house. He'll be bursting to tell me all about the game, but I am sure he would much rather share it with you."

Brad looked at Chris, who nodded. "Of course, Herr General. It would be our pleasure," he said.

They watched the bundled-up general walk out the door, then Chris turned to Brad. "Well, what do you think?"

"I think this opportunity to visit the general's desk might be too good to pass up."

"Or it's a setup." Chris gestured at the hall table. "The general forgot the bottle of port he brought from the cellar to take to Madame Gastain, which means that maybe he has a date with her after all. I guess we have to take a chance and let the cards fall where they may. You go do what you have to do, and I'll stand watch in case he comes back for the port. I'll say you're in the toilettes."

The general did not return, and ten minutes later, Brad rejoined Chris uneasy but keyed up. The Minox camera in his pocket held a photocopy of the list of names and addresses of the Abwehr's undercover agents operating in the United Kingdom. Hans and Wilhelm arrived, and Brad had to wait until he and Chris walked out together to tell him of the list.

"Where did you find it?"

"On his desk tucked into a photo album under a stack of books. My guess is that he stuck it there out of sight until he could lock it up for safekeeping. I put the list back exactly in the position I found it, so if the general does suspect us and took note of the books' order, he won't notice even a corner out of alignment. I felt the list worth taking a shot of, Lapwing. The names could be the real deal."

"I agree," Chris said, "but it sure smacks of a setup to me. The general leaves us alone supposedly to visit a woman supposedly not expecting him, giving us all the time and opportunity in the world to help ourselves to a highly secret list of foreign agents within an easy search of his desk. It's almost amateurish when you think about it." He drew his scarf higher on his neck against the cold night air but felt another kind of chill creeping in.

"I'll attach a note of our suspicions when I pass off the list to a cutout and let the major decide if it's too much of a risk to act on the information," Brad said. "I figure it will take a couple of days to check out its legitimacy. If he does decide to take a chance on the names and they prove phony, we'll know for sure that we were set up."

"And if they're authentic…and the agents are rolled up…"

"Then the general will know the information came from somewhere," Brad said, "but I believe he'd suspect his own men first, the reason those names were on his desk and not locked up at his headquarters. Nobody trusts anybody in his outfit. In any case, we should have time to get out. I figure we have two days before we know if we have to cut and run. Labrador will leave us a code signal. Remember it's a squiggly line drawn somewhere in our symbols."

"And if the major decides *not* to act on the information, we're safe," Chris said. "I'm going to call in sick, since we'll have to check the mural hourly. How about you? Can you arrange for time off?"

"My schedule is flexible," Brad said. "We'll have to be careful of the beat cop—" He stopped talking and stared, and Chris looked to see what had cut off his speech. Madame Gastain's mansion was totally dark, buttoned down for the night, no light shining in her drawing room window, or in any other part of the house that they could see, yet they'd not met the general on his return home.

"Maybe he got lucky, and they've retired to her bedroom," Brad suggested.

"Maybe," Chris mused, "or maybe not. Limpet?"

"Yes?"

"Pray that we're boxing at shadows."

That night neither could sleep and spent part of it packing for flight, making sure of their explosive devices and of instant access to their cyanide pills. Chris did not regret the risk Brad had taken. He would have done the same. It was part of the job. If the list of German spies proved legitimate, the worth of the intel was staggering, but finding it on the general's desk had been too easy. They both agreed to that. The Abwehr chief might be careless once, but not twice, especially when he planned to be out of the house while guests were about. No German head of intelligence would be that trusting of anyone to go off and leave a classified document of such importance slipped hastily between the pages of a book on his desk. But the deed was done. They had only to wait to see what became of it.

When Major General March returned to his house that evening, he made immediately for the stairs and Hans's room. He had not gone to Madame Gastain's for a nightcap but walked in the opposite direction. He would not have imposed his company on the widow unannounced, and he would see her Saturday evening when they attended the premiere. The cold fog, turning to frost, had drawn around him like an icy blanket, and he would have rather been anywhere than walking the dark, deserted streets of an unfamiliar neighborhood this time of night, but he'd had to give his mousetrap time to be sprung. Frankly, he thought it would net him nothing but the assurance that there were no mice running free in his house.

"Did you set aside the wineglasses and mark them by name?" he asked his aide.

"I did, Mein General. They are in a sack on your desk."

"Thank you, Hans."

General March descended to his study. Donning gloves, he carefully inserted the classified document listing the insertions of Abwehr agents into England, Scotland, and Ireland into the sack containing the wineglasses. In the morning he would carry the lot to Abwehr headquarters and have the fingerprints on the glassware compared to those on the document.

CHAPTER FIFTY-FIVE

A sick ache filled his chest, radiated down his arms, burned like a lump of coal at the back of his neck. Achim would have thought he was having a heart attack if he had not known the source of his pain. His hopes, his dreams, his future lay broken back in that priest's hole in Mademoiselle Dufor's apartment. Bernadette Dufor was a *spy*, a conniving, deceiving, lying spy, a traitor to his belief and faith in her—in *them*!—and in the mural as simply a painting. He had been deceived into protecting a spy's mode to communicate with her cohorts in the French Resistance or whatever rotten group she was working with. From the beginning, he had suspected the painting of being a clandestine tool and should have bypassed his ox-headed commander's objections and gone straight to the Gestapo with his suspicions.

Then he would have been spared the agony he suffered now.

The shock of his discovery had forced him to his bed Saturday. He'd deserted his post and staggered home to crawl under his loving grandmother's quilted tribute to her grandson and pull it over his head. His bed and quilt had been his haven to take his disappointments and shattered trust since he was a child. In it, he could disappear from the world's cruelties—his father and stepmother, his teachers, the bullies at school, the girls he had admired who had laughed at him, of whom Mademoiselle Bernadette Dufor had turned out to be the worst. In this dark, quiet retreat, this cocoon, he could nurse his injuries, plan his revenge. It took him the rest of Saturday and all of Sunday and Monday before he emerged from the swaddle of his bolt-hole.

It was now Tuesday morning. He was at his post, careful to have arrived after Mademoiselle Dufor left for work, and he had formed a plan. He would not turn her in to the Gestapo. He would wait until the Vichy government's new paramilitary police force went into operation on the thirtieth of January. His application into the Milice had already been approved on the contingency that he prove himself worthy to belong. This he would do by handing over Mademoiselle Bernadette Dufor. What an entry permit! By then, he would have had time to widen his net to snag the others involved and to learn the mural's code. That should buy him a seat in the organization—and a fairly high one, too. He couldn't wait to see Mademoiselle Dufor's face when she and the others were arrested and her precious mural literally wiped from the face of the earth. He had been raised Catholic, not that much of it had stuck, but he remembered the peace prayer of Saint Francis and the one line the nuns beat into him that he should live by: *Where there is hatred, let us sow love.* Thinking of Bernadette Dufor and his former feeling for her that now tasted like ashes in his mouth, he revised it: Where there was love, he would now sow hatred.

Monsieur Stephane Beaulieu was not at breakfast. He had not answered Dirk's tap on his door, either, as he passed it to go downstairs. Madame Dupree told him that the engineer had left the boardinghouse earlier than normal—"Right at the lift of curfew," she said.

Dirk panicked. God! Had the man skipped town? Had his escape been a topic of the collusion Saturday at the bookshop? Dirk had planned to waylay the Frenchman this morning to insist that they talk. He'd tell him to call his bosses and say that he was sick, and Dirk would give the captain the same story at breakfast. He was even prepared to put on a show of an upset stomach if the bastard was reluctant to allow him the day off. After giving the situation a lot of thought since his discoveries Saturday, Dirk had decided to approach the Frenchman and lay out what he knew. He was ready to get the ball rolling for a ride out of this hellhole country before the mountain trails closed and the train rails got snowed under, or—God help him!—the invasion came before he got out and he was shot as a traitor.

"Do you know how to get hold of him?" he'd asked Madame Dupree.

"No, monsieur sergeant."

She's lying, Dirk had thought, and he wanted to slap her. The proprietor of a boardinghouse not having on hand a work phone number for her tenants in case of an emergency? Who did she think she was kidding?

"Was he off to work?" Dirk asked.

"I assume so."

"Where does he work?"

"I do not know, monsieur."

Dirk raised his voice. "What the hell *do* you know about your tenants?"

Madame Dupree answered calmly, impaling him with a stare like a dentist's drill. "Since the German Army invaded my country, as little as possible, monsieur."

The other boarders had answered his questions with a shaking of heads and a shrugging of shoulders. Nobody knew where Monsieur Stephane Beaulieu worked.

Yeah, sure. Right. Since Saturday, Dirk's head had been buzzing with unanswered questions like flies captured in a mason jar. What was that café meeting about? What were those people up to, Chris especially? What were they planning? Their escapes? Had Nicholas Cravois attended and then slipped out unseen? Who was the group working for? The Resistance, OSS, SOE? Would they be willing to help him get out in exchange for what he knew? He would not even consider involving Chris. Dirk would leave without his friend ever knowing that he'd been here, seen him, and pretty much got the gist of what he'd signed up for.

Maybe someday, when the war was over and they were home again...but for now the Frenchman was his key out the door. Without him all would be lost.

"Madame Dupree, was Monsieur Beaulieu carrying a bag when he left?"

"I did not notice, monsieur."

"No, of course not."

His performance at breakfast had not been necessary. The captain had immediately granted his request. "Of course, Sergeant. We can certainly do without you."

So he had a whole day ahead of him but was still no closer to holding his ticket to freedom. He'd never been one to wait for a slow elevator. He always took the stairs, arriving at his floor out of breath, and feeling like a fool to find that the slow cab had gotten there before he did. So, unable to hang around and wait for the Frenchman to return, Dirk caught a train to Honfleur with the intent to confront Nicholas Cravois, the legendary Black Ghost. To assure that he'd get back alive, he would tell the Resistance leader that he had taken precautions to guarantee his safe return back to Paris, then offer him a trade: the Black Ghost's help to get to Switzerland in exchange for Dirk's silence about Stephane Beaulieu.

The man's agreement would depend on what and how much the Frenchman meant to him.

His knees shook at the thought of meeting the great man, and Dirk lost his nerve to walk boldly up to the house and knock on the door where he'd seen him and Stephane Beaulieu step out together. Instead, he hid out in the churchyard across the street and glued his eye to the same small opening in the cemetery wall, but he saw no one leave or enter the house. After an hour of unproductive surveillance, tired of standing, of being cold, he thought *to hell with it* and walked quickly to the house across the street.

The door was opened by a woman Dirk judged to be a cleaning lady from her faded kerchief and apron and the aged and weary look of someone who'd scrubbed floors all her life. She carried a broom and started when she saw his uniform. Dirk guessed he must have interrupted her sweeping.

"Oui, monsieur?"

Dirk, pencil poised above the folded underside of a letter-sized sheet of paper, asked officiously in his sketchy French, "I'm taking names of the residents on this street, madame. Who lives here and how many?"

"No one now, monsieur," the woman answered. "The owners have gone to Switzerland. I do not know their names. I was hired to clean the house in their absence."

"I must see for myself." Dirk brushed by the woman into a hall flanked by several rooms. The air held the staleness of a vacated house. White sheets shrouded the furniture. The kitchen showed no signs and gave off no smells of recent cooking. Mattresses were bare. Wardrobes, empty.

The charwoman followed him, still holding the broom. After his quick search, Dirk spun to her. "*Danke*, madame." But as he started to leave, he decided to cast caution to the wind. He unfolded the letter-sized sheet to expose its face. It was the WANTED poster of Nicholas Cravois. "Have you ever seen this man?"

The woman peered at it, then shook her head. "No, monsieur."

"Have you ever heard the name or met Stephane Beaulieu?"

"No, monsieur."

"Danke."

On the way home, to soothe the frustration of a fruitless mission, Dirk stopped at a bakery patronized by Germans and treated himself to several *canelés*, luscious little custardy cakes flavored with rum and vanilla and enclosed in a thin, caramelized shell. Had he glanced back over his shoulder, he would have seen the charwoman without kerchief and apron and broom set off in the opposite direction in a rush of her own that belied Dirk's impression of her age and profession.

CHAPTER FIFTY-SIX

Late Tuesday morning, a white-coated figure from the fingerprinting unit at Abwehr headquarters laid a manila envelope upon the desk of Major General Konrad March. "The report that you ordered, Herr General," he said. "Do you wish me to interpret?"

"*Nein danke*. I'll take it from here."

Konrad stared at the face of the evidence that would either clear or implicate Barnard Wagner or Claus Bauer of suspicion of espionage. If found guilty, for whom, for what organization he was working, Konrad would soon learn. He wouldn't guess the French Resistance. The tutor and fisherman were German. The French underground would not involve nationals of the enemy country, not even declared anti-Nazis. The French wouldn't have trusted them. No, the young men would have been planted at the behest of a foreign service like the OSS or SOE, or internally by the SS or SD investigating his own loyalty to the regime.

For most of the night, unable to sleep, Konrad had grappled with the question of whether either of the men could possibly be a spy. Was he snatching at empty air? The cheese was still in the trap when he'd checked. Nothing had looked disturbed, but well-trained intelligence agents would know to leave things exactly as they were. Logic argued for the young men's innocence. Konrad reminded himself that neither young man could have anticipated that he'd be invited into the home of the chief of German military intelligence in France as social companions to himself and his son.

But then, sometimes intelligence opportunities simply appeared at the feet of a spy engaged in another operation. Barnard Wagner's mission could be to report on German military activity along France's waterways, or Claus Bauer's to pass on information gathered from his Nazi students' loose discussion of their fathers' dinner table conversations with their mothers—shallow picking grounds for intelligence in Konrad's opinion, but thus were treasures found among rubble. Konrad believed he could rule out casual curiosity. Neither young man seemed of the nosy disposition to snoop through their host's personal papers, especially those of a high-ranking Abwehr officer. The old adage "Curiosity killed the cat" was never truer than now in German-occupied Paris.

Konrad pulled in a breath and opened the envelope from which he withdrew two reports. One applied to the fingerprint images found on a wineglass marked A, the other to a matching glass designated B. Alongside each image were the prints lifted from the sheets of German agents operating in the United Kingdom. Konrad let go his breath. The prints on the list of names matched those on wine goblet B.

Barnard Wagner.

Konrad dropped back into his chair. His good friend the fisherman, his little boy's kickball *Kumpel*, was a spy. He should have paid more attention to that dart of doubt about Herr Wagner's authenticity when he'd overheard his conversation with Captain Allard on his boat back in September: *That wouldn't have been by design, would it?... The less you know, Captain.*

So who was he working for, this young German he once thought of as a simple, ordinary fisherman—the Americans, English, or Nazis? Who had planted him next door with his fishing tackle and flies to angle his way into the general's warm regard and into the heart of his son? Konrad could, of course, reel in Captain Allard to question him, but he'd allow him to be for now.

Konrad picked up his desk phone and dialed a private number. In case someone in his department traced the call, the number would be found to belong to a legitimate recipient, one the Abwehr chief would have reason to contact from time to time, despite the enmity between their organizations. "Good morning!" Konrad said heartily to the person on the other end of the line. "I have that report for you. I'll send it through the usual channels."

Two hours later, dressed in civilian clothes and having driven himself in his personal car to a wooded park in a quiet neighborhood of Paris, deserted this time of day in the week, Konrad sat down to await the person he had arranged by code to meet. Shortly he saw him emerge from the canopy of bare-limbed trees that stood like sentinels along the path. A painting Konrad had seen recently popped into his mind. The reach of the gray, naked arms of the trees toward the overcast skies and the man walking under them in his black SS uniform with its red armband, reminded him of the artist's rendering of nude Jews lifting their arms in anguished appeal toward heaven against a background of blazing ovens. Konrad quelled a threat of nausea and stood, removing his glove.

"Derrick," he said, smiling, and extended his hand. "So good of you to meet me."

Colonel Derrick Albrecht drew off his glove as well and accepted his hand. "My pleasure, Konrad. What has happened?"

The men sat down on the bench, and Konrad poured two cups of steaming coffee from a thermos he had brought. "I've discovered that my next-door neighbor is a spy," he said.

"Good heavens! Madame Chastain?"

"No, thank God. Her tenant living in the apartment above her garage. He works as a fishing guide for a company whose business is conducting river fishing tours. He and I share in common an obsession for fly-fishing, and he and my son share a passion for kickball. They play a game together most afternoons. My son is silly about him. I am fond of him, too."

"Ah," said Derrick, his tone understanding. "A sad situation."

Konrad asked calmly, "Is he one of yours?"

"No."

"You're sure."

"I'm sure."

"The Waffen SS?"

"I would know of it."

"The Gestapo?"

"They would not dare intrude on my territory."

The questions were asked and answered in a spirit of friendship at odds with men who worked as heads of intelligence organizations that despised each other. In 1938, Hitler appointed the Sicherheitsdienst, a division of the SS known as the SD, as the Nazi Party's military arm of intelligence. Its job was to detect and expose members of the German government, intellectual elite, clergy, and military hierarchy who opposed the Nazi regime and to eliminate them by any means necessary. To carry out these orders, the SD dispatched spies and informants not only into the departments of government officials but also into the divisions of the German Army to gather intelligence against those suspected of treason. The task of ferreting out enemies of the Third Reich among the less-exalted ranks fell to the Gestapo.

From its creation, conflict had risen between the Abwehr—Germany's oldest organization of army intelligence, headed by Admiral Wilhelm Canaris—and the upstart amateur Sicherheitsdienst, directed by the admiral's archenemy, Heinrich Himmler. The Abwehr, whose purpose was to protect Germany from domestic and foreign espionage, despised the SD's mission and the methods it employed. The new organization siphoned off materials, resources, and manpower needed by the Abwehr, undermined its intelligence reports, got in the way of its activities, and generally tromped on the Abwehr's toes. Recently, Hitler had ordered the SD to investigate several Abwehr officers suspected to be involved in anti-Hitler plots.

By all appearances, the same dislike flowed between Major General Konrad March and Colonel Derrick Albrecht, but appearances could be deceiving. The counterintelligence chief of the SD and the head of the Abwehr in France were members of a very private club of brothers-in-arms mutually engaged in highly secret affairs.

"Are you going to bring him in for interrogation?" Derrick asked after Konrad had explained the basis for his suspicions.

"No. I will allow the buck to graze unaware of my gun scope until I discover who he's *not* working for. I'll learn soon enough. That list of names was authentic. If my English assets are rolled up, I will know the SOE or OSS is running him. If they are left alone…" Konrad shrugged, leaving it unsaid that Barnard Wagner would be in the employ of the

SS or Gestapo or an entity within his own ranks seeking evidence to bring the charge of treason against him.

Derrick nodded approval. "A good move. This way you've ridded the Reich of what—fifteen assets?—in strategic positions to cause damage to the Allies. Let's hope your spy is with the Brits or the Americans. What are you going to do with him if he is?"

"Ply him with intel that will send his bosses into tailspins of exuberance."

"Be careful, Konrad, I beg you. The Americans or English may have planted him, but that doesn't mean our brother organizations aren't interested in you."

Konrad replenished their coffee cups. "I intend to be very careful. I am in love."

Derrick cocked his head in surprise. "Oh, really? Who?"

"The beautiful Madame Adeline Gastain, my neighbor."

"Is she in love with you?"

"I have a glimmer of hope that someday she might be. I am taking her to the premiere of *Les Visiteurs du Soir* Saturday night."

"I will see you there!" Derrick said. "I am taking

the beautiful Mademoiselle Veronique Colbert, my fencing partner at L'Ecole d'Escrime Français."

"You speak of her as if *you're* in love, *mein Freund*."

"I very well could be."

Konrad cocked an eyebrow. "Is she in love with you?"

Derrick shook his head. "No, sadly, and I've not a glimmer of hope that she ever will be."

CHAPTER FIFTY-SEVEN

Returning to his boardinghouse after work Tuesday, Bucky had felt his heart "go back on him," an expression that his dear Oklahoma grandmother, now deceased, would use to describe her reaction to a shock. Each day, going and coming from the boardinghouse, Bucky looked for a black mark on the right underside of the first step. That it was never there was no surprise to Bucky. He did not expect to hear from his father again until the war was over.

But Tuesday afternoon, his usual cursory glance stuck to the black mark as if glued to it, his father's instructions resounding in his ear. *Should I need to contact you, you will find a black mark on the right side of the first step of your boardinghouse. Couriers are too risky. Go to the tree.*

Making the trip to the plane tree in Passy-Auteuil at that hour would have meant the risk of being caught out after curfew. He would have to wait, trapped, until the following morning, so Wednesday, he was up and gone from the boardinghouse the minute curfew was lifted. The day had not fully broken when he arrived at the tree across from his aunt's house and withdrew a message from its hiding place. It was short but succinct. The message warned that on Tuesday an Abwehr sergeant who appeared to be an American had called upon the house by the quayside in Honfleur and inquired of the caretaker about Nicholas Cravois and Stephane Beaulieu. Bucky remembered the silent-footed woman in the faded kerchief and apron who had served him and his father tea. He hoped she was long gone by now.

Sweat broke out on his face. How the hell had Dirk Drechsler, that bumbling fool, discovered the house in Honfleur? The only explanation was that he had followed Bucky to it. Did that mean he had also tailed him to the café in Montparnasse Saturday? Was that the reason for his curious questioning of Bucky's whereabouts that day?

Bucky sat down on the park bench and pressed the heels of his palms to his temples. The rush of blood to his head had made him dizzy. Because of his stupid carelessness, Dirk Drechsler now knew of his connection to Nicholas Cravois and possibly of his association with Liverwort and—oh God—the guy's hometown buddy, Lapwing! What was he to do now? Split and run while he had the chance? He was as brave and tough as the next man, but as the major had warned them many times, nobody held out under torture. If he broke, they'd set a trap for his father at the hole in the tree and for Dragonfly at the mailbox. They'd arrest Madame Dupree…

But wait a minute! He must think. It was now November 4. His trip to Honfleur had occurred Sunday, October 11, three and a half weeks before, about the time Dirk had taken a special interest in him. Bucky now understood why. At least that mystery was solved, but the puzzle he couldn't work out was the sergeant's motive for keeping the information to himself. The capture of Nicholas Cravois would have promoted him to general. Drechsler could have hurried back to Paris from Honfleur and reported his findings immediately, but he clearly had not. Even when Liverwort had shown up at the boardinghouse the following Sunday and added to his suspicions, he'd still not shown his hand. But why? Bucky wished he could talk to Lapwing about it, help him get a read on his confounding childhood friend.

Bucky got up to stamp feeling back into his numb feet and started to walk. Walking helped him to think. The pressure in his head relented. Ever since that Sunday, he had felt Drechsler wanted something from him and was only waiting for the right moment to spring it on him. He had an airtight case for Bucky's arrest if he'd followed him to the café, but the turncoat had kept his silence, so he wouldn't split just yet, or report his discoveries and suspicions to the major. Major Renault would pull him and the others out for sure, no discussion about it. Bucky would go back to the boardinghouse and take a chance that his and his teammates' perception of Dirk Drechsler was right on the money. The guy hated the people and the job he'd signed on to and wasn't about to interfere with the factions that could bring them down. He was desperate for an end to the war so that he could go home, the sooner the better. The sergeant might even be turned to work for the OSS, a mole right under the Abwehr's noses. Whatever was at stake, Bucky would keep the L pill within reach of a quick swallow. For the sake of his father and the team, he wouldn't be taken alive.

Tuesday afternoon, Bridgette returned to the convent to find that Achim was back at his post. This morning as she'd left for work, she had mixed emotions about his continued absence. She had begun to worry that something had happened to him, but that morning right after the lift of curfew, she'd found a note from Limpet, their fisherman, on the floor beneath the letter drop asking for a cutout and immediately transmitted the request to the major. He'd come back with the message: *Done. Usual time and place*, and Bridgette had felt relief that she could relay it to Limpet by code without being under the watchful eye of Achim.

As Bridgette approached the convent, she could see that Achim was deep into study of the mural and frowning. Her heart jumped. Had he discovered the extra detail on Limpet's code symbol? She put on a happy face. "Achim! It's so good to see you! I've been worried about you. Have you been ill?"

"You could say that," he said in a tone absent of the cheer of his usual greeting. He pointed with his truncheon at the mollusk. "That wasn't there before."

Bridgette, surprised at his abrupt manner, said,

"Oh, you do have an eye. Yes, the inspiration hit me this morning. From time to time I feel I must add some other touches to the mural for greater depth. Do you like what I did to the limpet?"

"Not particularly," he said, his eyes roving the mural. "Gilding the rose, if you ask me. I see the *nose tweak*, as you called it—the diagonal line—has disappeared."

Bridgette retained her smile despite the clear note of insinuation that the mark was more than a harmless prank. "Yes, I found the perfect solution to eradicate it as if it had never been," she said.

"You should not have touched it. In the future, should other *nose tweaks* appear, you are to let them be until I can investigate further, do you understand?"

Bridgette felt a flare of resentment. What in the world had gotten into him to set her back to square one with him? "It's my mural, Achim. It should be for me to decide what to do about such marks."

He turned to her, eyes cold. "It is now the property of Paris because it appears on a public street. I am a servant of the people, so it is for *me* to decide if such marks should be erased. They could mean something seditious."

Bridgette forced a laugh over a catch of panic in her chest. "Seditious? Oh, Achim, that's ridiculous."

"You laugh at me, mademoiselle?" he said, his voice pitched high in indignation. "You will not do so when I am a member of the Vichy police and am in a position to treat such impudence as it deserves."

Bridgette's mouth fell open. "Achim..." Her voice dropped to a gentle plea. "What has happened? You're not the same. Have I done something to offend you?" She moved closer, but he stepped back as if she'd breathed dragon fire. For an instant his hard gaze softened to something like sorrow, but it vanished as quickly as a switched-off light.

"I am perfectly fine," he said coldly. "Now I must see to my duty. Good evening, mademoiselle."

Bridgette observed him walk away to assume his "duty," which consisted of walking a few yards to plant himself in full view of the evening metro rush, leaving her to push open the heavy courtyard door that he had come to perform as a routine courtesy upon her return in the evening. It could be a flimsy, petty thing that had set him against her, Bridgette told herself. Achim Fleischer was soon to be inducted into the Vichy Milice, that ultra-hated body of French police that discouraged associations with people of their jurisdictions, and he might have recognized his friendship with Mademoiselle Dufor as no longer appropriate. But Bridgette remained unconvinced. Hatred had flamed on his face, the kind that stemmed from deep betrayal, but when had she betrayed Achim Fleischer? A greater concern was his suspicion that the mural was more than an aquatic landscape. Bridgette would give him a few days. Maybe she could worm out of him the reason for his change of mood before deciding whether to report his about-face to the major.

An hour after he'd dropped his need for a cutout into the mail slot, Brad had passed by the wall again with hope that Labrador had acted upon his request. His hope was rewarded at the glance of the dark parallel lines cleverly stroked in as part of the shading on the mollusk, and he'd taken off to meet his cutout to deposit the treasure he'd found in Major General March's study. The brush pass went off without a hitch. Brad expected the list of German agents to arrive in Bern today. Major Renault would act fast once the names were in his hands, and then he and Lapwing would know whether to scram or to stay in place. The waiting would be terrible and require a risky number of passes by the mural. The cop had not been there this morning or on Monday, and Brad had hoped he'd disappeared for good.

In midafternoon, on the chance there would be a message for him and Lapwing, he hurried off to check the wall again. The all clear signal was to be a small circle inconspicuously drawn within the details of their symbols. The code mark would mean that the agents were legitimate. The worry then would be whether the general suspected Barnard Wagner and Claus Bauer of leaking the information. Somehow Brad believed he would not. Some other poor soul would take the rap, but the judgment of whether or not to pull him and Lapwing out of France would rest with the major. If the list was bogus, then their exfiltration was a certainty. The squiggly line would tell it all.

No squiggly line was in sight, but the policeman was and had returned to stand guard with an air of renewed commitment to his job. Brad, peacoat collar turned up, beret pulled down, shoulders drawn against the cold, hurried past him without so much as a glance at the mural, an ordinary fisherman on his way to get out of the weather. But the policeman had noted Brad's walk and figure and outer attire, the details by which he could identify those who belonged in the neighborhood, those who did not, and those who appeared more often than they should. The seaman was what he called a "familiar." Achim's vigilance was sharper now. He would no longer look for anyone or anything out of the ordinary on the street, but for the common and usual, the familiars.

CHAPTER FIFTY-EIGHT

The list of German agents was in Alistair's hands by the end of Tuesday, November 3. Suspicious but guardedly elated, he relayed the information to the director of MI5, the United Kingdom's domestic counterintelligence and security agency headquartered in Thames House in London. MI5 immediately initiated a roundup of the people named on the list. The following morning, a postal clerk in Brighton, East Sussex, was therefore surprised when he answered his doorbell and found himself surrounded by a swarm of His Majesty's finest. The same held true for the keeper of a lighthouse overlooking the coast of Dover, a door-to-door salesman working for a vacuum cleaner company in Whitby, North Yorkshire, and a political science teacher who had retired to the village of Southwold in Suffolk. Within the next few days, MI5 and other government intelligence departments throughout the United Kingdom had quietly gathered into their net other residents of cities and coastal and inland villages, until their interrogation rooms were filled to bursting. The list of spies working for the Germans in the UK was legitimate.

Near the end of the week, Major Renault sent word to that effect to Brad and Chris via cutouts but, surprisingly, did not command them to abandon their posts. The men had expected the order because their access to Major General March's desk would put them immediately under the Abwehr's suspicion. By Saturday, no squiggly lines had appeared on their symbols, but their flight bags remained packed. They would give it another week before drawing a full breath. On the other side of the city, shortly after the roundup began, Major General Konrad March and Colonel Derrick Albrecht tapped glasses filled with a fine French Merlot in celebration of a successful coup.

By week's end, Achim Fleischer had compiled mental notes of familiars who passed the wall more than twice daily. At the top of his list upon whom he would keep a sharpened eye was the strapping young man huddled deep in his peacoat that he'd noticed on Monday, followed by another familiar of equal build and outer swaddling, this one a blond man about the seaman's age. In his position of authority, Achim could have stopped them at any time, asked for their papers, and questioned their business in the area, but he preferred to wait for more rope by which to drag them into an interrogation cell—not, of course, at the office of his district commander, but in January at Milice headquarters in the free zone of Vichy France.

Wednesday, Dirk Drechsler had been waiting for Bucky when he returned to the boardinghouse from Honfleur in late afternoon. "Monsieur Beaulieu, may we talk?" he had asked quietly.

The anxiety chewing away at Bucky's insides bit harder, and his fingers closed around his belt buckle containing his L pill. "Of course, monsieur," Bucky said. "Where do you wish to converse?"

"I don't want to cause you trouble, Stephane," Dirk had said when they were seated in the relative warmth of the sergeant's room. "You got to trust me on that. Let me put all my cards on the table..."

By the end of the conversation, Dirk had confirmed Bucky's guess of the reason that he'd held off blowing the whistle on him. The boy wanted out, and he wanted Nicholas Cravois to arrange it.

"By Thanksgiving," Dirk had said hopefully, but did not threaten "or else." What date did Americans celebrate this holiday? Bucky had asked. The fourth Thursday of November, Dirk had answered. Ah well, Bucky said uncertainly. Monsieur must understand that General Cravois might not be able to arrange for his disappearance so soon. These things took time, careful planning, but he would see what he could do. Dirk had not argued the point or demanded the impossible, but Bucky had concluded for himself that if he failed, the sergeant would choose to improve his miserable situation with the Abwehr by turning him in. Each had held on to his secrets. Dirk did not divulge his friendship with Christoph Brandt or that he'd seen his knockout blond friend at the café, and Bucky did not volunteer the information that he was an American or that he was the son of Nicholas Cravois.

Saturday, Admiral Wilhelm Canaris arrived as the guest of his protégé, but informed him immediately that he would return to Berlin on a night flight, thus relieving Konrad's fear of a disruption of his date with the widow. The admiral had come only to warn his friend that suspicions of his own anti-Nazi activities were growing at the Reich Chancellery. He wanted Konrad to prepare an exit plan "should the hammer that falls on me, fall on you."

Konrad's stomach had knotted, for unbeknown to his superior, Konrad was as deeply involved in conspiracies against the Third Reich as his commander. He had thought it best not to involve the admiral in his activities, since he had enough of his own to concern him, and the less each knew of the other's work, the safer. But Konrad held one card that his mentor did not. His discovery that Barnard Wagner was an undercover agent working for either the English or the Americans came with an unexpected benefit. It provided a channel of escape for himself and his son.

At the reception for the viewers of the private showing of *Les Visiteurs du Soir* Saturday evening, conversation paused at the entrance of the handsome Colonel Derrick Albrecht and the new dazzler on his arm, Mademoiselle Veronique Colbert, an instructor of foil said to be his match on the piste. Victoria in her ivory satin gown and Derrick in the black jacket and white-lapelled formal uniform of the SS made quite a stunning pair. Victoria's beauty outshone even that of the film's starring actress, Arletty, as, cocktails in hand, they made the rounds of the Nazi elite, Victoria feeling as if she were moving in a den of snakes dressed in formal attire. A tense moment came when she and Colonel Albrecht encountered the commander in charge of the Abwehr in France, on his arm an extremely attractive woman introduced as Madame Adeline Gastain. Their two organizations were known to hate each other, and the men would have crossed metaphorical swords had the ladies not responded warmly to each other's introductions, complimented each other's gowns, and expressed enthusiasm for the film.

Victoria worried how the evening would conclude. Would Derrick Albrecht invite himself to her apartment to share one of the bottles of the Bordeaux delivered with the boxes of food? How would she handle him? But at the door of her hotel, under the eye of the concierge peering through the glass from her station inside, Colonel Derrick Albrecht merely bowed over her hand, clicked his heels together, and said, "Thank you, Mademoiselle Colbert, for the most enchanting evening of my life. Regrettably, I am afraid that I have a pressing matter to attend to tomorrow and will be unable to keep our scheduled appointment. I will look forward to our bout Sunday next. *Bonne nuit.*"

Sunday in Bern, Major Alistair Renault felt a special need to spend the day in a church where he might find a moment's peace while he waited to learn Dragonfly's fate. Any day he expected to receive word that one or all of the team had been arrested. Henri, his ubiquitous eyes and ears in Paris, had reported that Victoria had been seen escorted by Colonel Derrick Albrecht to a cinema premiere and that Sister Mary Frances had notified him that the beat policeman had turned against Bridgette. The classified list that Brad had passed on from Konrad March's desk Alistair now suspected to be too much of a windfall.

"The general's tired." Wild Bill had made light of Alistair's suspicions that Brad and Chris might be under surveillance. "Fatigue makes us sloppy, which he's already demonstrated once. Sometimes even I am slack in giving due diligence to classified material."

The chief of the Abwehr in France, careless? Maybe, maybe not. Wild Bill had been ecstatic over the intel. At Milton Hall, the SOE had brought out the champagne, but Alistair's nose, equal to his unimpeachable gut, had caught a waft of something about it that he didn't like.

The other odors drifting out of Paris were as worrisome. The plethora of highly secret material Victoria was feeding them—how was she coming by it? Colonel Derrick Albrecht should have already picked up on Victoria's native tongue by now. Why hadn't she been arrested? Same for Bridgette, if the policeman had caught on to the clandestine activities going on behind his back. Alistair questioned why the American turncoat had not squealed on Sam Barton to his superiors, and why Brad and Chris had not been rolled up. Aware that he had left top secret material on his home desk, it stood to reason that they would be the first persons the general would suspect of leaking the information to the Allies, but they remained untouched. Why?

None of it made sense to a spymaster familiar with the sleights of hand, the illusions, the trickeries of play in the espionage game. His nose, his gut, told him that his kids were either being played by high-level Nazis working against the regime or being set up in a cat-and-mouse game in which they were the mice in a cage of ocelots, their wiles and wits their only defense of play.

THE GAME

1942–1944

CHAPTER FIFTY-NINE

The week of November 9, 1942, broke fair and calm. Sunny days and fluffy clouds afloat in a sea of blue skies offered respite from the former dark weeks of dripping rain. While the German Army, in violation of a 1940 armistice, expanded its occupation of France by seizing Vichy France, the country's supposed Free Zone, other war news held slivers of hope that the Allies were making headway against the Axis powers. In North Africa, German-occupied Algeria, a province of France, was liberated by U.S. troops with the assistance of a band of French Resistance fighters. In the Pacific, the Americans won a decisive victory against the Japanese on Guadalcanal. In Libya, the British Eighth Army recaptured Tobruk, a port city strategic to the Germans' plan to move into Cairo and take over the Suez Canal.

In the City of Light, while most Parisians took a little heart at the unfolding developments spread by word of mouth and garnered from underground newspapers and hidden radios tuned to the BBC, the team of Dragonfly went about their week with an eye constantly cast over their shoulders, senses alert, nerves taut, the phrase "jumping at shadows" never more clearly understood and felt. Victoria's glance at a headline in *Le Temps* as she hurried through the hotel lobby to work Monday had caused her to miss her step and almost lose her footing. The accompanying news item stated that Beaumont Fournier's death had been ruled a homicide by potassium poisoning. The police had tracked the author's movements during the week to the day he was last seen, Saturday, October 31. According to his butler, he had left his residence to pay a morning visit to the office of Colonel Derrick Albrecht, the counterintelligence chief of the Sicherheitsdienst, headquartered at 84 Avenue Foch, and then to the Ritz Hotel, where he was to meet the actress Michele Morgan for lunch. According to both parties, Beaumont Fournier did not show up. Their statements had been corroborated by Colonel Albrecht's aide and the maître d' of the hotel restaurant. When questioned about the nature of the writer's visit, Colonel Albrecht had professed no idea or even knew to expect him, since no appointment was on the books. The police were continuing the investigation.

Victoria felt goose bumps rising amid the same unease that had disturbed her when she had first heard the news of his death. She shook the suspicion from her head that Derrick Albrecht was somehow involved in Beaumont Fournier's death. Again she told herself that the colonel was responsible for enough crimes without adding the murder of the writer to the list. What reason would he have? He barely knew the man.

The concierge had emerged from her private rooms behind the registration counter with a special smile for the hotel's beautiful young benefactor. Victoria always had to keep in mind that the woman was neither friend nor foe, but a survivor. She would go in whatever direction the stream flowed to stay alive and preserve her hotel. "I thought I'd find you here," the concierge said. Victoria was always the first in the lobby this time of morning and the first to glance at the newspaper before the residents passed it around among themselves over their morning coffee in the salon.

The concierge's eye fell on the headlines. "I see you've read of the murder of France's most prominent author and the involvement of your colonel," she said. "I wonder if nowadays someone in his position would be held accountable for a crime against a Frenchman?" The woman looked clearly worried. Her question was really meant to inquire of Victoria if the residents' windfall of foodstuffs and heating would be suspended should the colonel be arrested.

"He is not my colonel, madame," Victoria corrected her, "and nowhere do I read in the article that Colonel Albrecht is suspected of killing Beaumont Fournier."

"Oh, you have to read between the lines," the concierge said. "He is at least suspected. Otherwise, why mention his name?"

The question was enough to add to the disquiet that had gnawed at her since Saturday, when the colonel had saved her coat from hitting the floor at the premiere. Her heart had grabbed when he'd caught the coat by its lining where she'd concealed her cyanide capsule. He'd given her a smile to say that all was well, and for the rest of the evening she'd had no reason to think otherwise, but he was a man of subterfuge, a practitioner of deceit, his charm and congeniality a mask. Had his hand felt the pill? A man of his experience in the espionage business would know immediately what it was and why it was there.

Her unease increased when the week passed and she didn't hear from him. She'd expected something—a note, chocolates, flowers, a bottle of wine—to be delivered to her door expressing appreciation for the pleasure of her company Saturday evening, but no such token arrived. Each day, Victoria had followed the stalled investigation into the mystery of the author's death that subscribers of *Le Temps* were finding a titillating change from the Nazi propaganda that usually made the headlines. Much was being made of the murder by publishers, editors, readers, fans, and the author's family and friends. It seemed that everyone who had even said hello to Beaumont Fournier was interviewed, including the actress Michele Morgan, but Derrick Albrecht's name was not mentioned again.

The Sunday morning after the film premiere, Derrick dispatched a coded message to his undercover radio operator in Long Island, New York. Wishing to keep his inquiry private, he handled the matter personally, sending the young SS sergeant at his electronic communications post off for coffee so he could transmit his encrypted text himself. Upon the sergeant's reappearance, Derrick gave him strict orders to leave the decryption of the return message to him. He did not expect to hear back from his Long Island agent until late Monday. The requested information would require his source to make a trip to Williamsburg, Virginia, and devise a careful strategy of approach to the documents clerk at William and Mary College.

On Monday, having slept only a few hours the night before and endured an aimless Sunday filling his time without the parameters of his fencing bout with Mademoiselle Colbert, he was back at his desk at Sicherheitsdienst headquarters earlier than usual to settle down to await his agent's report. He already knew the truth it would contain, but he wished it confirmed. He was a man who made sure his ducks were lined up before taking aim.

Setting his morning cup of coffee before his chief on his desk, Karl observed, "You are not yourself today, mein Oberst."

"Not since Saturday night, as a matter of fact," Derrick said, sipping his coffee.

"Mademoiselle Colbert would make any man not be himself, if I may be so bold to state an observance, Herr Colonel." The aide had served as the couple's driver Saturday night, and the appearance of Mademoiselle Colbert stepping from the hotel entrance in her evening finery had challenged his military training to keep his attention eyes front.

"It would be difficult not to observe the obvious," Derrick said. *Very difficult, indeed, more's the pity*, thought Derrick as Karl left the room.

The only jarring element to her appearance had been her coat. It was her everyday coat, an incongruous contrast to her elegant satin gown. Derrick had thought she should be swathed in fur. When he offered to check it, she'd said that she would keep it should she get cold. He had pointed out that the hem would only drape to the floor from the back of her chair, and he would make sure the room temperature would be to her liking. She had yielded it reluctantly, and he had understood why when a clumsy oaf ran into him and he'd grabbed the inside of her coat before it fell to the floor. Instant recognition of the thin-walled glass capsule in the lining shot through him like an electrical charge. It was an item routinely searched for in garments worn by captured enemy agents. Derrick couldn't be absolutely sure of its compound or purpose, but if it wasn't a cyanide pill, what was it doing concealed in the lining of Mademoiselle Colbert's—Victoria

Grayson's—coat? He could draw only one conclusion: The astonishingly beautiful woman whose coat he held was a spy.

She'd been standing not three yards away, drawing eyes, but hers were on him. She had witnessed the mishap and his rescue of the coat, and Derrick's trained eye saw her pale slightly and a swallow move down her throat, betraying the question flashing in her gray-green eyes. Had he discovered the pill? He'd sent her a smile of assurance—*Saved by the bell!*—while he waited his turn to check the coat.

Late in the afternoon, the sergeant he'd spoken to yesterday appeared before his chief's desk. "Your transmission is about to come through, Herr Colonel."

Derrick hurriedly took his seat before the telegraph machine and transferred the coded message to a sheet he deciphered at his desk. The information was as he'd expected and had carelessly not thought to research. The college transcript of Victoria Grayson, aka Veronique Colbert, revealed her secondary academic discipline as German.

CHAPTER SIXTY

Monday, November 9, began on an uneasy note for Chris also. During a break in gym class, a student approached Chris's back carrying a balancing pole. Chris, seeing its shadow on the gymnasium floor, had reacted with "the slip," a sudden rotation of his body to avoid an attack from behind, one of the maneuvers taught during OSS training sessions on defensive tactics. Embarrassed, he apologized to the startled student who had almost received a kick in the groin. Louis Mueller had observed the scene and hurried across the floor to confront him. After a friendly clap on the boy's shoulder, Chris quickly sent the student on his way before Louis could reach him.

"My God, what was that all about? You nearly scared that boy shitless!"

"One of the defense techniques I've been teaching the class," Chris improvised.

"Since when have you included such maneuvers into your track-and-field curriculum?"

"You don't approve of teaching defense tactics to our young warriors, Herr Mueller, especially if they are unarmed with an opponent holding a weapon at their back?"

"That's not the point!"

"What is?"

At a loss for a comeback, Louis dismissed the argument with a frustrated wave of his hand. "You've received a message."

A current of nerves skittered through Chris. Was the message from Major General March? The director would not have bothered to deliver it otherwise, may not have even given it to him. He had not seen the general since having dinner with him a week ago Monday—strange, since the man usually made a point to arrive at the completion of his son's tutoring sessions to question how he had fared, and Limpet had not encountered him on the riverbank the Sunday before, his neighbor's usual day to throw in a line from his back forty. Also, this morning the sports director had greeted him with a smirk and glint in his eye that made Chris think the man had discovered something about him over the weekend that was his to know and for his instructor to worry about.

"What does it say?" Chris asked.

The director's face reddened with rage from the implication. "It came by phone! Major General Konrad March wishes you to dine with him and his son tonight after your tutoring session."

"How kind of him. I can use a good meal."

As Chris stepped by him to pass, Louis said, "That was a military maneuver you just demonstrated for the boy. Your file never said anything about your having had army training. Where did you learn it?"

"In martial arts school when I was a boy. I had to learn to defend myself because of this." Chris held up his thumbless hand.

"As well you should have," Louis snarled.

Chris chastised himself as he walked away. *Get hold of yourself! You're jittery as a worm in a hawk's nest!* Louis Mueller would file away that block-blow among all the other scraps of suspicions about him. That sly look Louis had given him that morning to imply some secret knowledge of Herr Bauer worried him. But that could just be Louis Mueller's mode of operation in keeping an iron grip on his fiefdom—making the staff think he had something on them in case they got out of line. Chris knew the waiting was getting to him. So far not a ripple had disturbed the relatively calm waters of his daily existence or, at last contact, of Limpet's, even though code marks on their symbols had confirmed the list of German agents as bona fide. Chris had considered that maybe the Abwehr had simply not gotten around to questioning the general's fishing guide and son's tutor, since they were on the tail end of the process of elimination.

Chris would find out this afternoon if Limpet was still safe. He had probably been invited to dinner as well. Wilhelm would have insisted on it. This past Friday, Chris had seen a fishing pole propped against the railing of Limpet's stable apartment when he'd arrived for his session with the boy, the signal Limpet had suggested when they met by chance at the bus stop on Tuesday.

Standing shoulder to shoulder, while Limpet pretended to scan the traffic, he had spoken out of the side of his mouth. "I'll leave a fishing rod outside my door on the days you come to tutor. If it's not there, you'll know I've been taken, so run for your life."

It was with great relief that Chris had seen the rod parked in plain sight against the landing's railing. The meeting at the bus stop where Limpet had mentioned his concern over the general's nonappearance on the riverbank Sunday was the only contact he'd been able to have with his teammate.

Chris had his own cause for concern. It was the general's practice to show up at least twice a week at the end of his son's math lessons to judge for himself how the boy was getting along, but he had not appeared. At such times, Wilhelm would show off his knowledge to his father and beam from his praise, and Chris thought the boy had missed his presence this past week. So had Chris, in the odd way a human being might miss a tamed and friendly bear he'd become fond of, even knowing that it could revert to its normal nature and turn on him any second.

If the weather had cooperated during the week, Chris would have suggested a round of kickball to Wilhelm after their lessons to include Limpet, and he might have learned what the general was up to, but the ground had been too wet to play. Hans had greeted him on his tutoring days with no glance of sharp-eyed suspicion, and Wilhelm had been his usual cheerful, chatty self, always glad to see him. He'd tried to finesse out of the boy his father's whereabouts, but Wilhelm had answered that he thought him very busy.

The man was certainly busy, but right now any

deviation from the norm was reason to worry. Dinner with the general tonight—if that was the purpose of the invitation—would reveal whether his fears were groundless or real.

From his office at Abwehr headquarters, Major General Konrad March put in a call to the counter-intelligence unit at SD headquarters and asked to speak to Colonel Derrick Albrecht. The staff member placing an invoice on the general's desk heard the request while he waited for his superior's signature and thought nothing of it. He was aware that from time to time, the two warring departments collaborated about sensitive intelligence matters in the interests of national security. "I will require you to assist in accommodating one of our guests," the general informed his intelligence counterpart. "He is not responding well to our attentions, and we've tried our best to cater to his every need. Do you suppose we might send him to you to try your hospitality?"

The procurement clerk flinched. The "guest" was a prisoner brought in last week for interrogation—an Abwehr major accused of handing over to the enemy the names of some of Germany's top spies in Great Britain. The "accommodations" referred to a smelly interrogation cell on the third floor. The clerk did not even wish to think of the SD's "hospitality."

"By all means, Herr General," Colonel Derrick Albrecht replied to Konrad. "When can we expect him?"

"I can send him to you immediately."

"We will be waiting."

The general hung up and, for the benefit of the clerk, signed the invoice with the sigh of one who has tried and failed. "I gave the man every opportunity to confess. His treatment is now out of my hands. Tell my sergeant to get the prisoner ready for transport."

"*Jawohl*, Herr General!" The young clerk snatched up the invoice to get back to his department. He had not been in his position with the Abwehr long enough to develop a stomach for the sight of a bloodied and frightened superior officer dragged from his cell to an even more hideous hell.

That night, Major General Konrad March was his usual gruff but hospitable self, betraying no hint that he might suspect that one of the young men he'd welcomed into his home was a spy. He had confiscated from a black marketeer a deluxe version of an

American board game called Monopoly, new to him and his son. The fisherman and tutor grasped the point of the game right away, and they played as a foursome until eleven o'clock, when Hans escorted a sleepy Wilhelm to bed. His guests were on the point of departure when the telephone rang in the library. "Just a moment, gentlemen, and I will see you out," Konrad, ever the punctilious host, instructed as he stepped from the room to answer the call. Brad tiptoed to the partially open door and cocked his ear.

"...And you have proof beyond a doubt that it was the major who betrayed our brave agents? A sad loss to us, Colonel. I was sure you could persuade him to talk," Brad heard him say.

Brad quickly rejoined Chris in the vestibule before the general reappeared with a sagging face. "Bad news?" Chris asked.

"I am afraid so. I've just learned that one of our own is a traitor to our cause. He disclosed classified information to an enemy intelligence agency. Well, good evening, gentlemen. Thank you for coming."

Outside beyond hearing range of the door, Brad spoke in a low timbre, coarse with guilt. "They tortured a poor guy into confessing that he gave the agents' names to the Allies. They'll probably execute him."

"Which means we're off the hook," Chris said, "but God have mercy…" He looked away, mouth twisting as if he'd tasted something bitter. "I wonder what other sins we'll have to live with and account for before this is all over."

CHAPTER SIXTY-ONE

Bucky waited out the week tense, as well, ready to leap out of his skin at the touch of a hand on his shoulder. It was now Monday, November 9, four days since he had left work early to drop a note in the tree at Passy-Auteuil asking for an urgent meeting. "In case of extreme emergency," his father had said. The "emergency" was a chip it galled Bucky to squander. Bucky wanted to hold it in reserve for a true crisis, for which the saving of the likes of Dirk Drechsler did not qualify, but he couldn't risk the traitor turning him over to the Abwehr. His other option was to depart the boardinghouse one fine morning and never go back, leave the sergeant to wait in vain for his evening return, but exfiltration wasn't the answer, either. He still had to get his hands on those blueprints of the gun facility underway in the French Alps.

For obvious reasons, he could not explain his need for the meeting in a note. It would have to be conveyed face-to-face. His father would take the simple message as urgent enough. *Beloved, we must meet as soon as possible but at your convenience.* Bucky speculated on pins and needles how long it would take for the note to be collected and in what guise he'd be contacted. The drop was made November 5, three weeks before Dirk Drechsler's Thanksgiving deadline. He visualized someone checking the cavity in the tree daily—perhaps his aunt's old retainer?—and seeing that it got to the proper recipient. Bucky was torn. He had little choice but to leave the summons, yet he was in a stew of agony that his response would expose the Black Ghost to increased danger. Dirk Drechsler wasn't worth it.

Bucky came within an inch of telling him so the previous Thursday night, when the traitor cornered him at the boardinghouse and spoke so close to his face in such a silly attempt to be secretive that a spray of spit struck his cheek. The idiot had thought his spring from bondage would materialize immediately. "Any news?"

"*Non*," Bucky gritted, pushing him back. "You must be patient, monsieur. I took the first step to honor your request only today. These things take time."

"Well, don't wait too long, amigo."

His contact came one day later, Friday, in the form of a jostle of his briefcase from his hand as he waited for the metro. "Pardon, monsieur," the man muttered, bending down to pick up the satchel. Handing it to Bucky, he turned quickly and headed off before it was possible to catch a glimpse of his face. Bucky at first suspected the man might be a pickpocket—Paris was rampant with them—and patted his breast pocket for his wallet containing his papers when he saw a corner of a note peeking from under the flap of the briefcase. He looked around to find that none among the self-absorbed, grim-faced crowd of metro riders had the slightest interest in the square of paper he slipped into his pocket. When the train was underway, he read that the meeting was set that evening at six o'clock in a convenient and accessible *bibliotheque publique*, a large public library a block from the engineering firm where he worked. The password to expect was *Victor Hugo*.

The place was an intelligent and logical choice. Bucky often went there after working hours to read in a relative haven of peace and quiet. The note had given no instructions where he was to meet his contact in the library. At a writing table? The reference room? Reading nooks? In the stacks? Which one? There were a dozen. He did not expect it to be Nicholas Cravois in person. He would send an intermediary, but was Bucky to expect a man or woman? How would the person identify him? Should he wear or have at hand some identifying flag like a scarf or particular book? Bucky supposed he was simply to show up and sit where he could be seen. The messenger would contact him. A few minutes to six, he had taken a seat at one of the tables in the main room facing the door, feeling exposed and thinking that he should be hidden in a corner where he and his contact would not be noticed.

At six o'clock, a wave of people dressed in overcoats and blowing out frosty breaths arrived—Bucky counted five from behind his newspaper—and fanned out about the room with the focused intent of regulars laying claim to their reading spots. No one paid him the least mind. Several minutes later a contingent of merry-cheeked university students blew through the door, laughing and chatting, falling immediately silent at the librarian's stern hiss. Without paying Bucky a glance, they selected a table in the far corner of the room where they could giggle and whisper over their homework out of sight of the martinet at the circulation counter. Bucky waited, growing more nervous with each passing minute.

An hour crawled by. It was getting on to closing time for the library and for him to catch his train to Saint-Michel. It was a trek to the station, and sometimes the train was delayed or full and he had to wait for the next one. Then factor in the walk to his boardinghouse, which would nudge the hour close to curfew. He must also figure in time for the meeting—that is, if his contact showed up.

She revealed herself ten minutes later. She stepped from the stacks behind the circulation desk, a librarian wearing an identification badge and carrying a load of books to be returned to the shelves. She passed by his table and said in a lowered voice, "Victor Hugo."

Casually, Bucky folded his paper, collected his briefcase, and rose. He checked his watch—*Still time to select a book before I have to leave*, it suggested to any who would be watching. To satisfy the chief librarian, busy at her command post but with her eye ever sharp on the field of engagement, he casually browsed shelves until he reached the one where the librarian had disappeared.

She was young, faintly pretty, and all business. Bucky thought she would eventually mature into the stern-faced, gray-haired spinster behind the circulation counter, the stereotypical librarian who would go home at the end of a day to her cat and one-room flat, if, in fact, his contact was a librarian. "How may I help you?" she said.

Bucky had explained. "You will be contacted," she'd said.

And so he waited, Dirk Drechsler hovering and fuming.

A ray of hope had appeared that Monday morning. As Bucky stepped out of the boardinghouse on his way to work, a check of the bottom doorstep called for a trip to the tree. He set off at once to answer the summons and would later explain his tardiness to his supervisor, his OSS facilitator, who would understand. In the park he found a single command in the depository: *Wait on the bench.*

Bucky followed the order, wondering how long he'd have to wait before someone showed up. He had not long to worry. Before his feet began to get cold, a man past middle age carrying a paper sack strolled into the park with the obvious aim to share the bench with Bucky. He surmised the man and his sack must be a regular visitor to the spot since a flock of pigeons in the bare trees appeared to be on the lookout for him.

The man acknowledged Bucky with a perfunctory nod as he sat down at the far end and opened the sack, apparently a signal that instantly drew the flock of birds down from the trees to swarm about his feet. Chagrined, Bucky watched him fling the bread, worried how his contact would know which of them to approach. The luxuriousness of the man's fur-lined overcoat and matching Russian-style cap, and the wanton sharing of a staple scarce to other Parisians, pegged him as a resident of the affluent neighborhood. Indeed, the sunny weather had drawn a number of his well-heeled contemporaries out of their doors to stroll arm in arm about the park.

While Bucky pondered what to do, the man said, "Victor Hugo used to sit here. Did you know that, monsieur?"

Bucky sucked in his breath. His contact! He took a stab at the appropriate response. "Victor Hugo. I've heard that name recently."

The man flicked a crust crumb to the frantically pecking pigeons. "Where?"

"In the public library not far from the Quai André-Citroën."

"Ah, yes. I was instructed to give you this to pass to your friend." He handed Bucky a folded note, its ends stapled together. "Tell him to follow the instructions printed inside to the letter. Now tell me what you know about this man, what you have observed of his character, personality, temperament, physical condition, predilections, ability to withstand hardship. Do express your personal feelings about him, monsieur. They are important."

Rattling the paper sack to show his feathered friends that it was empty, the man folded it and stowed it in a coat pocket—everything was worth saving these days—and sat back with crossed arms like a theatergoer waiting patiently for the play to begin. Meanwhile, Bucky considered his impressions of Dirk Drechsler. He understood that his assessment was needed to determine the type of cargo his father's associates would be hauling. The route out of France to safe territory would be rough and treacherous, certainly not for the weakhearted or untrustworthy. Other people would be involved, indispensable, brave people risking their lives to return an American traitor back to his homeland. Bucky had no choice but to describe the man he'd observed Dirk Drechsler to be—indecisive, bumbling, easily misled, self-serving, desperate, but intuitive and perceptive.

"I wish I had more positive qualities to relate," Bucky said when he had finished.

"Tell me one thing more," the man said as he rose to leave. The flock, having pecked the ground clean, had abandoned him and taken off to the trees in a single flight. "Do you believe the man to be a danger to you if his demand is not fulfilled?"

Bucky hesitated. "He wouldn't want to be, but..." He lifted his shoulders.

"But he is what he is, no?"

"Yes. That's why he's dangerous."

CHAPTER SIXTY-TWO

That morning, Sister Mary Frances encountered Bridgette coming down the stairs on her way to the House of Boucher, and said, "*Ma chère*, may I have a word in private?" and with a swish of her habit headed to her office before Bridgette could answer.

"Of course, Mother," Bridgette murmured. *A command, then, not a request*, she thought, and followed the black-robed figure down the hall to the dark-paneled chamber where even angels would take care to tread lightly. What in the world was up? She'd never seen the mother superior look so grim.

Inside the "castle keep," as the nuns fearfully but affectionately referred to the mother superior's office, its keeper turned to her. "Mademoiselle Dufor, I fear we have a problem."

Bridgette's heart sank. Uh-oh. *Mademoiselle Dufor*, not *Mademoiselle Bernadette*. That meant trouble. "Oh?"

"Yes. You'd best sit down."

Bridgette sat. Sister Mary Frances spread the folds of her habit on the seat behind her desk, folded her hands on the surface, and addressed Bridgette in the tone that supported her exalted title and no-nonsense reputation. "I believe Achim Fleischer has found you out."

"*What?* How?"

"The inexplicable change in his behavior toward you this past week confirms a report that I received early this morning. A neighborhood resident finally had the courage to come forward. It seems that in the late afternoon a week ago this past Saturday, he saw Achim Fleischer sneaking down the fire escape from the attic floor of your room while the convent body was at vespers. My informant did not want to get involved with the French police, but his conscience got the better of him and so he came to me. You were out at the time, had gone to meet some friends for tea, as I recall."

It was the Saturday that Bridgette had met the team at the book and tea shop. Confused, she said, "But why would Achim have been on the attic floor?"

Sister Mary Frances tipped her head back and leveled a gaze at Bridgette through her bifocals. "Really, my dear child, need I explain? He took advantage of our absence to search your room. He may have been looking for contraband, but my instinct tells me that he wished to learn more private details about you as a woman. That would be typical of the sneaky student I knew."

Realization dawned. "And he found the radio," Bridgette whispered numbly.

"I believe he must have. Did you notice anything ajar, out of place, in your quarters?"

Bridgette thought back. "Yes, my nightgown had dropped from its peg to the floor. I didn't think anything about it at the time, but I was surprised because I always hang it by the inside loop." Horrified by what this would mean, Bridgette said, "But if he discovered the radio, why hasn't he had me arrested?"

"I would guess he is waiting for the right moment, perhaps when he's joined the Vichy Milice. Either that, or up to this point he hasn't had the heart. Regardless, you must contact your superior about this change of events and seek another place for your operation immediately. I am sorry, *ma chère*, but I cannot have the convent placed in jeopardy."

The mother superior stood up from her chair like a dark, unbridgeable wave rising from the ocean. "Perhaps now would be a good time to do so, don't you think?"

"Yes, Mother." Bridgette stood in obedience to her dismissal, cold to the core, her appointment with Madame Richter for the second fitting of her ball gown forgotten. Oh God, the drop box, the mural, her lodging, the ideal location for the radio…all to replace. She went immediately to her attic room to notify the major.

His long years running clandestine operations had rendered Alistair immune to the unexpected disasters of the sort contained in Bridgette's transmission. Calmly, hardly without drawing a breath, Major Renault coded back: *Do nothing. Sit tight.* Immediately afterward, he put in an SOS call to his man in Paris. "I will see to it," Henri said.

At the end of his shift late that afternoon, Achim Fleischer stood on the metro platform waiting with a crowd of other passengers, determined to be among the first to step aboard and grab a seat. At the whistle of an oncoming train barreling up the track, he trusted the status of his uniform to allow him to disregard a metro official's warning to step away from the edge of the platform. Within a minute of the passengers' surge forward before the train stopped, the air was rent with the screech of locomotive brakes, frantic whistle blowing, and human screams. A man—the puffed-up policeman, so Achim was later described by a witness—had fallen into the path of the arriving train. The death was later declared an accident. The victim had been bumped to his demise by the indifference of the crowd—a lesson in personal safety and moral behavior that rail passengers should bear in mind for the future, metro authorities advised.

Monday night at the prescribed time of eight o'clock, Bridgette received a transmission from Bern: *All is taken care of. Stay put.*

Later that evening, Sister Mary Frances received a visitor, a Frenchman of the type rarely invited into the convent, never into her private quarters, and certainly not at that time of night. After hearing the news he had been dispatched to impart, the mother superior crossed herself. "God have mercy upon his soul," she said, to which the man replied, "Amen."

That afternoon in a back hall of the boardinghouse, Bucky passed the note to Dirk, who read it with an ear-to-ear smile. "Hot diggety dog! Thanks, buddy," Dirk said. He punched Bucky's shoulder playfully. "Looks like my ride is on the way! I'll know more when I meet with somebody tomorrow afternoon who'll tell me the drill."

"Sssh!" Bucky cautioned him.

Dirk put his finger to his lips. "I won't say another word, amigo."

You shouldn't have said that much, Bucky's glare said to him and watched the sergeant swagger off to join the German boarders drinking schnapps in the lounge, his smirk as clear to read as a schoolgirl's taunt on a playground: *Yay-ya-yay, ya yay yay! I've got a secret!* After a couple of steins of beer, who wouldn't take bets that the fathead wouldn't slip in a boast that his days among his tormentors were numbered? Bucky didn't give a Billybedamn for the consequences to Dirk Drechsler, but he did for the lives of his father's men.

Bucky stewed over the situation until he was able to speak with the turncoat privately the following evening to learn the details of his defection. At breakfast, the captain noticed his sergeant's happy mood and inquired what accounted for the sudden bounce in his *Hintern.*

Bucky winced when Dirk threw him a quick wink down the table and replied with appalling recklessness, "Wouldn't you like to know?"

The captain and lieutenant went back to their sausage and eggs, plainly disinterested in what had put a spring in Sergeant Drechsler's posterior, but it was that sort of mindlessness that had forced Bucky to stalk the front windows waiting for his return that evening. The sooner the man was out of here, the safer for him, his father, the team, and his mission. "Well, monsieur?" he said when he finally appeared.

The sergeant's scowl told the story. "I'm not going," he said, his voice sour with disappointment. "It's too dangerous, too difficult. I'd never make it. I might as well die here where I'm warm and my belly's full and I'm relatively safe rather than starve and freeze to death trying to make it across the Pyrenees in winter. No thanks. I might think about it again in spring, but for now, I'll take my chances getting home again after the war is over."

"Well, what did you think the route would be like, monsieur?" Bucky snapped. "A walk in the park, as you Americans say?"

"I thought we'd go by train."

Bucky got it then. The team had exploited the sergeant's weaknesses that Bucky had described to the bird man and used them to dissuade him from making the attempt at escape. Drechsler had been given the full picture of the hardships and danger and deprivation, and he had chickened out, saving his father's rescue teams the waste of time and effort in hauling Drechsler to the Spanish border—unless, of course, they had meant to put a bullet in him at the start to spare themselves the trouble of dealing with him. But where did that leave Bucky, son of the Black Ghost? He was now even more exposed to the danger of the sergeant's tongue.

Two days later, Unterfeldwebel Dirk Drechsler, American born and reared, disappeared off the streets of Paris, never to be seen again. There were no German reprisals. A typed letter left on his desk in his Abwehr unit stated that he was on his way back to the United States and declared his absolute loathing for the captain, his lieutenant, the Third Reich, Adolf Hitler, and the Nazi Party.

CHAPTER SIXTY-THREE

Once again, Colonel Derrick Albrecht found himself in a situation where he had to decide what to do with Victoria Grayson, now proven to be a foreign undercover agent he was almost certain worked for the OSS. He had not made contact with her since the night of the premiere almost a week before. She must be wondering what he was up to, what he had in mind for her attentions beyond their Sunday bouts. It was now Friday, November 13, a date on the calendar purported by much of the world to be an unlucky day. Bad things happened when Friday fell on the thirteenth of the month. His mother never put a foot outside the door on that day. She claimed personal experience to support the belief that it was the most dangerous twenty-four hours on the calendar. Derrick wondered if Victoria believed in the superstition. He would predict she'd scoff it off as nonsense.

He should get up and go, he thought, release Karl to his own Friday evening diversions and call it a night, as his long-ago Harvard friends would have said. He had nothing he wanted to do and nowhere he particularly desired to be, although that was not exactly true. He had canceled his evening with Celeste. They were to meet her friends at a popular cabaret, but he was in no mood for the frenzied atmosphere of a smoke-filled dance hall loud with people desperate to forget that the war was happening. Celeste's cronies were a brittle-witted, caustic-tongued assortment of artists, writers, musicians, and film people as shallow as their talents, and they had begun to bore him.

Thus he remained in his office enveloped in the fragrant smoke of a Montecristo swirling under the light of a single desk lamp. He could think most clearly and dispassionately about the duties of his job here in his cold, impersonal office rather than in his hotel quarters, where familiar objects made him long for home and family. Somehow his brief acquaintanceship with Victoria Grayson had unlatched the door to the memories of the untroubled boy he had been in those days, so in contrast to the man of his later years.

But then, in those days, Germany was not at war.

Glorious Victoria... Whatever should I do with you, my beauty? It had taken him almost a week to decide while he fought the temptation to call on her. His immediate thought upon discovering the cyanide pill had been to get her out of France before someone else got onto her and her luck ran out. He would return her unmasked but unharmed to whatever American mastermind had thought to plant the perfect woman in his path. And what a brilliant scheme it was!

Known for his own brilliance at the manipulation game, Derrick was amazed at the subtlety of it. Victoria's controller had inserted a fencer of foil at L'Ecole d'Escrime Français with the belief that her skill with the blade would reach the ears of Colonel Derrick Albrecht, Germany's own champion of the sport. Curiosity and the thrill of challenge would have lured him to take a look and test her mettle, and after that first Sunday... whoever was pulling the strings had simply allowed Colonel Albrecht's natural inclination toward a woman of Victoria's beauty and breeding to take its course. One thing would lead to another, and she would end up by the colonel's side at Nazi functions and eventually in his bed while collecting intelligence like daisies in a field.

But how could the man in control of the wires not have expected the mark's trained ear to detect his marionette's American accent? Had he counted on Derrick Albrecht turning a blind eye to her nationality out of fondness for America and his respect and fascination for a beautiful woman? The bald assumption of it and the arrogant disregard for his operative's life angered him, and Derrick thought that if he ever got his hands on the orchestrator, he'd rip his throat out. What if the plan had failed? What if the puppeteer had misjudged the colonel's attraction to his plant once she was exposed? She would have already been before a firing squad.

There was also another part of the plan that Derrick could not reconcile to the woman he had come to know. Victoria had no intention of sharing his bed. She had given no indication that she shared even a mite-sized attraction for him. In the vetting process, how could her controller not have discerned that a woman like her would never agree to seduce a man she found contemptible? He was, as far as the OSS knew, a key player in the greatest evil ever perpetrated against mankind. His country had initiated a war that had killed the love of her life.

So in reexamining his first perceptions, he had come to believe that Victoria Grayson had not been placed to capture his eye, and he might have given her controller too much credit. Colonel Derrick Albrecht had not figured into the OSS plan at all. He was simply an unexpected intruder onto the playing field of Victoria Grayson's mission at the fencing school.

Thus he had reconsidered his plan of action. More was at stake than his feelings for her. He must think of his country and do what he could to get it out of this insane war, and he had decided to allow her to proceed with her mission, believing herself still undetected. Like Konrad's two spies, unaware that they were playing into his hands, he would use Victoria Grayson as a funnel to channel top secret information to assist the Allies in bringing Hitler to his knees.

But he had to be even more careful to protect his position that in turn would protect Victoria. Derrick had pursued this intent since September 1, 1939, when the Waffen SS massacred two hundred Jews at Będzin, Poland, along with some members of the nobility who were lifelong friends of his family, including Derrick's beloved godfather. Derrick's father, disgusted by his son's misguided but patriotic decision to join the Waffen SS, had declared, "The Nazi Party's establishment of a thousand-year reign is the delusion of a raving lunatic. The Third Reich is nothing but a castle built on sand within sight of the oncoming tide. Germany is doomed unless something can be done to stop that madman."

Derrick, highly decorated, awarded the Knight's Cross by Hitler himself, and well regarded within military circles, had come to agree with his father's view, but it was too late to withdraw from the Waffen SS without raising suspicion of his loyalty to the Führer. Not only would he be arrested for treason, but Himmler would go after members of his family, their titles unable to save them.

Originally, Derrick had hardly thought about his decision to join. The SS was formed to save the German people from its enemies. It was the elite organization of the Nazi regime. Reared in a world of elitism, it was only natural that he take his proper place in the highest echelons of the German military.

How naïve he had been! Plucked from the regular army of the Wehrmacht before he barely had time to serve, he had not been indoctrinated into the mind-set of the SS. He had been spared having to attend Bad Tolz, the SS officers' training school that required Hitler's paramilitary "elite" to renounce belief in God, kill their parents if required, desensitize themselves to human suffering, and overcome every moral inhibition.

But he had played his part with the worst of them, and he, too, would burn in hell for the atrocities in which he had participated, even if the laws of men did not catch up with him first.

By 1940, Derrick was eager to atone for his crimes and willing to take on the clandestine task of rescuing German military officers, political figures, and clergymen suspected of treason against the Third Reich from torture, imprisonment, and death. This he accomplished by spiriting them out of the interrogation cells of the Abwehr and SD to purported graves, bogus interrogation sites, concentration camps, and firing squads. The deliverance of these men involved nerve-racking, dangerous machinations. The slightest false move could result in the undoing of Colonel Derrick Albrecht, his family, Major General Konrad March, and the two men of his SD staff loyal to the cause of freeing Germany from Hitler's stranglehold.

The latest candidate for rescue that Konrad had sent over from Abwehr headquarters, a Wehrmacht major, was a case in point. Already suspected of treason by the SS, he had agreed to be the scapegoat for the leak of the German agents. He was arrested, "interrogated," and his "corpse" transported out of Paris. The man had made a slight noise in the wooden box used to transport him from his cell to the "disposal sites" where he would be deposited into friendly hands. A lance corporal on his staff exclaimed, "Wait! I thought I heard a sound coming from inside the coffin. Should we open the lid to see if the traitor is still alive?"

"Too bad if he is," Derrick said coldly. "He'll find it much more pleasant being buried dead than alive."

The corporal had laughed. "*Jawohl*, Herr Colonel!"

Derrick took a final draw of his cigar before extinguishing it thoughtfully in the brass ashtray bearing his family's coat of arms. Victoria Grayson…He knew, of course, exactly what his plans were for her, but first he had to obtain irrefutable proof that she was a spy. This he would accomplish on Sunday at the fencing school.

CHAPTER SIXTY-FOUR

Bucky heard about Dirk Drechsler's defection Wednesday evening, November 13, when he returned to the boardinghouse at the end of his workday. Madame Dupree met him at the door before he had finished scraping his shoes on the front porch mat. "Come to the kitchen," she said in a lowered voice. He followed her without comment, slipping by the door of the living room unseen by the other boarders, who were conversing in animated tones. "What's happened?" he asked after Madame Dupree had closed the door firmly behind them.

"Your American friend has deserted and gone back to America," she whispered. "The sergeant left a note to that effect. Captain Achterberg has just informed us." His landlady's lips arched into a rare smile. "We don't have to worry about him anymore, eh, *mon ami*. He's—how do you say?—out of our hair."

"He's gone for good?" Bucky could hardly believe it.

"From under this roof at least. If he's found before he can get out of France, he'll be shot. A manhunt is on for him." She released a blissful sigh. "I can already breathe easier. You should, too, Stephane."

"Yes…" Bucky said doubtfully. The thought he'd had earlier of the rescue squad using a bullet to spare themselves the trouble of dealing with the American traitor might not have been an idle one after all. He wondered if his father or the major had ordered the alternate plan to get the sergeant out of France. Uneasy in his mind, Bucky joined the others in the living room to hear the report of Dirk's desertion. "He won't get far," the captain was saying to his colleagues and the agog Frenchmen. "Damned American. I knew never to trust the quisling. It will be the firing squad for him if he's caught."

He won't be caught, Bucky could have told them, suddenly sure of Dirk Drechsler's fate. The poor sap should never have left Texas. Somehow, he'd have to let Lapwing know that he no longer had to fear running into his best friend from childhood. Bucky suspected that he would be sad, but he could breathe easier, too.

On Tuesday evening, the day the story ran in *Le Temps*, Bridgette said to Sister Mary Frances, "Do you believe it was an accident?"

"What else could it be, *ma chère amie*? The metro platform at rush hour is one of the most dangerous places in Paris. Achim was standing too close to the tracks, no doubt to bully his way to be first onboard. He had been properly warned and chose not to listen. It was due to his own nature that he met his untimely death."

Untimely, my eye! thought Bridgette, looking hard at Sister Mary Frances. Achim's "accident," only hours after she informed the major of the mother superior's report, was too timely to be anything but deliberate. A chill seized her. She had not anticipated a drastic and permanent removal of the threat to her safety.

Sister Mary Frances placed cool fingers to Bridgette's cheek. "You must carry on as you were, my child. You are fighting on the right side—God's side—to rid the world of a great evil. Sometimes the greater good requires casualties. Achim was on the wrong side."

Bridgette stared at her. Good Lord! The mother

superior *was* in on this somehow. The nun had an idea of what had happened to Achim Fleischer. "Live in peace, my child," the woman advised kindly. "Achim now is with God. I will pray that he is shown mercy."

It would be a while before she would live in peace, assuming she ever would, Bridgette thought, swallowing down a surge of nausea. Achim Fleischer most certainly would have denounced her to the French Milice. His former feeling for her had been as dead as a dried flower pressed in a book, but still... Bridgette sighed. The only peace for her, the only comfort, was the knowledge that Achim no longer presented a threat to the safety of her friends.

By Saturday, Brad and Chris were feeling relieved of the anxiety that had plagued them night and day all week, but they could not shake the guilt over the interrogation of the innocent Abwehr officer who had been blamed for their crime, never mind that the man, by virtue of belonging to the Abwehr, had likely committed crimes of which he *was* guilty. They were now living the reality that the major had warned them about: "No one completes their missions with clean consciences. Dirty dealing is part of the job."

Nonetheless they were grateful they no longer had to sleep with an eye open and look over their shoulders with every step. All indications were that the general had never once considered that Brad and Chris might have been involved with the rollup of the Abwehr's spies.

On Saturday also, by a stroke of luck, Chris managed to free himself of the dark cloud under which he'd been living. He was spending the morning in Les Halles, Paris's central fresh food market, the "belly of Paris." Chris could picture what the exposition looked like before the occupation, the teeming Saturday crowds and the sprawl of carts and stalls overloaded with fresh produce, cheeses, meats, breads, and pastries that had been in operation for eight hundred years. There were still foodstuffs to buy but in scarce supply at exorbitant prices. He had just emerged from one of the labyrinthine underground alleys, where he'd haggled down the price of a bottle of wine for the general and a fortune-telling game for Wilhelm, when he spotted Louis Mueller in civilian clothes with a man unknown to him. They were laughing with abandon, an activity of which

Chris had not thought Louis capable, but something about their absorption in each other, subtle though it was, made him say to himself, "Well, I'll be!"

Curious if he had misunderstood, he decided to follow the pair.

According to the tour books, Les Halles had been a favorite hangout of homosexuals and lesbians ever since the French Revolution had eliminated laws declaring same-sex relations a criminal offense. While German violators of the Third Reich's law against homosexuality would have been prosecuted, the occupying authorities pretty much turned a blind eye to French offenders. They believed the French were beyond saving from moral corruption anyway. Subsequently, tucked among more sedate establishments were bars, cafés, salons, and spas of long standing that catered exclusively to these clientele. It was toward one of these that Louis and his friend seemed headed.

Chris followed them to a small underground café in an alleyway and took the chance that after a few minutes he could enter without being noticed. As expected, the bar was dimly lit with low lights and the haze of cigarette smoke permanent to such establishments and beginning to fill with the lunch crowd. Chris managed to melt in, unseen by his target, and maneuvered within shooting range of his Minox. Less than sixty seconds later, the moment he had anticipated arrived. With a twinge of regret (a man's love life should be his own affair, but his own life was in danger), he snapped a picture of Louis in a deep kiss with his lover. Chris took a number of shots more to make sure of the scene that would remove Louis from his life and slipped quietly out to grab a bus headed in the direction of a trusted photography studio that developed film with no questions asked. That afternoon an envelope containing photographs of Louis with his paramour along with an anonymous note of explanation was on the way to Gestapo headquarters at 11 Rue de Saussaies in the eighth arrondissement.

CHAPTER SIXTY-FIVE

Victoria left for L'Ecole d'Escrime Français on Sunday worn out from sleepless nights and nerves strung tightly as fiddle strings. She had still not heard a peep from Colonel Derrick Albrecht. In the past, to remind her of her Sunday appointment with the colonel, a message was left with the concierge, but none had been relayed for today. Did that mean he had no plans to show up? The idea that he wouldn't, and the fear or hope that accompanied it, was laid aside when Victoria rounded the corner of the fencing school and saw the colonel's staff car parked in its usual spot and Karl behind the wheel. Derrick Albrecht had arrived early. Did that deviation from his normal routine mean anything? Seeing her come into view through his side window, the colonel's driver hopped out to open the school door for her.

"Good afternoon, Mademoiselle Colbert," he said. "A lovely day for a change."

"Yes, it is." Victoria agreed with a quick search of his stolid face and saw nothing that warned of trouble ahead in the fencing hall. "*Merci*," she said.

"Always my pleasure, mademoiselle."

Well, we'll see, Victoria thought, entering the building. It occurred to her that she did not know Karl's last name, so she must address him only as *monsieur*. "Herr Karl" seemed too familiar, beyond a latitude of friendliness she felt comfortable to go. She sensed him a man of many titles in the service of his lord and master—driver, aide, confidant, body guard, torturer, assassin—whatever duty required. He was always unerringly polite to her, thoughtful even. After the premiere, he had produced a blanket to wrap around her against the cold—his idea, not his boss's. *Thank you for your foresight, Karl. I am sure mademoiselle is most grateful*, the colonel had complimented him in German.

Victoria reluctantly climbed the stairs to the top floor of the fencing school. She was wearing her usual coat after a long deliberation about whether to exchange it for another and resew the L pill in its lining, or to continue wearing it with the hope that her worry was unfounded. If in fact the colonel had felt it and the capsule was missing, the lining obviously resewn, he would have proof to support his suspicions. In any case, both options would doom her should he investigate further.

The salle was deserted. Victoria had expected to find him in his whites, whipping the air with his foil.

"Good afternoon, Mademoiselle Colbert," the colonel's voice called out from the conference room. "I am in here."

Mademoiselle Colbert. Cautiously, Victoria drew toward the open door of the room and halted at its entrance. Colonel Derrick Albrecht was in civilian clothes—tweed, corduroy, leather—the kind of attire the Virginia hunting gentry wore on their country estates. A tweed cap such as the sort worn by a golfer lay on the table. "You're early," she observed.

"I wished to arrive before you dressed for our bout."

"I thought we were fencing today."

"It's too beautiful an afternoon to be indoors, don't you think? So, no we're not. I took the liberty to arrange a little trip."

"A trip?"

"A trip. Prepare for a surprise."

"A surprise," Victoria repeated. There were surprises and then there were surprises. A surprise from a suspicious colonel in the SS could hold very unpleasant connotations. "What kind of surprise?"

"It wouldn't be a surprise if I told you, now would it?" He held out his arm. "Shall we go?"

"Where to?"

"Part of the surprise."

With Karl at the wheel and the top of the staff car lowered to allow the sun on their faces, Victoria watched Paris slip by with growing unease. It was one thing to be an American innocent caught behind enemy lines, quite another to be caught as an American spy. "Where is Karl taking us?" she asked when they entered the countryside. She pretended casual disinterest, but she could not hear the wind for the drum of her heartbeat in her ears.

"Part of the surprise. Enjoy the ride," he answered.

Because it would be her last? Victoria glanced at his profile, stoic, unreadable. Perhaps it was the civilian clothes, but he seemed a different person from the man she knew, a stranger, even. She much preferred him in his military uniform, a cobra out in the open rather than a rattlesnake camouflaged in the bush. He held his head slightly back, his face tilted to the sun, and did not speak as the car sped along, seemingly interested only in the pleasure of the sunlit day.

After a five-mile drive, her heart rate increased when Karl turned through a pair of majestic gateposts flanking the entrance to a road that wandered darkly through an evergreen forest. A few hundred meters later it forked off between a storybook chateau atop a far hill and a stone folly in the opposite direction. Karl took the road toward the folly.

The colonel spoke for the first time. "Count Darold Archambault's country estate. He and his family have retired to Switzerland for the duration of the war."

Haven't they all? Victoria thought and wondered numbly if the duke had confiscated it for his own use. Ancestral strongholds like the count's held dungeons.

In Victoria's experience, follies were usually erected by people who wished it known that they had money to waste on nothing. This one at least had value in that it overlooked gently rolling acres that reminded her of the green splendor of English downs. It was enclosed except for its front and back entrances and came equipped with a stone slab table with benches on either side and a fireplace stacked with wood.

"Karl, if you will do the honors," Colonel Albrecht instructed in German, gesturing toward the trunk, and offered a hand to Victoria to help her from the back seat. "A perfect place for a picnic, no?" he said in French.

"A picnic?"

"Of the American variety. I had it prepared especially for you. Fried chicken and potato salad. Apple pie for dessert, a taste of home."

"That's the surprise?"

"Yes. Are you pleased? You looked…frightened when I first suggested a surprise. What did you think—that I had something else of a more nefarious nature in mind? Now why ever would you assume that?" There was a light in his eye—playful, ironical. Was he toying with her? Victoria felt another roll of unease. Something definitely was going on here.

"Can you blame me? I never know what to expect from you, Colonel Albrecht."

"Derrick, please. Have we not agreed to first names, and have I not assured you that you have nothing to fear from me? Come, let us walk while Karl prepares the fire and table."

The colonel walked toward a snow-covered crest still holding some of its green against the approaching winter. The forest, deep and dark, the trees' outer branches sparkling with snow, stood guard behind it while a swath of open country threaded with a winding creek lay before it. The frosty country air smelled fresh and sharp, carrying scents of pines and clean water, and Victoria drew in a halting breath to steady her nerves as they walked along.

"That breath had a shudder to it," Derrick commented, and observed before she could respond, "This is a rather wonderful place, isn't it? I must bring you here in warmer days. The valley is blindingly green in the spring."

Victoria glanced at him. He spoke of a future, but he was a master at psychological manipulation—*The best interrogator we have without resorting to...other methods*, an SS colleague once remarked to her. She offered no comment. She was safer keeping silent. If he knew she suspected he was onto her, any response would sound forced. If she'd misread him, no harm done. He knew that he could expect nothing from her.

The colonel did not touch her except to take her upper arm occasionally to assist her over a rough spot on the pebbly path. The afternoon was still cold, but it felt almost balmy after the miserably frigid and wet weather of previous weeks. Any other time, with anyone else, Victoria would have enjoyed the pastoral getaway from the grimness of Paris.

At the crest of the hill they stopped to admire the

sweeping view. "This place reminds me of my ancestral home in Germany, the reason I enjoy coming here," Derrick said in English. "Have you ever been to Germany, Victoria?"

"No," she said.

"My home is in Franconia in Bavaria, thought of as the land of sausage, beer, and lederhosen, but it is so much more than that." He spoke with nostalgia, his gaze wistful on the sweeping vista before them. "The region is the most beautiful in Germany, possibly in all of Europe. It is an area of alps and lakes and striking castles and towering rock structures that date back to the Jurassic age. Our lovely little villages and gardens are so picturesque, postcards can't do them justice."

"You sound homesick," Victoria commented.

"I hope to return to it after the war, perhaps never to leave it again...one way or the other."

Victoria could not resist asking, "You don't plan to stay in the SS, help your Führer crack the whip to ensure the thousand-year reign of the Third Reich?"

"There will be no SS. There will be no Führer. There will be no Third Reich." He turned to her with a thin smile. "Shall we go back? The fire should be going by now."

He had never spoken so directly of his feelings about the future that Hitler envisioned for Germany, although Victoria had come to believe that he did not share the maniac's delusion. But was the colonel's blunt, seditious opinion meant to put her off guard? She studied him in silence for a moment until the peace and quiet were suddenly shattered by the roar of a motor engine racing up the road toward the folly. They turned to see, skimming along the border of hedgerows, an SS staff car with its red-and-black Nazi flag whipping from the antennae and its back seat occupied by two uniformed officers. Victoria went numb. She should have known. They had come for her. This had all been a game.

"Let's go," the colonel ordered tersely and gripped her arm. One of the car's passengers, a major, hurriedly disembarked from the vehicle and came flapping toward them in his leather coat. They met halfway. The usual stiff-armed salutes and *Heil Hitlers* were exchanged, and the major, grim-faced, glanced toward Victoria. In German he asked, "May I speak freely, Herr Colonel?"

"Yes, my companion does not comprehend German."

There followed a rapid trade of questions and answers while Victoria, limp with relief, stepped away from the men to admire the view but within hearing range of their conversation, unaware that she was recording every word of crucial intel they spoke. After a while, the colonel broke off from the major and stepped to Victoria. "My deepest apologies, mademoiselle," he said in French, "but we must get back to Paris immediately. An emergency has arisen."

"A pity," she said. "I was so looking forward to the fried chicken."

CHAPTER SIXTY-SIX

Monday afternoon of the following week, November 16, as Louis Mueller was preparing to leave for the day, he heard the outer door of the Sorbonne bang open and the loud rush of feet toward the entrance of the staff offices. Startled before he had time to become frightened, Louis popped up from his desk at the appearance of three men wearing the slouch hats and ankle-length black cowhide coats of the German Gestapo charging into the school facility. One spotted the astonished Louis in his glass-enclosed office and led the march through his door to confront the sports director, who was staring at them openmouthed. The Gestapo spokesman held an envelope in his hand.

"Herr Louis Mueller?"

Louis swallowed hard. "Yes."

"You're under arrest for sodomy!"

Louis's face bloomed a tomato red. "*What?*"

Chris and the other instructors who had not yet left for the day peered out their cubicle doors to investigate the source of the disturbance. The leader of the black-coated pack slapped the envelope onto the sports director's desk. "Are you the man in these photos?"

Eyes bulging, cheeks pulsing like bellows, Louis picked up the envelope and slowly withdrew a number of photographs. He nodded meekly. "Yes."

"Come with me!"

Rough hands seized him and lugged him from his office under the astounded gazes of the lingering staff and arriving janitorial crew. Before being yanked over the threshold of his fiefdom that he would never see again, Louis threw a wild-eyed look at Claus Bauer watching from his cubicle door. Their gazes locked. Chris kept his perfectly still, with not a hint of guile in it, but Louis's flared in shocked recognition of his denouncer as he was dragged away screaming by the men in whose hands he had planned to deliver Claus Bauer.

A drop-jawed instructor next to Chris said, "Herr Mueller, a queer? Whoever would have guessed?"

"Whoever indeed?" said Claus Bauer.

Derrick finished composing his note to Victoria Grayson and affixed the seal of his family crest to the flap of the envelope. It contained his written apology for cutting their picnic short yesterday and an invitation to make it up to her by taking her on another drive through the countryside to a small inn that offered spectacular views and served the finest lemon sole in France. Would she be free this Friday, November 20? Enclosed was a telephone number where he could be reached. After summoning Karl to arrange a courier to deliver it to the fencing school this Monday morning, Derrick settled back in satisfaction to finish his coffee.

Victoria Grayson had taken the bait and proved beyond doubt that she was a spy. Now he hoped whoever she was working for would swallow it as well. The whole dramatic scene at the folly had been staged as a setup to lure her to make contact with whomever she was working for. Upon their return to Paris, excusing himself for a matter of urgency, Derrick had instructed Karl to take him to his headquarters first before driving Mademoiselle Colbert to her residence. He'd then gone to his rooms at the Crillon to await the report from his wolfhound, now in place to follow her as soon as she left the hotel. No one was more skilled at shadowing than his longtime investigator. Derrick had not been surprised to see the man's face fall as he gave him his instructions. Though Derrick trusted him and Karl above all men, the confidences he shared with them were limited to a need-to-know basis. Neither ever questioned his orders or asked for information beyond what they were given, but like all men after having seen Victoria Grayson, his wolfhound was saddened that such a beautiful woman should fall under the suspicion of the counterintelligence head of the Sicherheitsdienst.

The sun had gone and a fire had been lit by the time his man knocked on the door of his private quarters. Derrick had a whiskey waiting. His wolfhound took it gratefully. "You were correct, Mein Colonel," he said. "Mademoiselle Colbert left her hotel almost immediately after her return and took the metro to Saint-Michel. At a house on Rue des Soeurs de Charité, next to the convent for which the street is named, I saw her slide a note through the mail slot, then she returned to her hotel."

Derrick nodded. "A dead-letter box. Any further observations?"

"A curious item. Some artist has drawn an astonishing mural on the convent's courtyard wall attached to the house. It's become a street attraction, apparently. A small group of Sunday strollers were gathered round."

"A mural of what?"

"A tropical scene. Blue water and seabirds and lily pads and other aquatic elements. There's a dog, too, and some dragonflies flitting about. Quite lovely. Quite peaceful. A pleasure to view."

"I doubt one has anything to do with the other, but it's worth watching. I'll put a man on the street immediately." Derrick offered his whiskey glass for a toast. "Good work."

"I am honored to serve, Mein Colonel," his wolfhound said, crystal rims ringing in the firelit room.

Now Derrick had to wait until time for Victoria's contact to react to her intelligence report. Derrick had chosen the target to eliminate the improbability that she reported to someone within the Nazi Party. If the chosen target remained untouched, Derrick would know that Victoria's contact was a member of an Allied intelligence agency. His bet was still on the OSS. It was an organization not easily deceived, and for some time Derrick had suspected that it was onto the game that he and Konrad were playing against the Third Reich.

Derrick had decided not to share his suspicions

of Victoria Grayson with his coconspirator. For her safety, there was no need for Konrad to know. His friend was already in danger because of his association with Admiral Wilhelm Canaris. Rumor was that Heinrich Himmler's vultures were beginning to circle over the admiral's head, and Derrick feared that whatever befell Canaris would befall his mentee. What his friend did not know, he could not betray.

The buzz of his desk intercom interrupted his ruminations. "Yes, Karl?"

"Chief Detective Maurice Corbett and an associate of the criminal investigation department of the French National Police are here to see you, Colonel."

Derrick stiffened. What the devil were they back for? He'd thought they were through with their questions. "Send them in, Karl, but make it clear that I can give them only a few minutes." He stood as they entered, the fledgling detective and his superior, the middle-aged police veteran whose deeply lined face appeared to have been stitched back together after falling apart at one point in his lifetime.

Well-seasoned, that one, Karl had commented after the man's earlier visit. And wily as a fox, too, Derrick had judged, a man not to be underestimated. The men removed their hats as they approached the desk, the junior officer's eyes sweeping the office nervously.

"To what do I owe the honor again, gentlemen?" Derrick asked.

Chief detective Maurice Corbett removed several blown-up photographs from a manila envelope. "We're sorry to bother you again, Colonel Albrecht, but I wonder if you wouldn't mind identifying this young woman for us." He spread the two photographs on the desk. They were of Derrick and Victoria Grayson seated at a table at the Ritz the first Sunday they met.

A chill swooped over Derrick. He forced up a smile and answered casually, "Why, yes, the young woman's name is Mademoiselle Veronique Colbert. She is a fencing instructor of foil at L'Ecole d'Escrime Français."

"How do you know her?"

"She's my fencing partner." Derrick sharpened his voice. "Now would you mind telling me how and where you got these?"

"Not at all. We found them in Monsieur Fournier's home in a hidden folder containing other photos showing persons of importance in compromising situations."

"Are you suggesting the man was a blackmailer?"

"It is an explanation we're considering at this point."

"Why in the world would he have included photos of Mademoiselle Colbert and me? We were having a meal at the Ritz after a bout," Derrick said, looking annoyed. He added nothing further. As a trained interrogator, he knew not to volunteer more information than was necessary to emphasize his innocence, a sure indication that he had something to hide.

"I am sure I don't know. We were hoping you could tell us."

Derrick said coldly, "There is nothing to tell. Perhaps Monsieur Fournier took the pictures to hold for the day there might be, but I can't imagine what. The reason is obvious, but valueless. At the time that picture was taken, neither Mademoiselle Colbert nor I were, and are still not, committed to other people."

Unless, thought Derrick suddenly, the folder included information on how the swine happened to know Victoria Grayson. He allowed a smile to skim his lips, totally without humor. "I might add, Detective, that it would be very dangerous business to attempt to blackmail the SS chief of the French counterintelligence division of the security services of the Reichsführer."

The senior officer returned the photos to the envelope. "Precisely my deduction, Colonel," he said, dipping his head respectfully. "We won't trouble you further. Good day."

For a moment after the door closed, Derrick stood chewing his lip. He didn't dare go to the fencing school to warn Victoria to be prepared for a police interview. Detective Corbett would be anticipating that move. He picked up the phone and placed a call on his secure line to L'Ecole d'Escrime Français.

CHAPTER SIXTY-SEVEN

Alistair, known around the OSS station in Bern as the man who never slept, ate, or left his desk, received and acted on Victoria's information with such speed and attention that, despite cigarettes becoming less available by the day, he allowed his Lucky Strike to burn to ashes in its tray. A Nazi informant in a Maquis cell had slipped word to the SD of plans to raid in two days' time a German radio receiver station set up in an unobtrusive farmhouse on the sea cliffs of Le Havre. This receiver was responsible for the loss of many RAF aircraft, as well as giving the Germans early warnings of Allied ships and planes approaching the coast of Western Europe. Colonel Derrick Albrecht's job was to arrange for an SS reception committee to thwart the raid and round up the saboteurs. Alistair's job was to alert the Maquis of the trap.

Task now complete. The Resistance fighters had been warned off, and the SS would have its men in position to repel an assault that would never come. Liverwort's intel had saved the lives of the brave partisans who would now live to attack another day. Alistair should be thankful for the miracle of Dragonfly's successful deflections of the threats to their covers these past weeks, sparing him that coronary he expected to suffer before he got them out. In three cases, the sure risks to their safety had been permanently eliminated, one by his hand, the others unknown. The policeman, Achim Fleischer, was no longer a danger to Bridgette, nor Dirk Drechsler to Bucky, nor Louis Mueller to Chris. Chris and Brad had missed the swivel of Major General March's eye when some other poor devil confessed to the theft of the classified list of German agents working in the UK. So for the time being, his chicks were free to continue to run.

However, Major Alistair Renault did not believe in miracles.

"For God's sake, Alistair, relax a little and treat those kids to a small reward for their good work," Bill Donovan ordered. "Christmas is coming. Think of something nice to do for them."

Alistair had thought and come up with the perfect

gift. He would allow his operatives to write to their families back home—their letters censored by him, of course—and Bridgette would leave the collection in the dead-letter box for Henri to pick up. His plan would call for two meetings at the tea and book shop, but the morale boost would be worth the risk of the group being seen together. One was necessary for Bridgette to inform the team of their surprise with instructions to slip their letters into the mail slot unaddressed, and another for her to distribute their families' replies. Considering the circuitous and unpredictable routes correspondence between France and the Allied countries were forced to take now, mail to and from the States would require weeks to cross and recross the continents, but their families' letters should be in the team's hands by Christmas, in all but the orphaned Bridgette's. He'd have to think of something special to do for her to compensate.

Colonel Derrick Albrecht had forewarned her by telephone of an imminent visit from homicide detectives of the French National Police, so Victoria was prepared for the summons to Jacques Vogel's office later that morning. "You have nothing to fear," the colonel had assured her after explaining about the police's discovery of the photos. "Simply pretend that you have no idea why they were in Monsieur Fournier's possession."

"What if he left an explanation of who I am and how he knew me?" Victoria asked.

"I wondered, but the detective didn't mention it, not to me."

"But he may to me. I'm the one Fournier meant to blackmail."

"Or me for consorting with an American. I could be blissfully unaware of your nationality, for all Fournier knew."

"Or he meant to turn me in to you. Perhaps that was the reason the man was on his way to your office the day he disappeared," Victoria said. There was an abrupt, strange silence as if she'd said something amiss. "At least, according to *Le Temps*."

"Ah, yes. I did hear that. In any event, the man never arrived, so his mission will remain a mystery."

After the police interview with Victoria, who claimed she'd never met the author and did not know why he possessed photos of her and Colonel Derrick Albrecht, the junior detective put forth a theory to his superior as they left the fencing hall. "Mademoiselle Colbert is a most beautiful woman,

Chief. She impresses me as the kind who wouldn't give that philanderer a lick of her spit even if he did try to blackmail her, especially if that SD colonel was bedding her. The scoundrel wouldn't have dared given her a side glance."

"And, of course, he would have kept in mind the danger to himself if he'd tried to blackmail the colonel," Maurice pointed out. "No, if he in fact did visit Colonel Albrecht that day, he had another reason in mind."

The junior officer looked at him in surprise. "You think the colonel is lying?"

"I think the colonel is protecting Mademoiselle Veronique Colbert."

While the new week of November 23 turned freezing under gray-metal skies, the team of Dragonfly enjoyed the relative calm that had come into their lives. Aware that their peace had been bought at the elimination of their nemeses, Bridgette, Bucky, Chris, and Victoria went about their jobs and clandestine activities feeling the release of the liberated, if the guilt of the culpable. The intel flowed, amplifying the wartime rationale "for the greater good" to justify the casualties. Brad succeeded in learning the details of the shipment of tungsten that allowed the RAF to blow it out of the water, creating for the Nazis an untold delay in their weapons manufacture that their regime could ill afford. One day the virulent-tongued Madame Richter, wife of the notorious commander of the Drancy transit camp in Paris, let fly before the ears of Bridgette the news that her husband would be accompanying a truck convoy loaded with Zyklon B pellets to the gas chambers at Auschwitz. Bridgette, kneeling on the floor to pin the hem of the woman's latest frock, invisible as usual to Madame Richter, listened as she explained that the pellets—"the very best thing for exterminating Jews"—converted to lethal gas when exposed to air.

"The guards throw the pellets through the vent holes, and the Jews are dead in twenty minutes," she said, speaking to the equally despicable wife of another high-ranking German officer. Within minutes of the woman's departure, a sick taste in her mouth, Bridgette took off for the convent to transmit the information to the major. Two nights later, he transmitted back: *Truck convoy hijacked. Diverted off course.*

Stephane Beaulieu had become so trusted and

well-liked at his consulting firm that the German engineer in charge of the "Mountain Project" invited him to make a tour of the facility in the French Alps, where they were constructing projectiles to annihilate the coast of Great Britain. Bucky committed the location and details to memory and drew blueprints of his own to slip to an OSS cutout.

By accident, Victoria learned the name of a mole working for the Nazis inside the American Embassy in Bern, and Chris was able to pass on a military strategy the Germans were planning to defend the coast of France against invasion.

Throughout the week, the mural remained undefaced. Bridgette had worried that without Achim's protection, the wall would be an open invitation for vandals and dabblers to have their way, but to her awed surprise, the fierce pride residents took in the painting and the intensified presence of the admiring German patrols were deterrents enough. However, on the morning of Saturday, November 28, streetgoers noticed a diagonal line drawn through the central dragonfly. The same person who had marked the dragonfly similarly once before had slipped the gauntlet to leave his calling card sometime in the night.

CHAPTER SIXTY-EIGHT

As the month edged into December and the year drew to a close, heavy snow began to fall in Paris, cloaking the city in an endless dreamscape of white, sculpting even the trash in the gutters into fantastical monuments of artistic wizardry, the glacial silence of the blanketed streets so deep that a mere cough sounded like a small explosion.

Parisians would have found the fairyland of snow-draped trees and downy rooftops, icicle-studded eaves, and lacy windowpanes a beautiful setting for the celebration of Christmas but for the rumble of German trucks transporting weapons and soldiers and the disturbance of bullhorns blaring German propaganda, oompah music, and the day's orders to the population. The presence of the Germans was like a fog of pollution hanging low over the city, and hatred for the occupiers increased by the day as their restrictions against French citizens tightened, reprisals for the Resistance's actions grew more frequent, and the hunt for food and fuel to stave off starvation and hypothermia became more desperate. Only necessity drove the conquered out to the streets from the dubious safety and warmth of their homes.

"And now *this*!" Major General Konrad March raged, slapping at a street poster of a public notice before his usual audience of Brad, Chris, and Madame Gastain, who had been invited to partake of fondue and wine and the comfort of a blazing fire in his house. "To think this—this *sacrilege* against the meaning of Christmas has been imposed on children in Germany and now in France!"

Throughout the day, German soldiers had been about the city tacking up posters and thrusting flyers into the hands of pedestrians that forbade any display of the Christian elements associated with Christmas. French newspapers had already lined up behind the Nazi pronouncement that Christmas had nothing to do with the birth of Christ. The holiday was derived from the ancient practice of celebrating the winter solstice and the rebirth of the sun. Santa Claus was a Christian concoction inspired by the Germanic god Odin. The poster provoking the general's disgust depicted a gray-bearded Odin astride a white charger with a sack of gifts on his back. The manger scene of Mary and Joseph and the baby Jesus had been changed to a garden strewn with wooden animal toys.

"That's not all," Madame Gastain said. "The shops have been ordered to replace their usual Christmas toys with facsimiles of tanks, fighter planes, and machine guns. In one store today, I saw that the star on top of the Christmas tree had been replaced with a swastika."

Chris said, "The posters went up in the school today. The staff has been ordered to instruct the students that Christmas is not about the coming of Jesus but the coming of Hitler and that they are to consider him the real savior of the world. He's to be called Savior Führer."

"*Verdammt noch mal!*" (Damn them!) Konrad exploded.

"I have lived too long," Madame Gastain sighed.

Brad and Chris had noticed that the general's tongue had become more unguarded around them, especially after he'd had a few glasses of schnapps. While not exactly careless, he was not as careful with the classified files he brought home, files that should have remained under lock and key at Abwehr headquarters, presumably because he did not trust his office staff. Brad reported that Konrad was also a little more open in discussing military matters with fellow officers aboard Captain Allard's boat.

"What do you think? Deliberately indiscreet?" Brad questioned Chris.

"I'm not sure... What's his game if he is?"

"Could be he simply trusts us?"

"I would think trust had been ironed out of him like the wrinkles in his uniform."

But none of the intel picked up from the study desk and the fishing boat had come back to point a finger at them, so the two young operatives carried on.

Victoria, also, was careful not to accept too readily Colonel Derrick Albrecht's trust in her. She could not fathom the man. How could a human being of such intellect, culture, and civility, an appreciator of the world's great art and music and literature, the epitome of civilized man, belong to an inhumane organization like the SS? Daily reports circulated of SS brutalities that curdled the blood. She had witnessed for herself an SS officer calmly pull out his gun and shoot a civilian on the street, leaving him to die in a pool of blood in the snow for no other offense than his failure to step out of the officer's way. The casual murder left Victoria so sick that she canceled an evening engagement with the colonel, unable to bear the sight of his uniform.

She no longer saw him alone. After their drive into the country to compensate for the aborted picnic, his invitations were to military social functions, dinner engagements with fellow officers, a cinema, or a restaurant party, his deportment toward her always meticulously correct and his company pleasant. The Nazi functions made her skin crawl, but they served up platters of intelligence that Victoria thought must surely water the mouth of even the jaded Major Renault.

Still, a small inner voice warned her to beware. A cobra lulled by the music did not mean that it was asleep.

Bridgette had no such fears. Free from Achim's watchful eye, convinced that he had not reported her radio, she enjoyed the luxury of concentrating on the mural as a work of art apart from its purpose as a code pad. Between the lulls in snowfalls, it grew in size and depth and beauty and led to pleasant acquaintanceships among the locals and even with the soldiers of the German street patrols. She began to feel at home in the convent. She enjoyed mealtimes and chess matches with the nuns in the evening. Several of the Sisters of Charity, without a hint that they knew what she was up to, volunteered to stand as lookouts to warn her of the approach of German direction finders during the times she was at her wireless.

Bridgette's one minor concern was the jealousy of several of Madame Boucher's designers, who were known collaborators. The French fashion world and its schools of design comprised a small, closed society. From her first day at the fashion house, the designers had covertly expressed their perplexity at how madame had happened to hire an apprentice unknown to their sphere and afforded her special treatment and leeway to come and go as she pleased.

"Always something to keep you on your toes," Bridgette sighed to the mother superior in confiding her impressions of her fellow coworkers.

"I will pray for your balance, *ma chère amie*, but you must take care," Sister Mary Frances warned.

With Dirk gone, Bucky, too, could now enjoy a relatively safe home and work environment. His greatest and constant worry concerned the safety of his father. The Black Ghost made weekly headlines in underground newspapers. One afternoon, as Christmas approached, Bucky returned to the boardinghouse after work to find a fresh black mark on the underside of the bottom porch step. His throat clogged with fear. Early the next morning, he arrived in the park when not a single footprint marred the pristine, snow-covered grounds. Gone were the birds and the man with his paper sack. He was alone. Bucky stuck his hand into the eye of the tree and withdrew a note. *My beloved, a Christmas package awaits you at CB.*

Bucky sprinted across the street to Claire Bellerose's house and rang the bell. It was instantly answered by his aunt's old butler and caretaker, who, without a word, thrust a wrapped package into Bucky's hand and closed the door. Taking the package to the bench in the park, Bucky unwrapped it. Tears immediately flooded his eyes. He held in his hands the yellow-fringed epaulettes worn by his father as a cadet officer and student at Saint-Cyr, France's foremost military academy. "Happy Christmas, son," read the accompanying note.

The Christmas letters to families were sent and received, an exciting event that called for another diagonal mark across the central dragonfly. In distributing them, Bridgette repeated Major Renault's orders. "Read and destroy immediately after reading," she said.

But of course none did, not immediately.

At the meeting, unless an emergency arose, the last

they expected to have together for as long as their missions took, Victoria made a suggestion. "What do you say that we make a pact to have another reunion, right here in this café at four o'clock on September twenty-third, 1962?"

Silence fell. All understood the psychology behind the proposal. Liverwort was asking them to declare their faith that they would survive to gather for a twenty-year reunion.

"Well, why not?" she contended, meeting their silence with a determined thrust of her chin. "Don't dragonflies always return to the river of their hatch?"

"That they do, Liverwort, that they do," Brad said. He reached forward to lay his palm on the table and each set a hand upon it. "To September twenty-third, 1962, right here in this spot in Paris," he said, and the others repeated in chorus, "To September twenty-third, 1962, right here in this spot in Paris."

Victoria and Bridgette were the last to depart the café and walked out together. "What about you, Labrador?" Victoria asked, her voice gentle. "Was there no one back home to write to you? No family, friends?"

"My family and friends are here," Bridgette said.

When she returned to her attic room that evening, a package wrapped in Christmas paper was waiting for her. The card inside read, "Merry Christmas from A. Renault." Bridgette smiled. The present was a box that contained one of her favorite things: Michigan cherry jams.

Nineteen forty-two drew to a close. By December 31, the war news appeared a shade brighter for the Allies. The Red Army had the Germans penned at Stalingrad, successfully stopping their further advance into the USSR. Field Marshal Erwin Rommel, commander of the Afrika Corps, was trapped in Tunisia, and the British won a strategic naval battle in the Barents Sea against German ships that had been dispatched to destroy fourteen of His Majesty's merchant ships carrying war materials to Russia.

On New Year's Eve in Bern, Switzerland, the teetotalling Major Alistair Renault accepted a glass of champagne at a station party and raised it with the office crew to toast all Allied agents working on enemy soil and pray they would make it back alive and well. For his team of five young operatives, Alistair still had his fears, but so far the mice had escaped the cats, and Dragonfly was still in the game.

CHAPTER SIXTY-NINE

Herr General, may I speak with you a moment?" Hans said, assisting Konrad March in removing his overcoat.

"Of course, Hans. You sound grave. Is it Wilhelm?"

"No, Mein General. May we speak in the kitchen?"

"Before my schnapps?" Konrad said, noticing that his aide hung up his coat without brushing the snow from its shoulders. He saw to the job himself. "You appear distracted."

"I am, begging the general's pardon."

"Lead the way then."

Now what? Konrad thought. He'd had a miserable day. All his days had been miserable for the past month, and it was only the beginning of February—eleven more months of misery to get through before it was all over, if the bleak start of the new year was any indication. Today, February 2, the battle for Stalingrad had been announced as officially over, which, as he and his colleagues had expected, had ended in disaster for Germany. Yesterday, he'd learned that among the quarter of a million Wehrmacht troops captured on Russian soil was his good friend Generalfeldmarschall Friedrich Paulus. Hitler had expected Friedrich to commit suicide before being taken prisoner, since no German field marshal had ever surrendered, but his friend had other ideas that had sent the Führer into an apoplectic rage. Konrad had been in meetings all day with members of the High Command. Everyone was worried that the Soviets, after two years of being pushed back by Nazi forces, would begin an advance toward Germany. Worse, what if the Russian victory turned the war in favor of the Allies?

Also, today the SS had intercepted and arrested a family of Jews about to enter Switzerland on an Abwehr pass signed personally by Admiral Wilhelm Canaris himself. When questioned, his nimble-witted mentor had explained that the father was an intelligence agent on a mission to Switzerland for his department. The SS was able to buy the story of the father as plausible enough, but for his wife, children, and grandmother? Konrad's hair had stood on end.

How long would it be before the head of Germany's military intelligence was discovered to be playing a double game? God, what a day! He needed his schnapps and a warm fire.

"Yes, Hans?" he said when they were in his aide's domain.

Hans lowered his voice as if the walls had ears. "It's about Herr Wagner and Herr Bauer."

"What about them?"

"They are Americans."

Konrad stared at him. "How do you know?"

"I overheard them speaking to each other—in English, with an American accent. I was behind the hedge in front covering the water pipes when Herr Bauer came for his tutoring session and met Herr Wagner on the street. Herr Wagner was taking in wood to Madame Gastain's. They did not see me and the street was deserted, so they thought it safe to speak softly in English. My ear is not mistaken, Mein General. As you know, my mother took in soldiers of the American Expeditionary Forces as boarders after the last war. I recognize an American accent."

"Could you understand what they were saying?"

"*Nein*, but I could make out a few American words."

"What were they?"

"Words like *zigzag* and *boondoggle* and *Archie*, meaning German antiaircraft fire."

Konrad mused over Hans's discovery in silence for a moment, then laid a hand on his aide's shoulder. "This information is to be kept between us until I can figure out what to do with it. Understood?"

"As always, Mein General," he said, looking crestfallen. "I regret having to report it. I would never have guessed the young men to be...spies. I quite like them, and of course Wilhelm—"

"Yes, yes, I know," Konrad agreed and let out a deep sigh. "It would seem there is no end to the ways in which people can disappoint us, eh?" He shook his head wearily. "*Danke*, Hans. Carry on."

As he left the kitchen, Konrad smiled to himself. Americans, huh? Why was he not surprised? The young kits had fooled the old fox. He had thought they were anti-Nazi Germans recruited by the SOE, but no, Americans, running for the OSS, even better to suit his plans. Konrad poured his first glass of schnapps of the evening and settled himself before the welcome warmth of his fireplace. The day had turned out not to be such a bitter pill after all.

Detective Maurice Corbett had an idea, spurred when he saw a French janitor vacuuming the carpet in the hall outside Colonel Derrick Albrecht's office after his last visit. It was a long shot and dangerous, but he thought he'd take it and without the assistance of his colleague. The lad was a good boy on all accounts, but he did not know him, and Maurice had learned that nowadays unknown quantities among the French could not be trusted. Some would betray their grandmothers for a loaf of bread.

He waited across the street from the Nazi-flag-draped entrance to SD headquarters for its counterintelligence chief to come through the door. Maurice had stood watch for days in a nearby shop to note the routine of Colonel Derrick Albrecht's departures from his office. It seemed the colonel preferred to take his noonday meals away from the premises. Who could blame him? The screams issuing forth from 84 Avenue Foch could sometimes be heard in the street. Maurice could imagine their effect on an empty stomach.

A German staff car drove up before the entrance, and an SS guard opened the door of the building before stepping back at rigid attention with an arm thrust out in a stiff Nazi salute. Colonel Derrick Albrecht strode forth, a striking specimen of Hitler's ideal of an Aryan male, tall, handsome, blond, confident, physically fit, scary as hell. Maurice waited until the Mercedes-Benz had pulled away and he was beyond view of the car's mirrors before walking across the street to the entrance, his papers already in hand, by all appearances just another Frenchman come to betray a fellow citizen. He showed the documents and his police badge to the guards, then headed down a hallway to the room marked CUSTODIAL SERVICES and BOILER ROOM that he had noticed on his previous visit.

He reminded himself again that in pursuing a certain line of inquiry into the murder of Beaumont Fournier, he put at risk not only his position as chief investigator of the homicide division of the French National Police, but also his person. His superior had ordered him to have no further contact with Colonel Derrick Albrecht. "The man says the author did not keep his appointment, and that's that," he'd said. "Why don't you believe him, Maurice?"

"Because the taxi driver said he let the author off at Sicherheitsdienst headquarters, and my cop's nose tells me the colonel is lying."

"Your nose could be wrong, and anybody could have gotten to the writer before he set foot inside the Sicherheitsdienst's door. The man wasn't exactly a saint."

"Nobody else but his butler knew he'd be there at that time of the morning. And wouldn't the door guards have seen something if he'd been abducted off the street?"

"So the butler says, for all he knew. And the door guards and colonel's aide confirm that the author did not show up. I believe them, and you need to, too, Maurice, for your own sake, regardless of your nose. I'm ordering you to drop the man from your suspect list, not only for the reasons that should be obvious to you, but because the man is probably a waste of time."

But Maurice's nose could not stop bothering him and neither could his professional conscience. Somebody was responsible for a French citizen's murder, and according to the agreement reached with the occupying authorities, French crimes committed on French soil were the purview of the French police to investigate and solve. Maurice supposed the key word in the agreement was *French*. It did not extend to Germans who murdered French citizens.

Maurice was well aware that his appearance back at SD headquarters would not go unreported, nor would his questioning of a member of the cleaning crew. He could be chasing after a wild goose besides. What were the chances he'd find the same bent old codger sweeping the floor down from Colonel Albrecht's office? Who would wager that the same janitor might have been plying his broom on the Saturday morning Beaumont Fournier purportedly visited Colonel Derrick Albrecht? More important, who would lay bets that a French laborer working in a department of the SS would speak to an inspector in the French police?

But there the old man sat, warming his hands before the furnace, when Maurice pushed open the door. Other custodians were in the room. Maurice discreetly showed his subject his badge and experienced a moment's surprise when the old man's murky eyes leaped to life with what seemed like an understanding of why he had come. Without a word, the janitor nodded toward the door and creaked up from his chair. Maurice took his lead and followed his shambling exit from the room.

In the hall, the janitor turned to him. "*Oui*, monsieur?" he inquired.

"I have a few questions. Are you willing to talk to the French police?"

"Depends on the questions."

"Were you working here and in this hall on the morning of Saturday, October thirty-first?"

"*Oui*, monsieur."

Maurice held up a photograph. "Did you happen to see this man here on that day?"

"*Oui*, monsieur."

Maurice stifled a start. "Did you see him go into Colonel Derrick Albrecht's office?"

"Oui."

"Did you see him leave?"

"*Non*, monsieur."

"No? Was that because you may have been somewhere else in the building when the man could have left?"

"*Non*, monsieur."

"In the boiler room, perhaps?"

"*Non*, monsieur." The man's tired old eyes glinted with knowledge that he had no intention of sharing. The janitor was fully aware of what had transpired on this floor the morning of October 31, but his noncommittal responses made clear that he would say no more on the subject.

"You were in the hall the whole time during this man's visit?" Maurice persisted.

"*Oui*, monsieur."

"And would you have seen the man leave?"

"*Oui*, monsieur."

"Merci, Oncle. Bonjour."

Maurice departed the building of horrors feeling as if its evil had permeated the wool of his overcoat like tobacco smoke caught in the weave. So Colonel Derrick Albrecht *had* lied. Beaumont Fournier had kept that appointment with the chief of the French counterintelligence division of the Sicherheitsdienst, and now he, as chief investigator of the homicide department of the French National Police, had to find out if the author had left as he arrived.

CHAPTER SEVENTY

Brad knew he should obey orders and destroy the letter from his mother to which the whole family, including his new stepfather, had contributed news. Rationing had begun. Meeker, Colorado, was virtually devoid of all its young men because of the draft, and the lumber company was short of manpower. The new house was under construction, Beata and Margie were taking tap-dancing lessons, and Bobby had an afternoon job as a stock boy at Shreve's grocery store. They were all praying for Brad's safety wherever he was, and they loved him very much.

Bobby had included his own note, which was especially touching and probably had been inserted unread by his mother. Brad could hear the boy's voice striving to be manly: "I've listed here the order of importance of those items I think you should know.

Your mom and sister are fine. That's number 1. Number 2 is that Jared is an okay guy, too. You can tell he loves your mom like my dad loved my mom. I remember that part from the old days. Number 3, he treats Margie and me as good as Beata which is saying a lot. You don't have to worry about that. I think that is about all. I miss you. It is empty here without you."

Brad had read the letter over and over, milking each line for every detail to make sure he had missed nothing. Apparently all was well in his family's household back in Meeker, Colorado. But while he'd almost committed the letter to heart, he couldn't bear to set fire to it, and there were no secure hiding places in his apartment. Finally he settled on simply tucking it into a book in plain sight, the best hiding place when nothing else was available. By now the general would have had his apartment searched as a matter of course, and no one else had reason to.

The day after Hans's revelations, the book was one of the first places the general looked after Brad left for work. He could not read the concealed letter, but he recognized its language as English. He now had evidence that his young friend was an American spy.

"It would seem, Herr Bauer," Jules Garnier said to Chris, "that you are now the new sports director of the Academy. I received my orders this morning."

Chris stared at the man in surprise. "How did that happen? I'm the most junior instructor here!"

Jules smiled. "My dear fellow, such considerations as rank and tenure—fairness—are rarely taken into account by the Nazis when extending promotions. Accomplishments are. You have done your job without intimidation and bullying while adhering to the party curriculum. The parents of the students in your pod praise you—and to the right ears, apparently. I received orders this morning to instate you in Herr Mueller's position." Jules's eyes twinkled, sharpening to a conspiratorial glint when he said, "You can expect more invitations to the boys' homes for dinner."

Chris took the news with mixed emotions. This "promotion" could mean that Major General March might reenroll his son in the school as an opportunity for Wilhelm to associate with boys his son's age. He would trust Chris not to ram the party line down Wilhelm's throat, but reenrollment would cut off Chris's access to his house and its vital source of information as well as the only occasions to pal around with Limpet. He would sorely miss them both. He'd come to look on the general's house as a sanctuary from his drab quarters and Limpet as a close friend. They were in sync about everything. Chris liked the fisherman's wise and tolerant ways. His Christmas letter from his parents had included no news of Dirk's return to New Braunfels, and Chris was now sure that his old friend would never be seen in their hometown again. He'd been sacrificed to protect Lodestar's cover. Chris had mourned for him, and Limpet had understood, despite that Dirk had been a traitor. "How can you not grieve for friends who make bad choices?" he'd said.

That afternoon when Chris announced his new position to the general, Konrad said, "I hope your new assignment will not mean that you will no longer be available to tutor Wilhelm."

"I had supposed that you might wish to reenroll your son back in school now that the sports director has gone, General."

The general smiled. "You supposed wrong, Claus. My son is happy as things are, and, selfishly, the household would miss your company. Can we count on you to continue with us?"

"Absolutely, Herr General."

Colonel Derrick Albrecht accepted the latest report on the activities of Rue des Soeurs de Charité. He thanked the man he'd assigned to watch the street and called off further surveillance. He had no need for additional information.

Derrick read quickly, thoughtfully, then filed the report in a drawer with others accumulated over the past three months. Only one question remained unanswered: Was Victoria acquainted with the other conspirators, all male, or did they work separately? She'd not been reported communicating or even being seen with the men at the same time. There were three of them: a seaman and two other men of undetermined professions. Photographs showed them young, early twenties, strong, fit, and attractive. Routinely, but separately, they were observed slipping messages into the mail chute of the house near the convent, now the canvas for a beautiful mural. Karl had driven him to see the house despite the risk that his staff car's presence on the street might warn the conspirators that the drop had been compromised. The mural was indeed something lovely to behold. Did this depiction of a peaceful scene of aquatic sea life have anything to do with the clandestine activity going on next door?

His wolfhound had nosed out information on the petite, blond artist as well. Mademoiselle Bernadette Dufor was a clothes designer working for the renowned fashion house La Maison de Boucher. Celeste was a patron of the place. Derrick would have to ask her if she knew her. Two details bothered him. According to his man's investigation, she had been hired about the time Victoria was employed at L'Ecole d'Escrime Français, seemingly out of nowhere, a graduate of a middling school of design in Lyons now defunct because of the war. No reputation of extraordinary ability preceded her that would justify a position at an esteemed fashion house, but the couturier who owned the place had been desperate to replace designers who'd refused to work in a house that catered to the wives of the Nazi invaders.

Coincidence? Derrick did not believe in coincidences. The other item was her place of residence. She lived within the thick walls of the convent, an ideal location to set up a transmission radio that might go undetected. Derrick would like to know how she came to reside in a house of nuns reserved only for their order, but his wolfhound had stopped short of presenting the question to the woman in charge of the place. "I am Catholic," he explained, "and I do not run afoul of a mother superior." He did, however, offer an opinion that ran contrary to Derrick's suspicions. "My observation of Mademoiselle Dufor has revealed nothing to indicate that she is aware of the purpose of the mail slot next door. It is my view, Colonel, that the artist is not a member of the cell."

That remained to be proved, but Derrick had no interest in flushing the chicken from its coop. He would not search the house with the mail drop or have the three men picked up for questioning. That would not suit his plans. If an OSS operation was being carried out on the Rue des Soeurs de Charité, he would allow it to be. He would not interfere with the game Victoria and her fellow conspirators were engaged in as long as they continued playing into his hands. His major concern was that they would get caught. He would have to take measures to assure that they were not. He would call in a specialized team for the task at hand.

CHAPTER SEVENTY-ONE

Nineteen forty-three progressed. The Allies were steadily making headway against the Axis powers on land, sea, and in the air. Throughout the spring that had merged into a hot, dry summer in Europe, enemy tides were turning. The Japanese were being pushed out of the Pacific Islands; Allied forces had begun a successful invasion into Italy that led to its unconditional surrender in September; and the North African Campaign had ended in May. Resistance organizations throughout occupied Europe were growing in numbers and successfully sabotaging Wehrmacht installations, German-controlled industrial plants, explosives depots, rail and communication lines, and rubber and steel works. In France, the elusive Black Ghost's Maquis group was terrorizing German patrols, convoys, and radio outposts, and forcing the Nazis to form protection units with soldiers they could ill afford to pull from their ranks. In his office at the Prefecture of Police headquarters in Paris, Maurice Corbett closely followed the news of the Allied advance and French victories, and patiently bided his time.

On into late fall and throughout the rest of the year, Dragonfly hovered close to waters teeming with an increasingly frantic enemy. Despite the extreme measures Nazi police organizations took to search out and punish Allied spies and informers, Dragonfly steadily provided critical information to the Bern station, a strong argument for keeping the team in place.

But Alistair could not shake his enduring fear that it was only a matter of time before his dragonflies flew into the enemy's mouth.

As 1944 began and advanced, the grounds were laid for Alistair's fears to materialize. A report was placed on his desk February 19 that elicited an expletive so loud that everyone in the building heard it. The startled desk sergeant outside his door jumped up and rushed into Alistair's office.

"What is it, Major?"

Alistair sat with his fingers kneading his temples. "Yesterday, Hitler relieved Admiral Wilhelm

Canaris of his command in Berlin and abolished the Abwehr. The organization is to be absorbed into the SS."

The stunned clerk asked, "What's to happen to Major General Konrad March?"

"How the hell do I know?"

Alistair immediately put in a call to Wild Bill Donovan, who was "unavailable." That meant that he was on a secret mission somewhere. "Tell him to get in touch with me as soon as possible," he ordered.

Drawing heavily on a cigarette, Alistair roamed his office. Nothing in the report said anything about Admiral Canaris being arrested or the reason for his dismissal. His removal smelled of the manipulation of Heinrich Himmler, who for some time had been suspicious of Canaris and had pushed to put the Abwehr under the control of the SS. If Canaris was discovered to be playing a double game, which he was, then his arrest was certain and where would that leave the admiral's close friend, Konrad March?

Alistair had never been sure that the two were in the game together or separately, but early on, he had suspected the major general of using Brad and Chris to channel information, always genuine, to the OSS.

Surely he shared the same conviction as the admiral's that Hitler was a madman sending Germany on the road to destruction. What else could explain the consistent flow of classified information to the ears and cameras of his fishing guide and his son's tutor?

If Alistair was right, with Canaris's arrest, the general would be one of the next cards in the deck to fall, and Brad and Chris along with him. Ditto for the rest of the team. Alistair knew his boss would direct him to wait and see if his fears for Dragonfly materialized, and only then get Dragonfly out. To hell with that. Alistair would obey his orders only to a point. He would decide himself when to extract his team.

The SS's takeover of the Abwehr in Paris was immediate and swift. No sooner had the admiral been informed that he would be relieved of his duties in Berlin than the commander of the SD, Derrick's superior, marched into Konrad's office in the Lutetia Hotel with his second-in-command by his side. While a contingent of SS personnel swooped through the rest of Abwehr headquarters taking possession of offices and desks, the SD commander proclaimed to Major General Konrad March that by decree of the Führer, the Department of German Military Intelligence in France was now officially abolished and its duties placed under the command of the Schutzstaffel. He would leave it to Colonel Derrick Albrecht, head of the counterintelligence section of the security service of the Reichsführer, to explain.

Konrad's friend and coconspirator played the part of the haughty conqueror well. With an icy gaze and tone that held years of hatred between the two organizations, Derrick announced to him that the general's department would fall under his jurisdiction. Major General March would retain a junior position unless, of course, he wished to transfer to another division of the Wehrmacht. Derrick would be taking over the major general's duties immediately. Konrad was to hand over the keys to all doors, filing cabinets, and safes, and see to it that all personal items were removed from his office. The colonel would be occupying both his own office at 84 Avenue Foch and the major general's in the Lutetia Hotel.

Konrad was assigned a desk in another room in the building that lacked all but the minimum ventilation and light. His function for the moment was to arrange the reassignment of his staff to other divisions within the German Army and to familiarize his new superior with the Abwehr's operation. Konrad would have been among the exodus to a post commensurate to his rank had it not been for the secret business he shared with the man who now occupied his office. To the few Abwehr men on his staff in on the conspiracy, he had presented the choice to stay on or to transfer to other commands. To a man they had agreed to accept demeaning positions in the SS to continue their rescue operations. In his organization, Derrick was not so fortunate to have such men on his staff. He could trust only one sergeant and a junior officer to assist with his clandestine activities.

With the absorption of the Abwehr into the SS, the two senior heads now had to be extra careful in making use of the *Nacht und Nebel* decree issued by Hitler, which gave intelligence organizations permission to ignore the agreements and procedures of the Geneva Convention regarding prisoners. Translated, *Nacht* and *Nebel* meant "night" and "fog," an apt name for the decree, since prisoners were hustled away under a cloak of darkness to some secret location where they would vanish without a trace, leaving their families never to know of their whereabouts. It was a loathsome policy meant to intimidate local populations into submission, but it provided Konrad and Derrick the perfect cover to arrange the escape of certain prisoners of state without questions being asked. However, on too many occasions, the victims had been whisked away prematurely, to the annoyance of other organizations wishing to question or make examples of them.

The day of the takeover, Konrad calculated how soon he had to get the wheels in motion to get his son out of France before Admiral Canaris was arrested. He had long expected that he himself would go down with the admiral's ship. It was for Wilhelm that he wished an escape route. He sent Hans to ask Barnard Wagner to come to his house the following evening and to telephone Claus Bauer at the school to say that he had something urgent to discuss with him.

The following evening, Hans ushered Brad and Chris into his superior's study without Wilhelm aware that they were in the house. No table of food or schnapps was laid out. Konrad was already seated behind his desk and gestured them to take a seat before it. He noted they showed him their usual deference, unlike the shift in the esteem colleagues and acquaintances were already paying him now that he had lost his exalted position. Nazi-controlled newspapers in Paris had been quick to report the Abwehr's abolishment and its chief's demotion.

The young men regarded him expectantly. Konrad interlocked his hands on his desk and said solemnly, "Gentlemen, I am aware that you are Americans working for your country's intelligence organization, the OSS." He raised a hand lest they speak. "Do not try to deny it. I have irrefutable proof, but you must not fear. I support your cause, and I have an extreme favor to ask of you."

CHAPTER SEVENTY-TWO

The following morning, Chris dropped a message for transmission through the mail slot that called for an emergency meeting with the Frenchman that day at the book and tea shop, usual time. He and Limpet had information that must be delivered face-to-face. That afternoon, at four o'clock, Brad and Chris entered the café separately. The CLOSED sign hung in the window. The Frenchman sat in his corner reading and smoking his usual vile-smelling Gauloises. Once the young operatives were seated, he moved to the table and listened patiently while Chris explained that Major General Konrad March had known for more than a year that they were Americans trained as OSS agents. He did not explain how the man had come by his information.

"*Mon Dieu*!" exclaimed the Frenchman. "And he hasn't had you arrested?"

"He wants an Allied victory as much as we do, it seems, to save Germany and France from destruction," Brad said. "At first, Lapwing and I wondered if he wasn't laying a trap for us, but when our intel proved genuine and we weren't arrested, we figured that maybe he was just being careless after all."

"So now the general feels that if Canaris is arrested for treason, he will be, too," Chris added.

"I would say he has a point," Henri said. "We have reason to believe that even Erwin Rommel, Germany's favorite general, is under suspicion. So what does the general want? Asylum?"

"Only for his son," Brad said. "He can't leave. He has too many people depending on him, he says. He's a soldier, and he loves his homeland. He will stay and fight until the bitter end."

"Let us hope he lives to see Germany's defeat. Where does the general wish to stow his son?"

"In Switzerland with an aunt, a Helga Wolfe. General March has asked that we use our extraction apparatus to get him out," Brad answered.

"Why doesn't he arrange to spirit his son out himself? He can't be without resources."

Brad shook his head. "He thinks it's too dangerous now that he's under the eyes of the SS and can be arrested at any time. Lapwing and I both believe the general is involved in more than he's letting on. We think he's connected with a network far greater than simply feeding us information. If that's the case and he's arrested and made to talk, his organization's safe routes will be compromised. He wants to see his son to safety while there's still time. We'd like to see that happen, too." He looked at Chris, who nodded in confirmation.

"What about you, my young friends? If your general falls, you will, too."

"The general will have enough to fill their ears without involving his fishing guide and his son's tutor. We can trust him on that. We will have time and ways and means to get out."

The Frenchman sighed. "I will report to the major."

Three days later, the general sat at eye level with his son and explained that he was sending him to be with his aunt Helga in Switzerland for a while, and that he would join him when he could. Hans was in the front hallway, handing off Wilhelm's luggage.

"Why?" the boy asked, eyes welling, lower lip trembling. "I don't want to go. I don't like Aunt Helga or my cousins."

He didn't, either, Konrad thought in despair. His sister-in-law was a bitch and her children were spawned in hell, but she was the one relative living outside Germany where his son would be safe. "It's not safe in France anymore, and your aunt is expecting you. You wouldn't want to disappoint her, now would you?"

"I wouldn't mind," Wilhelm said, his voice wobbly.

Konrad reached out and drew his child hard against his chest. He would have sobbed, but he couldn't let on that this might be the last time he would hold his son. "I love you, my son. Always remember that should it be a while before we see each other again."

"But you'll come for me, right, Papa?"

Hans saved him from answering. Coming into the room, he announced quietly, "The driver is here, Herr General."

"Can I say good-bye to Herr Wagner?" Wilhelm asked.

"He's not here, son. I'll say good-bye for you. Now we must go downstairs."

Taking Wilhelm's hand, following Hans, father and son descended the wide staircase. At the door, Hans, struggling to hold back tears, said his good-byes before Konrad knelt and hugged his son close again. He pressed his lips to the boy's forehead and said, "*Auf wiedersehen*, my son. God be with you, until we meet again."

That night, uninvited, Brad rang the general's doorbell. When Hans answered, Brad knew at once from his swollen eyes and drooping face that Wilhelm had gone. The major had come through. Hans, incapable of speech, merely nodded toward the study, where Brad found the general slumped in his fireside chair, the glowing embers highlighting his vacant, tear-streaked gaze and the empty bottle of schnapps on the table beside him.

"In my country, there is a saying that misery loves company," Brad said. "Want mine?"

"Have a seat," the general said.

The following day, February 24, Colonel Derrick Albrecht's surveillance man called at the colonel's quarters in the Crillon Hotel to deliver his latest reports. For more than a year, he and his relief crew had occupied the site of a closed bistro across the street from the Convent of the Sisters of Charity. There was a mural on the convent wall, a beautiful thing that would be a tragedy if it were defaced. Its protection was not part of his duty, but if the situation came to that, he would make its preservation his business to the perpetrators' regret.

Though his job as a surveillance expert was occasionally boring, he had never tired of it. He was well paid for doing virtually nothing, and people watching was one of his favorite occupations, the reason he was so good at what he did. Nothing got by him. He enjoyed observing the pretty artist add touches to her painting, and he welcomed the opportunity to read and to teach himself French while making sure no movement on the street escaped his surveillance. The imagined consequences of missing something important that should be reported to the chief of the SD's counterintelligence department in France allowed no room to fall down on his job.

Based on his surveillance experience, the sleights of hand with which three men and one woman regularly slipped messages into the correspondence chute of the house beside the convent, as well as the care taken to appear natural, confirmed beyond doubt that they were members of a subversive organization using it as their dead-letter box. In his reports, he referred to them as the seaman, the Greek god, the briefcase, and the Goddess. He expected Colonel Albrecht to have had them rounded up by now, but the colonel had ordered him and his relief to stay at their post and report at once any activity or person that appeared to be a threat to the group.

One had appeared today.

Derrick heard him out in silence, a tingling along his neck. "A Citroën Traction Avant?" It was the Gestapo's car of choice, the most sinister sight on the streets of Paris.

"Yes, Herr Colonel. Black as the devil's heart, three men inside, unmistakably Gestapo."

"And they stopped before the mural?"

"For twenty minutes. Each man got out and took a look. I thought they might mar it in some way, but they didn't. It was hard to say what they were thinking."

"You say 'looking.' Casually? Intensely?"

"I would say intensely. Each looked as if he were inspecting it."

"And the car did not appear to be cruising the street?"

"No, Herr Colonel. The mural seemed to be its destination. The car moved on once all the men seemed satisfied and were back inside."

"If you see further Gestapo activity on that street, you're to report immediately to me, understood?"

"*Unbedingt*, Herr Colonel."

When his surveillance man had left, Derrick mulled over the report. The mural's increasing attraction was bound eventually to have reached the ears of the Gestapo. Anything odd and unusual, be it innocent as a child's toy or innocuous as a work of art, roused their suspicion. Their intention today might have been simply to analyze it to determine if it was deserving of the Gestapo's attention, and then moved on, satisfied that it wasn't. He would rely on the alert attention of his specialty surveillance team to make sure.

CHAPTER SEVENTY-THREE

Gradually, the cards began to fall. There were a few traces of sun in the months before the skies darkened entirely. On Friday, February 25, Brad was able to report Wilhelm's safe arrival in Switzerland to his father. The general called together his usual guests to celebrate the news with a bottle of champagne, but there was little to be done to relieve the sepulchral silence in the house without the presence of his son. Madame Gastain offered some comfort: After good nights were said to Chris and Brad and the general left to walk her home, he did not return. His neighbor had taken pity on him and invited him to stay the night.

Rumors were flying that an Allied invasion was imminent, perhaps on the northern coast of France in the spring, when the weather was more favorable.

In March, a stroke of good luck favored Bucky when he was tapped to go along with an engineering team to check out the structural readiness of the massive Atlantic Wall, designed to protect Nazi-occupied France from an Allied invasion by sea. The sight of the 1,670-mile coastal defense system would be indelibly imprinted in his memory as long as he lived. Stretching from Norway along the Belgian and French coastline to the Spanish border were miles of barbed wire and an endless chain of impregnable bunkers from which the Germans could mow down landing forces the moment they hit the beaches with full protection from return fire. Mines by the thousands were strewn along the shoreline attached to steel-and-concrete spiked structures designed to halt tanks, troop carriers, and other amphibious landing vehicles in their tracks. At high tide the invaders would approach the beaches without seeing the traps, and at low tide the sight of their awesome and deadly numbers would dissuade even the most determined forces from launching an invasion by sea.

Sick at heart, his imagination rife with the horror of such an assault and the casualties of the brave men who might try it, Bucky recorded details of the enemy's coastal defense fortification in a report so meticulous that it served as one of the major consultation sources to the Allied strategists planning the invasion.

On March 4, Admiral Wilhelm Canaris was put under house arrest, but weeks passed and no word came of the admiral's out-and-out incarceration. A rumor circulated in Konrad's office that his former chief was to be assigned a government job of minor importance in Berlin. But Konrad didn't trust Himmler. He knew how the Nazi chief of the SS worked. Play the fish along until it was time to sink the hook deep, then yank it from the water. So Brad and Chris, unknown to Konrad, concocted a plan to keep the general safe if the worst came to Admiral Canaris. They had decided that when the time came to run, they were taking the general with them to Switzerland, where he would reunite with Wilhelm and remain until the end of the war.

By April, classified intel was dropping before the team like a windfall of apples. With tensions running high in the Vichy government and the German High Command, Chris received fewer invitations to the homes of the academy's students, since the fathers could not be counted on to make it home for dinner, but their sons had no qualms about repeating their fathers' explanations for the activities that kept them from the family table.

At the House of Boucher, frantic wives and mistresses openly discussed their husbands' and lovers' military strategies to counter the oncoming tide. In Bucky's engineering firm, it was nothing for desperate German engineers to invite the French into meetings once conducted in hush-hush secrecy, and Victoria could hardly keep up with the flow of classified information bandied about in the fencing school and the trickle collected from the colonel.

The result was that the team made almost daily passes by the dead-letter box.

Colonel Albrecht's top stakeout expert kept his vigil and saw nothing amiss on the street of the Sisters of Charity to rouse his suspicions, though he worried a bit about the frequent passing of his four targets along the street that might establish a pattern of interest to anyone else watching. And then on his watch one morning in late May, his surveillance sharpened when a blind beggar wearing dark glasses took up a sitting position before the wall with his tin cup, cane, and a sign reading: PLEASE SHARE FOOD. The watchman observed him intently all day, saw him plead pathetically with passersby, some who dropped a few coins into his cup, and one who gave him a small wrapped package revealed to be bread, which he tore into immediately and consumed as fast as he could. The surveillance expert took every watch after that and after a few days, strolled by the man to check him out himself. He decided the beggar was harmless. In fact, a position by the mural before a convent was a smart place to beg, especially since the artist who lived in the convent—such a lovely little thing, always fashionably dressed—took pity on him and put something for breakfast into his hands every morning as she left for work. The veteran stakeout man knew that any occurrence unusual to the street was worth reporting, be it large or small. You never knew, but if he reported the beggar, the poor man would be dragged into SD headquarters, questioned unmercifully, and when proven harmless, cast out onto the street frightened and confused and without aid to return to wherever he called home. The watcher would spare him that.

On June 4, Konrad imparted good news. The admiral had been released from house arrest and assigned the meaningless job as head of the department of Mercantile Warfare and Economic Combat Measures. The posting was an insult to his rank and former position, but the demotion meant that he was free. Champagne corks popped in the general's house that night.

Shortly thereafter, Dragonfly made its first costly

mistake. The chance encounter of the whole team meeting on the street at the same time had not yet occurred in their almost two years on the mission, but on this first Tuesday of June, in the late afternoon of a slate-gray spring day, they happened to stroll up the street simultaneously. Despite the hour of the day, no one else was on the street but the beggar, busily eating a bag of pine nuts someone had placed in his lap.

Everyone shot looks up and down the street for signs of activity, saw none, and as one body, embraced and engaged in a quick conversation.

Uh-oh, thought the stakeout man from his vantage point, now having proof that the agents did know one another, including the artist. For the colonel, that would raise another question, regarding the real purpose of the mural. The group had been unwise to converse within hearing of the beggar. In this climate, not even a blind man begging for his food could be counted on to be trusted. He observed the five quickly break apart, four to slip their messages through the mail slot and the artist to hurry into the convent. Presently, a patrol of the hated French Milice strolled into sight, explaining the hasty retreat. The watcher lowered his attention to make notes of his observations, and when he glanced up again, the beggar was gone, his cup, cane, and bag of pine nuts scattered where he'd sat. Madly, the stake-out man stowed his pen and notepad and took off for SD headquarters.

He was forced to take the metro, which was aggravatingly late as usual. Waiting impatiently, he tried to calm himself with the rationalization that the Milice, a gang of bullies who had turned on their own countrymen, had simply been resorting to their usual tactics of preying on the helpless and weak. In the few minutes of writing his report, they had dragged the beggar away, disregarding his belongings, to torment him simply for their pleasure and amusement. They might have even decided that the beggar's presence was a desecration to the mural, if they were capable of such sensitivity, but the surveillance man's experience argued against hope. The blind man, he understood now, could see as well as anyone and had been planted by the Gestapo. He had fallen for a ruse as old as his profession. The colonel would have his head on a pike for his mistake, but even more important, if he did not act, those young people would be in the Gestapo's hands by nightfall.

When he finally arrived at SD headquarters and asked to speak to Colonel Derrick Albrecht, he was told by a desk clerk that the colonel was in a meeting and under no circumstances would he disturb him. The flurry of activity and the sounds of ringing telephones, teletype machines clicking, typewriters clacking away, and the tight faces of the SD staff told the stakeout man that something serious had happened. On the metro, he'd been aware of an atmosphere of suppressed excitement. Passengers had seemed more restive than usual, but he'd been too absorbed with his own set of worries to wonder why, and he knew better than to put the question to the desk sergeant. "Please, it's urgent, Sergeant," he pleaded.

"I will not risk my neck for yours, whoever you are," the sergeant barked. "Leave your message. I will get it to the colonel when the meeting is over."

The watchman handed over his report. "You must get that to him as soon as possible," he said, "or it will be *your* neck in the noose."

It was the sixth of June, 1944. In the predawn darkness of that morning, American, British, and Canadian forces, in simultaneous amphibious attacks, had come ashore on five separate beaches along the Normandy coastline. The Allied invasion of France was underway.

CHAPTER SEVENTY-FOUR

The Allies' landing on the coast of Normandy came as a surprise to the Germans, who had believed poor weather conditions would delay the invasion. That day, troops had been allowed to relax from their guard duties along the Atlantic Wall and other coastal defense fronts, numerous senior officers had not returned from their weekends, and many German artillery units and their commanders were on maneuvers away from their posts. Even Field Marshal Erwin Rommel had treated himself to a few days' leave to attend the celebration of his wife's birthday. Parisians learned about the landings when news filtered into their city through underground newspapers, hidden radios tuned to the BBC, and pamphlets distributed secretly by the French Resistance. The French citizenry was jubilant. Liberation was at hand.

Tuesday night, Bridgette slept with her small bed pulled close to the armoire should the major contact her beyond their normal transmission times. He seemed never to go to bed. Sure enough, before dawn on June 7, she was awakened by the clickety-clack of an incoming message and leaped out of bed to transcribe it. It was an alert from Major Renault. That morning, just as a pale daybreak allowed enough light to see, Bridgette defied curfew to slip out of the convent with her paintbrush to stroke in the code signal on a liverwort plant to warn Victoria that her safe house had been compromised. The girl had nowhere to go should she have to go on the run.

Three days passed before the desk clerk to whom the stakeout man had entrusted his message happened to remember to give it to Colonel Derrick Albrecht on the morning of Friday, June 9. "For you, Herr Colonel," he said. "It was delivered by some man off the street who said it was important. You were in a meeting, and I did not wish to disturb you."

When Derrick read the message, the desk clerk, already a tangle of nerves, blanched when he saw the colonel's jawline tighten and his eyes shoot flames when he looked up from the report. "When did this arrive?"

"Why, uh, Tuesday at noon, June sixth, I believe, Herr Colonel, and uh, another message came for you...yesterday...from Major Schultz at Gestapo headquarters. You were in a meeting then, too, with orders not to be disturbed."

"You idiot!" his superior thundered. "I should have you shot!" He barked for Karl, who came running. "Get me to Gestapo headquarters quick!" Derrick ordered.

By then four members of Dragonfly had been arrested and taken to the dreaded address at 11 Rue de Saussaies in the eighth arrondissement, referred to by Resistance fighters as the "street of horrors." The roundup of the team had begun on June 7. That evening the beggar was back at his site when Bridgette returned to the convent. What happened? she asked him. Where had he gone? She'd been concerned when she saw him missing and his cup and can and bag of nuts strewn on the street. The beggar spat into the gutter and replied that he'd been dragged away by the filthy Milice, who'd questioned his blindness and accused him of faking it to get money and food. They released him when they realized their mistake and even brought him back to collect his cane and cup. Somebody had made off with his bag of pine nuts.

The man did not point her out that day or the next to the aproned hireling sweeping the stoop of a shop a few storefronts down. He would save her for another police unit from which he would collect a bounty that, added to the Gestapo's reward, would amount to more than what they would pay him for all five together.

The first to fall under the point of his cane was Victoria, the signal that brought three leather-coated, slouch-hatted men running from the shop like rats scuttling toward cheese. They approached her as she was studying her code mark, jerked her hands behind her, and bound them before she could pull the thread to her cyanide pill. Led away, she glanced at the sightless beggar, who was drawn up against the wall as if struggling to determine what the commotion was all about. *It was you*, Victoria thought, sickened at the team's own blindness in not seeing that the man could be a Gestapo plant. It was only a matter of time before they were all rounded up.

At Gestapo headquarters, her face inscrutable but her heart pumping so hard she thought it would burst through her chest, she was made to sit before the desk of a Gestapo major. "You are Mademoiselle Veronique Colbert, foil instructor at the L'Ecole d'Escrime Français, are you not?" he addressed her in French.

"I am."

"I thought so." He nodded at a guard, who yanked Victoria to her feet and took her to a squalid prison cell where she was bound to a chair under a hot ceiling lamp. Through walls marked with scrawls of fear and defiance and last endearments to loved ones—*Never confess! I am afraid. Don't talk. Keep the faith. Simone, I love you*—she could hear moans of torture in the next room. How long would it be before they came for her, she wondered, her stomach clenching as she imagined herself stripped naked before her interrogators went to work on her. She and Labrador had been warned to expect it. Major Renault had told them that stripping a woman down to her birthday suit was a Gestapo torture technique, designed to humiliate and demoralize the victim and make her more vulnerable. *Be prepared for that mortification if you're caught*, he'd said, but she and Labrador had agreed that they could not possibly gird themselves for that kind of violation. She would hold out as long as she could. Had the others also been arrested? How long would it be before they broke? It was Labrador they had to keep safe.

An hour passed. Thirst made swallowing difficult,

and sweat broke out from the heat of the lamp in the airless room. Victoria's bladder began to fill. Her limbs ached from their bound positions, and her hearing numbed from the steady pound of her heartbeat and the cries of the suffering. The breathing and mind exercises to steady the nerves taught in training proved useless. After a while, Victoria's eyes closed and her head fell forward as she waited for the cell door to bang open.

Finally the day and moment arrived and two men walked in, one a colonel in the Sicherheitsdienst and the other the major who had interviewed her. Victoria's mouth fell open. The Gestapo man pointed at Victoria. "Is that her?"

"Yes!" Colonel Derrick Albrecht snapped. "That is my bout partner at L'Ecole d'Escrime Français."

The major said, "When it came to my attention that the woman consorting with the three men we've also picked up was your fencing partner and…your special companion, I thought it wise not to begin questioning any of them until I had informed you of their arrests. I felt sure you would like to conduct the interrogation yourself. They are all coconspirators who we believe are American agents, probably OSS, masquerading as French and German citizens. They have been relieved of their cyanide pills." The major's proud tone asked for a pat on the back for his decision to contact the counterintelligence chief of the SD that he secretly despised. It stung him that the Gestapo, considered made up of the less educated and desirable segments of German society, was subordinate to the more refined and cultured SS.

"Your wisdom is to be commended, Major Schultz," Derrick said, staring hard at Victoria. "My office has had the three men in your cells under surveillance for some time until we could round up the whole group. Your informant, the blind beggar, got into the game late." He walked to stand in front of Victoria, drawing off his glove. "But this one I did not know about." He drew back his hand and slapped her hard across the face. Blood spurted from her lip. "Deceiver! Spy! You'll be sorry our swords ever crossed when I get through with you! Major, have your men load up the whole lot and take them to the van I have waiting," Derrick instructed. "I have a special cell prepared at the Lutetia Hotel for the likes of them." Without another look at Victoria, he left the room, the Gestapo chief following.

"What do you intend to do with them, Herr Colonel?" he asked.

"If they survive their interrogations, the men will

be deported to the work camps, the woman to the firing squad."

"Ah!" The major's eyes lit up. "In that case, with your permission, of course, I and my men would like to witness the execution, if you'd be so kind to let me know the time and place."

Derrick paused in drawing on his glove. Giving the major a cool look, he said, "SS executions are conducted privately, Major Schultz. They are not for public show unless to set an example."

The major responded with a knife-thin smile. "Surely you do not consider the Gestapo the public, Herr Colonel, and I was thinking of the execution more as a morale boost to me and my men, rather than an 'example,' but if nothing else, a reward for *my* office's success in bringing in the agents."

After another moment's silent regard of the major, Derrick acquiesced with an indifferent shrug of his shoulders. "Very well. If you wish."

"So you'll be sure to inform us of the time and place," the major persisted. "It will be so good for my men to witness the results of their labor."

Flinty-eyed, Derrick said, "You will be informed, Major. Now have your men release the prisoners into the custody of the SS."

CHAPTER SEVENTY-FIVE

Assisting the German Gestapo in Paris was an auxiliary police organization called the Carlingue but contemptuously and fearfully referred to as the "French Gestapo." Its members had been recruited from the belly of France's criminal underground and wore the same black military uniform with modifications as special units of the SS. Anytime one of these men strolled into a civilian establishment, hearts seized and breaths stopped. So it was that Madame Jeanne Boucher, formidable couturier of the House of Boucher, met the pair of uniformed men from the Carlingue as they entered the fitting room where garments on half-dressed models were in the last stages of preparation for the fashion show scheduled for the following Saturday, June 17. Such interruptions as the Allied invasion of France offered no reason for Madame Boucher to cancel a fall showing that had been in the planning stage for a year.

Despite the gallop of her heart, the couturier marched up to the men in black and spoke directly into their faces, successfully obstructing their goggle-eyed attention on the underwear-clad mannequins, and demanded the cause of the intrusion. The pair were of the lowest grade in their organization—boys, really, barely out of the pimple stage. Jeanne Boucher recognized them as hardened criminals no less dangerous for their youth, but obviously unsure of themselves in a place of such intimidating opulence.

The lance corporal, the older of the pair, answered in a voice that had to be cleared by a nervous cough. "We are here to see Mademoiselle Bernadette Dufor," he said. "She is to come with us."

"By whose authority?"

"Ours," the younger and bolder one growled, not to be put off by madame's haughty manner and the grand surroundings.

"I am afraid that will not do. Let me see your papers authorizing your orders. Mademoiselle Dufor is the designer for your superior's wife. She is due for a fitting today. Madame will not be pleased if her designer is not here." Jeanne's pointed eyebrow allowed the obvious to speak for itself. She had no idea of the name of the boys' superior. Her pronouncement was a lie to stall the little thugs long enough for Bernadette Dufor to slip from the room and take off.

Bridgette inched toward the door, and the lance colonel, looking uncertain, said curtly, "Very well. We'll be back with the proper papers and Mademoiselle Dufor better be here."

They had turned to leave when one of the designers pointed at Bridgette and said, "She's right there."

The men spun around and spotted Bridgette almost at the door. The lance corporal raised his voice. "You will come with us, mademoiselle. If you resist, you will be shot." He kept his hand on his holstered pistol as the pair moved toward Bridgette and quickly grabbed her arms.

"May I ask why I am being arrested?" she asked.

"You are not being arrested. Our orders are to bring you in for questioning."

"Why?"

"You have been reported."

"For what?" Bridgette glanced at the designer who had pointed at her, the woman looking frightened as the eyes of the others turned coldly upon her.

"You will be told!"

All stood watching with frozen faces as Bridgette was marched out, then Madame Boucher whirled to the designer who had given her away. "You whore!" she screamed and slapped the terrified woman's face. "Get your things and get out! You are fired! And when France is liberated, I shall make sure that you are hunted down and feathered and tarred as a French collaborator!"

"No! No! You must believe me, madame. I am not a French collaborator! I am not responsible for Mademoiselle Dufor's arrest. I regret pointing her out—"

Jeanne drew back her hand again, and the designer scurried out of the room, the hisses and boos of her fellow coworkers following her.

Bridgette was taken to 93 Rue Lauriston, a quiet little street in an unobtrusive neighborhood in the sixteenth arrondissement that housed a soundproofed third floor where the French Gestapo took French Jews, Resistance fighters, and various other enemies of the Third Reich, and subjected them to the most vicious interrogations of all their brother police organizations. Bridgette was plunked down and shackled to her chair in a hall on the first floor of the three-story building. Now and then when a door opened at the head of the high flight of stairs, she could hear faint screams of torment coming from above. As taught, she breathed slowly in and out in an effort to remain calm and detached while considering the facts of her situation.

Typically, the organization's arrests were made in dramatic fashion by men in the upper grades, not by pipsqueaks like those sent to fetch her. She must not be that important a catch. At first she'd leaped to the possibility that one of the team had been caught and made to talk, but if so, she would now be upstairs with the rest of the tortured and damned, so she tried to ease her concern on that score. Her accuser was probably the designer who'd denounced her out of jealousy with no real proof of her guilt. She had not officially been arrested but merely brought in for questioning. She held on to that slight difference as a reason for hope.

She sat an hour as Carlingue staff members, carrying papers, appearing busy, and looking harassed, came and went by her chair, paying her no mind. *They should look worried*, Bridgette thought. This morning, June 9, Madame Boucher reported that the Allies had gained the beachhead at Normandy. The couturier speculated that they would be in Paris in two months' time. Finally a door opened to the office across from the corridor, and out walked a captain considerably older than the others of his rank. He looked like someone's grandfather, bent, tired, and overworked. Frowning over a report, distractedly, without a glance at her, he ordered the hall guard to unshackle her hands. Released, the guard pushed her forward to follow the captain into his office. The door plate read CAPITAINE AXEL GUERIN CHARGE D'AFFAIRES. "Sit down," the captain said vaguely, as if she were the least important item on his overflowing agenda.

Bridgette prayed that she read his disinterest correctly and that his grandfatherly manner suggested sympathy for a young girl brought in on a trumped-up charge. She straightened primly in her chair and set her face in an expression of bewildered innocence. The captain laid down the report and reached for a sheet of paper that he scanned quickly. "It says here that you are the artist responsible for drawing a mural on the convent wall of the Sisters of Charity. Is that right?"

"Yes," Bridgette answered in a tremulous voice, wondering how the designer who might have betrayed her would know that. "I did not realize that I was doing anything wrong. I had the permission of the mother superior. I thought...the painting would bring pleasure to the people in the neighborhood."

The captain looked up and his tired gaze flashed surprise as if just now finding this young thing before his desk, merely a girl dressed in stylish, grown-up clothes. "You were reported speaking English to several passersby familiar to the area who also seemed to know the language. How did you come to learn English, Mademoiselle—" the captain referred to the sheet "—Bernadette Dufor?"

Bridgette could feel herself grow warm. Did that mean that the rest of the team had also been arrested? Were they here? Were they the ones being tortured in the room upstairs? She ran her tongue over dry lips. Oh, God, the blind beggar! He was the informer.

"I…my aunt," Bridgette said, improvising as she explained. "She married an American soldier after the First World War. He taught her English, and she—she taught me some of the language."

"Your aunt and the American soldier…they settled here in France?"

"No, they went to America."

"Then how did you learn the American language? Did you live there, too?"

Bridgette wet her lips again. "No, they—they divorced and she returned to France. That's when she taught me. She—she's dead now. She was killed in the Allied bombings of Saint-Nazaire in November of 1942."

"That is sad, the fate of so many," the captain said, his sympathy sounding genuine. "Who were the passersby with whom you were speaking English?"

Bridgette grabbed a few seconds to think. If the captain had to ask who they were, they were not in the room upstairs. Either that or they had not talked. Maybe they had managed to escape the dragnet. Or they could be here, and the captain was on a fishing expedition. Either way, she was cooked, and all she could do was stall the inevitable.

"I—I really don't know their names. I just know they are German and French residents of the neighborhood and pass by the mural often. They admired it greatly. I... heard them speaking English, not very well, and I just thought they'd picked it up on their own, like me, and I could practice mine."

The captain gave her a grandfatherly look of exasperation over the tops of his glasses. "Did you not realize, young woman, that in these times such a conversation overheard by the wrong people could get you into trouble, which apparently it did. These English-speaking residents—male or female?"

"Three men, one woman."

"You know where they live?"

"No sir."

The captain consulted the sheet again. "It is suspected that the mural is something other than a pretty painting. It is a means to communicate with the French Resistance."

"Oh, no sir!" Bridgette said, waving her small, delicate hands in protest. "I assure you it is nothing of the sort. I—I am an artist, you see, and I—I just wanted a creative outlet, and the wall was there, and the mother superior said I could draw on it, and I thought the mural would offer a relief from the ugliness of war and—"

"Yes, yes, I quite understand," the captain said, stopping her flow. "And it does at that, your mural. I've seen it." He consulted the sheet again. "So you live in the convent?"

"Yes, Capitaine, the sisters were kind enough to rent me a room."

"Ah," said the captain. "I am familiar with the place as well. Quite a sturdy structure. Thick walls." Suddenly his eyes behind his spectacles sharpened, all traces of grandfatherly geniality vanished. "Well, Mademoiselle Bernadette Dufor, I will be ordering your room at the convent searched for anything of a clandestine nature. My men are not likely to find anything of that sort, are they?"

Bridgette's breathing stopped. She must give nothing away of her panic. "Of course not, Capitaine."

"Good." He summoned the desk guard outside his office. "Take mademoiselle back to her chair in the hall until I call for her." To Bridgette he said, "You will remain there until your story is confirmed, and then we will see about letting you go."

CHAPTER SEVENTY-SIX

Karl's military demeanor slackened when he saw the beautiful Mademoiselle Colbert directed out of Gestapo headquarters with her arms tied behind her back. Roughly hustled along with her were three men unknown to him, equally bound. The two Gestapo men pushed the four captives none too kindly into the back of the waiting van especially equipped to transport persons of interest to various interrogation sites. Karl had to keep himself from coming to Mademoiselle Colbert's aid, the impulse abandoned when he saw Colonel Albrecht coming down the steps wearing a face he knew only too well—tight, implacable, unyielding.

"Drive us to 45 Boulevard Raspail," he instructed.

Karl reacted with surprise. "Not to 84 Avenue Foch?" Boulevard Raspail was the location of the

Lutetia Hotel, former headquarters of the Abwehr. The cells in the SD headquarters contained means to induce prisoners to talk, whereas the Abwehr's interview rooms did not, except for one, known as Cell Block B, that had been reconfigured to meet the standards of the SS.

"To Boulevard Raspail, Karl," Derrick repeated tersely.

"Yes, Herr Colonel!" Hope sprang in Karl's breast for Mademoiselle Colbert.

At the Lutetia Hotel, Karl stayed with the van, not daring to check on the prisoners inside, while Derrick took off through the arched entrance. Without breaking stride, he barked to his desk clerk that he wanted to see Major General Konrad March in his office immediately. The clerk had the former head of the Abwehr in tow within two minutes.

"He's in a foul mood, Herr General," the clerk warned Konrad as he knocked on his superior's office door, and Derrick's harsh command, "*Komm herein!*," confirmed it. The colonel was in the process of lighting a cigarette. The sergeant beat a hasty retreat, closing the door quickly and quietly, and Konrad said, "I thought you'd given that up."

"Certain situations call for the restoration of certain

broken habits." He offered Konrad his gold case of American Chesterfields.

Konrad declined. "What's happened?"

"I've got your fisherman and son's tutor outside in my van, Barnard Wagner and Claus Bauer." He handed Konrad the three captives' identity papers. "Major Schultz at Gestapo headquarters had them rounded up for interrogation. They were overheard speaking English together and were reported to the Gestapo by one of their informers posing as a blind beggar."

Konrad sought a chair to sit down. "How did they happen to end up in your hands?" He wasn't sure what to say.

Derrick pulled up a chair close to the general's so they could speak in low tones. "They are Americans, members of the same cell working for the OSS, Konrad. Your fisherman and son's tutor knew each other before they ever met at your house. Perhaps you figured that out."

Konrad was genuinely surprised. He'd thought the boys had simply recognized each other as Americans and learned they were working for the same outfit after being sent to gather intelligence on their own, Barnard on his fishing boat, Claus in his schoolroom. This he explained to Derrick, adding in disbelief as he rubbed his forehead, "*Gott!* How could I have thought it simply a stroke of good luck that their paths crossed mine?"

"Don't feel bad, Konrad. I was blinded, too. Mademoiselle Veronique Colbert is one of them, part of the same cell. She is an American, also. Her name is Victoria Grayson from Williamsburg, Virginia."

Konrad's jaw dropped.

"Yes," Derrick confirmed. "I have known of her nationality since the beginning, but not that she was a spy. I made the discovery quite by accident, the night of the premiere, and I have been using her to channel information to her OSS sources, as you have Herr Wagner and Herr Bauer."

"And you didn't tell me!" Konrad accused.

"Come now, General. You know why I couldn't risk your being in possession of that knowledge any more than you could chance telling me that your friends were Americans and your son's tutor was also a spy."

"Yes, yes, of course," Konrad said, mollified. "I quite understand. Do please go on."

"The third young man I know little about. His cover name is Stephane Beaulieu, an engineer employed at the Barousse Consulting Firm of Civil Engineers near the Eiffel Tower, also an American.

I suspect that a fifth member is involved—the artist responsible for drawing a mural on the wall of a convent located in the Latin Quarter. The wall is next to a house with a mail depository in the door that serves as their dead-letter box. I believe the mural to be a medium for communicating in code."

"How do you know all this?"

"I've had the cell under surveillance for some time," Derrick said and gave him a short briefing on how he'd come by his discoveries. "I didn't know who your young friends were until I saw their names on their identity papers," he concluded.

"Why did Major Schultz call you?"

Derrick blew out a final stream of smoke and crushed the butt of the Chesterfield in a tobacco tray on his desk. "Because the major knew that Mademoiselle Colbert and I are well acquainted."

"Of course," Konrad said, understanding perfectly. "And you've got them all in the van? We're to put the *Nacht* and *Nebel* plan into place?"

"With one exception. Mademoiselle Colbert is to be executed."

Konrad's ruddy skin tone whitened to the shade of a boiled potato. "My God, Derrick, why?"

Derrick snapped a flame to another cigarette. "Because I made the mistake of saying that I intended to have her set before a firing squad for playing me for a fool. Major Schultz asked if he and his Gestapo pigs could watch the execution. Good for his men's morale to witness the results of their labor, he said. I was forced to agree to his request."

"The swine," Konrad said. "But of course you're not going through with it?"

"I have to. Otherwise, I might be accused of going soft on an enemy spy. Hitler is about over the edge. He's ordered Himmler's eye on every department under his command, convinced that with the way the war is going, some of us might be inclined to switch loyalties. I've got to take this step to avoid suspicion."

"But, my God, Derrick, you…you have feelings for this woman!"

"All the more reason why her death is necessary, Konrad. My attraction to her is well-known and documented. The execution of the beautiful woman I've come to care about will play well in my favor with Himmler and prove my loyalty to Hitler. Your young friends and the engineer will simply disappear with no eyebrows raised, but if I don't go through with this execution, I could be the one before a firing squad and our entire operation blown. I plan to arrange it for day after tomorrow, and I need your help."

The search of Bridgette's room was over in less than half an hour. The two French Gestapo men knew the hidden cavities to look for. They came down from the attic carrying the wireless set concealed in a suitcase, the mother superior hovering anxiously in her black robes at the foot of the stairs.

One of the men set the case on a refectory table and opened it. "Did you know anything about this, Mother Superior?" he demanded.

Sister Mary Frances pretended shock and shook her wimpled head. "No, I did not. All I know about Mademoiselle Dufor is that she is employed as a fashion designer at the House of Boucher. What has happened to her?"

"She's been arrested on suspicion of being an enemy spy." The man snapped the case shut. "This proves it."

Sister Mary Frances made the sign of the cross. "Oh dear. Where has she been taken?"

"To our headquarters on Rue de Saussaies, where she will be interrogated." He would have questioned the mother superior further to determine her involvement, but in France, unless for justified cause, the Catholic Church was off-limits to the French Gestapo, most of whose members were reared in the Church.

The moment the two men left, Sister Mary Frances put in a call to the burly Frenchman whose name she did not know but who had left a number for her to call him should an emergency arise regarding Mademoiselle Bernadette Dufor. She laid a hand on her heart to calm her fear that he could not be reached, but he answered on the second ring. "Mademoiselle Bernadette Dufor has been taken," she informed him without preamble.

"Who by?"

"The French Gestapo. They were just here and found the radio. She's been taken to their headquarters at 11 Rue de Saussaies."

"*Merci*, Mother," the Frenchman said.

Sister Mary Frances hung up, trembling. If ever she believed in miracles, she must do so now. It would take one to deliver sweet Mademoiselle Dufor from the hell into which she had fallen. She left her office and set off down the corridor, announcing to the nuns that they were not to disturb her, that she would be unavailable for the night. Once inside the walls of the convent chapel, she knelt on a pew bench, clasped her hands, and began to pray.

At La Maison de Boucher, Madame Jeanne Boucher heard, "*Madame Boucher!*"

The assault on her ears could have been mistaken for the shriek of a bull elk. Jeanne hurried into the salon.

"Yes, Madame Richter?"

In a ghastly gray frock of many folds, its originator unknown, Madame Richter sailed toward her with all the intent of a pirate frigate ready to commandeer an undefended ship. Jeanne swore the woman got uglier at every fitting, her ill-favored looks and figure made worse by a meanness that leached from her entrails. "Where in God's name is Mademoiselle Dufor? She was to fit me today."

Playing the role of so many of her indifferent countrymen, Madame Boucher lifted her shoulders and displayed her palms in typical French style. "I would assume at the headquarters of the French Gestapo. Two members of their body arrested her this morning."

"Mademoiselle Dufor?" the woman shrilled her disbelief. "Whatever for?"

"Oh, one of our designers denounced her for no other reason other than she was jealous of her from the first day of her employment here."

"The bitch should be sacked. What am I to do now?"

"I did sack her, but have no fear. I'm sure one of our other designers would be happy to assist you in every way possible."

"The devil they will! I must have Mademoiselle Dufor!"

"I'm afraid that is impossible, madame. My hands are tied."

"Mine aren't. My husband has authority over those imbeciles of the French Gestapo. Mademoiselle Dufor will be back here this afternoon. Prepare my gown for my fitting." And with that Madame Richter sailed out, leaving Jeanne staring after her in astonishment. Rescue was on the way for Bernadette by the last person on earth she would have expected to save her.

CHAPTER SEVENTY-SEVEN

At the van, Colonel Derrick Albrecht ordered Mademoiselle Colbert brought inside the former Abwehr headquarters while Karl was to drive the others to an alternate location for the interrogation of prisoners. "Put them in the cell with the window overlooking the courtyard," Derrick instructed.

"And Mademoiselle Colbert?" Karl dared to ask.

"She will remain here." Derrick turned on his heel and struck off again for his office while Victoria was hoisted from the back of the van by SS personnel under the worried eye of Karl, unable to prevent her rough handling. Victoria managed to exchange only a brief glance with her three teammates before she was whisked away and the van doors slammed shut.

Her hands were rebound immediately after being

untied to relieve her of her coat and to allow her to go to the toilettes, then she was taken to an interrogation chamber, where once again she was left under a hot, blinding light. Swallowing down nausea from a dry mouth, Victoria wondered if here she'd be made to strip. The colonel would like nothing better than to see her nude. Presently, he entered with a female SS corporal. He carried an instrument kit that looked like a metal plumber's box with a swastika emblazoned on the lid. Victoria could see nothing in his face and manner to suggest that he was the man of civility and courtesy that she knew. He ignored her as he set the box upon the table.

"Corporal, take the prisoner back to the toilettes," he ordered. "I don't want a mess in here, but keep her hands tied until she is in the stall, then retie them when she leaves, and when you return her, make sure we are not disturbed."

"*Jawohl,* Herr Colonel!"

The corporal, an oak tree of a woman, had been transferred from 84 Avenue Foch to Abwehr headquarters at the colonel's request and was familiar with the contents of the black box. As she directed the prisoner to the toilettes, she studied Victoria's face with its cut lip and said in fragmented French as she untied Victoria's hands, "You'd better get a good look at that pretty *Gesicht* of yours in the mirror while you're in here, mademoiselle. It will be the last time you'll ever see it as it is now."

Once re-bound and in the chair under the harsh ceiling light, the colonel dismissed the corporal and locked the door behind her. His glance fell on her cut, still-bleeding lip, and Victoria, glaring at him, expected him to produce another white handkerchief, but he walked around her chair. She flinched, expecting a blow to her head, but he merely checked her bonds. He then pulled up a chair directly in front of her and leaned close. "Listen to me very carefully, Victoria. I know you are an OSS spy. I suspected you were when I found that cyanide capsule in the lining of your coat, and I knew it for sure the day of our picnic when you swallowed the major's report hook, line, and sinker, to borrow a phrase from American slang. I know about your cellmates in the van, the dead-letter box, the artist. Your cover is blown. The SS shoots enemy spies. So now you must do exactly as you're told, you understand? Your execution is scheduled for the day after tomorrow, and I must prepare you for it." He opened the black box.

After giving Henri instructions to clear out the house with the mail slot of any evidence identifying it as a dead-letter box, Alistair informed his decryption clerk of Labrador's compromised transmission signal. Any information coming in from that quarter was to be discounted. He was to be informed when the first false transmission came in, proof that his radio operator had been taken and made to talk. Alistair returned to his desk with his head ready to explode. The glass of water he reached for shook in his hand, and the dribble he swallowed passed over his tobacco-coated tongue like acid and burned his throat going down. Bridgette had been arrested by the French Gestapo, the most barbarous of the Nazi police organizations. It would be only a matter of time before they broke her, that kitten with the heart of a lion. The others would be snagged at the letter drop unless their facilitators could get word to them quickly enough to save them. Alistair sat down heavily at his desk, put his hands together, and squeezed shut his eyes. He was not a spiritual man for all his love of liturgical music, but he commenced doing the only thing he knew now to do. He prayed.

"Well, Mademoiselle Dufor, it would seem that you are not as guiltless as you sound and certainly not as innocent as you look. A wireless transmitter was found in a hidden cupboard in your room at the Convent of the Sisters of Charity."

The captain addressed Bridgette in the late afternoon, after she'd sat for three hours shackled to her chair in the hall. She had not yet been dragged up to the third floor like several other struggling prisoners shoved through the doors of the headquarters of the French Gestapo, but she had endured her own brand of torture waiting for the moment when she would join them. Finally, the captain once again had her deposited before his desk, where he looked at her hard and long, as if searching for something he had missed before.

"Can you explain its presence?" he asked.

The captain hoped that his stony gaze and her fear of the upstairs cells would be sufficient to loosen her tongue, and they could get this over with. He was tired and wanted to go home. The girl might have fooled him, but he was inclined to believe his first impressions of her. She was probably a very good dress designer, and she clearly possessed talent as a painter, but that little blond head was too innocent to worry with wireless sets and code murals and secret messages passed on the sly. No search revealed an encryption pad by which to check her handwriting, and the mother superior of the convent declared that if her boarder had been transmitting messages, she would have known. Nothing the informant, posing as a blind man and beggar, had brought to the Carlingue had panned out. The informant's claim that the mail slot in the house next to the convent was a dead-letter box proved false. It was a storage room for sewing materials in line with Bernadette Dufor's work, and a check of the mural found nothing to indicate that it was any more a code device than his wife's grocery list. The stone painting was an amazing piece of artwork. Demolishing it would incite more trouble in that district than the French police were capable of handling at this explosive time. The captain believed her story about her divorced aunt, too, and a French interpreter of English could detect no trace of an American accent in her French speech. The damned informant had misread her.

But there was the point of the wireless to be explained. "Well?" he demanded.

Bridgette had her story ready. "I...was approached by two men of the French Resistance demanding to use my room to operate their wireless set. They would transmit their messages while I was at work and during the hours the nuns were out of the convent," Bridgette said, doe eyes beseeching the captain to believe her. "They wanted the convent because its thick walls provided protection from the German direction finders. They would not take no for an answer."

"How did they know about your room and the hidden alcove?"

"They said a former nun who left the order told them."

The captain had heard of a nun joining the partisans, reputed to be a crack shot. "How could they force you to permit them to use your room?"

"They…threatened to kill me and the mother superior. When I refused, they pushed a French policeman, known in the neighborhood as the guardian of the wall and protector of the mural—the sweetest man who ever lived—into the path of an oncoming train as proof they meant what they said."

The captain had read of the policeman's death in the papers. Shocking.

"And how would they have gained access to your room without being noticed?"

"They entered by the fire escape when I was at the fashion house. I…was to leave the attic window unlatched and my door unlocked."

"What about their names? What did they look like?"

"I do not know, but I would recognize them again, that's for sure."

The captain made a note. "Did you ever learn their call signal?"

"The what?"

"Never mind. Did anybody else in the convent know what was going on?"

"No, Capitaine, no one." Her voice had faltered to a frightened whisper.

The captain believed her. Every point of her story bore out as the truth. He should have her arrested for her cooperation with the Resistance, but the girl had had no choice. She was clearly innocent of covert activity. "Very well, Mademoiselle Dufor," he said, riffling some papers to appear official, " I see no reason to detain you longer—"

Suddenly the door burst open, and the German SS commandant of the Drancy internment camp, accompanied by a woman and several other SS men, filed into the room. Behind them, the captain's desk clerk lifted his shoulders and spread his hands in frightened apology for the break-in.

The captain leaped to his feet. "May I help you, Herr Commandant?"

"That's her," the woman said, pointing at Bridgette. "That's my designer."

"She is coming with us, Capitaine. Madame Richter has need of her services," her husband ordered.

The captain would not have dreamed of protesting. Besides outranking him, the commandant was a member of the SS. The French captain acquiesced gracefully and quickly, glad to be rid of the problem of Mademoiselle Bernadette Dufor. "She's all yours, Herr Commandant," he said.

CHAPTER SEVENTY-EIGHT

Saturday, June 10, 1944. Madame Gabrielle Dupree took her derringer from its hiding place under a floorboard and slipped it into her apron pocket. If it was discovered on her, she would claim that it was for self-defense against the growing unrest in the streets now that the Allied invasion was underway. People's houses were being broken into with impunity since domestic burglaries were not high on the response list of the French police.

This Saturday was the fourth day that Monsieur Stephane Beaulieu had not returned to the boardinghouse. He had not appeared since he left the house for his engineering firm the morning of Wednesday, June 7. She'd been looking for him that afternoon because she had a treat for him—an apple, one of several kindly shared by a widower friend who had a romantic interest in her. Her instincts told her that Stephane had been arrested; otherwise, he'd have let her know that he would be away, as his work sometimes called him to be. Apparently he had not talked, or at least not involved her and the boardinghouse, but Gabrielle was prepared in case they came for her. She had nothing to live for and nothing to fear from dying. She believed in a merciful God. She had no surviving child, and no family, not even a pet, no close friends to speak of, and she had finally given up the attempt to get over her husband's death.

Some pains, time did not heal. Time only made them worse. Her husband could have risen above his grief, comforted by and grateful for her memory, but she was a cynic at heart and for Gabrielle, memory was only a mocking reminder of what she had lost. She missed Stephane Beaulieu, the only person who'd warmed a spot in her heart since her husband and son were killed, and now he was gone, too. She would pray and light a candle in Saint Mary's to give him an early release from his agony.

Madame Jeanne Boucher listened halfheartedly as one of her designers whined about the lack of cooperation from one of the runway models. "She's taking advantage of the pinch we're in and threatening to leave the show if we don't let her wear the shoes she prefers, madame. You must say something to the little witch. Those shoes will *ruin* the look!"

"Let her wear the shoes," Jeanne said, wearily waving her away. As of only yesterday, she would *never* have bowed to a model's demands, scarce though fashion mannequins were in Paris since the war. Jeanne would have stormed out of her office with guns blazing, fired the impertinent little parvenu on the spot, and dressed Isolde from the accounting department in her place. Isolde was of the perfect weight and height for the runway, and with a little coaching she would be ready for her debut by the evening of the showing on the seventeenth. The couturier of La Maison de Boucher had worked such miracles before. But today, Saturday, June 10, she could think of nothing but her premonition that she would never see Mademoiselle Dufor again. Madame Richter had not returned Bernadette for her fitting yesterday as threatened. Jeanne had heard nothing from the woman since, and the hellcat had not responded to messages the couturier had left with her maid.

What had happened? Had the woman been unable

to convince the French Gestapo to let Bernadette go? Had she failed to save the child from the dungeons at 93 Rue Lauriston? Would the Gestapo bastards soon be coming for Jeanne Boucher as a facilitator for the American OSS?

Or...?

Madame Jeanne Boucher called herself a fool for not thinking of another possibility from the beginning. She doubted that even Madame Richter had thought of it at the time. But now, knowing the evil of which the woman was capable, Jeanne was certain she would not be returning her designer for her fitting. In fact, they would never see Madame Richter in the House of Boucher again. That was a blessing for which Jeanne should be grateful, but not for the curse it would mean for the courageous little Bernadette Dufor.

The shock of her new line of thought compelled Jeanne to unlock a drawer, remove a bottle of gin, and take a long swig. Then she stood and straightened the peplum of her jacket. She was in no mood for sass from a bony clothes hanger who would still be waiting tables if it hadn't been for the scarcity of the mannequins who'd fled Paris at the outset of the war. Jeanne had changed her mind. The girl would wear the proper shoes or else.

Karl was in a state of quiet frenzy. A graduate of a military academy, albeit an undistinguished one, he had been disciplined to obey and never to question a superior's orders. This grounding in obedience had been reinforced by a stint in the Waffen SS before Colonel Derrick Albrecht plucked him from the ranks to serve him in the Sicherheitsdienst, primarily as his driver but with the understanding that he was to become his man of all purposes. Karl had gladly accepted the assignment. To serve an officer of Colonel Derrick Albrecht's superior caliber was an honor, no matter what he should call upon him to do. The insubordinate urge to question the colonel's decisions, motives, and methods had never tempted him.

Until now.

Karl had noticed the bleeding cut on mademoiselle's lip on Friday when he thought the colonel had rescued her from Gestapo headquarters. He hadn't questioned his superior even when he'd seen her hands bound like the other prisoners and treated as roughly right under the eyes of his idol. She was loaded into the van with the other prisoners and forcibly taken inside the Lutetia Hotel. Karl had not seen the colonel since his return to the van an hour later with the order to drive the three captives to an SS location in a remote area of Paris specially prepared for certain kinds of interrogations and secret executions. When he learned Mademoiselle Colbert was to remain behind, Karl had drawn a tenuous breath of relief for the beautiful woman. The fate of the men in the van was sealed. They would not be leaving the special camp alive.

But what of Mademoiselle Colbert's fate? Karl had not liked the angry set of the colonel's face the last time he'd seen him. "Mademoiselle Colbert...is she all right?" he'd dared to ask.

"Better now than she will be," he'd said.

Karl had been shocked.

Several other odd things happened on that trip. At the camp from which no prisoner returned, he'd expected to be met by SS men whose organization controlled the execution center, so he'd been surprised to see two soldiers from the Abwehr come out to take charge of the prisoners, with no presence of the Schutzstaffel about. Karl had brushed off the manning of the camp as part of the SS's attempt to assimilate the Abwehr into its more extreme operations, the camp being one of them.

Karl had then assisted in unloading the men and

taking them to a room with a barred window and no glass that looked out on a stained, bullet-ridden execution pole in a courtyard enclosed by a wall peppered with evidence of what had occurred there. It was a gruesome view, but the Abwehr trainees had clearly misunderstood their orders, for they planned to shackle the three prisoners in the same room. There was comfort in shared misery, so what was the benefit of that tactic to their interrogator? The prisoners would be able to get their stories straight, discuss their strategies, take courage from one another. It was an infraction of procedure, but the trainees' ignorance was no concern of his.

Back at 45 Boulevard Raspail while waiting further orders, Karl had grabbed a member of the colonel's office staff to ask what had happened to the beautiful French prisoner brought in earlier, and his hope for Mademoiselle Colbert and his trust in Colonel Albrecht's protection of her had plummeted.

"She's been taken to Cell Block B," he'd answered. "Colonel Albrecht has already begun the interrogation. Too bad. A woman like that..." He'd shaken his head.

Karl had been speechless. No, the colonel would not have subjected mademoiselle to the treatment that went on in that place, not the woman he deeply admired and had grown extremely fond of—even loved, if Karl's observations had not deceived him. But rumors were floating around the hotel that she had indeed been taken to Cell Block B. Gruesome sounds of her torture could be heard issuing from the locked room. Karl couldn't believe it of the man he'd come to know and respect. It was with mixed relief, then, that eventually someone had come with a message from the colonel instructing Karl to go home. He would not be needing him until 0500 hours—five o'clock—Sunday morning. His aide would be spared from laying eyes on his fallen hero until then.

CHAPTER SEVENTY-NINE

Before dawn broke on Sunday, June 11, 1944, only a few SS and Abwehr personnel were gathered in the Hotel Lutetia to witness in solemn silence as the prisoner in Cell Block B, hands bound behind her, shuffled from her cell through the lobby by two SS men with a grip on each arm. A couple of cleaning women suppressed gasps at the state of her bruised and bloodied face, her chopped-off, sweat-darkened hair, stained clothes, and head lolling forward like a doll with a broken neck. "Take her to the van," Derrick ordered.

Karl's jaw sagged when he saw Mademoiselle Colbert dragged through the doors of the hotel. Two SS men had come out to stand by the back doors of the van, which they immediately threw open to hustle the prisoner inside and off the street as quickly as possible. Karl stepped forward with a cry of protest that he could not suppress. "Herr Colonel—"

Derrick raised a hand to stop him. "Enough, Karl."

Karl stepped back, cognizant of the rank of the man he addressed, and felt his heart shatter. He knew the destination of the van. "As you say, Herr Colonel!"

Floodlights stabbed the fog and darkness. Karl drove Derrick's staff car behind the van driven by a member of the recently absorbed Abwehr. Besides the broken prisoner, inside the interior were four other members of the former German intelligence agency. Karl recognized them as members of a special military squad who, this morning at first full light at his colonel's command, would fire their rifles at Mademoiselle Veronique Colbert.

Bucky heard jackboots on the floor outside their cell room's door and was the first to jump out of his sleeping bag. "Is it finally happening?" Chris asked, getting quickly out of his. Ever since they'd been locked in Friday afternoon, they'd asked themselves what in the hell was going on. They'd expected to be strapped to a chair and the screws put to them by now. Instead, their blindfolds had been removed and hands unshackled, and they'd been able to move about the room freely. Throughout the rest of Friday and Saturday, under the level of Abwehr rifles, they'd been allowed to visit an outside latrine one at a time, given water, blankets, hot meals, and at night even a wineskin of burgundy. Sleeping bags had been brought in for the nights and removed the next morning.

Meanwhile, they'd been conscious of the barred window with its full view of the killing courtyard gazing upon them like a leering evil eye, even at night when the stars winked mockingly at them from their distant spheres. The men had tried to question the guards, but were ordered, "*Sprich nicht!*" (Don't talk!) The building remained quiet. No audible evidence of torture could be heard through the walls. What in God's name was going on? Where was Liverwort? What had happened to her? Had Labrador been warned about the blind beggar and escaped to her safe house?

"Yes, I believe they've finally come for us," Bucky answered Chris, striving to remain calm. "These last days were just to soften us up for the business to come. Good luck, guys."

"To you, too," Brad said, swallowing at the hard

knot of fear that had formed in his throat. Chris nodded, beads of perspiration popping out on his forehead. In the tense silence, they waited for the door to burst open. Minutes passed. They smelled coffee and heard sounds of increasing male activity—German—and then in the guttural din, one woman's voice, plaintive, frightened, familiar, speaking in French. The three captives gasped. "*Liverwort!*" they said together.

They rushed to the door and Chris raised his fist to pound on it, but Bucky forced back his hand and whispered sadly, "We can't help her, Lapwing. She wouldn't want us to."

"He's right," Brad agreed softly. "They'd pound us to a pulp right before her eyes. Let's spare her that."

Chris nodded and Bucky let go his arm. They listened in stricken silence for further words from her, but heard nothing more from Liverwort. Brad put an ear to the door. "They're leaving, going outside."

They turned questioning eyes to one another. What was happening? German babble filtered in from the courtyard, and they hurried to the barred window, jostling for viewing room. A group of Gestapo and SS men, many with coffee cups in hand, were assembling around the perimeters of the courtyard wall where they continued to talk and jest like spectators at a soccer game. A photographer in civilian clothes was adjusting the lens to his camera.

"Oh, God!" Chris moaned as a unit of four Abwehr men carrying rifles marched in through the courtyard entrance and took their positions along the firing line. Rifle butts to the ground, they stood at parade rest with legs apart, one hand on their gun barrels, the other at the smalls of their backs.

"They're an execution squad!" Brad gasped. "They're going to execute Liverwort!"

Presently, as the dawn illuminated the grisly scene, an officer wearing the red Nazi armband and black uniform of the security service of the Reichsführer strode into the courtyard, jackboots gleaming, and took his place to give the order to fire. The straining eyes at the window recognized the SD colonel who had taken personal possession of Liverwort while they were ordered on to this godforsaken place. Shortly, to the applause and cheers of the spectators, two Abwehr men dragged the battered prisoner into the courtyard to the pole set in its center.

"Oh, my God!" Brad cried at the sight of their nearly unrecognizable friend.

"What did they do to her hair!" Chris exclaimed.

"Jesus!" Bucky choked out. "What did they do to *her*?"

Gripping the bars, their eyes and mouths open in appalled disbelief, the men watched an Abwehr soldier secure Victoria's hands behind the pole. The photographer lined up his tripod and silence fell as another soldier walked toward the victim carrying a black hood. The colonel barked the execution squad to attention while the soldier solemnly drew the hood over the victim's head, then the SD officer signaled the men to raise their rifles to the firing position. Instinctively, the three prisoners at the window, as if they could pluck Victoria to safety, thrust their arms through the window bars as far as they could reach and screamed as one voice, "*No!*" just as the colonel ordered, "*Fire!*"

Tears forming, Brad and Chris stepped back from the window with slumped shoulders and bowed heads, unable to bear the sight of Victoria's bullet-ridden body sagging and hanging limply from the pole. Only Bucky, eyes clouding and throat burning, witnessed a burial team rush out to unleash her body and wrap it in a covering. Brad and Chris raised their heads in time to see it carted out like a rolled rug while the spectators disassembled and filed past the SD colonel to shake his hand and offer congratulations. They were still staring, sorrow boiling to rage, when the man, the courtyard cleared, turned his face to the window. Immediately the captives began to hurl invectives at him, mindless of the punishment they'd receive for the insult, but the colonel merely responded with a small smile and walked away.

Karl drove carefully, slowly to avoid the roll of Mademoiselle Colbert's shrouded body in the back of the bumping van. He still couldn't believe it. Colonel Albrecht had ordered the execution of the magnificent woman that Karl thought had finally won his heart. Karl had thought he'd surely change his mind at the last minute, but he had proved himself an indoctrinated officer and son of the Schutzstaffel first and foremost, after all. Once Mademoiselle Colbert had been delivered into the hands of the same Abwehr soldiers who had taken charge of the other three prisoners, the colonel had ordered him to park the van some distance from the camp compound and to remain with it. Karl did not have to question the reason. His superior wanted him as far removed from the scene of the execution as possible, but he could do nothing about the sound of the volley of shots. The crack of the rifles had sent him blurry-eyed and stumbling headlong to the riverbank to heave his breakfast into the water.

He'd adjusted his expression to reveal nothing of his rage and disappointment when the colonel signaled him to bring the van around to collect mademoiselle's swaddled body, beginning to leak blood. He expected to be instructed to take it to the usual burial fields where attendants waited with shovels and rakes, but again his superior surprised him.

"You are to drive Mademoiselle Colbert's body to Count Darold Archambault's country chateau, where you'll be expected, and then you're free to enjoy the rest of your Sunday, Karl," he said.

The nonchalance with which the colonel could wish his driver a pleasant Sunday after what had just transpired was the final straw. Monday, Karl would ask for a transfer back into the Waffen SS with a request to be assigned to the medical unit as a driver for the evacuation of the wounded. The war was nearly over anyway, and the Allies were winning—a view he thought the colonel shared, but now he couldn't be sure of any views of his superior. At least the man had the decency to have mademoiselle buried in a pleasant place. She had been enthralled by the area of their destination the day of the picnic that never occurred. At the colonel's insistence, Karl had taken the fried chicken and apple pie home to share with his wife.

After hours of numb driving, Karl turned the vehicle onto the road that led to Count Archambault's country estate, and at the fork took the route to the chateau. No sooner had he pulled before the massive front entrance than the double doors opened, and Mademoiselle Celeste, his superior's mistress, stood posed in the wide-oaked frame, elegantly dressed as always, and in her hand, the usual cigarette burning in its long, slender holder. She smiled at Karl and came forward with several servants who hastened to the back of the van. Then, like a flare in the night illuminating battle-shattered ground, thunderstruck, Karl understood.

CHAPTER EIGHTY

On Monday, listening to the latest news from his man in Paris, Alistair's hope for Dragonfly sank. The team was lost. His facilitators had reported in—Madame Dupree, Jules Garnier, Jacques Vogel at the fencing school, and Captain Ballard. Bucky had not been seen at the boardinghouse since Wednesday. Chris had not shown up at the academy nor Brad on the captain's fishing boat. Rumors were that Victoria might have already been executed, and Bridgette would be shot once they'd wrung her dry. So far, at least, the little spitfire had not given up her call signal. Her radio remained silent. Fighting down a surge of biliousness at the cost of her stubbornness, Alistair placed a call to Wild Bill Donovan.

The rest of Sunday the three prisoners were treated with the same solicitousness as the other days of their confinement, but in their grief over Liverwort they could neither eat or sleep, so they were already awake at dawn on Monday when their cell door suddenly flew open, and they were yanked from their warm nests to their feet by four Abwehr guards. Before they could catch their breath, their hands were tied behind their backs and black hoods were pulled over their heads.

"What's happening?" Chris asked in German. "Where are you taking us?"

"Sprich nicht!"

"To the post in the courtyard, where else?" Bucky said.

"What? Before the first act?" Brad said.

"Sprich nicht!"

They were pushed roughly out of the room and building, the hoods keeping them blind to their surroundings, and nudged forward by rifle barrels past the courtyard, still smelling of cordite, on a long, stumbling trek until they were ordered to halt in a place strong with the odor of automotive fuel. One by one, with the assistance of a man stationed inside, they were lifted up into a conveyance they soon realized was a prison van. Once plunked down on a row of seats, they heard him jump out, the door slam closed, locked, and smacked to alert the driver of the all clear, and they were off to God knew where.

Bucky had an idea but did not venture it. He would bet this trip was a "night and fog" operation, devised as a way to get rid of people with no questions asked. They would be taken to a deep ditch already dug in some remote, unknown location and instructed to kneel by its edge so that after being shot in the back of the head, they would pitch forward, and their burials would be a simple matter of throwing dirt over their bodies. Nice German efficiency. No report would be filed of their names and deaths. He and the others would disappear from the face of the earth like a vertebrate species gone extinct. His family in Oklahoma and his French father and the families of his fellow dragonflies would be left always to wonder where they were and what had happened to them.

"Why do you suppose they treated us so well if they're going to kill us?" Brad asked.

"Another form of torture like Lodestar suggested about our good treatment. Butter us up before putting us under the broiler," Chris said.

"They wanted us to witness the execution," Bucky said quietly. "That was part of the torture, too."

"Then why didn't they interrogate us afterward?" Chris asked.

"Because they'd already gotten all they needed from Liverwort. Why waste time on us? The cell of Dragonfly was defused and no longer a danger to them," Brad said.

Chris moaned. "Oh, God, that means they got Labrador, too. So where are we going now?"

"Take a stab," Bucky said.

Following a moment's silence, Brad nodded. "Right."

After what seemed an endless drive, perspiration running into their eyes under the hoods, the clangor of pedestrian and vehicle traffic signaled they were entering a large city. Bucky was surprised. He had been listening for country sounds like farm machinery and cowbells and flowing creek water. Perhaps they could simply be passing through Paris on the way to their final destination, but then eventually the van turned away from urban noise into a quieter area disturbed only by children's voices and laughter and the strike of a rubber ball that indicated a soccer game was being played.

"Where in the bejebus are we?" Brad asked.

Soon the vehicle stopped. The prisoners' pulse rates soared as the door to the van opened and fresh air flowed in. A man got on and handed them down to two other pairs of hands that helped to steady them on solid ground. "Quickly now," one of them said, and still shackled and hooded, they were hurriedly steered up a flight of steps to a stoop. They heard the ring of a house bell and the sound of a door opening. "Step inside," they were ordered, and behind their hoods, Brad and Chris sniffed a familiar smell. Heavy footsteps approached.

"Gentlemen," Major General Konrad March said quietly. "You may remove their hoods and release their hands now."

CHAPTER EIGHTY-ONE

Bridgette heard the bedlam coming from outside the window of her sewing room and thought she recognized its cause before getting up from the cutting table to peer through the small square of glass. The other internee, who'd brought in her supper last night, had warned her to expect it.

"Don't look," she'd advised. "The sight will just add to your nightmares." But Bridgette was determined to record every incident of her captors' brutality here in the SS-controlled internment camp, and someday, if she survived, bear witness of them to their judges and juries. Her diary would be a bolt of muslin on which she'd record dates, times, and names of those responsible for the monstrous offenses against human beings that went on behind the electric-wired fences where Jews were held until their transport to the extermination centers in France and Germany. Her roll of cloth might be the only surviving document of the kind of horror going on now.

The scene would be impossible to describe in depth on fabric. Under a rain of punches and kicks, truncheons, whips, and rifle butts, amid cries and wails of protest and pain from the recalcitrant and rebellious among the families wrenched apart, hundreds of Jewish men, women, and children of all ages were being packed into a string of city buses conscripted from the Paris public transit system. The buses were headed to the train stations, where the latest internees selected for disposal would be loaded into boxcars bound for the crematoria.

Bridgette drew away from the window, shaking, her stomach turning and ears ringing from the bawls of human suffering. Madame Richter had explained the deportation process to her the first hour of her arrival yesterday. *Let me make one thing perfectly clear, Mademoiselle Dufor*, she had said. *There is no escaping Drancy, and if you do not do what you are told*—when *you are told—you will be on one of those French green-and-white transit buses that you will see pull out of here tomorrow, as soon as the gas chambers are ready to receive another load of Jews. As long as you are of use to me, you will live. Otherwise, you will not. Do you understand?*

Bridgette had understood. By "use" to her, she was to design and sew Madame Richter's clothes. She would require many garments for many occasions—*to wear when my husband and I are safe in South America*, she'd said, *where we will reside should the Allied invasion prove successful. They dress well in the circles in which we will move, and I will* not *be outdone.*

This was expressed on a tour of the deplorable facilities Madame Richter assured Bridgette would be her lot if she disobeyed. Over the past months, Bridgette had heard a smattering of stories spread by the French Red Cross of the camp's squalid conditions and prisoners' misery, but seeing evidence of them with her own eyes defied the imagination. The tour included a circuit of barrack rooms built for two but that housed twenty or more inmates. The prisoners slept on metal beds with no padding or blankets and lived without running water, working lavatories, or sufficient light. Bridgette's stomach heaved from the stench that hung over the courtyard, lined with buckets to catch rainwater for drinking. Flies swarmed about open latrines, food tables, and clothes hung out to air for lack of water to wash them.

"Seen enough?" Madame Richter asked as Bridgette lowered her eyes to keep from looking at a man whose emaciated face was covered in boils.

"*Oui,*" she said.

She was given a tiny room at the back of the camp commander's spacious house with the use of a latrine built on the side of the house for servants. It was an airless closet with a hole in the wood for elimination and contained no bathtub or shower. Adjoining her small living space was a larger room equipped with a table, chair, and Swiss-manufactured Bernina sewing machine. Piled in a corner were sewing materials and countless bolts of fabrics of every description—ransacked, Bridgette was certain, from French textile warehouses.

Bridgette knew that Madame Richter was right. There would be no escape from this place enclosed by barbed wire, overlooked by watchtowers, and patrolled by guards with machine guns and watchdogs. She was here for the duration of the German occupation when, but for the delay of only a few minutes—the cruel fate of it made her want to empty her stomach—she would have been set free and on her way to her safe house.

CHAPTER EIGHTY-TWO

Following a soft knock, Brad heard a hushed appeal through the door of the guest room in Major General March's house, where he had spent Monday night. "Herr Wagner, may I speak with you a moment?"

Recognizing the voice, Brad tossed back the covers. It was not yet dawn, but he'd been awake since midnight, too high-strung from the roller coaster of the last forty-eight hours to sleep. He opened his room door to find Hans dressed in an army-issued wool robe and a night cap. Brad was in pajamas that he'd packed along with a few other things from his room over Madame Gastain's stables. "Is my ride here already?" he asked. He and Lodestar and Lapwing would be leaving sometime after morning curfew, going separate ways in different vehicles to their safe houses.

"*Non*, Herr Wagner. I have come about another matter."

Brad invited him in, and Hans cast a look toward Major General March's room at the end of the hallway before entering. "I regret to disturb your sleep," the aide said, speaking low, "but before the household is awake, I've come with a grave proposition that I hope you will accept. It has to do with the general's concern for the safety of his son."

Surprised, Brad said, "Isn't Wilhelm safe at his aunt's in Zurich?"

"For the time being, yes, but the general and I fear the day will come when he will be arrested. If that happens and he refuses to cooperate under interrogation, Reichsführer Himmler's policy now is to incarcerate members of the prisoner's family as leverage to get them to talk. Wilhelm will not be safe even in Zurich. He will be kidnapped and brought back to share the same cell as his father. Also, Herr General believes that should something happen to him, without his protection, and if the money dries up, he cannot be sure the aunt will treat Wilhelm kindly." Sweat stood on Hans's brow despite the night's frigid temperature.

"What can I do to help?" Brad asked.

"I have come to propose that you take Wilhelm with you to America."

Stunned, Brad stammered, "Hans, I'd love to, but

I—I can't promise he'd be any safer with me. I have no idea of my escape route and its hazards. I may not even make it out of France." By what method he and the others would be extracted, Brad couldn't even guess—by car, train, plane, ship, or on foot? Would their exfiltration take hours, days, weeks? Where would they be headed—to Spain, Switzerland, Gibraltar? The answers to these questions would not be answered until they got to their safe houses and made contact with Major Renault.

"You'll be safe with this." Hans handed Brad an SS-issued travel pass bearing his cover name, occupation, and all the official signatures and stamps. "Herr General arranged one for you and your comrades to carry with your papers to guarantee unquestioned passage to your ultimate destinations. He…doesn't know that I took this one to show you. I must return it to his desk before he discovers it missing."

Brad stared at the pass, hardly believing his eyes. With this impressive authorization, he and his teammates could get into safe territory without challenge. German officials had stepped up their scrutiny of forged passes, but not even the sharpest trained eyes could doubt this document's authenticity.

"Will you do it?" Hans asked. "You may be Wilhelm's only chance at survival."

Brad thought of two ragged, frightened, and starving children on the bank of the White River in Meeker, Colorado, in September 1938. What the hell. How could he say no? With hardly a pause to consider, Brad said, "I'll do it."

Hans grabbed Brad in a bear hug, his eyes moistening. "*Danke*, Herr Wagner," he said. "With all my heart I thank you." Getting hold of himself, he released Brad and took back the pass. "Now I must return this downstairs. The general will soon be up. He does not sleep long these days. Once he's down, you must present my proposal but not that it came from me."

As he turned to go, Brad said, "Wait a minute, Hans! What about you and the general? Since he believes he'll be arrested, why can't you both come with me, and you guys take Wilhelm and lie low in Switzerland until this is all over?"

Hans said quietly, "*Mein General* is under constant scrutiny. He would not get far before he was discovered missing. Besides, my superior is a professional soldier and general officer, Herr Wagner. He would not dream of deserting his post and the responsibilities that rest on his shoulders. As for me, I must remain with him."

"But if he doesn't make it, he would trust me to

take his son and only child to a foreign country to be raised by strangers?"

"*Ja*," Hans answered. "He knows you to be a good man and that you would take care of his little boy. *Auf wiedersehen*, Herr Wagner. *Gott sei mit dir.*" He held out his hand.

Brad clasped it hard. "God be with you and the general, too, Hans. I hope we'll meet again. I'd like nothing better than to welcome you and the general to my hometown in the mountains of Colorado. The area is a fisherman's paradise."

Hans's resigned shrug expressed sadly that such a pleasure was not likely to be. "Little Wilhelm is very fond of mountains," he said.

With the aide gone, Brad dressed hurriedly. The SS passes should convince Lodestar of Major General March's trustworthiness. Yesterday when the hoods came off, and the general had greeted Barnard Wagner and Claus Bauer as old friends, he'd been puzzled. What was going on? Of course it hadn't taken a minute for Brad and Lapwing to realize that the general had learned of their arrest and orchestrated their rescue. Lodestar had taken some convincing. "You can trust him," Chris had assured him. "If and when we get out of this mess, you'll be enlightened at our reunion in New

York. Until then, the less you know about him, the safer he is."

Last night over schnapps, the general offered no information on how they came to be sitting in his house rather than a Gestapo or SS cell, but Lodestar could not resist asking, "The woman your men executed—could you not have arranged for her escape, too?"

"She was one of you?" the general asked.

"Yes," Lodestar said. "She was definitely one of us."

"I'm sorry, I didn't know. But I could not have helped her even so. Any assistance from me on her behalf would have aroused suspicion from the SS. The woman was the... special project of the SD officer in charge of her interrogation and... execution."

Brad and the others exchanged a look. The SS colonel had to be the linguistics expert the major had feared would expose Liverwort. Their friend should have listened, and now it was too late.

The sun was up and curfew was only an hour away when Brad slipped down the stairs to await the general. Minutes later, he appeared at the head of the staircase and descended while buttoning the cuffs of his uniform shirtsleeves. "Did you sleep well?" he asked.

"As well as could be expected," Brad answered.

"Let us go into my study," Konrad said. "I have something I wish to give you and your comrades when they join us, a little parting gift to ensure your safe arrival at your destinations."

A fire had been laid in the room, comfortable and familiar, but Brad would not be sorry to leave this place that he had come to regard as a tenuous harbor from the storm. The general handed him the pass, issued by the security service of the Reichsführer and signed by a Colonel Derrick Albrecht. Brad pretended surprise and said, "Now I have something to give you if you are willing to accept it, General. I know that you are not happy with the arrangements you've made for Wilhelm. Would you consider allowing me to take him to America with me until you can come for him?"

Konrad blinked as if he'd not heard Brad correctly. "You would do that—take Wilhelm with you to America?"

"Yes, if you agree."

Hope shone briefly in the general's eyes, then died. He shook his head. "But you don't understand, my friend. I may not be able to come for him. I...don't expect to survive the war, you see. What happens to my son in America should I perish?"

Brad replied, "Then he will simply become a member of my family, but you're his father. He could never forget that, and I won't, either. He'll have a good life. That I can promise you."

"My young friend..." Konrad began, but his voice faltered, and tears filled his tired eyes. He settled for pumping Brad's hand. "My gratitude is endless."

"I'll take that as a yes," Brad said. "Now we must hurry, General. We don't have much time. I will need documents, Wilhelm's birth certificate, christening record, passport, anything you have, to establish who he is as well as a letter from you to his aunt authorizing me to take Wilhelm with me. I will leave you my address where you can reach me after the war is over."

CHAPTER EIGHTY-THREE

She's waiting," Celeste said. "In the drawing room. She cleaned up very well, rose from her bath like a phoenix from the ashes. The artistry of her demise was amazing and would have fooled me if I hadn't been aware of the ruse. A shame about her hair, but I reshaped it and put a curl to it, and it will return to its former glory."

"As so many things won't," Derrick said.

"No," Celeste concurred.

In the hall, his former lover's bags were packed by the door waiting for the chateau's old retainer to carry them to Karl, who would drive Celeste back to Paris. Derrick bent to kiss her cheek. "Thank you, *ma chérie*—for everything."

"I would say that it was nothing, but it would not be the truth, Derrick. I will miss you." Gently, she cupped his jaw with her hand, her look soft with affection and pity. "My poor *bien-aimé*, I do see the attraction of her charms to a man like you."

Derrick took hold of her hand and pressed it to his lips. "But I yearn for a star too far. Is that what I read in those wise and lovely eyes? Yes, I know. You will be in danger from the Resistance once the war is over. I will not be able to protect you. Where will you go?"

Celeste laughed. "To the man I jilted in Spain who still loves me and sends me flowers every week. Where else?" She took back her hand. "It is you for whom I fear, *mon chéri*. Please take care."

"As best I can," he said and kissed her cheek again.

Trailing a light scent, she left him, but at the open door, she looked back. "Tell her good-bye for me, will you? I quite liked her, you know."

Derrick nodded. "*Au revoir*, Celeste." He stood gazing after her until the old retainer had closed the door behind her, a chapter closing in his life. Then he walked into the drawing room. It was Tuesday, June 13, 1944.

That same afternoon, in his office at the headquarters of the Prefecture of Police, Chief Detective Maurice

Corbett rose from his desk to greet the woman ushered into his office and introduced as Madame Florence Bisset. He judged her age to be in the middle forties, but the working life of a charwoman and years of hunger and worry put her a decade older. Maurice's heart twisted for her. He invited her to sit down. "How may I be of help, madame?"

He'd already been told by his assistant that she worked as a cleaning woman in the offices of SS headquarters at 84 Avenue Foch, Maurice's reason for agreeing to see her. He couldn't place her among the few members of the custodial crew he'd briefly glanced at in questioning the hall janitor last February, but then most women of her mold looked alike. Before she answered, her eyes darted fearfully about the room as if afraid the walls were listening. "You may speak freely, madame," Maurice encouraged. "Only you and I are here."

Nervously fingering the crucifix around her neck, the woman spoke in almost a whisper. "I did not know if I should have come... but my priest told me that to earn God's forgiveness I must confess to you."

Maurice felt a tickling along his spine. Madame Bisset knew something about the murder of Monsieur Beaumont Fournier. "What must you tell me?" he coaxed kindly.

In a shamed voice, Florence Bisset confessed. Saturday morning, October 31, 1942, she'd happened to see Colonel Derrick Albrecht's aide leave his desk outside the colonel's office to go down the hall to the men's toilettes. Urged by a sudden impulse, spurred by hunger, she'd knocked softly on the colonel's door and, hearing no answer, opened it to find the room empty. The cleaning help was not to enter SS offices unless their occupants were present. But each morning these rooms were provided fresh croissants for the officers to enjoy with their coffee, the colonel's usually left uneaten and given to his charwoman to take home to her family at the end of the day. Florence Bisset had slipped in to take a few to feed her own starving family. She had just filled her apron pockets when she heard Colonel Albrecht outside his door conversing with his aide, who had returned to his desk. She'd bolted into a cleaning supply closet because there was no other place to hide, and there she was forced to remain until—until…

"Until when, Madame Bisset?" Maurice prompted, his heart holding—he had waited nearly two years for this—and the rest of the story tumbled out.

Sometime afterward, worried that she would have to spend the rest of the day in the closet, she heard the colonel's aide enter and announce the name of a visitor. She recognized it. It was the name of France's famous author, Monsieur Beaumont Fournier. He had come with news of someone he wished to warn the colonel about, a woman. Madame Bisset could not remember the name. It was not familiar to her. She had heard the colonel offer him coffee. The next thing Madame Bisset knew, there was a discussion between the colonel and his aide over plans for the removal of a body. From what she could gather, it was that of the author. He had died in his chair. She had been terrified that they would place it in the cleaning closet, but God in His mercy had spared her. She heard the colonel instruct the aide to return with something large to wrap the body in, and they would carry it out by the colonel's private exit, which they did, and it was then that she had made her escape. She had wondered why the colonel had not reported the death to the authorities and left it to them to take charge of the body, but then she had read in the paper of it being found in the Seine and that the authorities were calling his death murder…

Maurice did not ask the woman why she had not reported her story before. The reason was obvious. He thanked her, assured her that he forgave her and that God did, too. She was not to share her story with anyone else. It was to be kept between themselves, her priest, and God, but when the war was over, and the time came when the Germans could be brought to justice, she would be called upon to bear witness against Colonel Derrick Albrecht and his aide, Karl Brunner. Would she swear before God to testify in court to what she had overheard and knew to be true, for only then could she be absolutely certain of total absolution for her sin of silence.

"I swear," vowed Florence Bisset.

"You are a brave woman," responded Maurice. "Now let's have your complete name and address, and the full details of your statement."

CHAPTER EIGHTY-FOUR

Victoria heard the voice of Derrick Albrecht in the hall and stood to face him from the fireplace as the lone servant in the house pushed open the drawing room doors to admit him. What was there to say until she was sure of his motives in bringing her here? What did he want? Why had he saved her and the others from death and by such risky, extreme, and extravagant means? Had he rescued her for himself? Was she a prisoner here? But then why had he set the others free—or had he? She had no idea what to make of him. He was an enigma, a constant variable, a never-ending surprise, as hard to grasp as a walking shadow cast by no form. His vicious slap across her face at Gestapo headquarters had convinced her that the game was over for all of them. She supposed he could forgive her much, perhaps even the shock and disappointment of learning that she was an enemy spy, but not the affront of using him to gain information. His aristocratic pride would not allow it.

He handed his gloves and hat to the waiting servant. "A bottle of 1943 Cuvee, *s'il vous plaît*, Alois," he said. After the servant had bowed and closed the doors, he turned to her. "Good morning," he said. "I see you've recovered well."

He looked tired, but as he drew closer to the fireplace, Victoria recognized something else beyond fatigue beneath the surface of his eyes.

"You're staring," he said.

He was not a good man. No good man would wear that uniform, but still her heart compressed with an emotion that she did not understand. "The others—where are they?"

"I've no idea. Yesterday, they were driven to the house of a colleague in on the ruse. If all went according to plan, they should be on their way to friendly territory by now."

"How do I know I can believe you?"

"You don't, but I can offer no further assurance." He paused to take in her dress. "You look lovely, by the way. Celeste chose well."

"She obviously knows your taste."

"No, she perceived yours. She has left the chateau with word that I tell you good-bye. She liked you."

"I liked her, too."

"I thought you two would get along. Now please move over. I wish to warm my hands. June is so unpredictable in Europe. Does your state of Virginia get these temperature drops in June?" He spread his hands, as finely tuned as a violinist's or a surgeon's, no stain of blood upon them.

Victoria ignored the question. "So please explain, Derrick. Why did you do it—save our lives? You went to great risks on behalf of myself and my friends at no small risk to your own."

During his orchestration of the sounds of her mock torture in Cell Block B—the slaps and punches and moans and groans—and the skillful application of false bruises and cuts and pig's blood, he'd refused to explain himself. *All in good time*, Derrick had said when Victoria pressed. *Meanwhile, if you and your friends wish to live, you will trust me and play along with this charade*.

Derrick poked at the fire. "That question is best answered over a glass of the first press of the grape," he said, referring to the bottle of 1943 Cuvee, one of the most expensive wines to be produced in France. Victoria wondered if the wine cellar of the count was also open to the disposal of the duke. "It's never too early in the day for champagne, especially in these times. Ah, here's Alois now," he said as the mantel clock struck ten o'clock.

They took seats on opposite couches while the servant poured the wine, leaving the bottle in an ice bucket on the table between them, and when they were alone, Derrick raised his glass to Victoria. "To your safe return to America to live a happy and fulfilled life, Victoria Grayson. That should answer the question of why you were brought here."

She stared at him. "That's the only reason?"

"The one and only. What else could there be?"

Her face warmed, but her gaze remained steady. "You know very well, Colonel. Or have I been flattering myself?"

He set down his champagne flute. "No, you've not been flattering yourself, but I accepted from the beginning that some hopes, dreams, desires, whatever word one wishes to describe yearnings, are never to be fulfilled. For the record, though, my hankering extended beyond sheer lust, as you continue to interpret my interest. You stirred longings of another kind on a purer and higher level. No need to go into them. I have been satisfied to believe that what could have been might have been at another, more benevolent time." He raised an eyebrow at her. "Do you deny it?"

Victoria forced herself to meet his gaze. She owed him a direct look and straight answer. It was true. After Ralph, if they'd met in a world at peace…"No, I cannot deny it," she said. Her eyes burned. "Derrick, how could a man like you become a part of an organization like the SS?"

He sighed. "At the time, I joined for the sake of my country. I foolishly believed in Hitler and his mission to restore Germany to its former glory. By the time I understood that my own work would perpetrate his madness, it was too late to withdraw without raising suspicion of my loyalties and endangering my family. But at least by staying in the SS, I could help save the lives of some of my countrymen."

Derrick picked up his glass again. "As to why the theatrical ruse," he continued, "one would not have been necessary if the Gestapo chief had not asked to witness your execution and bring along his underlings. As it was, I had no choice but to make your torture and execution appear real to secure my own credibility and safety."

He took a sip of champagne and added wryly, "In certain quarters, to those with a skewed view of heroism, I am quite the man of the moment. My personal sacrifice for the greater cause earned favor in high places. Most certainly, your execution left no question of my allegiance to the Third Reich to those who doubted it. The regard in which I held my bout partner was no secret to those interested in the affairs of Colonel Derrick Albrecht."

"You…are not who you pretend to be, are you?" Victoria said, beginning to realize the dangerous game he was playing. "Are you a double agent?"

He laughed shortly. "Not exactly. A double agent plays both sides. I am on only one side, and that is what is best for Germany. I belong to a group secretly formed to oppose Hitler and his regime. My mission is to save like-minded countrymen accused of treason from fates worse than death while carrying out my other unsavory duties. You dropped into my life as an unexpected means to broaden my range of activities. My hope was to pipe classified material through you that would save lives on both sides and bring an early end to the war." He reached forward to refill his champagne glass.

Victoria's remained untouched. "So the drama that day at the folly was a setup."

Derrick tipped his glass to her. "I would apologize for the deceit if I meant it."

Amazed, Victoria shook her head, her throat going

tight. He could have secured his future by going through the real thing, the torture and execution, and spared himself the enormous task of pulling off an incredible scheme to save her and the others, but he had not. For her sake, he had imperiled himself, his organization, and even his family. How did a woman reconcile her feelings for a man like that?

"You put your life on the line for me," she said.

"My life was already on the line."

"I am grateful, Derrick."

"I have stated what I wish in return—for you to live a full and happy life. That pinnacle is often unachievable for most people, but I would like to be promised that you will at least attempt to honor my request. Do I have it?"

Tears finally spilled. This man induced emotions in her that bounced around like Ping-Pong balls. Through her blurred vision, she saw him stand and produce a white handkerchief. "I never thought I'd see those for me," he said.

She took the handkerchief and wiped at her tears. "Well, you have."

"Do you promise?"

She said, "I promise."

"Excellent. Now we must discuss the next step from here. You will leave in the morning at daybreak. Karl will deliver you to your safe house, where you will be handed over to your contacts—" At her frozen look, he said, "What's wrong?"

"My safe house. It's been compromised."

"How do you know?"

"I was informed shortly before I was arrested and before other extraction plans could be made."

"Even though your safe house has been compromised, do not you have another means of getting out of France?"

Victoria shook her head, trying to think. Her revelation had clearly unsettled him. Why not offer his own avenues to get her out of France? "Our radio operator was the go-between to our handler," she said. "I don't know what has happened to her, if she escaped the roundup or not. I don't know her address, where she works, or what name she goes by. There is only the mural..."

"The aquatic landscape on the courtyard wall of the convent?"

"Yes. What is the problem with getting me to safe territory through your own channels, Derrick?"

"The risk is too great for two reasons," Derrick said. He got up from the couch, looking worried, the champagne forgotten, and returned to the fire. "Our refuge sites are within France and Germany.

We have no means to get you beyond their borders. Also, the Gestapo has made sure Paris is buzzing with your execution, the lover of the SD chief of counterintelligence and the principal instructor of foil at L'Ecole d'Escrime Français. They're trumpeting it as a triumph of their detection and a warning to others. Your picture made the front page of *Le Temps*. You were known to many: your students, my associates, the residents at the hotel. Many witnessed you fall before the firing squad. You are supposed to be dead. A chance recognition of you, no matter how well disguised you'd be, would put you, me, and my entire organization in danger. Your extraction must come from the OSS. Is there a way to notify the radio operator that you are still alive and need help?"

"Yes!" Victoria said. "A diagonal mark drawn across a liverwort, my code symbol on the mural. It means to meet at a book and tea shop at four o'clock the day it appears—La Petite Madeleine, near the Catacombs. If our radio operator hasn't been extracted or arrested, she will see the mark and know what it means. She'll know it was left by me and be at the café unless she smells a trap. Tell whoever you send to mention the Rose Main Reading Room of the New York Public Library. She will know then that he can be trusted."

"The Rose Main Reading Room of the New York Public Library," Derrick repeated. "I know the place well. I was once introduced to T. S. Eliot there."

"One other thing. If you see a V in the Labrador's ear, that will mean she has been compromised and has left Paris. Will you be sending Karl?"

"No. I will go," Derrick said.

HOME

June 1944–September 1962

CHAPTER EIGHTY-FIVE

A copy of *Le Temps*, printed Monday, was on Alistair's desk at the Bern station when he arrived on Tuesday, June 13. Its headlines screamed FRENCH WOMAN WORKING AS SPY FOR THE AMERICAN OSS EXECUTED! Several pictures of Victoria, one of her with her face bloodied, and another of her tied to the execution pole, her hooded head lolling forward, were accompanied by a detailed article describing her and the execution ceremony. It included the name and position of the SS colonel who had personally given the order to fire. Typically, the Gestapo and the SD kept their executions under wraps, not have them displayed on the front page of an occupied country's most influential newspaper for the world to see. The publicity of Victoria's murder was intended to frighten and intimidate a French populace growing rebellious against its German invaders.

Alistair tried not to think of Victoria's ordeal at the hands of Derrick Albrecht when he learned that she was a spy, but somehow, amazingly, since *Le Temps* made no reference to her as an American, she must have managed to keep that information from him. A wave of grief washed over him. There was also no mention of the others caught in the net. By now they most likely would have met the same fate. They were not as newsworthy as Victoria, well-known fencing instructor and lover of one of the most dangerous Nazis in Paris.

At three o'clock that afternoon, his secure line rang. The caller was Henri. "I've news, perhaps hopeful," he said. "A mark has appeared on the mural. I pass the wall every day, and the mark was not there yesterday. It does not look like the work of vandals because no other part of the painting was touched. Could it mean something?"

Alistair pressed the receiver to his ear. "What does it look like—the mark?"

"It is a diagonal line drawn through a liverwort."

"What! That can't be! The mark is code from Liverwort to my radio operator to meet at La Petite Madeleine at four o'clock today!"

"And... I assume that is impossible?"

"Yes," Alistair said simply. Henri would have figured out that Liverwort was the French OSS spy reported executed in today's *Le Temps* and that his radio operator was Bernadette Dufor.

"Could it be that one of your other operatives could have given up the code sign under interrogation, and the mark is designed to set a trap, which would imply—"

Alistair tried to quell a burst of excitement. "—that one of the team is still alive and on the loose. There is only one way to find out. You know what to do, my friend."

"*Oui*," Henri said.

Ten minutes until four o'clock that afternoon, Derrick entered the book and tea shop. Only the proprietor—or the man he assumed to own the shop—was present behind a counter. Business did not appear prosperous enough to employ more help, and his apron implied he did double duty as waiter and bookseller. He regarded Derrick's appearance more with curiosity than suspicion. What was a man dressed like a rich country squire doing in a shop like his?

"Good afternoon," Derrick said in impeccable French. "Tea?"

"In the back room, monsieur. Allow me." The man came quickly from behind the counter and led Derrick to a table in the tea shop. "I'll take this chair," Derrick said, choosing one that faced the entrance of the tearoom rather than the one the proprietor offered of a murky view of the courtyard.

"Very well, monsieur. I'm afraid our tea selections and pastries are limited today."

"I will take what you can provide."

Bowing away, the owner flicked a glance at the Frenchman in the corner. Henri continued reading, having shown no interest in the man who had entered, but he recognized him without doubt. No verbal exchange in faultless French, no English-tailored suit, could disguise the SS chief of the SD's counterintelligence division in France. A nerve pulsed in Henri's temple. The man's appearance could mean only one thing: The name of the café had been given up as a meeting place for Alistair's operatives, and the SD chief had come to spring the trap himself. His presence did indeed imply that at least one of Alistair's dragonflies was still alive, or had been yesterday.

The proprietor brought in the tea. "I'm expecting

someone," Henri overheard the SS man tell him. "A petite, blond-haired woman. Would you please show her in? I may have to ask you for another cup."

Henri's fellow confederate bowed. "My pleasure, monsieur," he said.

Mon Dieu! Henri thought. The man was expecting the operative Henri had guessed to be Labrador, whose undercover name was Mademoiselle Bernadette Dufor, Alistair's radio operator. Did the man not know that she had been arrested by the French Gestapo? It was well known that the one group did not speak to the other. Had he come to arrest Mademoiselle Dufor in person?

Time passed. The trap had been laid, but no one appeared to step into it. After an hour, Henri wormed his body out between chair and table as if tired of sitting and drinking watery tea. He left a few centimes for the proprietor and walked leisurely by the man at the other table to hurry his report to Alistair.

Derrick sat two hours, the tea barely drunk, the unidentifiable pastries uneaten, before deciding to leave. The radio operator was not coming. Victoria was now without a contact to arrange her extraction unless he could think of another course. The possibility of reaching out to Swiss authorities to contact the OSS crossed his mind, but he dismissed that idea. He knew no one personally whom he could trust or who would trust him, the man who had ordered Mademoiselle Veronique Colbert's execution. Victoria would have to remain at the chateau until he could decide what to do. He knew of no other place safe for her.

Alistair pounced on the phone the moment it rang a few minutes past five o'clock that afternoon. "Bad news," Henri said immediately and related his report. "Obviously, the French Gestapo and SD do not communicate."

"It will be only a matter of time before news filters to the SD that she's in the hands of the Carlingue," Alistair said, "and that will be the end of the roundup."

"Has she given up her call signal yet?"

"No. Not a transmission has come in. They either haven't broken her, or she's dead."

"It is all very puzzling, Alistair."

"Isn't it?"

"Not the least of which..." Henri paused. Alistair lost a breath.

"Go on."

"Don't you think it odd, *mon ami*, that an SD chief would take the time and trouble and the bother to appear in civilian clothes in person, alone, to make an arrest, even if important? One would think the SS would have a cadre in hiding in the café."

Alistair thought, then asked, "Did you see any sign of an SS presence on the street when you left the shop?"

"No, and another strange thing. According to Phillipe, Colonel Albrecht sat a full two hours waiting for your agent before he left. Now why would an officer of his important status do that?"

Alistair stared into space. Henri was right. Things weren't adding up. "I can't answer that, Henri."

Breaking the connection, Alistair looked at his doodled collection of dragonflies on his desk. Until Henri's call, he had thought of brushing them all into his wastebasket in a fit of despair, but somehow, despite having no more expectations of Dragonfly's survival, he felt a tiny flicker of hope and chose instead to sweep his doodles into a desk drawer.

CHAPTER EIGHTY-SIX

The evening of June 13, Derrick returned to the chateau to find Victoria waiting anxiously. She could read from his expression that his mission had failed. "She didn't come, did she?" she asked.

Wearily, Derrick handed hat and gloves to Alois and made for the liquor table. "I regret to tell you that she did not. I saw no V in the dog's ear. I waited over two hours and no one appeared. Today I made inquiries and managed to find out why." He looked at Victoria, dreading to tell her the news. "You'd better have a drink. It's not good."

"Tell me," she whispered.

"I questioned her employer, the couturier, Madame Boucher. She last saw your friend on June ninth, when she was led away by two men from the French Gestapo. Their commander didn't recognize the name when I inquired, but I did not believe him. I am well experienced in detecting liars. An hour later, he called back to report that their records showed that his office had indeed arrested your friend but that she had been sent to the Drancy internment camp on June tenth."

"Well, can't you use your influence to get her out of there?"

Derrick said gently, "Two days ago she was deported to Dachau concentration camp because of overcrowding."

"Oh, God..." Victoria sank to the couch, and Derrick placed the glass of whiskey on the table in front of her. "Dachau...the camp with the crematoria..."

Derrick turned to fill his own glass, feeling the burn of shame creep up his neck. "It doesn't mean that she will be gassed, Victoria. She's not Jewish, and apparently she managed to avoid revealing that she is an American OSS agent. Otherwise, she would have been shot."

Victoria pressed her hands to her cheeks. "First in the hands of the French Gestapo, now Dachau. She'll never be able to endure what they do to people in those camps."

"Perhaps she will, Victoria. From what I have

gathered, she is a strong young woman." But Derrick could see that she didn't believe what he himself could not. Dachau was the training ground for the SS commanders of concentration camps, and the prisoners were used as subjects for practicing techniques of persuasion. Worst of all, the camp had been established as a laboratory for the conduction of medical experiments, with the inmates used as guinea pigs.

"Of course I will continue to make inquiries and use my influence to do what I can," he said. "If she can hold out to the end of the war, which can't last much longer, she'll make it. The Allies have managed to dig in and hold a number of beaches along the French coastline despite enormous German resistance, and I expect they will be in Paris by August. France will be entirely liberated before winter."

"Little good the liberation of France will do Labrador," Victoria said dully, unconsoled. "There's still Germany to invade…"

Derrick took a seat beside her on the couch and took hold of her limp hand. "Victoria, I am sorry for your friend, but we must now talk about you. We have no options left to get you out of France. That means that you must stay here at the chateau until it is safe for you to leave. You cannot afford to be seen by anyone but Alois. A chance glimpse of you by a delivery boy, a daily hire, a groundskeeper or farmer or hunter on the downs where you like to walk, and you could be reported. Once the Parisians are free to exact their vengeance, they will descend upon this place like avenging angels. It won't help that the chateau belongs to a count who deserted France before the first German arrived. You will be dragged out and made an example of as a French collaborator, or worse, the lover of an SS colonel in the despised Sicherheitsdienst."

"Well, if I must stay, I must, and when the Allies arrive, I'll go to Paris and get in touch with the American military—"

"No, Victoria! You don't understand," Derrick said. "The city will not be safe for you even when it is liberated—especially then. The Parisians will be after blood. One glimpse of the beautiful French instructor of foil—one who roused such admiration and sympathy from her countrymen when they believed her executed by the Nazis—and they will be on you like a pack of jackals. The French do not like to be duped."

Victoria, bewildered, withdrew her hand. "Then what am I to do, Derrick? I can't stay here forever!"

"No, of course not! I am saying that you must stay here until I can personally contact your army to send someone for you. Only in their protection will you be safe."

"How do you plan to do that—contact the American army?"

"Leave that to me. I'll get word to you as quickly as I can make arrangements." He finished off his drink in a single swallow and stood. "Now I must go."

Victoria stood also, stricken by a sudden awareness. "Derrick…When will I see you again?"

He took her hands into his. "My dear Victoria Grayson of Williamsburg, Virginia. I do not anticipate the pleasure of meeting you again."

"Derrick, I—"

"Shush," he said, drawing her into a light embrace, and brushed his lips across her hair. "No need to say anything. You leave me with memories that I shall treasure as long as I live. I ask only that you remember me with kindness and keep to the promise you have made." He released his arms and stepped back, his long gaze into her eyes storing the last time he would see her. "*Au revoir*, Mademoiselle Colbert. Remember to wait for my call."

Stunned at the suddenness of his departure from

her life, her chest swelling with a pain beyond her understanding, Victoria watched speechlessly as he collected his hat and gloves and, with a nod and a last glance at her, stepped through the doorway and was gone.

CHAPTER EIGHTY-SEVEN

Alistair was at his desk, June 19, when one of the staff handed him a transmission from a woman who managed a safe house in Barcelona. LODESTAR HAS ARRIVED AND IS READY FOR PICKUP, the code message read.

Shocked, disbelieving, Alistair shot up from his chair so suddenly, his head swam. "Oh, my God," he said and fell back down on the seat, too woozy to stand.

He was at the airfield when a Swiss Red Cross plane delivered Bucky to the tarmac. Alistair's eyes filled when the long-limbed Oklahoman stepped down the flight ramp. As they embraced, he noticed a sprinkling of gray in the boy's brown hair and the lines across his forehead and around the eyes that had not been there before. He had just turned twenty-five.

In the airfield office Bucky described the horror of Liverwort's execution and recited the astonishing events that had delivered him and Lapwing and Limpet from suffering the same treatment and death. Alistair's heart swelled. What of Labrador? Bucky wanted to know. Alistair had to tell him that she'd been taken by the French Gestapo shortly after their arrest. There had been no word of her since.

"You think she's dead?"

"I have no hope for her."

Bucky looked away, eyes watering. "Damn!"

"I have something for you, Sam," Alistair said, and deposited a box on the table. "Madame Dupree, thinking you were dead, sent a few of your personal effects to me to see that they got to your parents."

The boy's disconsolate face flashed surprise as he opened the box, and Alistair discerned why. The box contained a pair of military cadet epaulettes. It didn't take much speculation to guess they belonged to his illustrious father, the Black Ghost. How they came to be in Sam's possession, Alistair would never ask. He would allow his agent's personal agenda for joining the OSS to remain his private affair. The important thing was that his quest had been successful.

"Welcome back, Sam," Alistair said, his eyes misting

again. "After a full debriefing, we'll get you on the first plane to Oklahoma."

Chris arrived next. Before leaving Major General March's house on June 13 to board the vehicles to transport them to their safe houses, the men of Dragonfly had clasped hands as comrades who have fought a long battle together but now must part to complete a final mission on their own: safe passage out of the country. Chris thought that his attempt had surely failed when an SS major boarded a train in Lyon and demanded to see each passenger's papers. He took one look at Chris, snatched his papers from his hand, and ordered him to stand up. Chris unwound from the overcrowded train seat under the hard study of the man clearly wondering why this six-foot-three young man of compact German muscle wasn't in uniform. When his scrutiny dropped to the SS travel pass, Chris saw a faint flash of surprise cross his face, but because the fancy had struck him to make him squirm, ordered, "Stay here!" and left the train with Chris's papers in hand.

"He's going to check to see if you are who you say you are," whispered the passenger in the seat behind him.

An hour dragged by, the passengers becoming more agitated with Chris for having caused the delay, before the officer returned. "All is in order!" he said, handing back Chris's papers with a respectful bow and military click of his heels. Chris expelled the air locked in his lungs. Apparently Colonel Derrick Albrecht, the signer of his travel pass, or someone in his office had vouched for him.

Brad was the last to step foot on safe soil. The delay in leaving France was due to a crucial change in the escape plan he insisted upon. After much arguing and cajoling, those in charge of his rescue operation were finally persuaded to alter his route from English-held Gibraltar on the tip of Spain to Switzerland, where he could look up Wilhelm's aunt.

Judging by Major General March's description of her, the sour-faced woman who had to be Helga Wolfe answered the door to her unappealing little house. As she opened the door, the raised voices of a boy and girl in a vicious argument surged around her like foul air. "Yes?" she said in the irritable voice of a woman hopelessly at the end of her patience.

Brad withdrew a letter. "My name is Barnard Wagner, and I've come on behalf of your nephew's father, Major General Konrad March—"

"*Herr Wagner!*" Brad heard, and suddenly Wilhelm came flying from a room off the hall and Brad, seeing his intent, bent down to scoop him up as the little boy ran past his aunt and leaped into his arms. "You've come! You've come!" he sobbed, fastening his legs and arms around Brad so tightly he could hardly breathe.

The situation was as clear to Brad as a Rocky Mountain stream. He held Wilhelm a little longer, the child's heart beating hard against his chest, then set him down and took hold of his hand. "You bet I have, buddy," he said. A surly boy and girl a few years older than Wilhelm had emerged to hang on to their mother at the door. Bullies to the core, Brad summed them up. Wilhelm wouldn't have stood a chance in that household. He said to Helga Wolfe, "Show me Wilhelm's room and I'll pack his things."

It was done in ten minutes, Wilhelm sticking close to his side. The aunt stayed downstairs. The children hovered in the doorway of Wilhelm's closet-sized room, mean little eyes alight with curiosity. "Where are you taking him?" the boy asked.

"As far away from you as possible," Brad answered.

It occurred to Brad as they were on the metro to present themselves to the American embassy that Helga Wolfe had never even looked at her brother-in-law's letter. He glanced at Wilhelm tucked beside him like an abused pup having found a safe shelter. Brad put his arm around him and drew him closer.

With the three boys and little Wilhelm now safe, Alistair felt the blessed relief that only a case officer and a runner of foreign operatives can know when his agents come home from enemy territory in one piece. Each and every one counted with him, but there were some whose safe returns struck a special chord in his heart. The same was true for their loss. The execution of Victoria Grayson and presumed death of Bridgette Loring would be a lasting grief. His radio operator's trail had ended at 93 Rue Lauriston in the sixteenth arrondissement, headquarters of the French Gestapo. Henri had managed to snuggle up to a female clerk working in the building who'd been willing to spill the little she knew of the petite blonde who sat for hours awaiting interrogation in the hallway, but she could supply no further knowledge. Mademoiselle Bernadette Dufor's name was not listed in the Carlingue's records of the dead or incarcerated. Inquiries from the organization's interrogators had yielded nothing. No coworker recognized the name Bernadette Dufor. The woman had simply disappeared.

CHAPTER EIGHTY-EIGHT

Alistair sat at his desk in Bern doodling. A report of OSS inquiries into the boys' return to the United States had come back with the information that they had arrived at their homes safely, and by now, the last day of July 1944, Alistair expected they would have picked up with their former lives. Christopher Brandt had expressed his desire to resume his profession as a math teacher and track-and-field coach while working on his PhD. He seemed unworried about finding a job. Male teachers were at a premium, since the war had siphoned off the able-bodied of his gender. Sam Barton—Bucky—planned to join an engineering firm in Oklahoma City that had kept a position open for him, and the son of Joanna Bukowski Hudson expected to return to his job at his stepfather's lumberyard.

He'd had no word of the men since, but he could picture their happy homecomings, guess at the questions they could not answer, conceive of the trail of mystery that would follow them until they were released from the bounds of the OSS's version of the Official Secrets Service Act, in effect for five years. Alistair expected that even then they would be disinclined to clear up the speculations and misperceptions of neighbors and friends and relatives about what they did for Uncle Sam in the years they were away, reluctant even to discuss the subject with the women they would marry. Their children would most likely never hear about what Daddy did in the war.

A rap on his door drew Alistair from his thoughts. His desk sergeant poked his head in and squinted. The window behind Alistair's desk reflected the full sun of high summer, so that upon entering the office the visitor saw only a silhouette of Alistair's head and upper body. It was an annoyance to those approaching his desk to have their vision blinded and being forced to speak to a blacked-out face. By late afternoon the sun would have moved on, but for now his desk sergeant, come to inform him that Colonel William Donovan had arrived, thought it prudent to suggest, "The conference room is available, Major."

"Not for our short meeting," Alistair said, continuing his doodling. He knew why his boss had come. "Show him in, Robert."

"Yes sir," the sergeant said, turning away with a sigh and rapid bat of his eyes.

"For God's sake, Alistair, move away from that window before it blinds me," Bill Donovan complained, entering like a force blown in by a strong wind, hand shielding his eyes.

"Hello to you, too, Colonel," Alistair said. "You're looking hale and hearty."

"Can't say the same for you. You look about as hale and hearty as week-old coffee dregs. What the hell is this?" Wild Bill waved Alistair's letter of resignation, effective upon the liberation of Paris, before his desk.

"What it looks like." Alistair made a motion to the sergeant to bring coffee and got up to move to one of the chairs reserved for visitors. "Good trip?"

"Tolerable, but enough about me," Bill Donovan said. He tossed Alistair's letter of resignation onto a table. "Let's talk about this. I know what's behind it. All your lambs didn't make it home to the fold, and rather than look at your glass as half full because three of them did, you'd rather consider it half empty because two of them didn't. Well, I don't accept your resignation, not without you hearing me out first. After that, you might want to tear it up."

Alistair sighed wearily. "I doubt it, but what's on your mind?"

"Congratulations, that's what, though I know my kudos will ping off you like BBs off a Sherman tank, but I'll give them anyway. You've done one hell of a great job running this station, Alistair, and your genius has paid untold dividends. The president wishes me to express his gratitude."

"Okay, accepted," Alistair said. "Next."

Wild Bill grunted as if that reaction was as expected. "I've come to offer you another job. German defenses of the entire Normandy front are collapsing even as we speak, and the Allies are steadily moving into France. It won't be long before U.S. Army tanks will be rolling down Paris's Champs Élysées. The Allied powers predict that France will be liberated by the end of August, so I accept that your job here is done. Now I want you to come home with me, Alistair—to Washington, D.C., that is. I will need you to help me administer the OSS when the war is over because it won't be over, not by a long shot. Our next enemy will be Russia. You can bet Stalin will force the Nazi-occupied countries liberated by his armies to become Russian satellites. The countries of

Eastern Europe will simply exchange one yoke for another, and there's talk of even Berlin being divided into eastern and western sectors. The West and its allies will have to face another world-domination threat, and the OSS has to be reorganized to deal with it."

"And you think I'm the man who can help you do it."

"Without reservation." Donovan paused and regarded Alistair in concern as the coffee was brought in. "You're just overtired, my good friend, jaded, and feeling the effects of bad health. You've been in the thick of it longer than any other case officer in the field, Alistair. You don't want to quit now. All you need is a change of scene and venue. A job that doesn't keep your nerves on end, and allows you three squares a day and a soft bed to lie down in at night, with the chance of getting a full eight hours' sleep." The OSS chief shot a glance at the rumpled cot in a corner of Alistair's office.

Alistair rubbed his neck thoughtfully, unsure if the power of suggestion had made his boss's proposal sound good, or if fatigue, lack of sleep and nourishment, worry and anxiety, too much caffeine and too many cigarettes, and the sick loss of Liverwort and Labrador had robbed him of the spirit and drive to go on, but he wouldn't fool himself. He hadn't really wanted to quit. He was just in a slump, and Bill was offering a way out of it, another opportunity to serve his country, the only mistress he'd ever cared about. He made up his mind without giving his boss's job offer another thought.

"What if I wrap everything up in the next few days?" he asked. "I have a competent man to leave in charge, and my operatives in France will be in good hands."

Bill Donovan reached for Alistair's letter of resignation and tore it in half. "I'll hold the plane for you," he said.

CHAPTER EIGHTY-NINE

Before daylight on August 15, 1944, Bridgette woke from her perspiration-soaked bed to the smell of smoke drifting through the patch of her open window. She looked out and saw, illuminated by the powerful beams of searchlights, members of the staff of Sturmbannführer Gottlob Richter, commandant of the Drancy internment camp, overseeing prisoners as they removed papers from file boxes and threw them into blazing pyres that had been built in the courtyard, creating a haze that hung as thick as fog in the cloying humidity. The smoke and heat from the fires had forced Bridgette to close the room's one window, which had been providing a little air to relieve the sweltering temperatures of Paris's unrelenting summer heat.

"Mademoiselle!" Bridgette heard the perpetually

anxious voice of Nicoline Arquette, a fellow captive and the Richters' cook and housemaid, whisper through the thin door of her room. Then came the sound of the key turning in the lock. At night she and Nicoline were locked into their rooms, set free by Madame Richter's hand only when the mistress of the house and keeper of the keys required their services. The lock sprang open and Nicoline, without Madame Richter, hurried in and quickly shut the door behind her. Her eyes looked ready to pop out of her head.

"What is it?" Bridgette asked, fearing to hear. "How did you get Madame Richter's keys?"

"She forgot to take them with her after she locked you in last night," Nicoline said in rapid French. "I was cleaning up the dishes last night when her husband stomped into the house all excited, and they shut themselves in the parlor where I couldn't hear them. Then he rushed out, back to his office, I guess, and she went off to her room and closed the door. When I finished cleaning the kitchen, she still hadn't come out. I went to my room and waited, but she never came to lock me in. All night I heard people coming and going from her room and madame hollering orders. About midnight, I peeked out. Madame's door was open, and I saw prisoners frantically packing and carrying out boxes and cases and luggage. Madame looked harried and scared, and she was still wearing the clothes she'd worn the day before. I popped my head back in before she caught me, and after a few hours it was quiet. I looked out again a half hour ago, but no one was about. I don't think the commandant came home last night. His door was open and his bed hadn't been slept in. That's when I sneaked out to the parlor, where I found madame's keys."

"What do you think is going on?" Bridgette managed to interject when Nicoline paused for breath.

"I think she's *left*!" Nicoline cried. "When I was in the parlor, I saw a van pull away from the house, and I'm sure madame was in it! She didn't answer her door when I knocked."

"Let's go see," Bridgette said.

Nicoline, sizably taller and larger than Bridgette but cowed by years of confinement and abuse, followed her dependable shield to Madame Richter's room. Bridgette knocked once, waited a few minutes, then pushed open the door. The room had been completely vacated. They stared with open mouths at the doors of closets and wardrobes and bureau drawers gaping emptily of their once overflowing contents.

"All those clothes you made for her..." Nicoline said in an awestruck voice. "They're gone. That's what she had the prisoners packing."

The smell of smoke had begun to seep into the room. Bridgette went to a window to look out again at the bundles and boxes of papers the prisoners threw into the fires with the systematic rhythm of a water brigade. Through the haze she could read the large print on some of the boxes: DACHAU, RAVENSBRÜCK, AUSCHWITZ...*My God!* she thought. The Germans were destroying the files of victims they'd deported to the concentration camps!

"What's that smell?" Nicoline asked nervously.

"Come look," Bridgette said.

Nicoline peered out. Her room was not on the side of the house with a view of the courtyard. "*Sainte Mère de Dieu!* What are they doing?"

"The Germans are burning evidence of their atrocities in the camp before it's liberated."

Nicoline stared at her. "Liberated?"

"I think the camp's liberation is near, Nicoline, and those monsters know it," Bridgette said, trying not to get excited. "Madame's hasty departure and that scene out there prove it. The commandant and his officers want no records left of the crimes committed here that they can be held accountable for."

"But, Bernadette, in the meantime, what will they do with us, the inmates?" A new fright in her eyes, she gasped, "Aren't we evidence as well of their crimes? Will they line us up and shoot us, so we can't bear witness against them?"

Bridgette reached up and removed a strand of rank hair stuck to Nicoline's moist cheek. Her partner in misery was thirty years old, with a striking bone structure. She must have been beautiful once and perhaps would be again, but after nearly four years of incarceration at Drancy in the grip of the Richters, the spirit that gave life to her beauty might never be restored. Even though Nicoline could not claim a drop of Jewish blood, she had been arrested while visiting a Jewish family during the first roundup of Jews in 1941 and interned in the camp. She would have been released had Madame Richter not recognized her as one of the chefs in their favorite restaurant. As Bridgette had been conscripted for her skills, Nicoline had been pressed into service for the Richters because of her culinary talents. Sturmbannführer Richter's appetites had extended beyond his appreciation of Nicoline's cuisine, however, and these he indulged with unrestrained gluttony on nights Madame Richter did not lock Nicoline's door to allow her husband access. Bridgette's heart wrenched on the mornings after she heard muffled screams coming from Nicoline's room to see the girl's once lovely face a wasteland of lost dignity and worth. When Madame Richter caught the commandant forcing himself on Bridgette and saw the blood on the sheets, she had pulled him off her in an inexplicable act of human decency and threatened to extinguish his firecracker once and for all if he touched her again. Apparently, in her thinking, it was one thing to ravish a woman already experienced in sex, quite another to rape a virgin.

"I don't believe we have to be concerned," Bridgette said to soothe Nicoline's worry. "They know the Resistance is knocking on their doors, and they wouldn't be able to dispose of so many bodies in such a short time. We'll be free soon, Nicoline. All we have to do is be patient and keep our nerve until help arrives."

But Nicoline would not be mollified. "What if the commandant returns and decides to shoot us so we won't testify against him and his wife for their treatment of us?"

Nicoline had a point that Bridgette had not considered, and it made frightening sense. As French citizens, they had been illegally imprisoned without charge, used as forced labor, starved, and beaten, and

Nicoline had been repeatedly raped. The commandant would want to dispose of them before they could air their accusations.

"Give me the keys," Bridgette said. "One of them has to open the bastard's private cache of guns."

They found the guns almost immediately, along with a stash of French francs and German marks locked in a cabinet in Sturmbannführer Richter's bedroom. After checking the chambers for a full round of bullets, the women helped themselves to two P08 Lugers, as well as the cash, hoping that when the commandant found the guns and money missing, he would believe his wife had taken them. The women would need funds once they were free.

The burning continued throughout the following day, August 16. Sometime late in the night Sturmbannführer Richter returned to the house. The women agreed that Bridgette would lock Nicoline in her room and keep the keys in her possession. "But…he will come for you if he finds my door locked, Bernadette," Nicoline said.

"Not to worry. I sleep with one eye open. I will hear him enter the house. The moment his jackboots turn in the direction of my bedroom door, I will welcome him with a surprise he won't live long enough to appreciate."

All night Bridgette waited to hear Sturmbannführer Richter stomp into the house, but when dawn broke, and she poked her head out her room, she saw no sign of the camp commandant. He had come and gone like a shadow, taking the packed bag on his bed with him and leaving the door to the locked cabinet open and empty of its remaining contents. Bridgette knocked on Nicoline's door, rattling the keys. "Nicoline, it's me," she said loudly, standing a safe distance from her door. "Richter looks to have gone. I'm going to unlock the door now."

When Bridgette turned the key and pushed the door open, she found Nicoline standing with the gun aimed at the doorway. Seeing Bridgette alone, she lowered the gun limply to her side. "Gone?"

"For good, it looks like." Bridgette put her arms around the frail woman's trembling body. "I think we're safe, Nicoline. Look outside."

From the windows, they could see SS officers and German guards hastily piling into a convoy of loaded jeeps and trucks and beginning an exodus toward the entrance gates of the camp. Some staff cars, no longer waving Nazi flags, roared past the line without waiting their turn, their passengers dressed in civilian clothes. "Rats deserting a sinking ship," Bridgette observed in disgust.

"You mean . . . they are truly leaving?"

"Before the liberators get here and shoot them or worse," Bridgette said, taking her arm. "Shall we risk stepping outside?"

Neither woman had placed a foot on the ground or felt the sun on her skin since being imprisoned in the Richters' house and forbidden to step outside on punishment of the whip. For Nicoline, the last day she felt the sun, such as it was in Drancy, was July 17, 1941; for Bridgette, June 10, 1944.

The courtyard with its still smoking pyres looked deserted of even the German guards who'd patrolled the area with unslung guns and dogs on relaxed leashes while the evacuation took place. The inmates were still in their quarters, ordered there to prevent their witness of the desertion that would mean the camp's liberation was at hand.

"What do we do now?" Nicoline asked.

"We wait until help arrives," Bridgette said. She jiggled the keys, still in her hand. "Meanwhile let's go unlock the cupboards for something to eat." It was the eve of the French Resistance's official liberation of the camp the morning of August 17, 1944.

CHAPTER NINETY

Upon the exuberantly spread news that Drancy prison had been liberated, a crowd rushed to be on hand to collect their loved ones when the gates opened, delayed when the Swedish diplomatic corps, anticipating chaos and a stampede in and out of the prison, took immediate control of the facility, aided by the Paris police and the French Red Cross. The Paris police held in check the lengthening lines forming outside the prison gates, photographs and flags and banners bearing the names of the imprisoned held aloft, while within, the diplomatic corps and volunteers handled the orderly release of the approximately 1,500 survivors of the camp, and the French Red Cross administered to the sick and infirm. While all were free to leave, and no inmates were held against their will, the exodus had to be done in a systematic and fair manner.

Bridgette, because of her short tenancy, was among the last to be checked off the prisoners' list. Nicoline, after a tearful farewell, had been released the first day in the care of a brother with the expressed hope they would one day reunite, but both knew they never would. They would have been too painful a reminder of a time they wished to forget. The date of Bridgette's liberation recorded in the annals of Drancy prison's infamous history was August 21, 1944.

Outside the prison, civilian volunteers had gathered with vehicles to assist in getting the last of the prisoners to their destinations. Carrying nothing but her roll of muslin, Bridgette singled out a horse-drawn wagon to take her to her safe house, should it still be in existence, and was about to board when "*Mademoiselle Dufor!*" rang out loud and clear. She wheeled toward the cry and saw Madame Boucher, elegant in red, frantically waving high a sign that read BERNADETTE DUFOR around the obstacle of a French policeman tasked to hold pedestrians back.

"*Merci*, monsieur, but I believe I will not have to trouble you after all," Bridgette said to the wagon driver, almost faint from the pleasure and relief of seeing the couturier. Tears trickled into big smiles as Bridgette, at eighty pounds, was swallowed in an embrace of red linen and a mist of French perfume.

Since the liberation, her OSS facilitator had been waiting outside the gates from morning until evening with hope of finding her among the survivors.

"How did you know that I was at Drancy?" Bridgette asked when they were on the way to the Convent of the Sisters of Charity, where Sister Mary Frances had "commanded" that she be brought if she were found. She would report to her safe house tomorrow, but for now she was eager to see Sister Mary Frances and the nuns again, sink into a bathtub of hot suds and water, sleep on clean sheets, and ditch the dress she'd worn every day for more than two months. It would be wonderful to feel the touch of clean fabric against her skin again, though it would mean a delay in contacting Major Renault to relieve his worry that she'd died in a cell of the French Gestapo. She did not want to meet him looking as she was now.

"I knew what that hellbat had in mind for you when she did not return to the salon," Jeanne explained. "We never saw her again. I was sure she'd had you imprisoned in Drancy, but of course I had no proof, not enough to report my suspicions to my OSS contact and get your people's hopes up that there you might have a chance to stay alive. The last I was able to report was that you'd been arrested by the French Gestapo. I kept trying to find evidence of my suspicions. I am acquainted with a doctor who was allowed to work in the prison, and I showed him your picture, but he said he never saw you."

"No, he wouldn't have seen me," Bridgette said. "I was never allowed outside."

"Not in all those months you were imprisoned?" Jeanne asked, aghast.

"For Nicoline, Madame Richter's cook and maid, it was close to four years."

"The unconscionable bitch!" Jeanne turned her furious gaze out the window. She had heard Madame Richter laugh and express her philosophy that in regard to servants, the harder you whipped a horse, the faster it ran, so she would not question Bernadette further about her treatment at the woman's hands. The answer sat in a filthy dress beside her, skin and bones without flesh, the pith of youth stripped from her, castrated—there was no other word for it—and smelling of the deprival of the most basic human needs. The flesh would fill out, the scars fade, the heart be restored, but the mind would remember...always. Such absolutes Jeanne knew from her own experience as a courier for the French Army, when she had been caught and incarcerated by the Germans during World War I. She noticed that the pad of Bernadette's needle finger had grown to the size of a cherry the color of a plum, callused to the hardness of a pit.

"What's going on?" Bridgette asked as Jeanne's Mercedes was forced to drive slowly to avoid hitting the growing number of pedestrians gathering in the streets.

"The liberation of Paris!" Jeanne replied excitedly. "The Resistance has the German garrison successfully under siege, and the Americans are making headway into the suburbs of the city. Many of the Germans have fled, and people are feeling free to come out of their homes."

Bridgette stared at the sidewalk cafés packed with Parisians where once German soldiers had lolled in their jackboots, their jubilation like the lift of a fog bank rolling into the streets. Paris liberated...She could go home now, back to the house on Elm Street in Traverse City, Michigan, back to its boredom and slumber, its humdrumness and routine, its peace and quiet...

Jeanne patted her hand. "France will soon be free as well, thanks to brave people like you and Sister Mary Frances."

"And to you as well, Madame Boucher," Bridgette reminded her and added silently, *And to Liverwort and Lodestar and Limpet and Lapwing*. A mental picture formed of her sitting alone in the Rose Main Reading Room of the New York Public Library, watching the door for arrivals that never came. She blinked to clear the image. "How did you come to know Sister Mary Frances?"

Jeanne explained that they'd met over concern for their petite Bernadette Dufor and become friends when they agreed to stay in touch to share news of her. Sister Mary Frances sometimes invited her to tea at the convent.

"Then you must have seen the mural on the wall," Bridgette said.

"Oh, yes. A beautiful piece of artwork—by your hand, I understand."

"Is it still there?"

"Indeed it is. The nuns and residents of the neighborhood have been fierce in seeing to its protection. Only one violator has dared to brave the ramparts to do mischief to it, and it was really nothing, a simple mark across one of those ribbonlike plants—" Jeanne broke off, seeing the sudden change in Bridgette's face. "It is nothing to be alarmed about, *ma chérie*," she said quickly. "It was made with a medium the rain has nearly washed off."

"Do you know when it appeared?"

"Shortly after you'd been arrested in June, I believe."

Bridgette studied the faint mark while they waited to be admitted through the courtyard door, locked now even during the day since the burgeoning unrest in the streets. Had Liverwort tried to contact her, not knowing she'd been arrested? Did that mean she was still alive? The major would be able to tell her that as well as the fate of the others. Hope, unfelt for a long time, suddenly bloomed like a dormant flower. What if they had all made it? What if they'd keep that date in the New York Public Library after all?

She heard the bolt being thrown, and Sister Mary Frances swooped through the courtyard door to drown her this time in swaths of black cotton and wafts of carbolic soap.

After sending Bridgette off for a bath and change of clothes, the mother superior placed a telephone call to a number locked in her private files. When the recipient came on the line, she said, "Mademoiselle Bernadette Dufor is here at the Convent of the Sisters of Charity, monsieur. She has just been released from Drancy, where she has been incarcerated since the middle of June."

Sister Mary Frances was quite sure the man she'd

met only once whose name she did not know was so shocked that he almost dropped the receiver. "*Mon Dieu!*" he exclaimed. "He thought she was dead!"

It was not for her to question who "he" was, so Sister Mary Frances responded simply, "I assure you that Mademoiselle Dufor is here, alive and in the flesh... what little there is left of it."

"I will make a few telephone calls and then come to you at once," Henri said.

Bridgette had finished her bath and changed into one of her dresses, which now appeared to have been borrowed from a woman three sizes larger, when a nun knocked on her door to inform her that a visitor had called for her downstairs. He was waiting in the mother superior's office.

"Who?" she asked, alarmed. No one knew that she was here.

"I don't know, mademoiselle. A Frenchman."

Ah, No Name, Bridgette thought, relieved. "I'll be right down," she said.

Bridgette heard the Frenchman expel a sharp breath when she entered the mother superior's office, but he recovered and rose gallantly to kiss her hand. "Mademoiselle," he said, "I cannot tell you what a pleasure it is to see you. I have now come to offer my assistance in getting you to the OSS French Affairs station in Bern, where arrangements are pending for your return to the United States."

"Where I assume Major Renault is waiting for me," she said.

"No, mademoiselle. Major Renault returned to America in July to resume his duties at his Washington desk. I come on behalf of his replacement in Bern." Seeing Bridgette's splinter-thin face fall, Henri hurried to say, "But you must not despair. He will be informed of your survival. I requested that his replacement let him know, and the major will be overjoyed at your return. Three of your number have already made it back and are now safely ensconced in their homes in America."

"Three? Who?"

"Your male counterparts."

"And... my female counterpart...?"

Henri's own face dropped. "I regret to tell you that she was executed by firing squad the eleventh of June."

CHAPTER NINETY-ONE

On Saturday, August 26, Chief Detective Maurice Corbett and his associate called upon Madame Florence Bisset at her apartment in a city that had gone berserk with joy over its just-announced liberation from Nazi tyranny. The policemen had feared Madame Bisset would be among the revelers, difficult to locate in the crush, and by the time they reached him, Colonel Derrick Albrecht would have flown the coop like so many SS officers when it became glaringly clear that the wolf was at the henhouse door. The German garrison had surrendered the capital to General Philippe Leclerc, commander of the second French Armored Division, the previous night. The City of Light was now back in French hands.

But Colonel Derrick Albrecht had not flown. The police personnel that Maurice had posted inside and outside the Hotel Crillon had reported the man was still in his rooms, as yet not taken into custody by the French or American army authorities—a glad surprise, but Maurice would need to hurry. He wanted to get to him before the military got their hands on him.

Paris's elation over its liberation was deafening and emotionally dizzying. All the church bells in the city were ringing, and it appeared that every French man, woman, and child who could walk or manage with crutches and missing limbs were out to greet the liberators in full force and voice. Waving flags to a cacophony of shouts, songs, sobs, cheers, and applause, the exuberant throngs besieged the soldiers in their armored vehicles and marching ranks with flowers, kisses, and wine—anything they could spare to express their gratitude to the saviors of Paris.

Madame Florence Bisset was not one of them. Her landlady had directed the pair of policemen to a Catholic church nearby, where they found her reciting the rosary and kneeling on a prayer bench in a pew with others who apparently believed that a house of worship was the place to be upon such a joyous occasion. Spotting her from the back of the church, Maurice whispered to his assistant to wait while he took a seat in a pew behind her and gently tapped her shoulder. Recognizing him, she nodded when he said quietly, "Madame Bisset, will you kindly come with us?"

They took her to Maurice's office at the headquarters of the Prefecture of Police, located on its natural island in the River Seine, quiet after the chaos of the day before.

After Madame Bisset had been seated in a chair to derive the most benefit from a rotating floor fan and served a glass of iced lemonade, the lemons confiscated from an arrested black marketeer, Maurice said, "Madame Bisset, will you still testify in court to what you saw and overheard in Colonel Albrecht's office on October thirty-first, 1942?"

"What I overheard, not saw," Madame Bisset corrected him.

"But you have no doubt that the voices you heard belonged to Colonel Derrick Albrecht and his aide, Karl Brunner?"

"Non."

Maurice slipped pen and paper across his desk. "Will you please write out your statement for purposes of securing a court order for the arrest of Standartenführer Derrick Albrecht?"

After arrangements were made for Madame Bisset's return to her apartment and the warrant secured,

Maurice and his assistant drove through the throngs to the Hotel Crillon. The Nazi banners once draped imperiously from its façade and the red flags of white discs and black swastikas flown along Avenue Foch had been pulled down and left burning in piles on the street. Maurice returned the salutes of the members of the police force stationed on the premises, instructed them to come with him, and took the stairs to Derrick Albrecht's suite of rooms.

From one of the open windows of his upper-story hotel suite overlooking the Place de la Concorde, Derrick observed the crowds of Parisians walking the width of the avenue arm in arm and singing "La Marseillaise," the French national anthem, heedless of the Third Reich's symbols smoldering at their feet except to stamp them into further oblivion. In his room, ceiling fans at full spin brought some relief from the sultry heat and smoke-laden air that mingled with the rich fragrance of his Montecristo.

Jacketless, shirtsleeves rolled up, Karl had nearly finished packing the last of the classified material. He assumed it had been spirited away from Derrick's two offices to keep it out of Allied hands, but his aide was clearly mystified, since the colonel's suite was no safer place to store them. Actually, unknown to Karl, Derrick fully intended to turn the boxes over to the detail of Americans sent to take him into custody. He expected their knock on the door at any hour.

By mid-June, he had landed on a scheme to get Victoria safely out of Paris and into Allied hands. Derrick had made contact with an intelligence officer attached to the U.S. Army's Fourth Infantry Division and offered himself as an enemy asset upon their arrival in Paris. An SS colonel in the Sicherheitsdienst with access to highly sensitive material would be considered a coup whose value would trump all other arresting bodies. His proposition had been snapped up immediately. He would be at the Hotel Crillon with the classified documents, he had told the officer. Derrick had rejected his initial impulse to base his offer on the rescue of Victoria at the count's chateau, reasoning that a preliminary evacuation in the current climate could easily be bungled or, more likely, agreed to but ignored, since it was not a top priority of the advancing forces.

So he would wait until he was face-to-face with a representative of the U.S. Army to disclose that an American woman and OSS operative awaited extraction in a chateau in the French countryside. That morning, Derrick had tried to telephone Victoria, but he had only reached Alois on a line with extremely poor reception. Derrick had made out that Mademoiselle Colbert was in her room and could not come out to the phone. Maids were cleaning the chateau for the return of the count and his wife in early September. Did the colonel wish him to convey his message? Derrick had shouted instructions that she was to remain at the chateau until a U.S. Army vehicle arrived to fetch her. He hung up deeply disappointed. The call would have been the last time he would hear Victoria's voice. He'd also had possibly good news to tell her, but the line had gone dead before he could relate it. Her friend, Mademoiselle Dufor, was not at Dachau. At least, her name was not on the camp's roll. According to the Drancy commandant, she had been deported in June. There was hope that the woman had managed to escape.

His eye on his aide, Derrick felt a swell of affection for the man who had served him loyally for six years. He had offered him a Montecristo, but Karl neither smoked or drank. He and the sergeant were soon to part. At best, Derrick believed he could talk the arresting authorities into allowing him to take off for his home in Germany to wait out the war like many other German soldiers who had already decamped. At worst, he could get them to agree to send his aide to an American prisoner of war camp until the war was over, which he expected to be in less than a year. He hoped that Karl would not think him a traitor. For his aide's sake, he had left him in the dark about his activities throughout their association. Derrick thought that Karl might secretly share some of his views of the Third Reich and, like him, felt as betrayed by its leader as did the superior officer he had served. In any event, Derrick would miss him and remember him as a superb soldier and man of honor.

He started when he heard the knock on the door.

"Shall I get it, Mein Colonel?"

"No, Karl. I will answer," Derrick said.

As long as he lived, Maurice Corbett would never forget the look on Colonel Derrick Albrecht's face at the appearance of the two French policemen he never thought to see again.

Cool as a lettuce leaf, the colonel pulled in a draught from his cigar, its smoke rich and fragrant, and expelled it through his finely shaped nostrils before he spoke. "Please come in," he said in perfect French. "You must forgive my surprise. I was expecting…other visitors."

"We are surprised to see you as well, Colonel. We would have thought you'd have been gone long ago with your fellow comrades."

"I had obligations that induced me to stay."

"Like destroying sensitive files of your organization's work here in Paris?"

"Something like that. Why are you here, Detective? I've answered all your questions to the best of my ability, and I am pressed for time."

"This won't take long." Maurice glanced at the colonel's aide, who had ceased packing and was staring at him in stilled surprise. "You are Sergeant Karl Brunner, I believe?"

"That is correct."

Maurice drew himself officially erect. "Colonel Derrick Albrecht and Sergeant Karl Brunner, we have come to arrest you for the homicide of Beaumont Fournier. You have the right to an attorney, to notify a relative and employer—"

The colonel waved away the charge with his cigar. "Don't be absurd. By what evidence?"

"A witness has come forward who will testify to your and your aide's poisoning of the victim, and we will call others who saw Monsieur Fournier in your office on the day of his murder, when you told us that he did not appear."

Derrick stubbed out his cigar. "Well, Detective, I am afraid I have to disappoint you, but representatives of the United States Army will be here at any moment to collect me for interrogation, and I am afraid their custody takes priority over yours."

"I am afraid I have to disappoint *you*, Colonel," Maurice said, and handed him the arrest warrant. "It is a matter of international law that when a crime is committed against a country's private citizen by a member of an invading army not in accordance with his military duty or orders, that country's jurisdiction takes precedence over any other consideration. The information is there in the warrant. Therefore, we must ask you gentlemen to come with us. I have policemen posted outside your door if you should decide to make this difficult."

Maurice had the strangely doubtful pleasure of seeing the SS colonel's handsome face lose a degree of color. No matter his part in the despicable organization in which he had served, something about the man impressed the hell out of him, which could not be said of his view of the author Beaumont Fournier.

"That won't be necessary, Inspector," Derrick said,

buttoning his jacket and straightening his tie, "but I have a very important request that I had intended to make of the American authorities, who are on their way now. It is a matter of freeing a young woman, a United States citizen and a member of the American OSS, from a chateau in the countryside. She has been confined there since June eleventh. And you are making a mistake in arresting Sergeant Brunner. Whatever you feel you can prove against me, he had no hand in it. Though I found the sergeant an exemplary aide in military matters these many years, I have never involved him in my private affairs, alleged or otherwise."

The aide uttered a startled grunt, whether at the news of the American citizen at the chateau or the colonel's defense of him, Maurice could not tell, perhaps both. "That remains to be reviewed, Colonel," Maurice said. "Sergeant Brunner is to come with us, and I assume you are speaking of Mademoiselle Veronique Colbert."

"The very one."

"I am sure we can take care of that matter from our headquarters as expediently as possible." He opened the door to admit the men waiting in the hall. "Gentlemen, if you please," he said, nodding toward Derrick and Karl.

CHAPTER NINETY-TWO

Victoria had become almost frantic. It was now August 30, six days since Derrick had left a message with Alois instructing her to remain at the chateau until a U.S. Army vehicle arrived to take delivery of her. Victoria had assumed it would come within days of the call. She had packed a few essentials and paced around the chateau, constantly gazing through its front windows expecting to see her olive-drab transport with a five-pointed white star on the side wheel into the car park. It had not come.

And now the count and his family were due back to the chateau in two days' time. They did not know that she was here, using their home as a hide-out. Even if they were willing to allow her to stay, what then? She could not remain indefinitely, and it would be unsafe for her to try to make it out of the city on her own. Since the evening of August 21, the Resistance radio station in Paris had been back on the air, and daily came news of the brutal public treatment and humiliation meted out to women accused of collaborating with the Germans. Reports of beatings and head shavings, even executions, and of women being driven naked through the streets were a common occurrence. One woman had been recognized and yanked out of a car in a funeral procession and made to lie in the gutter while a crowd threw sewage and urinated upon her. Derrick had warned her of this very retribution and wouldn't have left her high and dry. She was certain of that, but what had happened to interfere with his plan for her? Had the liberating forces arrested him before he could set it in motion?

Her whole being had gone numb at the possibility. Alois, her only human contact beyond Derrick since June 11, had painted a clear picture of what the German occupiers of his country, especially the officers of the SS and Gestapo, could expect if they were captured by the rescuing authorities. To her question of what would happen to Derrick should he fall into their hands, Alois had replied, "There will be a military trial when the war is over. If conducted by the French and he's found guilty of the offenses against the French people, he will be guillotined. If by the Allied liberators, hanged."

Victoria had listened in shock. Guillotined? Hanged? Derrick Albrecht was guilty of offenses against the French people, certainly, but at great risk of his own life, he had also saved the lives of countless others, including her and her fellow dragonflies. He did not deserve to die in such a way. "Are French military courts ever open to hearing pleas of mercy for the condemned?" she'd asked.

"If there is reason for clemency, *oui*, but—" Alois shrugged and showed his palms "—they rarely listen. On the other hand, American and British courts are reputed to be more tolerant."

Victoria trusted the old wizened servant to know what he was talking about. He was an astonishing fount of information, a consolation and a lifeline to her during her months of confinement. Self-taught despite his servant status, the man would have done honor to any number of disciplines taught in the Sorbonne. There was also the surprise that Alois possessed a hidden radio tuned to the BBC around which they gathered nightly for news of the war. She'd sought him out in the kitchen one morning when the walls had begun to close in. She'd wanted to ask him about the history of the chateau and the count and his family. Before long, they were breakfasting together every morning and meeting for a glass of wine in the evening. She helped him cook their meals, learning his culinary secrets, and worked with him in the garden.

Whichever military court tried Derrick, Victoria vowed that she would return to France in Derrick's defense. She'd get the boys to speak for him and Major Renault to present intelligence documents as proof of his aid to the OSS. She'd place ads in newspapers pleading with those whose escapes he'd arranged to come forward and testify on his behalf, even enlist her family's own battery of lawyers to represent him if need be. She could not—*would* not—let him die. Imprisonment, yes, but not death.

Late that afternoon, she peeked out a front window at the crunch of auto tires turning into the car park and immediately took off to her room. Minutes later, she was called out of hiding at Alois's announcement that the French policeman who had called at the chateau was there to see her and insisted on speaking with her. "A matter of great importance," he said.

Victoria answered the summons apprehensively. The detective with the apologetic air and sharp eyes who had visited her at L'Ecole d'Escrime Français was standing as if he hadn't time for a visit when she joined him in the drawing room. "Ah, Mademoiselle Colbert, a pleasure to see you again," he said.

"I'm not sure I can return the sentiment, Detective. Why are you here?"

"I come at the behest of SS Colonel Derrick Albrecht," he said. "He has asked that the Paris police provide an escort to see you safely delivered into the military care of your countrymen. You are an American, I believe. The duke has told us all about you."

"*You* have come? But...I don't understand. He told me to expect a United States military escort."

"There was a change of plans. I apologize for the length of time required to make arrangements for your departure from my country, but—" a sigh and roll of eyes "—I had to consult my superior, who had to take the matter to General Leclerc, who had to consult with the American authorities before I was given permission to carry out the duke's request. I am now authorized to see you to an airfield where a military aircraft waits to fly you to America."

"But I still don't understand. I assumed Colonel Albrecht had contacted the American military for my extraction. How did the French national police become involved?"

"Colonel Albrecht is now in the custody of the Prefecture of the Police. I was the arresting officer."

Victoria thought she had misheard him—she *wanted* to have misheard him. Derrick in the custody of the French police, not the liberating or American military authorities, and arrested by this man? That could mean only one thing. *Oh God.* She felt faint suddenly. "Colonel Albrecht arrested by the French police? Whatever for? On what charge?"

"For the murder of a French citizen, Monsieur Beaumont Fournier."

Before Victoria could ask any more questions, he said, "I am sorry, mademoiselle, but we must leave now for your plane."

On the drive in an official car of the Prefecture of Police, she asked in despair, "Why did he do it? What was his motive?"

"To protect you, Mademoiselle Colbert. Monsieur Fournier meant to turn you over to the Gestapo—an abomination, the colonel said, that he could not allow. I must say that I quite understand his motivation, even if I do not approve of his solution to the problem."

Dumbly, feeling sick, Victoria asked, "What will happen to him?"

"He will be tried for homicide."

"And if found guilty?"

"French courts are not disposed to be merciful in the case of willful murder of one of their own, especially if the accused is a member of the German Schutzstaffel. However, the duke comes from an important noble family in Germany with many powerful connections among the French elite, so their influence may carry some sway in his punishment."

"I must see him," Victoria declared.

"I am afraid that is impossible."

"Why? You are in charge."

"Because Colonel Albrecht does not wish to see you. Your appearance in Paris…It would put you in grave danger. He was quite adamant about it, and in any case, time does not permit a visit to the prefecture. I am sorry, mademoiselle, but we must make haste. I was made to understand the plane is on a tight flight plan."

At the airfield in the shadow of the huge U.S. Army transport plane's wing, Maurice handed Victoria a note as she prepared to board. "From Colonel Albrecht," he said. "I was instructed to give it to you at the plane shortly before you were up and away. *Au revoir*, Mademoiselle Veronique Colbert. Safe trip home."

From her window, Victoria watched the detective

brave the whip of the C-47's takeoff, hat removed, to see her on her way before he turned to walk back to the police car. Airborne, Victoria tore open the envelope. "Remember your promise to me. Yours always, Derrick Albrecht."

CHAPTER NINETY-THREE

One by one, the lives of Dragonfly fell into place while the war raged on in Europe. All but Victoria, whose return to the United States had not been documented, were issued letters bearing the seal of the U.S. State Department to present to employers to explain the applicant's missing two years as "time served in the national interest of the country."

Bucky went to work for a civil engineering firm in Tulsa, Oklahoma, an hour-and-a-half drive from his hometown. At a stopover on his return home from France, he had telephoned his parents to alert them that he was on the way, and his father's bellow of joy and his mother's cry of "*Oh Dieu merci!*" were ringing in his ear all the way to Oklahoma City. They were at the station when the Santa Fe steamed in, looking as if they'd been standing on the platform all night in case they would miss it.

Three days later, helping Wilhelm down, Brad stepped onto the platform of the Glenwood Springs railroad station. "Is this the village where you live?" Wilhelm asked in a wondering voice and held Brad's hand tighter.

"No, buddy," Brad said in German. "Remember that I told you that I live in Meeker, an hour away." He scanned the platform for his family, disturbed and not a little disappointed at the lack of a reception committee. From Washington, D.C., he'd telephoned his home number to find it had been disconnected. He realized that the number had probably changed since his family had moved into the new house, but the operator had told him that none was listed for Jared Cramer and explained that phone hookups for new residences took weeks, if not months, to be installed because of technician and material shortages. Brad had then placed a call to the lumberyard and asked to speak to Jared.

"He's not here," said a young woman whose voice Brad did not recognize.

Could he leave a message? Brad had asked.

"Sure, wait till I find a pen. There's one around here somewhere."

Where in the world had Jared dug her up? Brad wondered. A secretary without a pen handy? Had he interrupted her painting her nails? "Okay, I got one," she'd said. "What's the message?"

Brad had explained who he was and gave her the approximate time of his arrival in Glenwood Springs and for his family to expect a guest as well.

"Okay, got it," the girl said and hung up.

Apparently the girl hadn't got it, or hadn't bothered to give it to Jared, Brad thought irritably. *Damn her!* Now they'd have to find a ride into Meeker with no idea of the address of the new house. He'd have to settle for being dropped off at the lumberyard. Some homecoming! Dusk had fallen along with the temperature. They were hungry and thirsty, and Wilhelm was shivering in his thin jacket.

Brad picked him up and wrapped him in his arms. The stationmaster obliged his request for a ride by conscripting his nephew to take him to Cramer's Lumber Yard.

"Looks like nobody's here," Brad said as they climbed out into an eerily quiet yard loaded with bundles of cut and processed timber. Where was everybody? It was a weekday, but not a soul was about. Even the saws were silent, and the office building looked deserted, not a light burning through the windows.

Wilhelm was shivering again, but not only from the cold. "Come on, Wilhelm," Brad said, starting toward the office building. "Let's go see what's going on."

He found the door unlocked and pushed it open. Immediately the room was flooded with light, and waves of warmth and the aroma of coffee and savory-smelling food rolled out to greet them as a chorus of "Welcome home, Brad and Wilhelm!" rang out. Brad stood dumbfounded until his mother and sister, Bobby and Margie, and Jared Cramer threw arms around him and Wilhelm, and the entire lumberyard crew surged forth to hug them. Only the girl that Brad guessed had taken his telephone message, pretty as a mountain peony, as it turned out, remained under the large WELCOME HOME banner, but her smile told Brad that her dumb-secretary act had been part of the conspiracy to spring the surprise on him.

Later, when the ballyhoo was all over, his mother explained that a State Department official had told her to expect him and Wilhelm at any time, so she'd had Laura, Jared's new secretary, alert them when he telephoned because it made sense that he'd contact the yard.

Brad could not have had a more moving homecoming. His family, with Jared now at the head of it, had kept a place waiting for him in the spacious new house. They'd set aside a bedroom for him, incorporating his things from the old house into the new furnishings. True Blue was in the garage, some of its parts and all its wheels replaced with new ones. A chair in which no one had ever sat was reserved for him at the kitchen table.

His heart ached at some of the differences time had wrought, but it soared for his family's newfound peace and security. A wedding portrait of his mother and Jared now occupied the position on the fireplace mantel where once his father's had been displayed in his former home. He would never see again the Beata of the picture he had carried in his wallet and for whom big brother, forgetting that little sisters grow up, had brought home French dolls for her and Margie. She had long passed the stage of play house and doll buggies.

Bobby had graduated from high school and now at eighteen was a man full grown, but Brad was saddened at the loss of the scrappy kid he'd left behind. He had enrolled in the Colorado School of Mines in Golden, where he planned to study mechanical engineering. His bags were packed almost before Brad could unpack his. "I want to design power-producing things," he said.

Jared…In Brad's absence he'd taken over his family, which was okay with Brad, but he was left with the feeling that he wasn't needed anymore except by Wilhelm, but his mother within minutes had taken charge of him, too. It had been the most moving moment of all when, in the bedlam of his homecoming, she had knelt before Wilhelm, the little boy pulling back against Brad's legs, and put her hands on his shoulders. Quiet fell, and his mother said softly in German, "Welcome to my heart, Wilhelm," and the little boy, as if in recognition of a haven he'd been seeking for a long time, had simply slipped his arms around Joanna Bukowski Hudson Cramer's neck and let her take him into her embrace.

So Brad had thought that after a good family visit, he'd move on, get a job on a fishing boat somewhere, until Jared had offered him a job he couldn't refuse. "I'm thinking of cutting my hours to spend more time with your mother and the family, something

I've waited to do until you came home," he said. "I'd like you to help me run the company, Brad, and when I retire, take over the business entirely if you're willing."

Brad had been willing.

CHAPTER NINETY-FOUR

Bridgette came home to a yard of groomed green grass and flower beds brimming with neatly contained peonies and dahlias, her grandmother's prized rose trellises pruned, and the bushes trimmed. She had dreaded the appearance of the lawn after two years' absence. *Gladys!* she thought.

In the house, everything was in perfect order as well: sheets on the bed, towels in the bathroom, food essentials in the refrigerator and pantry, utilities working. Even the telephone had been reconnected. Bridgette set down her luggage and picked up the receiver. She was grateful and moved, but sadly, she and Gladys could never be best friends again.

"Gladys isn't here," Mrs. Bradbury said. "It's been a while since she's been home."

"Oh?" Bridgette said, surprised. "She's living in

Detroit, then? She must have taken the elementary teaching job there?"

"No, she lives in Fort Worth, Texas, home base for American Airlines. Our Gladys is now a stewardess for the company, would you believe? Right after...she left college, she decided to forgo teaching and try her wings at something else, literally." Mrs. Bradbury laughed. "She's been with them for two years now."

Dumbfounded—Gladys, an American Airlines stewardess?—Bridgette asked, "But...who, then, is responsible for taking care of my grandmother's house while I've been gone?"

"Oh, that was me. I just couldn't bear to see Angelique's immaculate little house at the mercy of rodents and bugs after you left, so I hired a yard man and a cleaning service to keep things up as she would have wanted. When I learned from the manager of Traverse City Light and Power Company that you were expected, I got everybody in gear to make sure all the power was on and things were ready for your return."

"That was extremely thoughtful of you, Mrs. Bradbury, but you must let me pay you for those services."

"No, Bridgette," Mrs. Bradbury declined gently. "It was the least my family could do after...what happened, but more than that, because of it, our daughter finally, of her own volition, cut the umbilical cord and discovered life outside the womb. She said it was what you'd want her to do, and that it was her only way to make up to you for what she had done. So now for the first time in her life, because of you, my daughter is independent, confident, truly happy, and utterly thrilled with herself."

"Mrs. Bradbury, I don't know what to say..."

"It's not necessary for you to say anything, dear. Welcome home, for however long that will be. I will tell Gladys that you called."

Within a week of returning to the little house on Elm Street, Bridgette contacted the head of the design department at Stephens College to inquire of openings for designers in the fashion industry. Less than forty-eight hours later, she received a call from Edith Head at Paramount Studios, inviting her to come to California for an interview. She took the first flight out of Detroit to Los Angeles the next morning, met the famous costume designer that afternoon, and by cocktail time she had signed a probationary employment contract with the studio.

Preferring to withdraw from the maddening crowds in New York, Victoria took a job as a French translator for a small publishing company in Toronto, Ontario, with access to a private plane and pilot that allowed her to fly to Williamsburg to spend weekends with her father and ailing mother. In Austin, Texas, Chris settled down into an academic routine at the University of Texas, became the secret heart swoon of the coeds, and spent most evenings running track.

But their days were not without moments of sudden pause in their activities that caught the attention of their loved ones and associates. Over his drafting table, Bucky would sometimes look up from his drawings in still and deep reflection unrelated to his work, and Bridgette would occasionally stop in midconversation as if interrupted by a voice in her head. "What are you thinking?" the pretty company secretary would ask Brad on their dates when he seemed far away, and he would reply: "Not thinking, remembering." Chris, poetry in motion on his runs, was noted to slow his pace as if stopped by an invisible force on the track, and from time to time, Victoria was noticed at her desk with her head cocked in the listening mode of someone engaged in dialogue with a visitor that only she could hear.

In mid-August of the year of their return, Bucky came home from Tulsa to find his mother in his room. He had not yet become acclimated to the city, nor had he developed an attachment to his apartment. He preferred to spend his weekends in his parents' company and the serenity and quiet of their home in Oklahoma City.

His mother turned to him, tears in her eyes. "Where did you get these?" she asked, holding up his father's gold cadet epaulets, which she had discovered when placing folded laundry in his drawer. Bucky had left the shoulder pieces there for safekeeping, his most precious possession, thinking that his apartment house was vulnerable to robberies. His American father was not home.

When Bucky did not answer, his mother said, "You know, don't you?"

"Yes, ma'am. I have for some time."

"How did you find out?"

Bucky told her.

"And you went to France to find him, didn't you? That's where you've been?"

"Yes, ma'am," Bucky said.

His mother pressed the epaulets to her heart. "How did you come by these, *mon fils*?"

"He gave them to me for Christmas."

"Then you found him?"

"Yes, ma'am, I found him."

"You must tell me everything, *mon fils*."

Bucky hesitated, but only for the seconds required to silence the reminder of the Official Secrets Service Act in his head. What could it possibly matter now? "*Oui, Mère,*" Bucky said.

One weekend later, from the nest of his armchair where he read the newspaper after dinner every night and offered opinions of its contents to his wife and son, Horace Barton commented, "Bad business over there in France. They found the tortured body of that famous French Resistance leader called the Black Ghost that makes the news over here ever so often." An August moon shone through the living room window sheers whose draperies had not been drawn for the night. *The Bell Telephone Hour* was playing on the radio, and under the lamplight Bucky sat reading and Monique embroidering a pocket for an apron held tautly in place on a tambour hoop.

"I guess the Nazi bastards finally caught him," Horace continued, "but it's believed he never gave up a word of information. For a Frenchie, he must have been one hell of a man. Says here that he came from wealth and was a marshal in the French military, but he tossed it all to go live in the mountains as a chieftain of a guerilla band to fight the Krauts. Did you ever know or hear of him, Monique?" Horace glanced over at his wife. "Name's Nicholas Cravois."

Monique seemed to be having difficulty drawing her needle through the fabric and hadn't been listening. Neither had his son heard a word. He was stroking his forehead in that way he had when concentrating hard on a book and had shut out the world. They rarely paid his views on the news front much mind, but that was all right with him. Horace took satisfaction in just having his family within sound of his voice in the evening, the radio playing softly, the room cozy and comfy. No matter what happened in the world, all was right in his.

In September, Victoria was asked to participate in a city fencing tournament. Suited in her whites, protective mask under her arm, foil in hand, she approached the mat at her turn of play and after the salutes, took her position on the en garde line. Suddenly a flood of memories swept over her, stunning her, and the foil's grip burned like fire in her hand. She dropped the blade, tore off her mask, and to the astonishment of her opponent and spectators, walked off the mat to the dressing room and was never known to pick up a fencing sword again.

CHAPTER NINETY-FIVE

That fall, Chris found Ernst Drechsler where he expected. "Ernst wanders off sometimes, and I don't know where he goes, but he always comes back," his wife had told Chris that morning when he went around to call for the first time since he'd been back in Texas. "I can't tell you how long he'll be gone, or I'd have you come in and wait. Would you like to come in anyway, Christoph? I have some brownies in the oven just about ready to come out."

"Another day, Mrs. Drechsler, when I have more time," Chris said. "Right now I'd just like to say hello to your husband before I drive back to Austin. I think I know where to find him."

Mrs. Drechsler, like everybody else in town, just wanted to pump Chris about where he'd been, what he'd been doing the past two years without once showing his face in New Braunfels or contacting his parents. The Brandts' explanation that he was off on some secret mission for the State Department was generally believed and accepted, but now that Chris was back home, confirmation of his activities would have been appreciated. It had not been forthcoming, so he was somewhat of a mystery man around town.

His homecoming had been less than what Chris had expected. His mother resented his "abandonment" of them bitterly, and his father, to appease his wife, took her side. Were telephone calls or letters too much for parents to ask of the son and only child they had nurtured and raised? It would have been one thing if he'd been over there in the line of fire, but whatever his job was for the State Department did not preclude him from contacting his family from time to time to save them the agony of worry. The misery that he had put them through for two years could hardly be forgiven.

Chris had been hurt and disappointed, the reason that he had moved quickly back to Austin and enrolled in the University of Texas to pursue his doctorate in education. He had the money for it without having to work, since two years' worth of uncollected wages were waiting for him in his bank account when he was discharged from the OSS. His parents had not approved of that decision, either. In the German manual of child rearing, deviation from parents' expectations was seen as a betrayal that carried a lasting sting, and things would never be right between them again. Chris couldn't help but compare them to Ernst Drechsler and his wife, who would have accepted Dirk back no matter under what black cloud.

Up until now, Chris had avoided the Drechslers, but he'd been back for more than three months, and it was time to make contact. He was worried about Mr. Drechsler. "Not the same since Dirk left" was the common comment Chris heard when he asked about him, and Chris's conscience prodded him to seek him out before he left New Braunfels with no plans to return anytime soon.

As Chris had expected, he found the older man fishing from his folding chair on the site of the Guadalupe River where Chris had spent most of his summer days with him and Dirk while he was growing up. His old fisherman's hat with its fly trophies pinned around the crown made him easy to spot. His fishing line hung limply in the water, and he was staring off into space as if the rod in his hand had been forgotten. Chris approached him quietly to avoid startling him.

"Mr. Drechsler?" he said softly.

"Ah, is that you, Christoph?" Ernst asked without looking around.

"Yes sir. Mind if I sit with you?"

"Be a pleasure," he said and reached into his pocket. "There's an extra chair in the car trunk," he said, handing a key over his shoulder. Chris took it and said he wouldn't be a minute. At the car parked under the same trees as always, he paused at taking out the extra foldup chair. *For Dirk?* he wondered.

"Not much action today," the older man said when Chris joined him.

"I can see that," Chris said. "How have you been getting on, Mr. Drechsler?"

"Oh, about the same as always since Dirk has been gone. Just waiting for the war to be over and my boy to come home. I imagine he's ready now and has been for a long time. I'm sure he's realized he made a mistake, but we'll just put it behind us and go on like nothing ever happened. We'll be moving once he's home and that will help."

"Oh? Where to?" Chris asked, his heart holding.

"We visited Oregon a while back, my wife and I, and we really like it. It reminded us of Germany—lots of forests and mountains and lakes, pretty farms.

Good fishing there. A change of scene where nobody knows us will do us all good."

"Have you... done anything about it? Bought some property there?" Chris asked.

"No. We'll have to see what Dirk thinks about it."

"That's good," Chris said. "Very wise."

"I think so." Ernst cast the line farther upstream. "Of course, if he doesn't come home, we'll stay here where the memories are... where you are, Christoph."

Chris swallowed down the balloon of emotion in his throat. Dirk was never coming home. That had been verified by Lodestar, but Chris would never—could never—reveal that reality to Dirk's mother and father. It was one of the many wounds of war he'd have to live with—the conflict between destroying a father and mother's hope for their son's return or preserving their faith that someday he would walk through the door.

"Tell you what, Mr. Drechsler," he said. "Let's you and me set a time to meet on the first Saturday of every month at this exact spot to do a little fishing during the season. What do you say?"

"I would say that would be most generous of your time, Christoph. I'd like that very much."

"All right then, it's a deal." They shook hands. "Now let's get you home. There's nothing biting today, and your wife told me she's got brownies coming out of the oven."

"No fish biting today, but there's always a chance they'll run tomorrow, right, Christoph?"

"Right, Mr. Drechsler."

CHAPTER NINETY-SIX

Nineteen forty-five began for Americans with the prediction that the war would be over by spring. In their far-apart locales, the team of Dragonfly marked September 23 on their new calendars with eager anticipation and prepared for their reunion in nine months' time. By February, Bridgette had reserved a hotel room near Bryant Park, close to the New York Public Library, and Victoria had made arrangements with a caterer to provide food and drinks for the group in her uncle's Fifth Avenue apartment the evening of the reunion. In March, Bucky booked his airline flight to New York City, and Brad asked Jared for time off. Both requests resulted in a surprise for Bucky and a shock for Brad.

"Tell me again why you are going to New York City," Horace asked Bucky.

"To visit friends, Dad," Bucky said, not for the first time. When he had first informed his parents that he'd be away the weekend of September 23, his American father had assumed that his trip to New York City pertained to business. Further persistent questioning revealed that no, he was going to meet some people for personal pleasure.

"Personal, huh? Have your mother and me ever met these friends you are meeting for personal pleasure?"

"No, Dad."

"Would we recognize their names?"

"No sir."

"Then…how do you know them?"

A look from his wife cut off the inquisition. It was another one of those times when his wife's eye and his son's tone warned him not to ask too many questions. Horace felt left out. They knew something that they'd chosen not to share with him, but he took no offense. The bottom line was that they had excluded him to protect him. He felt it down deep, just as he'd become convinced that his boy had been involved in something more dangerous during the war than sitting it out for two years behind an engineering drafting board in a secret government facility. His mother had intuitively known it when he left for Washington in 1942, supported by the fact that they didn't hear from him but once in all the time he was away. What kind of peacetime job would keep a man from his family that long? But now, his wife was working out of more than her intuition. She knew something that her husband was not privileged to know.

But he didn't need to know. He'd served in war, by God, and he knew that the bravest men didn't always wear uniforms. The look he sometimes glimpsed in his son's eyes was the same hollow gaze of war veterans everywhere, so it was time to let Bucky—Sam, his son—know that he knew.

From his reading armchair, he glanced at his wife embroidering in hers. "Monique, honey," he said, "could you excuse us men for a while?"

Monique cast a startled look at her husband. Never had he asked her to leave the room for a private conversation with her son, and he had not said *please*. She was expected to go. "Of course," she said.

When she'd gone, Horace looked at Bucky staring back at him, puzzled. "Sir?" he said.

"I don't know what this trip is all about, son. All I know is that you have my blessing and that you go knowing how very, very proud I am of you. I ask your forgiveness if I've given you reason to think otherwise. No father in the world could be more proud of his son. You understand what I am saying?"

"Yes, Dad, I do."

"Well now, that all ironed out, let's call your mother back in."

Joanna said to Brad, "You must have some new clothes for your trip to New York City, *Sohn*. We can't have you looking like a ragamuffin among these people you're going to meet."

Brad had been unable to come up with a plausible excuse for going to New York City. When he asked Jared for time off, he'd said that he couldn't give him a specific reason but to trust him that it was important. His mother's concern about his clothes was just another way of worming the information out of him. "It's okay, *Mutter*. The guys I'm going to meet don't dress well."

Joanna's eyebrow shot up. "Then one of them must be Alistair Renault."

His eyes betrayed him. He was never good at evading the truth. "I thought so," Joanna said, turning away. "As if it wasn't enough what that man stole from me, he had to take my son from me for two years of my life. Now what does he want? You must tell me."

Surprised, Brad said, "What...did he steal from you?"

"My heart. He stole my heart, *Sohn*, and I never got it entirely back. He never knew."

"What? But I thought that you and *Vater*..."

Joanna turned to him. "No, your father was my second love...and choice. Again, Alistair never knew, and neither did your father."

Brad didn't know that he wanted to hear these revelations this late. Was his mother telling him that...His face must have flamed with his shocking thought, for she patted his cheek. "No, *Sohn*, it is not what you are thinking. Look at your father's picture. You two could have been bookends."

"Then why are you telling me this?" Brad demanded.

"So that you will understand why I do not want him back in my life, my home, my family. My life is...content, and I don't want him—" she struggled for an American word "—*messing* it up. He is not to come here anymore while I am here, understood?"

Brad stared into her eyes. He couldn't believe it. My God, after all these years and two men that she loved and who loved her, the flame still burned in the heart of Joanna Bukowski Hudson Cramer for the man in brown, and Alistair Renault, still carrying the torch for his mother, never knew.

Many frustrating attempts and jumps through numerous bureaucratic hoops had failed to put Bridgette in contact with Major Alistair Renault at OSS headquarters in Washington before it was abolished in October 1945. The telephone number on the organization's initial recruitment letter had become invalid. Desk clerks she spoke to referred her to other departments who referred her back to the desk of her original inquiry. She thought that if she heard the excuses *classified* and *on behalf of the national interest* to deny her access to her former case officer one more time, she would leap through the telephone line and strangle the person at the other end. She was now convinced that Major Renault had never been informed of her release from Drancy. He would have gotten in touch with her otherwise. Her telephone number in Traverse City had been disconnected after her house was put up for sale and sold within a week, but she'd left forwarding information to her new address in Los Angeles, and the major had access to the OSS's endless resources to track down missing persons.

She would never forgive the case officer in Bern for failing to notify the major that she was still alive. Before being airlifted to Milton Hall, protocol demanded that Bridgette meet for an informal and unnecessary debriefing with the major's replacement, only to find that he'd been called out on an emergency. His fill-in did not recognize the name Labrador or Dragonfly. The station was in a state of high anxiety and turmoil over incoming intel of the betrayal of a legendary and important Maquis leader to the Gestapo by a member of his own guerilla band. The case officer had had little time for her, but he thanked her for her work and sacrifice and said he would let his chief know that she'd stopped by. Before being pushed out the door, Bridgette had managed to stress the point that Major Renault would want to know that she'd survived Drancy, but apparently it had fallen on deaf ears.

Victoria likewise experienced the same sense of urgency to inform her case officer that she was alive and well, at least in body if not in spirit, but she presumed he was still in France and she would have to wait until the reunion to present herself in the walking flesh. After Labrador failed to appear for the meeting with Derrick, there had been no way for Victoria to inform the major of the ruse of the firing squad. As far as he and the boys knew, she was buried somewhere in France. Victoria hoped that none of them had weak hearts when she strolled into the Rose Main Reading Room of the New York Public Library, alive and well.

Alistair, too, marked his calendar. By his calculation of the Allies' progress in Europe and the Pacific, the September date Dragonfly had set aside for their reunion would occur this year. He planned to keep it whether the surviving members did or not. Men who were tighter than knitting balls in the thick of battle, once they were out of it and the smoke cleared, their most ardent intentions could unravel in the peace and quiet of home. He didn't expect it with the three remaining men of Dragonfly, but it might happen. He would see.

Meanwhile, in his new job he was engaged in contending with the challenges the Soviet Union was expected to present to America and its democratic allies after the war was won in Europe. He currently occupied a different desk in a different office under a different title—all very secret stuff, since his boss was virtually alone in anticipating the threat that the pathologically suspicious-minded Joseph Stalin posed to the free world.

But the war in Europe still lingered tenaciously on, and in early spring, Alistair received a report that made him blanch. In the early hours of April 9, Admiral Wilhelm Canaris, sentenced to death for masterminding a failed 1944 assassination plot against Hitler, along with his protégé, Major General Konrad March, who allegedly participated, were marched naked to the gallows at Flossenbürg concentration camp. The brutal details of their hanging by piano wire were sure to be reported by the press, and before Brad could read them, Alistair called him at Cramer's Lumber Yard in Meeker, Colorado, hoping to find him there rather than at home. He was in luck. Alistair had not wanted to risk hearing Joanna's voice.

That evening, Brad invited Wilhelm for a walk after supper. They returned an hour later, Wilhelm with swollen red eyes. After Brad had seen the boy to bed, the family gathered around. "What happened?" Joanna asked.

"The Nazis hanged his father."

After their expected reactions to the news, Bobby, home from college for the weekend, asked, "Does that mean we get to keep him?"

Brad looked at him with a tenderness so great that

he could hardly speak. “Yes,” he said. “We get to keep him.”

Two weeks later, on April 23, the Flossenbürg concentration camp was liberated by American troops, and on May 8, 1945, the Second World War ended in Europe.

CHAPTER NINETY-SEVEN

September 23, 1945, fell on Sunday. At two o'clock that afternoon, quiet tears streaming down her face, Victoria sat by her mother's hospital bed and held her hand as her life slowly ebbed away. Her father and brother stood behind her, each with a consoling hand on her shoulders, surprised at the emotional intensity of her grief. The death was not unexpected, and her family had said their good-byes to wife and mother some time ago. Elizabeth Grayson had suffered from heart problems for years, coupled by a quick and devastating onset of Alzheimer's disease detected shortly after Victoria went away. By the time she came home, the mother she knew and loved was gone. Her final heart attack had occurred at four o'clock that morning.

Her brother bent to her ear. "There are times you just have to release and let go, sis. It's for the best."

Victoria shook her head. "No, not this time," his sister said, her tears shed for those she could not release and let go.

Victoria had been summoned home from her uncle's New York City apartment where she had arrived the day before to finalize plans with the caterer. On the way to the municipal airport, she had the taxi drive her to the New York Public Library before it opened to drop an envelope through the mail chute. It was addressed to Major Alistair Renault with instructions to the librarian that he would be meeting with three male associates at two o'clock in the Rose Main Reading Room. The enclosed letter included her full name, address, and phone number and explained the circumstances of her survival. The taxi driver saw his fare pause with her hand on the mail chute after releasing the letter and bow her head in dejection, or maybe in prayer that it would reach its destination.

The librarian to whom it was handed diligently followed instructions but she saw no man enter the library in a military uniform wearing the rank of major—no serviceman, period. A number of meetings were going on, one a study group of college students, another a congregation of three men she took to be researchers, another a gathering of old codgers who used the library as a hangout, and in a far corner some sort of gleeful reunion consisting of four men, one much older and shabbier dressed than the others, looking nothing like a military officer, and a woman, a very pretty young lady sporting the latest in fashion.

That afternoon before she left for the day, the librarian debated what she should do with the envelope. If it were her, she would want to know that it had not been delivered. She decided to open the envelope with the hope it contained a return address. By the time she finished reading the contents she had lost her breath. What a tragedy that the letter had not been delivered, but at least the sender would know that the New York Public Library had done its duty. She wrote a note expressing as much and enclosed it and the letter into another envelope addressed to the sender and dropped it in the mailbox on her way out.

CHAPTER NINETY-EIGHT

SEPTEMBER 1962

Alistair sat doodling, his thoughts pulled away from the manuscript he'd been working on since reopening Dragonfly's files. He'd decided to write that book after all, as of yet missing a title, but it would come to him. It was a time for deep thinking. In less than two days, he would return to France, his first trip back since leaving for Washington, D.C., in July 1944. He was going into Paris early, staying at a small hotel he'd favored before the occupation when he'd gone to the city to arrange for safe houses and assets and facilitators in preparation for the war to come. On Saturday, September 22, he would join the others in the hotel Bridgette had managed on such short notice to arrange for them in the Latin Quarter. "A quiet, non-touristy place removed from the maddening crowds," she'd told them. They'd have dinner together Saturday night, visit what remained of the mural as a group on Sunday, September 23, and from there go on to La Petite Madeleine to arrive by four o'clock that afternoon. The book and tea shop was still there, open on Sundays and apparently thriving, she reported. She had checked. Whether the original owner was still around, she couldn't say, since the team had never learned his name and Alistair had not given it.

To go to Paris or not to go to Paris had been the topic of conversation a couple of years ago as the date of the twentieth reunion drew closer. Without Liverwort, what was the point? Nobody but the wives of the male members of Dragonfly wanted to go to the restored City of Light, and there were other places closer to home and less expensive where they could include their teenaged children. They'd tabled the decision until the first of the year, when Bridgette suggested they go to a beach resort on Hilton Head Island in South Carolina over Labor Day weekend in lieu of the twenty-third—what did the date matter now, anyway? So plans were formed and reservations made.

What Labrador suggested, all agreed to and willingly, including Alistair. Still no bigger than a minute, but possessing managerial skills sharper than ever, she remained the undisputed leader of the group, taking it upon herself to arrange all their get-togethers and to serve as a source of cool advice the boys still consulted even as they neared middle age. Alistair would have expected their wives to be resentful of their dependence on her, but they adored her, as did their children. She was the one divorced dragonfly in the group with no children of her own, but she basked in her role as aunt to the boys' progeny.

So it was she who had a few days before offered the opinion that they should go to Paris for the reunion after all, "Just in case there was something to John Peterson's story." Even after all these years, Bridgette still held a scrap of hope that the faint diagonal line somebody had drawn too late through the mural's liverwort might have held meaning. If Liverwort were alive, she'd be there, she maintained. She wouldn't have forgotten the rendezvous point, date, and time, and she'd show up at the book and tea shop on September 23, 1962, at four o'clock, no matter what. They could count on it.

If they decided to go, it would be just the four dragonflies and the major, all agreed. The occasion was not to be a family vacation to a city that held so many memories they would each just as soon forget.

Would the Paris of today prove cathartic, a way to shake off the miasma of cobwebs that still clung, or would the visit revive nightmares long chased away by the joys of survival? To prevent the trip from being a total bust should Liverwort—Victoria Grayson—not appear, all but Bridgette would be arriving a few days early, staying in accommodations of their own choosing until they met up at the Hotel La Rose. The others had people they wished to look up from the occupation years who, like Alistair, had left France without arranging a means to stay in touch. For him, it was Henri Burrell, his man in Paris, but Bridgette had learned through Parisian fashion sources that her close contacts—Madame Jeanne Boucher and Sister Mary Frances—had died a number of years ago.

But Alistair had another mission as well. Within three days of contacting his former colleague at CIA headquarters in Langley, he received back a report on John Peterson. The man was deceased, but his common-law wife was still alive. Her name was Raina Desjardins, and she lived in a French village in Normandy called Lion-sur-Mer.

Alistair had done a lot of thinking since reading John Peterson's last chapter of facts or fiction. The doodles on his desk proved it. If the execution had indeed been a ruse designed to fool the SS, the only person in command who could have pulled it off was the head of the counterintelligence division of the SD, none other than the notorious Colonel Derrick Albrecht. Had he fallen for Victoria Grayson and orchestrated her mock death to save her life? The world would never know. John Peterson had not mentioned the name of her savior in the book, and Colonel Derrick Albrecht had been tried in a French court for the murder of France's contender for the Nobel Prize for Literature and executed by guillotine in late 1945.

Over their rods and reels and fishing lines cast into the White River, Bucky and Chris and Brad had met to discuss the validity of John Peterson's claim and to consider Bridgette's suggestion that they go to Paris. With Alistair, they routinely got together for a weekend in Meeker during trout season, the date marked on the calendar months beforehand, but this meeting was slipped in on a moment's notice because Bridgette had to know their decision to make the appropriate reservations. Alistair, his lungs no longer able to abide the high altitudes, could not be with them. He had been coming to Meeker for the group's get-together since Joanna and Jared, now in their sixties, moved to Florida to relieve their arthritis and left Brad with the company and the new house.

Their wives and children had given them flak for even considering going to Paris, especially without them. The trip would mean canceling the Hilton Head plans, and the time wasn't convenient for the men to be away for so long from their jobs. Brad would have to cancel a trip to East Texas to oversee a crucial logging operation. Bucky was working under a deadline for an engineering project that if successful would mean a bulge in his company Christmas stocking, and Chris had appointments with master's degree candidates for whom a delay in discussing their thesis topics would sorely affect the completion of their graduate work.

In other words, a lot of people were going to be pissed if they went to Paris. Were the sacrifices worth it on the off chance that a woman they had not seen for eighteen years, who was most likely dead, would keep an appointment made twenty years ago? After all this time, would she remember it—or them, for that matter—even though her image was as indelibly imprinted in their memories as a carving on stone?

At the first reunion, the major had filled them in about Victoria Grayson and how she'd come to make the acquaintance of the man who'd ordered her execution, SS Colonel Derrick Albrecht. Yet he had been the man to sign the SS passes to get out of France that they'd held on to, his signature clear. Chris remembered the haughty SS major's about-face when he returned to the train after verifying the name on his pass. It didn't make sense that the SS officer who'd given the order to execute Victoria would sign off on their means to escape from the torture and death he'd dealt her. It was another mystery that supported the ruse theory. "Remember it was Liverwort—Victoria—who suggested the time, date, and place," Chris reminded them.

"She was adamant about it," Bucky said. "Of all of us, she was the one who most wanted to stay in touch."

"Maybe it's just strong wishful thinking on my part because her execution damn well looked real enough, but I have a strong sense that there's some truth behind Peterson's story," Brad said. "He got too many facts right."

"If that SS colonel arranged her escape, wouldn't it make sense that she would be in on the ruse, too?"

"Well, there's only one way to find out," Bucky said. "Let's go ask her."

That decided, the men packed rods and reels and headed home to make their flight plans. Dragonfly had a long-standing meeting in Paris they must attend.

CHAPTER NINETY-NINE

Two days before her departure to Paris, Bridgette put in a telephone call to her best friend. He lived in California, across the country from her home in New York City. She was surprised to reach him so quickly, since he was a senior homicide detective in the Los Angeles Police Department and was often out on assignment. Even at his desk, though, if he was busy, he'd ask the dispatcher to take the party's name and number, and he'd get back to them, but he always answered if the caller was Bridgette.

He snatched up the phone immediately. "Hey, Slugger, great to hear from you. What's up?"

Years ago, Bridgette had ceased to be annoyed by her ex-husband's nickname for her. She understood that then, now, and always, Bridgette Loring was the love of his life. Their marriage had been a mistake, entered into because the sight of Steve Hammett, solid, stable, and steady, a reminder of her unadulterated childhood, walking into her office at Paramount Pictures wearing a chest full of medals and ribbons, a master sergeant's stripes on his sleeve, and the Forty-fifth Infantry Division's gold Thunderbird patch on the left sleeve of his uniform, made her fall in love with him.

"Hey, Slugger, remember me?" he'd said.

She'd whirled around from the cutting table with a cry of disbelief and all she could say was, "Do you still carry my yearbook picture in your wallet?"

"Yes, ma'am," he said. "It's right here." And he'd pulled out the photo, limp and faded, to show her. "Your letter to me, too, written from Stephens College."

She'd asked him how he knew where to find her.

"Your pal Gladys told me when I was in Traverse City on furlough this week. She happened to be home, too. Imagine clingy, insecure, stay-at-home Mommy and Daddy's little girl, Gladys Bradbury, an American Airlines stewardess traveling the world."

"Yes, imagine that," Bridgette said. "And you flew all the way to California to...see me?"

"Who else? I had to make sure that you were okay." His gaze probed her face. "*Are* you okay?"

"I am now," she'd said.

She still possessed the letter Steve had written to her at Stephens College informing her of his coming deployment overseas with the Forty-fifth Infantry Division. His unit had been first on the scene to liberate Dachau concentration camp in April, so when she'd gone against orders and told him about her incarceration in Drancy prison to explain the cause of her nightmares and disinclination for sex, he had understood.

In the end, love was not enough. He had his needs and she had hers. Their worlds collided. Steve loved California, and after his discharge from the army he applied to and was accepted into the LAPD academy. A year into the marriage, Bridgette was offered a job in New York City working for the widely acclaimed fashion designer Norman Norell, the first in his ranks to see the need for a line of clothes created for the petite woman.

They were divorced after eighteen months, parting in sorrow and tearful embraces on the courthouse steps but united in a friendship that had withstood the erosion of time and distance, other loves and losses, and the incompatibility of their interests, tastes, and pursuits.

So her ex-husband and best friend listened with

a heart gone cold when she told him that she was flying to Paris the following day, the city of her nightmares and aborted youth. She had not wanted him to worry when she missed their Sunday phone call that weekend. During their marriage, she'd mentioned her special friend who'd been reported executed. She had been a part of the OSS group in which Bridgette had served but never elaborated on. He and Bridgette had been married when she came back from their reunion in New York City wearing a small dragonfly tattooed over her left breast, right over her heart. "Don't ask," she'd said, and he never had. He figured the tattoo had to do with "the boys" and the old man she called "the major" that she'd gone to meet. Steve approved of their close and abiding ties. Bridgette needed a family.

"So even if she is alive, what if the woman you remember has changed and...she doesn't feel as warmly about you after all these years?" he said.

"Then she won't show up at the café," Bridgette said.

Point taken, Steve thought. She'd always been one step ahead of him in the rationale department, but he still didn't want her to go. "Yeah, but to go back to that city, Bridge...Do you know what you're risking?"

"I do," she said.

"If she's still alive, can't the boys bring back the information that will put you in touch with her again anywhere but Paris?"

"They could do that, yes."

"Then why the hell are you going?"

"To go forward, Steve, sometimes you have to go back," she said.

CHAPTER ONE HUNDRED

Paris in September. Warm days, cool nights, sublime sunny skies. It was the Paris of his mother's time—more modern, of course, but the magic that was the city of Monique Barton's growing-up years had been restored. Bucky especially noticed the flowers. They were back in parks and on street corners and balconies, in the bicycle baskets of cyclists and the mesh bags of shoppers, explosions of intensely hued cosmos, Japanese anemones, dahlias, and the last of the season's roses, a stable landscape around which the renewed, chaotic, glorious energy of Paris swirled.

Intent on his mission and destination, Bucky took in the differences between the Paris he'd left and the city to which he'd returned with only a cursory interest. Now, like then, he wished to find his father. His first stop after settling into his hotel in Passy-Auteuil was the villa of his aunt. He would visit Madame Dupree and the boardinghouse later, if they were still there. Now, like then, Aunt Claire did not know that he was in Paris. In fact, Bucky felt himself not that much changed since the last time he'd pressed the bell of her house.

A maid opened the door, and Bucky delivered the introduction of himself that he'd rehearsed in 1942. She ushered him into the pleasing sunlit room that he remembered, and he took a seat in one of its sumptuously upholstered chairs. His aunt, silver-haired but still slim and willowy at sixty-two, rushed into the room minutes later, expressing in fluting French her joy and surprise at seeing him, her dulcet voice sobering when she answered the question her nephew had come to ask: Where was his father buried?

"I will take you there," she said.

First, Bucky told her, he had one more thing he must do and explained.

He walked across the street to the park where he'd met the man feeding the pigeons that cold winter day and made for the plane tree by the stream. The hole in the trunk was still there and Bucky, taking a chance that it was not the habitat of a creature that would take issue with the intrusion, thrust in his hand. His fingers felt something like age-stiffened plastic. Gingerly, he drew out the item and his heart began to pound as he unwrapped the waterproof covering of an envelope. He opened the flap and removed a letter dated August 17, 1944. "Dear son," it began.

Alistair quickly located the house of Raina Desjardins in Lion-sur-Mer by consulting the fountain of all information in a village, its local priest. He had decided not to telephone beforehand in case the woman should put him off. He'd determined the best approach was simply to knock on her door with John Peterson's book in hand—a gift from his local library, since only one other person had checked it out, and Alistair was a generous contributor at fund-raising time. He found her at home, a place from which she rarely stepped foot except to tend her garden, according to the priest. "A bit of a recluse and unapproachable since her paramour died," he'd said. "We in the parish look after her as best as she'll let us."

But Raina Desjardins invited him in almost

eagerly when Alistair explained in French in his most golden tones that he was an admirer of the late John Peterson's work come from America to have a word with her about it, if she'd be so kind. He put her age at a well-worn seventy-something, and her house smelled of deeply embedded cat urine, but thank God the offenders were nowhere to be seen, Alistair thought, as he took a seat in her cluttered living room. Dogs were his choice if one must share a habitat with a four-legged creature. He declined her offer of tea and got right to the point, designed to flatter the author's scholarship and remarkable attention to detail. Raina Desjardins preened at the praise and said that she would provide what help she could.

Alistair said that he was especially interested in the source that John Peterson had consulted for the last chapter of his book. Alistair thought he might know him and would like to make contact while in France.

The woman had to retrieve her reading glasses to refresh her memory of the last chapter. "Oh, yes," she said, tapping her finger on the final page. "I very much remember Jean telling me about the man who told him this story. He couldn't believe his luck in meeting him. The rest of the chapters are made up, you see, figments of Jean's imagination, but this one was true. He'd always wanted to write about spies, and talking with this man gave him the idea for the subject and title of his book. They met in a bar in Germany."

"Do you know his name?"

"No. It's been so long ago, but..." Raina Desjardins brightened. "I still have Jean's journal of notes for his book," she said. "Perhaps the name is in there. Would you like to see it?"

"Yes, I very much would like to see Mr. Peterson's journal," he said. "I am so fascinated with my fellow countryman's work."

Alistair accepted a cup of tea after all, and his hostess left him alone to read while she went out to check on her garden. The journal was a mess. It would take patience to slog through his scrawl, but his hopes were up at the woman's mention of the man in the bar, and he owed it to Dragonfly to leave no stone unturned. They all had begun to believe there was definitely something to Peterson's story. Even if Victoria did not show up at the tearoom, Alistair was willing to believe that didn't mean she wasn't still alive. If there was a chance of finding a name, a scrap of information that might lead to her current whereabouts, his time and effort in a house that smelled like a litter box would be worth it.

He found it halfway through the author's notes. His lungs protested from his excitement at the discovery and sent him into a fit of wheezing. The source was Karl Brunner. He claimed to be the driver of an important colonel of the SS in France during the German occupation. He would offer no further information on himself or persons or official positions for the author, but Alistair did not need them. He recognized the speaker as the driver for Colonel Derrick Albrecht, and knew the identity of the woman the colonel had rescued from execution. The whole conversation between John Peterson and the drunken German sergeant was laid out in black and white in the pages of the author's journal. It told of the respect and admiration the driver had for his superior and of the colonel's love for his beautiful French bout partner, a fencer of foil, who did not return his affections. When his superior discovered her to be a spy for the Allies, he concocted a scheme to save her from the firing squad, the plan matching almost word for word the text of the last chapter of John Peterson's narrative. In his journal, but not in his book to protect the driver, the author had even included a paragraph in Karl Brunner's own words: *He loved her. He would have done anything for her. He even murdered for her. He poisoned a famous French author to save her from the Gestapo, an act in which I took part, but he refused to the end to implicate me to the French authorities. I was allowed to go free, but he went to prison, and the French eventually chopped off his head. After his execution, I took to bouts of drinking when the memories became too strong.*

John Peterson did not mention that the woman the colonel saved from the firing squad was an American, so Alistair assumed that he believed, like the driver, that Victoria was French, thus the reason he claimed that she lived somewhere in Europe.

Alistair managed to draw in a deep breath, unmindful of the room's stench. "Well, I'll be damned!" he said. "Well, I'll be damned."

Brad and Chris stood before the imposing mansion once occupied by General Konrad March. "Looks the same, doesn't it?" Brad said.

"Exactly as I remember," Chris agreed. "I wonder if the people who live there now are the original Jewish residents or their children."

"The owners might be if they managed to get out of Paris before they were arrested."

"General March didn't seem the type to live in a house confiscated from a family hauled off to the cattle cars," Chris said.

"Madame Gastain would know." Brad gestured toward the mansion next door. Hers was the next stop, the second for both of them. Brad's first call had been to Captain Claude Allard, his OSS facilitator and owner of the fishing tour company where he'd been planted. The barnacled old riverboat captain's jaw dropped when he happened to glance through his office window to see Brad stroll up the walkway to his boat to report in like always. He'd thrown open the door and met him halfway, arms wide and welcoming, exclaiming in French, "My boy! My boy! We thought you were dead!"

Chris received the same shocked, warm welcome when he visited the home of Jules Garnier, retired director of personnel at the Sorbonne. His wife ushered him into the garden where her husband was pruning roses. "Look who's here," she said, and Jules turned at her voice to squint at Chris through eyes clouded with cataracts. "Holy Mother of God," he let out. "Are my eyes deceiving me at last? Can it be true? Herr Bauer, is that you? Are you really alive?"

Brad pushed Madame Gastain's doorbell, he and Chris wondering aloud if her old butler would answer. Ancient when they knew him in 1942, the longtime family retainer had most likely gone to his heavenly reward. Neither was prepared when Hans Falk answered the door. After sharing a few seconds' mutual shock of recognition, Hans said with a stiff little bow like always, "Gentlemen, how nice to see you again and looking so well. Should I let Madame Gastain know that you've come to call?"

Americans did not stand on ceremony when occasions called for emotional displays. Brad and Chris hugged him, and he returned their hearty embraces, tears in his eyes. They went into the drawing room that Brad well remembered and filled in one another while they awaited Madame Gastain's entrance. Hans went first. When the general knew he was soon to be arrested, he'd dispatched his aide to the priest's hole in his neighbor's house next door. He did not witness Major General March's arrest and would always regret not being by his side, but that was not what the general had wanted. When his mistress's old butler died in 1945, he had stayed on as his replacement. He did not wish to return to the country that had executed one of its finest and most dedicated soldiers and general officers. Madame

Gastain was well, except for occasional bouts of arthritis. They would find her charming as ever. She'd had to sell most of the house's Old Masters, but they had fetched enough money to keep the mansion almost in the style to which it was once accustomed. Now Hans wished to hear of Wilhelm. Was the boy happy? Was he getting on well in America? How old was he now?

To Hans's questions, Brad answered yes, yes, and twenty-six. He had graduated Regis University, a prestigious Catholic institution in Colorado, and was studying to become a priest. Again tears clouded Hans's eyes. "His father would be proud," he said.

CHAPTER ONE HUNDRED ONE

Are we ready?"

"We're ready."

"Then let's go," Bridgette said.

It was the afternoon of Sunday, the twenty-third of September, 1962. Alistair and the team of Dragonfly had registered at the Hotel La Rose throughout the day on Saturday and assembled for dinner that night. It had been a sober meeting lightened by reports from Brad and Chris and Bucky of their reunions with the people they'd flown in early to see. Chris had even managed to find the farmhouse whose owners had hidden him from the Germans at the risk of their lives the night he'd landed in France. The couple was gone, the farm now run by the teenaged son who'd been complicit in concealing him in the hayloft, but the grown man well remembered the experience of the boy.

Bucky had visited Madame Dupree, who still ran her boardinghouse, but the property was up for sale. "I'm too worn out and out of patience to run it anymore," she told him. "The males of this current generation…they are not made of the stuff of the men of your youth." When she'd opened the door to him, the brave, worn face that had seldom been touched by a smile, at least not when Bucky had known her, had registered such an explosion of recognition that it was like the sudden burst of sun over a dark landscape. She cried his name and cupped his cheeks between her palms. "I must make sure that you are real," she said. "My hands will tell me what my eyes cannot believe."

Bridgette added a touching report of her own. The day before, she had visited the House of Boucher and was spotted by one of the designers still around. Bridgette had not meant to make herself known, but the designer had been genuinely glad to see her and insisted on taking her up to the showroom. Displayed on the wall under glass for all to see were drawings of Bridgette's fashion designs, including those with which she'd worked miracles to reshape the lumpy body of Madame Richter. "It was Madame Boucher's wish that the drawings remain there always as a lasting tribute to your talent and courage, Mademoiselle Dufor," she said.

Bridgette did not mention her visit to Drancy. Against her intention, that morning she had taken her courage in hand and boarded the metro to the U-shaped complex in the northeastern suburb of Paris. She had long ago ridded herself of the physical reminder of her time in Drancy by donating her roll of muslin to the Holocaust Museum in Jerusalem. At the open gates, she had not entered but stood looking in. *How time changes things*, she thought, taking in the building that had been returned to its original purpose, public housing. She observed people coming and going about their daily business in the courtyard where thousands had languished and died, saw children at play, women gossiping, bicycles parked, and toy vehicles strewn in front of apartment doors, window boxes brimming with flowers. She had expected ghosts to run out to meet her and suffering voices to fill her ears and her flesh to rise at the very memory of the Richters, but the place held no power over her. Her breathing remained steady, her heart rate calm. Steve would be proud of her. She was glad that she had come.

Alistair kept a lid on his news. If Victoria appeared at the café at four o'clock, his information would be a moot point anyway, and if she did not, he would wait to share the content of John Peterson's notes until they were back home and his source at CIA headquarters confirmed one way or the other Victoria Grayson's existence in the United States, but for now he thought it best not to get their hopes up. He did, however, have a surprise to spring on the group. Henri Burrell, his man in Paris, would be joining them at La Petite Madeleine.

They were now off on the final leg of their journey in a rented van. All would be flying home tomorrow, back to their lives and the loved ones they had left. But first to the street of the Sisters of Charity to pay a visit to the mural on the convent wall that Alistair had never seen.

"Oh, my gosh!" Brad exclaimed when they drew up before the painting.

Slowly, their faces tight with emotion, the members of Dragonfly descended from the van and approached the nautical landscape. A man passing by took them for tourists. He lived in the area and was accustomed to the reverence visitors showed the star attraction of his neighborhood, a commemorative World War II memorial. The mural, slightly faded but clear in detail, was in reality more beautiful than Alistair could ever have imagined. It took his breath away.

It had been preserved under a layer of Plexiglas and beside it, bolted into the stone wall, a bronze plaque stated in French: THIS MURAL WAS PAINTED AS A WAYSIDE SACRAMENT TO BEAUTY FOR THE PEOPLE OF THE RUE DES SOEURS DE CHARITÉ IN DEFIANCE OF THE UGLINESS OF WAR. CREATED SEPTEMBER 1942. ARTIST'S NAME UNKNOWN.

Not a mark desecrated its plastic surface but for a single line in crayon drawn diagonally across the flat body of a liverwort, easily wiped off. Alistair and the four members of Dragonfly stood motionless before the code signal, then turned to stare in speechless wonder at one another. Finally, Bridgette said, "We'd better get a move on, boys. Liverwort is waiting for us."

They found her facing the door in her usual seat in the café, the same look of expectancy and hope and fear on her beautiful face that she'd worn all those years ago when she'd thought they were lost to her.

"Hi, guys," she said, rising, tears filling her eyes.

Saturday evening in New York City. The Westminster chimes of the Waterbury standing sentinel in the hall struck six o'clock as the September sun lowered over the treetops of Central Park. Sunday had just gone past the hour of midnight in Paris. The distinguished man sitting guard over the telephone in his Park Avenue apartment had been waiting for the instrument to ring all day, though he had known not to expect a call until after four o'clock in France. That was the time his wife was to keep an appointment in Paris at a tea shop with friends she'd not seen in eighteen years. She was to let him know if they'd shown up.

Or not.

It was the "or not" that most worried him, but at least his wife would have some form of answer to the question roiling around in her head for years: Were her friends from the war years still alive? He knew very little about the circumstances behind the question. Victoria had allowed him only a few glimpses into a two-year stretch in her past that otherwise was uncomplicated history. All he really knew was that in those two years, she and these particular friends, all Americans—three men and a woman—had served together in the OSS as a group working in Paris during the war. After all these years, she'd not been able to free herself from the hope that they had survived. He had accepted but not been able to understand her enduring devotion to four people whose real names she did not know, nor where they came from, what they did for a living, or a single detail about their backgrounds. "It is hard to explain," she'd said.

So he had given this trip his full support and blessing with his own hope that it provide his wife some kind of liberation from that time. Maybe then she'd open up about those years, the men she'd known that he suspected still hovered in her memory. One he knew about. Her brother, Lawrence, had confided that she'd been madly in love with a man she'd known since childhood, an RAF pilot shot down over France. "Somehow, sis tracked down his grave outside Paris and brought his body home for burial in Williamsburg, and after that, she let him go, Richard," Lawrence had told him. "It was what Ralph would have wanted." The other man was unknown, but Richard suspected that he was someone she had known in Paris who was dead, too, a casualty of that time.

It was the little things that made him think the effects of that man still lingered. "You do not fence anymore. Why?" he'd asked when he saw dozens of pictures of her in full fencing gear in a family photo album along with shots and newspaper clippings of her awards and wins in foil. She had removed the album from his hand. "It wasn't fun anymore," she'd said. Later, her father had told him that his daughter had not fenced since her return from "over there"—his name for France and her period in Paris.

When they were dating, she had a nasty fall and scraped a side of her cheek. He'd pulled out a handkerchief to dab at the blood, but she'd jerked her head aside, a strange look in her eye. "What's wrong?" he said, alarmed that she'd mistaken his intent.

"Nothing," she said. "I just…had a moment of déjà vu."

There were murmurings in her sleep, unintelligible but uttered with a pathos of conscience that could come only from a well of deep remorse. What in the world had happened "over there"? After a while, the murmurings ceased, especially after the children came. One day he asked her, "Victoria, are you happy?"

"Of course I am, just as I promised."

"To who?"

She'd kissed him. "To a friend I made in France," she'd said.

And then there was the day a dragonfly had lighted on her hand. They were having a picnic with the girls by the lake in Central Park, and she had been fascinated by the swarm of dragonflies playing around near the surface of the water when suddenly one of the little fellows darted away from the group and made a beeline for Victoria's hand. The girls had squealed, but his wife had stared at it with a look and smile he'd never forgotten. After a few moments, it flew away, and she said, "Richard, do you believe in... signs?"

"Do you?" he'd countered, knowing instinctively that the dragonfly had something to do with "over there."

"Yes. I believe that one just landed on my hand."

"Then there must be such a thing," he had said and noticed that in the years following she appeared more at ease with her past.

The phone rang, the sudden explosion of sound in the quiet room jarring. He was alone in the apartment this evening. He had dismissed the servants for the night; the cook had left supper for him in the oven, and his daughters, seven and five, were at their grandparents' home in Connecticut for the weekend. "Hello," he said with a clutch in his voice.

"Richard, my love, I am sorry for the late hour. I... have been engrossed."

Richard, my love. She had never called him that, and there was a warmth in her voice that he'd never heard before.

"Was your trip successful?" he asked, his heart stilled.

"Very. I will be coming home tomorrow. I have much to tell you. Much to share. It's time, Richard."

"I'll be waiting," he said.

Two years later, a nonfiction book appeared on the *New York Times* best sellers' list written by an unknown author but a well-known legend in the field of which he wrote. The intriguing title had caught the nation's attention as well as the striking jacket cover. It featured a mural of a stunning seascape painted on the ancient courtyard wall of a convent, and above it in raised lettering, aptly titled from the content and rave reviews, *The Mark on the Wall.*

ACKNOWLEDGMENTS

A close friend, Terry Jo Gough, presented me with a gift after my first novel, *Roses*, was published. It was a polished block of gray stone and on its face was written, "Once in a while right in the middle of an ordinary life…love brings you a fairy tale." As with all T.J.'s gifts, it was most appropriate, and it sits now on a special shelf in my office where my glance can fall upon it as I drink my morning coffee. It is a reminder that this writing journey of mine has indeed been the stuff of fairy tales brought to life by the love from family, longtime friends, fans, and readers. Without your interest and confidence in my literary endeavors, I may not have stayed the course. So thank you, each and every one. You are held dear in the ordinary life of this writer.

Beyond that fold, I owe my thanks to several

gentlemen for the contributions they made to the most challenging novel I have ever written and for which I take full responsibility for any and all mistakes in translation. My immeasurable gratitude goes to Daniel Joseph Bryant, whose vast knowledge of the hierarchal structure and inner workings of the German Army and SS set me on sound footing on uncertain ground more times than I have breath to thank him for. Without your guidance and assistance, Daniel, *Dragonfly* might have floundered in a mire of fruitless research. I will be forever grateful for the divine intervention of your email.

I am in debt to Rev. Dr. Richard O. Knott Jr., who inspired the character of Brad after I heard one of his magnificent sermons based on fly-fishing. Richard shared with me his own experiences as an avid fly-fisherman and plied me with books on the skill and magic and beauty involved in casting out a line where the wild fish run. Thank you, Richard, for a glimpse into a world I would never have known.

Contributing also to this novel in ways beyond my stock of words to describe was Jackie K. Cooper, fellow writer and film and book reviewer, formerly for the Huffington Post. Jackie has been an ardent supporter of my books from the get-go, but I especially valued his belief in this novel because it kept me on task and on track when an illness might have prevented me from reaching the finish line. Thank you, my friend, Jackie, forever and always.

Words fail me, too, in expressing my gratitude to Johanna Castillo of Writers House for guiding *Dragonfly* through the publication process and to Millicent Bennett, executive editor of Grand Central Publishing, who took the novel to her heart. Johanna and Millicent...how great thou art.

And thank you, Arthur Richard Meacham III, my love of fifty-two years and the best fairy tale to come true in my otherwise ordinary life.

ABOUT THE AUTHOR

Marie Langmore/Langmore Photography

Leila Meacham is a writer and former teacher who lives in San Antonio, Texas. She is the author of the bestselling novels *Roses*, *Tumbleweeds*, *Somerset*, and *Titans*. For more information, please visit LeilaMeacham.com.